# Desperate Measures

Wally
  What can I say
after all these years.
    Thank
  May's you
        10/11/03

# Desperate Measures

Mary E. Young

iUniverse, Inc.
New York Lincoln Shanghai

# Desperate Measures

iUniverse, Inc.

For information address:
iUniverse, Inc.
2021 Pine Lake Road, Suite 100
Lincoln, NE 68512
www.iuniverse.com

ISBN: 0-595-27868-X

Printed in the United States of America

*O Mein Papa*

# Acknowledgements

Writers are fond of saying that ours is a solitary occupation. Nothing could be further from the truth. We rely on friends, family, research professionals and many others who offer support and ideas, sometimes unwittingly. Among the many people who did so are (in alphabetical order, so as to avoid choosing who helped most: Bernice Boughner, Lillian Burnsfield, Helen Corbin, Valerie Haas, Chris and Leslie Hoy, Tom Legendre, Doug Laurent, Doyle Mullican, Stewart Rooth, Rosaline Williams, Geoffrey Woodhouse, countless librarians and dozens of friends who have been listening to this story for so many years.

I send a special thought to my deceased father, Franklin Lewis Young, Sr., for this is his story.

# CHAPTER 1

▼

## November 1, 1945

From where he stood on the Adams Road Bridge, Dan Kirk could see two police officers knee deep in the icy Clinton River, trying to reach a woman's body caught face down on a cluster of rocks near the shore. The corpse looked to Dan's trained eye to be just over five foot with short, auburn hair. The jacket of her beige suit billowed out from her torso, her bright red fingernails a sharp contrast to the murky brown-green water around her. An officer reached out and grabbed her right foot but lost his grip when the shoe came off in his hand. As he took hold of her stockinged foot and eased the body toward him, her full skirt floated up around her waist. Underwear still in place, Dan noticed. No rape. Another officer standing on the shore helped pull her ashore, laying her face up in the tall grass. Dan headed across to the center of the bridge where Lieutenant Cunning-ham stood.

"Morning, Stan," Dan said.

"Dan." The lieutenant gave a curt nod without taking his eyes off the action below, puffing on his ever-present pipe.

"What gives?" Dan asked.

"We got a call from one of those two guys over there," he said, nodding toward two men standing at the north end of the bridge. Each had his right arm looped around a .22 rifle. "They were driving around out here looking for some good hunting spots and saw her. I called you at the newspaper office when I got the call because I figure there's not going to be any identification on her. Never is when we find one out in the sticks like this. Maybe we can get something in this afternoon's paper."

Dan pulled the collar of his coat up against the cold, damp Michigan morning and glanced at the sky. Thick blue-gray clouds crowded each other overhead, obliterating the sky. Wisps of filmy fog clung to tree branches like a cat's cradle stretched between a child's fingers. Yesterday's rain would turn to snow today, he figured. His trench coat flapped loosely around his tall, lanky, thirty-eight-year-old frame. Bright, blue eyes blazed out from beneath his brown fedora, taking in the details of the work going on at the riverbank. He scribbled a few descriptive details in his reporter's notebook then glanced sideways at Lieutenant Cunningham who was re-lighting his pipe.

Stan's years of sitting in police cars on stakeout, poring over paperwork for hours and eating heavy meals before going to bed at night showed in his paunch. Shorter than Dan, he was also more pale. The aroma of the cheap tobacco he smoked hung in the air around him. He pushed his hat to the back of his head where it hung precariously. His sharp eye and retentive memory caught the details Dan saw, but he felt no need to write them down.

An officer standing farther along the bridge called to the Lieutenant who then shuffled through the gravel to look at something on the ground. Dan followed. The men gazed down at a cranberry red stain. Streaks through it gave the impression it had been a bigger stain that someone had tried to clean up by throwing some of the pebbles away. Stan told the officer to scoop up the pebbles for analysis later and he and Dan strode back across the bridge as the officers arrived at the roadside carrying the woman's body. They laid her face up and Cunningham reached down to close the eyelids in the water-puffed face. Mascara blotted her lower eyelids. She appeared to be barely out of her teens. One of the officers dropped a purse next to her head and it landed with a thud. Stan knelt on one knee next to the body, turning its head to one side then to the other, noting a bullet hole that pierced the left temple then ran through to the right.

"Looks like a .38," he said as Dan wrote. He turned the corpse's hands over and back, ran his hands down her legs and up the back of her neck. He rolled the body to one side and examined her back. "No other injuries. Doesn't look like she struggled."

It wasn't the first time Dan had seen a dead body, of course. He'd been the police reporter at the *Detroit Free Press* for six years. A dead woman, though, was rare and a little tough on him. This one was less battered than many. Most met their demise at the hands of an enraged husband or boy friend. Broken bones, bruises, cigarette burns or ligature marks usually marked the bodies of the dead women he had seen. The woman on the ground before him was unmarked except for the bullet holes. He scribbled in his note pad. Beige suit, flowered blouse, wedding ring (not expensive), jade ring and gold bracelet, both costume, new and expensive shoes. Stan reached into the woman's jacket pocket, extracting a theater ticket for last night's performance at the Bijou in Detroit. He stood up with a groan and nodded to the ambulance attendants who loaded the body and drove away, the crunch of the vehicle in the gravel breaking the heavy silence of the countryside. He picked up the purse, peered inside then turned it upside down. Five small rocks fell out.

"I figured," he said, handing the purse to an officer standing nearby.

Dan glanced at his watch. Eight-thirty a.m. Still time to get something in today's paper if he got going. Stan's thoughts ran along the same lines. "Can you make deadline?" he asked.

"Yeah, if I get going."

"Do me a favor. Leave out the description of the jewelry. We can use it to help identify her."

"Got it."

On his way to the car, Dan stopped to speak to the hunters who had found the body, but they had no information to offer but their names: Ralph Summers and Otis Weaver, two local farmers. On the drive back to the office, Dan remembered another murder of a woman in Detroit about three weeks ago. Mrs. Lydia Thompson had been found dead in her back yard, bludgeoned to death. She was the wife of a wealthy automobile dealer who, he recalled, had an alibi for the night his wife died. He'd been with his mistress. Mrs. Thompson's Russian-born father was being investigated for the murder, the last Dan remembered. He made a mental note to follow up on that case. The theater ticket in the pocket of the woman just found in the Clinton River meant she had some connection to Detroit. Two dead women in a month was unusual, even in Detroit where violence had always been part of the city's complexion. He wondered if there was any connection.

# CHAPTER 2

▼

As soon as the afternoon papers hit the streets, phones began ringing at Dan's desk and at the Oakland County Sheriff's office. Callers had an unending stream of suggestions about who the woman in the Clinton River might be. Some were crying when they called, hopeful the woman was a missing wife or daughter. She was positively identified by the callers as a lost sister from Algonac, the wife of a man from Dearborn, the neighbor of a couple on Belle Isle, a missing celebrity from Hollywood. Both Dan and the sheriff's deputies made notes of each of the calls for further follow-up. No callers were able to accurately describe the jewelry the woman found in the Clinton River was wearing. Two callers claimed responsibility for the murder. Dan recognized their voices from confessions they had made to previous murders. Over lunch at the Woolworth's counter, he reviewed his notes but found no leads.

That evening and the next morning calls continued to pour in, over a hundred in all. Even after all these years on the paper, Dan couldn't believe what some people thought they read. Despite his detailed description of the woman and her clothing, callers insisted the woman was really fifty years old or plump or wore slacks or had red hair. He addressed the regular callers by name.

"No, Eleanor. I don't think there's a mistake. She is definitely a small woman. I saw her."

"Hi, Elmer. Good to hear from you. I'll check into it."

Dan was sometimes tempted to let the newsroom secretary filter his calls, but he never knew which ones would pay off so he took all the calls himself. The anonymity of the telephone seemed to encourage people to unload their most intimate secrets to complete strangers, however, and he ended up listening to long stories about families, disappearances, financial troubles, and sexual exploits.

Twenty-four hours after the story about the body in the Clinton River hit, Dan got a phone call from a woman who said she knew who had been pulled from the river. This time, the caller was able to describe the jewelry he had seen on the corpse. Dan got her name and phone number and called Lieutenant Cunningham, offering to give him the information the caller provided if he could be in on the interview.

"Hell, no," Stan roared. "We don't even know if she knows what she's talking about, and I sure wouldn't want you to waste your valuable time till we do know. You let me check it out first." His voice mellowed a bit. "Look. I'll have this woman meet me at the Davis Funeral Home. You come out there at five-thirty tonight. We should be done by then, and you can talk to her if you want."

Dan gave Stan the woman's name and number then called his hockey coach to say he wouldn't make that night's game.

The Davis Funeral Home served as the county coroner's office. Dan arrived at the somber building on Eighth Street at five-fifteen. The receptionist told him the Lieutenant and three other people were inside viewing the body of the woman found floating in the Clinton River. He paced the waiting room till the four emerged down a hallway. There were two women and a man with Stan. One woman looked to be in her mid to late twenties, her brown hair pushed back from her face. The other woman, also brown haired was maybe ten years older. Both wore plain woolen coats, no makeup, and no jewelry. The man was much older, maybe mid-fifties with wire-rimmed glasses, a rumpled gray hat, and a tweed coat. Dan moved toward them, but Stan stepped in front of him, his back to the reporter, blocking Dan's approach to the three people. As he talked quietly to them, they glanced over the lieutenant's shoulder at Dan. The man's mouth quivered. First one, then the other, and finally all three nodded. Stan walked over to Dan.

"These people have identified the woman we found. Her name is Twyla Larson. They worked with her. They're pretty shaken up, so go easy," he said. Dan pulled his notebook from his overcoat pocket and strode easily over to the three people. "My condolences on the loss of your friend," he said, removing his hat. "What can you tell me about her?" They all fidgeted, then the man spoke up.

"She was a lovely woman. Lovely. She worked hard and minded her own business. I can't imagine how this could happen."

Dan noticed glances passing between the two women as the man spoke of the dead woman.

"What is your name, sir?" he asked.

"Robert Gaines. I was her supervisor at work."

"Where is that?"

"Carrier Tool and Die in Detroit."

"Mr. Gaines is right," the older woman said. "She was so sweet. It had to be some madman that did this." Dan sensed a hollow sincerity in her voice. Maybe the man was also this woman's supervisor, and she thought she had to agree with him. He talked with the trio for a few more minutes taking down their names and phone numbers. They said they didn't know where Mrs. Larson lived, but they did know she had a twin sister in Detroit somewhere. Dan headed to the Carrier Tool and Die Company.

Carrier was one of dozens of companies that had sprung up since the end of the Depression to provide parts for the burgeoning automobile industry. When the war broke out, their efforts had been redirected to military products—tanks, airplanes, munitions. Since the war ended last summer, though, many of the factories had closed, at least temporarily while they re-tooled to return to their pre-war functions. Dan figured Carrier had remained open because its products had a wide variety of usages. As Dan stepped into the front office, he could hear the hum of machinery through the wall. A stout woman with heavily rouged cheeks eyed him suspiciously before waddling to a file cabinet, extracting a folder, and grunting out Twyla Larson's address. Despite the woman's obstinacy, Dan pressed her for anything else she might know about the dead woman. She didn't know anything, she insisted. As Dan was leaving the office, she called after him, "I don't socialize with the people in the factory, but you might check around back. The security guard seems to know everything that's going on."

Dan thanked her with a tip of his hat and closed the door behind him. He circled the dirty white building wondering how the workers could tolerate the noise inside for a full shift. The smell of engine exhaust and grease drifted out of the high windows making him a bit nauseous. In the back of the lot, he found a security guard who identified himself as Clifford Malin, a fortyish man with a doughy face and a lump of a nose. In the shadow of the brim of his hat, Malin's eyes squinted and darted. He tightened and loosened his lips as Dan talked to him. His suit and silk shirt were too expensive for the job he had.

"Yeah, I knew Twyla. Everyone knew Twyla, if you get what I mean," he told Dan. "She was quite a rounder." His voice was soft with a hint of a southern accent. His eyes danced around as he spoke, not looking directly at Dan for long.

Dan raised his eyebrows. That didn't sound like the woman her supervisor had described, but if what Malin was saying was true it would account for the glances he saw pass between the two women at the funeral home.

"Why do you say that?" Dan asked.

"Hell, cuz I knew her. Bumped into her all the time at one nightclub or another. She was always with someone, mostly guys. The last few weeks she had some problems and was always in tears. She started to ask me for help a time or two, but she never finished what she was saying. I don't know what her problem was. Men, I figure."

"Wasn't she married?"

"Sure. Most of these women here are married. Their husbands aren't back from overseas or maybe they won't be coming back. Hers, Twyla's, was due home any time. I figure that was part of her problem. Probably couldn't get rid of a boyfriend."

"Why would she come to you for help?"

"I don't know, maybe because I've known her for a while, maybe because I carry a gun sometimes. I do some private dick work on the side. I used to be a cop. Maybe she wanted me to put the muscle on someone. I don't know."

The two men talked a few more minutes before Malin said he had to make his rounds. When he left Carrier, Dan headed for the address the woman in the office had given him. It was a modest structure owned by the Searle family where Mrs. Larson obviously rented a room. Dan's knock on the front door was answered by a boxy, middle-aged woman with her hair tied in careful knots on each side of her head. Her apron bore the markings of dinner in the making.

"Mrs. Searle?" She nodded. "I'm Dan Kirk from the *Detroit Free Press*. Can I come in a minute?" She hesitated before opening the door and letting him in. She offered him a seat on the sofa and perched on the edge of a chair across from him. The room was immaculate with antimacassars over the back of every chair and the sofa, family pictures on the buffet, and handmade doilies on the tables.

"Mrs. Searle, did you read in the paper about the woman found out in Oakland County?"

Mrs. Searle gasped and put her hand to her mouth. "My daughter told me. I say to her it couldn't be." Her speech was clipped with an eastern European accent. "Please, don't tell me," she said and stood up. She went to the foot of a staircase in the hallway and called upstairs.

"Lillian! Come down here! Get your father!"

She returned to her chair and faced Dan. "Please, Mr. Kirk. Wait for my family."

A pretty teen-aged girl in the uniform of St. Mary's School bounced down the stairs and into the room. "What, Mama?"

"Get your father. Be quick."

The girl left the room, returning a few minutes later with a heavy-set man who was wiping his hands on a rag.

"What is it, Mama?" he asked. Mrs. Searle reached her hand toward her husband. He crossed the room and took her work-gnarled hand in his own. With her other arm, Mrs. Searle reached toward her daughter.

"This is Mr. Kirk. He is reporter with the newspaper. He want to talk to us."

Dan explained about the woman found in the river but didn't mention the bullet hole in her temple. Mrs. Searle and her daughter both broke into tears.

"I just knew it, Mama," the daughter cried. "When I read it in the paper, I knew it was her. You thought I was crazy, but I knew."

When someone knocked on the door, Mr. Searle let his wife's hand drop and crossed the room to open the door. Dan saw Lieutenant Cunningham framed in the doorway and knew his own interview was over. Once inside the living room, Stan jerked his head toward the door, signaling Dan to clear out.

Driving back to the newsroom, Dan wondered about the mysterious Mrs. Larson. According to the security guard at Carrier, she was a party girl. That wasn't unusual these days. As difficult as war is on those in the battlefields, it is just as trying on the ones left behind. The imminence of death pervaded daily life. Sometimes, the only solace is in someone's arms. But Dan was having trouble getting hold of exactly who the murdered woman was. Her supervisor and the people she lived with obviously thought she was a sweet, loving woman waiting for her husband. Malin's opinion couldn't have been more to the contrary. It was hard to say what the two women from the funeral home thought. One thing was certain. She didn't die with a bullet through her skull because someone thought she was a sweetheart. Unless she was a sweetheart to the wrong person.

# C H A P T E R  3

▼

It had been three days since Twyla Larson had been pulled from the Clinton River near the Adams Road Bridge. Dan Kirk had been calling Stan Cunningham almost hourly, but the Lieutenant was ignoring all messages. Frustrated, Dan decided to pay another visit to the Searle home where Twyla Larson had been living. He needed to decipher the mystery that was Twyla Larson. Was she an adoring wife or a rounder as Malin characterized her? What had she done to end up with a bullet through her skull? He had to know more.

The smell of fresh baking permeated the Searle home. Sitting at the kitchen table, Dan munched on a warm slice of cinnamon-laced apple pie and sipped a cup of strong coffee, a special treat for a single man who mostly ate at diners. He asked Mrs. Searle for more information about her former lodger. She seemed to want to give him what information she could but obviously found it difficult to talk about Twyla, stifling tears as she talked.

Mrs. Searle said Twyla had been an ideal roomer, considerate of the rest of the family, tidy, undemanding. She went to work every day on the bus that she caught down at the corner next to the fire station. Sometimes she came home on the bus, but if she worked late, one of her friends would drive her home. Twyla was gone a lot in the evenings, Mrs. Searle said. She had a twin sister across town she visited frequently or went to the movies with some of the women she worked with who, like Twyla, had husbands or boyfriends overseas. On some weekends, she went to see her parents up in Port Huron, a small town on the lake about sixty-five miles away, but she worked a lot of weekends. She was saving money for the day her husband would return from overseas and they could start their lives together, Mrs. Searle assured Dan.

Dan realized that with all the time Twyla spent away from her landlady, she could be up to just about anything. He asked Mrs. Searle if Twyla got many phone calls. Not many, Mrs. Searle said, mostly her sister and friends from work. Once in a while, a man would call but Mrs. Searle didn't ask who he was. Twyla was a pretty woman, and Mrs. Searle could understand why men would be attracted to her, but Twyla never gave them any encouragement. She loved her husband and looked forward to his return.

"Once, though, I hear her get very angry with this man," Mrs. Searle said. "It was two, three weeks ago. She tell him he should do something for her, I don't know what, or she go to the newspaper. It don't make any sense to me, but I don't ask no questions."

"How long did Mrs. Larson live here?" Dan asked.

"She move in two years ago. She live here two years," Mrs. Searle nodded, wringing her hands as she talked. After a pause she added, "Except for that little bit when she live with her girlfriend."

"When was that?"

"Let me see. I think she move out in July or August. Yes, that's right. She move out right after Independence Day picnic. Then she come back."

"Who was the girlfriend?"

"I don't know. She not tell me. She say girlfriend's husband die in Japan and she stay to help girlfriend till she feel better."

After getting the name and address of Twyla's sister, Dan asked to see her room. It was small, tucked at the back of the house next to the kitchen and made all the smaller by two bureaus and a twin bed pushed up against the walls. A dressing table stood beneath the only window in the room. Dan pulled open a couple of drawers in the bureaus and found them packed with neatly folded sweaters, blouses, and lingerie. In the closet hung tailored suits and coats, more blouses, and three rows of shoes. The drawers of the dressing table were empty, and Mrs. Searle said the police had taken all the papers from the drawers with them.

On one end of the dressing table stood a photograph of Twyla and a man in military uniform. Mrs. Searle said it was the Larsons' wedding photograph. Twyla wore a simple, short-sleeved dress with a gardenia and rose corsage that must have cost her husband a week's pay. The groom wore an army uniform with lieutenant insignia on the hat. Dan heard sniffles from behind him and turned to find Mrs. Searle daubing at her eyes as she looked at the picture.

"It so sad," she mumbled. "First he leave her and now she leave him."

"What do you mean he leaves her? You mean because he's overseas?"

"No. I mean he is going to divorce her."

Mrs. Searle said several weeks ago Twyla received a letter from her husband. She was in her room reading it when Mrs. Searle took in a piece of pineapple upside down cake, Twyla's favorite. She noticed Twyla was crying. After some prompting, Twyla said the letter from her husband asked for a divorce. Mrs. Searle had been shocked to hear that Ernie, Captain Larson, wanted a divorce. The couple seemed so much in love, Mrs. Searle said. They wrote frequently. Twyla had been buying dishes and linens to begin a new life with her husband when he returned from the war. Ernie had been sending money home every month for Twyla to put in the bank. Twyla, too, was adding money to the account. They would use their nest egg to build a house, Twyla had told Mrs. Searle. From everything Mrs. Searle knew, the couple was very much in love. This divorce made no sense to her.

After he left the Searle home, Dan stopped at the Alibi Club and called his office. Stan still had not returned the reporter's calls and he decided to head out to the sheriff's office.

Wading through four inches of wet, sticky snow, Dan crossed the parking lot and entered the Oakland County Sheriff's building in Pontiac, stamping his feet and leaving little lumps of snow where he stood. He asked the desk sergeant if Stan was in. Heaving his corpulent frame from his chair, the sergeant strolled slowly down a hallway behind him. In a few minutes, he returned and signaled Dan down the hallway that ended at Stan's office. The Lieutenant sat behind a desk littered with files, half empty cups of cold coffee, and overflowing ashtrays. The air in the room was thick with smoke from the Lieutenant's pipe. Scraps of daylight peered through a dirty window behind the desk revealing a dusting of dead flies on the windowsill. The wooden floor was knicked and scraped from years of use but shined from a recent waxing. It was about the only clean surface in the room, Dan noted.

"Been trying to call you," Dan said, shoveling a stack of files off a chair and sitting down. He stretched his long legs past a stack of files on the floor.

"Yeah, I know. There's a lot going on here. What do you need?"

"Anything you got on the Larson murder. Like have you heard from her husband?"

"Yeah. He called from New York and should be here tomorrow. The goddam military can't find their ass with both hands and a flashlight. They showed he was in England and he's in France, so it took some time to find him. In fact, we didn't find him. He found us. The poor old bastard read about his wife in that military newspaper they put out and wired us. He had to convince the brass that this is an emergency before he could get a leave. It's a wonder we managed to win the war."

Dan leaned back in the chair and looked at Stan through narrowed eyes. "What kind of woman do you figure Mrs. Larson was?"

"What do you mean?"

"I've been talking to her landlady and some of the people at the plant where she worked. I get conflicting stories. Someone says she was a rounder and someone else says she was a loving wife waiting patiently for her husband to come home. Mrs. Searle, the landlady, said her husband wrote asking for a divorce."

"Tell you what," Stan said. "Here are her letters and bank statements. Take them into one of the interrogation rooms and read them, then we'll talk."

Dan scooped up the file and headed back down the hallway stopping at the first empty room. The aroma of years of sweaty bodies, cigarettes, and cigars would likely never be cleared from the room, Dan thought. He wondered vaguely how many men—and maybe a few women—had bled on these floors, cried over the table, been slugged, smacked, and punched in here.

After organizing the letters into date order, he began to read. There were letters from Mrs. Larson's mother up in Port Huron that was mostly motherly stuff—family news, admonishments to eat right and not work too hard. There were letters from a lady friend, Mary something or other, she didn't sign her last name, also in Port Huron, filling Twyla in with chatty news about the weather, mutual friends, guys this Mary was dating, her job. Part of one of her letters caught Dan's eye. "I sure miss the good times we had and I know it's as hard for you to come up here to visit as it is for me to come down there. But I have to tell you I'm pretty worried about you. You seemed to have made some rough friends and I don't want to see you get in trouble. When I saw all that money you were carrying around, I worried even more. Don't you think that you should be putting that in the bank? You could get robbed, you know."

Ernie Larson, Twyla's husband, was a prolific letter writer. He wrote with a flowery, adolescently poetic style in a wide, looping hand. He told of things he had seen overseas, men he knew who had shipped out after their injuries or died. And he obviously couldn't wait to get home to bed his wife. No letter ended without at least a few sentences of how much he missed her physically. Some letters were nothing but talk about what he was going to do with her when they were reunited. A brief thought about what he was doing in the meantime scampered through Dan's mind. He read more carefully when he came to the letters of the last several weeks. The last one was dated October 20, 1945.

"Thoughts, dreams, hopes, and God knows what of you run through my mind continuously," Ernie wrote to his wife. "Why? Only because I love you. Whatever the postwar era brings to us, I want to enjoy life with you. Even if things come a little tough for a while, I'm sure you'll stick with me—I'm that sure of your love for me."

Ernie wrote that he had received his orders to ship home and was scheduled to catch a troop transport November 10. "But I'll believe it when I'm actually on the boat," he wrote. Not only was there no mention of a divorce, Ernie Larson's letters were filled with longing and desire for his wife. Could Mrs. Searle have misunderstood what Twyla said?

Dan wondered about the money this friend Mary had mentioned. Twyla apparently worked regularly and her husband sent money home, but she was also buying all those clothes and household goods. Now there's mention of a purse full of cash. The factories had been paying pretty well during the war years and there was plenty of overtime pay to be earned, but it still seemed unlikely anyone could accumulate all those things plus a bank account. Dan reached for the stack of bank statements.

The account had been opened nearly three years ago at the Michigan National Bank in Allen Park. Most of the statements showed regular deposits, weekly, probably from Twyla's paycheck with one larger deposit each month, probably from money Captain Larson sent home. Every week or so there were other deposits of smaller amounts. Dan wondered about their source. The account reached a high of four thousand dollars. But six months ago, withdrawals started. First, the withdrawals were twenty-five and fifty dollars, but then they became larger. Five weeks ago, she withdrew thirteen hundred and fifty dollars. At the time of her death, the account held only a dollar and sixty-eight cents. On a note clipped to the latest bank statement was a note in Lieutenant Cunningham's writing that read "Where are the war bonds?"

Dan sat staring in front of him trying to make sense of all the information he had gathered. The letters and bank statements created more questions than they answered. He leaned back in his chair considering what his next move should be when he saw Clifford Malin, the Carrier Tool security guard, pass by the door heading toward the Lieutenant's office. Dan would give the two some time together while he made some notes before asking Stan more questions. When he saw Malin leave, he stacked up the papers in front of him and went down the hallway.

"I think I have more questions now than I did when I came in here. Did Twyla's landlady tell you about the letter asking for a divorce?"

"She did. But I can't find any such letter."

"What's this note about bonds?"

"One of the people that came out to the funeral home yesterday told us that they heard Mrs. Larson had three thousand dollars in war bonds. So far, we can't find them."

"What did you want to see Malin about?"

"I didn't. He came in here saying he had some information about the murder. He seems to think there was a boyfriend that can explain where all the money went."

"How did he know about the money?"

"He said Mrs. Larson came to him during the summer all upset that she had loaned somebody some money who wasn't repaying it. She asked him to help her collect the money. He apparently wasn't very successful."

"That's curious. He told me she came to him a couple of times but never told him what she wanted. What's the boyfriend's name?"

Stan shook his head. "Not yet. Not till we get a chance to check him out."

"Have you talked to Mrs. Larson's twin sister?"

"As much as we could. Her husband came out for an additional ID on the body just so we had someone from the family. We talked to him. It was rough enough on him. The poor bastard must have felt he was looking down at his own wife laying there. They were identical twins, you know."

"One last question. You remember that woman that was axed in her back yard? Lydia Thompson? Do you think Mrs. Larson's murder and Mrs. Thompson's are related? I mean, two women killed so close together seems kind of odd to me."

"Don't have any idea. I'm not in on the Thompson case. Why don't you poke around with the Detroit boys and let me know what you find."

The drive back to the newsroom from Pontiac was painfully slow. The snow fall of a couple of nights ago had been light, but when it melted, it turned the roads to mush, freezing at night into hard ruts like a giant stretch of corduroy. The sun punched through the clouds this morning, softening the frozen mud just enough for Dan's car to sink slightly and slow his progress. Dan dug for a full minute with his right hand through the loose papers, candy wrappers, and dried sandwich crusts piled on the seat beside him before he realized he no longer needed to be concerned about his gas ration tickets. He twisted the dial on the radio till he found Bob Crosby and the Bobcats swinging out a tune. As he picked his way between and around the ruts the best he could, he noticed a dull ache creeping into his shoulders from the effort.

Arriving at the office, he stood next to the car, flexing his broad shoulders to relieve the tension. His thoughts were consumed with Twyla Larson and he was trying to piece together what he knew of the Lydia Thompson murder.

Inside, he typed up an eight-inch side bar first with excerpts from Captain Larson's letters to his wife before tackling the main story. He told of the couple, married three years then separated by war, Twyla working as a drill press operator to earn money she and her husband would use to start a new life together when he got home. He handed the story to the copy boy then banged out a six-teen-inch story with details of the investigation into the woman's murder. This one told of how homicide detectives had detained two of the people who had identified Mrs. Larson's body for further questioning.

Dan had learned that the man and one of the women he had met at the Davis Funeral Home had not been as forthcoming as Lieutenant Cunningham had wanted them to be, so he had had them locked up as material witnesses. It seems that Robert Gaines, Twyla's supervisor had not been at home the night Twyla was dumped into the Clinton River, despite the fact it was his wife's birthday. He told police he had taken his car to be serviced at a shop on the corner of Gratiot and Conner then went to Grand River Avenue to another shop to have a tire repaired. He said he had visited several taverns alone before returning home between ten and ten-thirty. Unfortunately, his wife said he didn't arrive home until midnight, maybe later.

Ruth Haskins, who had also identified the body at Davis Funeral Home, said she rode home with Twyla on the streetcar on the night before she died. She said Twyla got off at McNichols Road and she continued on to Seven Mile Road. Unfortunately for her, other employees said that she, Twyla, and Robert Gaines had all left the plant together.

Dan had also obtained the name and address of the dead woman's parents up in Port Huron and included that in his story, adding that Mrs. Larson's mother had collapsed when told about her daughter. "I told her recently to quit work and come home," Mrs. Van Buren had told police officers.

Dan handed the second story over to the copy boy before heading to the paper's archives, a windowless room deep in the bowels of the building. The block walls gave off a musty, damp odor that he thought seemed so appropriate for a place referred to as The Morgue. Mrs. Hutchinson presided over the files here and was fastidious about it. That meant that invariably reporters could find what they were looking for. She was also a fount of information. She seemed to not only have read the newspaper everyday for the eighteen years she worked there, but to have retained it all in her mind. Often, a reporter would ask for a given file only to have Mrs. Hutchinson return with three others that were related.

No one seemed to know anything about Mrs. Hutchinson. She was a fixture in the building, like the glaring lights over her head, a resource you used and never thought about afterwards. Dan wondered if she ever felt that way. For the first time, he took a real look at her. It would be hard to say how old she was. Her short platinum hair was swept back from her face and fell in soft curls behind her ears. Tiny lines around her eyes betrayed what? Worry? Laughter? Her makeup was heavy but impeccably done. Her rather ample breasts sagged under their own weight and a small stomach protruded beneath her belt. When she turned away to retrieve the files, Dan noticed she had a nicely rounded ass and strong calves. She returned with the file on Lydia Thompson and Dan smiled at her. "Thanks, Mrs. Hutchinson. Does anyone call you anything besides Mrs. Hutchinson?"

"No. Mrs. Hutchinson is fine." Her smile was tight, but Dan thought he saw a flash of surprise or pleasure in her eyes. Then it was gone and she was Mrs. Hutchinson, the archivist. He took the file to a nearby table and spread it out. He thought he heard Mrs. Hutchinson humming.

The file held not only the published articles about the Thompson murder, but notes reporter Martha Shaw had made on the case. Mrs. Thompson and her husband were estranged. Their address was listed on Nottingham Avenue in Detroit. The street struck a familiar chord with Dan and he wrote it down. Three weeks ago, Mrs. Thompson had been found axed to death in her back yard. A barber and a beautician had been held in the slaying but were cleared after passing lie detector tests. Now the police seemed interested in the dead woman's father, a man born in Russia named Alexei Skirski. Nothing indicated why the police thought the father had any responsibility for his daughter's death. Back upstairs, Dan found Martha Shaw at her desk tapping out a story on her Smith Corona. He asked her if she had any updates on the case, in particular, why the police were interested in Mr. Skirski.

"I don't have any idea what they are thinking. I can't see anything that would make them think he could do it. They had a fiery relationship, but a father taking an axe to his daughter? Not likely. You ask me, I think they're just out of leads, and he's all they have. One of the officers told me that maybe the father was upset about the impending divorce, old-world values and all that. Plus, I suppose she was keeping Daddy in pretty high style with her husband's money. Could have been afraid of losing it, I guess. But axing your daughter to death is a pretty extreme way of showing disapproval, you'd have to say."

At his own desk, Dan checked the address he had written from the files in The Morgue and he realized why it was familiar. Mrs. Thompson lived in the same block on Nottingham Avenue as Twyla Larson's twin sister did. Was there some connection like a convoluted case of mistaken identity? Were the three women involved in something? If so, Theresa, Twyla's twin sister may be on someone's death list.

Dan glanced at his watch. Malin came on duty at Carrier Tool in about an hour. Dan could grab a sandwich at the Alibi Club on his way over. He arrived at Carrier just as Malin was clocking in. Malin greeted him with an affable smile and suggested they walk together as he made his check-in rounds at the gates and the tool crib.

The Carrier factory housed several acres of groaning, grinding, twisting machinery that made some kind of metal parts for something else. Not being handy with anything besides a typewriter, Dan had no idea what the various black and chrome pieces were that came chunking out the end of the three assembly lines. They could be something that goes into Ford's Tri-Motor airplane, a Dodge truck, or a Chrysler marine engine. Hell, for all he knew, they went into toasters. A double row of windows paraded twenty feet over the heads of the workers. Even in the depths of winter, some of them stood open to vent exhaust fumes and body heat. They also admitted the brisk Michigan winter air. Occasionally, a blast of the icy wind skidded over the heads of the workers, sending chills and stiffening fingers. The damp, snowy smell tumbled with the aroma of machine oil, exhaust fumes, and the sweat of the workers to create a sweet, pungent yet clean aroma. Since the end of the war, Carrier had reduced its work force like most war plants. Every third post on the assembly line and at the machines stood empty. A few men had returned to reclaim their jobs, but mostly women counted, sorted, drilled, and punched at Carrier's.

Dan followed Malin around the periphery of the plant as the guard checked doors and windows and logged in that he had done so. At the tool crib, he checked locks on drawers and cupboards then went out into the yard and patrolled the perimeter of the property for anything out of place. Though he talked easily, his body was anything but at ease. If they were standing still, he shifted from one foot to the other. As they walked and talked, his hands were always in motion, taking his hat off and putting it back on, lighting or putting out a cigarette, rubbing his face. Dan was aware again of a slight southern drawl. Malin had a long stride and, like the first time they talked, didn't look directly at Dan.

At the back of the property, Malin led Dan into a Quonset hut identified by a freshly painted sign as Building 14. At the back of the building stood a row of wooden tables bearing rows and rows of neatly arranged clay pots. Some had lush green heads of plants emerging from them while others bore fragile, pale shoots of plants. Dan recognized a few from having helped tend his mother's garden as carrots, tomatoes, and green beans in varying stages of growth as well as flowering plants he couldn't identify. Glancing around, he saw barrels of potting soil and fertilizer and a few bottles of liquid plant food. Stacks of unused, scrubbed pots stood in the corner.

"This your garden or the company's?" he asked.

"I guess you could say it's some of each. I started it, but Mr. Carrier reaps some of the rewards. Nothing like a fresh tomato on a January salad to keep the boss happy. I rotate the plants from his office through here so he always has the nicest looking ones up front. He lets me use this space and his water."

Dan asked Malin about the story Lieutenant Cunningham related concerning Twyla's asking Malin for help in collecting some money from someone. Malin said it was an ex-boyfriend who had taken the money. Malin was able to pull a few strings with his former colleagues and get a confession out of the boyfriend, but, as far as Malin knew, no money had been forthcoming. He said the boyfriend hung out at the Blue Orchid on Brush Street and Big Bill's Pool Hall. His name was Vince Di Grassi.

"She told me she moved in with him last summer and bought him clothes and a 1941 Packard. He always promised to pay her back and never did. I guess when she found out her husband was coming home she was pretty upset."

"What were you talking to Lieutenant Cunningham about? Cops and private eyes aren't legendary for their warm, wonderful relationships."

"Just trying to help. I don't want to see anyone getting away with murder. Besides, I was on the force myself. Professional courtesy, I guess you'd call it."

"Does that mean you have some idea who did it? You think this Vince Di Grassi murdered her?"

"I don't know, but he seems like a good prospect for it. He couldn't pay, she was going to go to the cops, he killed her."

"But I thought you said she came to you, not to the cops, and that she never did tell you what was troubling her."

"I couldn't help her. I told her to go to the cops and have his ass arrested. As for not telling you about it, I guess old habits die hard. Cops and reporters also don't have warm, wonderful relationships."

The two men had made a complete circuit of the property and were back at the front gate. The reporter slid his notebook into his overcoat pocket with one hand and extracted a pack of cigarettes from the opposite pocket, offering one to Cliff. They were quiet a moment as Dan lit the cigarettes and inhaled deeply from his.

"So you were on the force, eh? Whereabouts?" he asked.

"Detroit."

"No kidding. Maybe we ran into each other somewhere. I've been covering cops for a couple of years."

"I doubt it. I left the force about three years ago." Cliff blew out a long pale stream of smoke and turned slightly away from Dan.

"What precinct were you in?" the reporter pursued.

"I got around." He dropped his cigarette on the ground and stubbed it out with his toe. "And right now I gotta go."

Driving back to the office, Dan wondered about Cliff's reticence on the subject of his police career. The ex-cops he had met were always more than willing to talk about their exploits in uniform. Why was Malin so tight lipped? He shrugged and reached to turn the radio on.

# CHAPTER 4

▼

Unable to locate Di Grassi, Lieutenant Cunningham turned what information he had over to reporters who pasted the man's picture on page 1A of the *Detroit Free Press* and the *Detroit News* for two days. Di Grassi's sister saw the picture and called him in New York, persuading him to turn himself in to the New York police. Following an arduous two-day car trip from New York City through snow and slush, two scruffy-bearded, belligerent New York City police officers handed Vince Di Grassi over to Lieutenant Cunningham.

Di Grassi was the type of man everyone—even other men—noticed when he walked into a room. Thick, black hair cascaded in waves over his forehead and sparkling hazel eyes gave the impression he knew how to have a good time. Finely-chiseled features and olive skin betrayed his Italian heritage and broad shoulders above a narrow waist gave him a sleek figure even in the baggy prison garb he wore. Well-manicured fingernails and smooth hands told Stan Di Grassi was not given to manual labor.

Di Grassi lazed diffidently in a chair across the table from the Lieutenant, his right arm over the back of the chair, his left leg stretched straight out in front of him, He answered questions but without the sense of panic most suspects exhibited during interrogation. He had turned himself in because he had nothing to hide, he said. He was in New York City when Twyla was killed and could prove it. He told Stan what he had already told the New York cops at least five times. He was employed by Queens Vending filling vending machines and collecting money. He had neither seen nor spoken to Twyla since he left Detroit months ago, he said. He was now seeing a woman named Hazel Bellson.

On the morning of the day Twyla was killed, Di Grassi said he ate breakfast at a diner on Woodhaven Boulevard then reported to work, making his rounds until five or six o'clock. After work, he went to Sullivan's Bar for a beer and a sandwich then went home to shower and have a nap. He was back at Sullivan's at eight o'clock and stayed till about eight forty-five when he walked to the subway to meet his girlfriend who was coming in from Long Island. They went back to Sullivan's and stayed there until eleven o'clock. Then they went to her place and had sex four times. Stan's reaction was the same as the New York officers at this last bit of information. He quit taking notes and looked up at the Italian stud in front of him, shook his head, and looked down again.

New York City police had confirmed Di Grassi's alibi, though they saw no need to embarrass Miss Bellson by asking how many times the couple had made love that night. On the night Twyla's body was dumped in the Clinton River, Di Grassi was in New York. No question about it. They also had confirmed that Di Grassi had been working both the day before and the day after Twyla died. There was simply no way he could get to Michigan and back and still be at work. Though they concurred that Di Grassi couldn't be a suspect in the Larson murder, the New York City police delivered him to Detroit as a material witness and because Michigan had an outstanding warrant on the man.

Cunningham figured Di Grassi could fill in some of the blanks about Twyla Larson's time in Detroit and, most particularly, about the missing money.

"Talk to me about all this money you got from Mrs. Larson," Stan said, flipping through a file in front of him.

"We're not going into that again, are we? I've already come clean on that."

"What do you mean you came clean? About what?"

"About the money I owed her. Check with your friends in Detroit. I signed a confession and everything. That private eye friend of Twyla's made my life miserable until I signed it."

"What private eye friend?"

"Cliff Malin. Talk to him. He'll tell you how he dragged me into his old precinct and made me sign that I took all this money from Twyla. Only a lot of it wasn't true. All I got from her was about eighteen hundred dollars. Most of that was for the Packard. I only signed about the rest of it because he said he'd have my ass in prison if I didn't. I don't know about the rest of the money. Maybe Malin's got it."

"How could he have put you in prison if you didn't take the money?"

"Come off it, Lieutenant. The police don't care if you're guilty. You guys get your jollies arresting someone and being a hard ass. Malin still has a lot of friends on the force. You should have seen the way he strutted around that station, like he owned the joint. He coulda gotten them to do anything he wanted."

"How well did you know Malin?"

"We weren't buddies, but I seen him around. Twyla knew him better than I did. She knew him long before I met her. I always thought he was jealous, but in a strange kinda way. Not like he cared we were living together, more like he was jealous of her time, like he wanted her to be available to do things with him when he wanted her, not out dancing with me. There was always bad blood between me and him. Then Twyla went to him about the money. I guess her husband was coming home and she wanted me to pay her back. Only I couldn't. I borrowed the money in the first place because I wasn't working. I sent her a couple hundred bucks since I've been in New York. I was trying to pay it back."

"What's this about you and Mrs. Larson living together?"

"We got us a little apartment for a few months last summer. She told her landlady she was going to stay with a girlfriend whose husband had been killed. It turned out not to be so good an idea, us living together, and she moved back into her landlady's."

"What do you mean Malin has a lot of friends on the Detroit force?"

"Are you kidding? Don't you know who he is? He was part of that mess a couple years back when all those cops went up the river. Only he didn't go with them. He got kicked off the force, but he must be connected, if you know what I mean. Never spent a day in jail. The Captain of the Bethune station where he used to work is still buddies with him. He let Malin use his office to get me to confess to this whole cockamamie story. I had to sign it. I didn't stand a chance."

Stan fiddled with his pencil as he thought a few minutes. A lot of men, well over a hundred, were involved in that mess a couple of years ago that Di Grassi referred to. One of them, Martin Flanagan, had been Stan's partner for the first couple years after their police training. But Flanagan had been bored with the petty crimes of Pontiac and wanted action, so he took a job with the Detroit force. Stan guessed he'd gotten the action he wanted. He also got twelve years in prison.

"Did Twyla go out with Malin much?" he asked, lighting a pipe and glancing at Di Grassi as he puffed.

"If you mean did they date, I don't think so. Sometimes when I wasn't in the mood to go out, she would call him and they would go nightclubbing together, but it was never a date thing. She just called him so she wouldn't have to go alone. Sometimes he called her, though and she'd run out of the place and not tell me where she was going. Hell if I know why, though. She never talked about him or what they were up to."

"But you're sure they knew each other pretty well."

"Damn sure."

Stan asked about the 1941 Packard. Blood red, Di Grassi said it was. He had bought it because it was a good deal, and he thought he could sell it for a profit. He would turn the profit over to Twyla to help pay back some of the money he owed her. Before he could sell it, though, he had an accident so he wasn't going to be able to get even the thirteen hundred and fifty he had paid for it. It still ran, though. He didn't know what she did with the car since she didn't drive. He left the interrogation room and told the desk sergeant to issue an all points bulletin on the car.

For two more hours, he asked Di Grassi to repeat his story—where he was when Twyla died, how well he knew her, how well he knew Malin. The room grew hot and thick with smoke and body smells. Dark stains grew under Stan's arms and his waist sweated under his belt. His mouth felt like an overfull ashtray and his forehead grew greasy. He needed air and a whiskey, but he kept questioning Di Grassi. Getting a person to repeat his story over and over often led to an arrest when the stories didn't match. But Di Grassi remained implacable. His hair stayed in place, his uniform unrumpled. He grew restless and paced the room, but he never got angry or threatened the officers in the room. And his story never changed. Finally, Stan stood up and stretched.

"I guess you're in the clear on the murder, but you'll be staying with us for a little while anyway," he said. "You should have been sending your ex-wife those child support checks."

After the prisoner was taken away, Stan sat mulling over his story. Either Di Grassi or Malin was lying and he began to suspect the latter. Di Grassi didn't seem to have anything to hide, but, if it was true Malin had been caught up in that scandal in Detroit a couple years back, he had plenty to hide.

A knock at the door interrupted his thoughts. A lean, pale officer stood in the doorway with a file folder in his hand. Stan signaled him in with two fingers. He had assigned the man to investigate any connection between Twyla Larson and Lydia Thompson figuring he would have access to files that Dan Kirk couldn't get.

"How's it going?" Stan asked.

"You know. Some you win, some you lose. I think on this one we got rained out." He handed the file folder to the Lieutenant. "You might want to go over this and see if I missed anything, but I can't find any connection between Mrs.

Larson and Mrs. Thompson. Not directly and not indirectly. I think it was just coincidence that Mrs. Thompson lived on the same street as Mrs. Larson's sister. Mrs. Larson and Mrs. Thompson didn't even get their hair done at the same beauty parlor."

Stan shrugged. "I'm not surprised. We've talked to a lot of people about Mrs. Larson and Mrs. Thompson's name never came up. And Mrs. Larson's sister and brother-in-law are squeaky clean. They don't even spit on the sidewalk. Thanks for looking into it, though."

Stan's thoughts returned to Cliff Malin. Reaching for the telephone, he dialed the Oakland Country Prosecutor's Office. When Howard Pitts answered the phone, Stan came right to the point. "Howard, I want to schedule a lie detector test. Yeah…for a murder suspect. Clifford Malin. How soon can I get him in?" After the prosecutor scheduled the test for that afternoon, Stan headed for Carrier Tool and Die to bring the suspect in.

Dan Kirk's curiosity continued to be piqued by who the real Twyla Larson was. Mrs. Searle told him that when Twyla left home the night of her death, she was headed for a dentist's appointment. A phone call to Dr. Arthur Wesley revealed that, not only did she not have an appointment, he didn't even take appointments on Tuesday evenings. Further, he said, he had completed Mrs. Larson's dental work a week and a half earlier. Whatever her destination, Dan realized she was going to great lengths to mask it.

Then there were the two people Twyla worked with who had been held for questioning. He wondered what they knew about this mystery woman. It was this lead he decided to track down next.

The windshield wipers of his Dodge could barely keep up with the snowfall as he inched his way across the city to the east side where Anna Harlow lived. He stopped the car at the curb in front of the address he had gotten from police records. It was a smallish house with crumpled paint on the eaves and at least two seasons of soot on the porch and the windows. The woman wasn't home, but her husband was.

"My wife has told the police everything she knows," the husband said through a torn screen door. Despite the biting November wind that wrapped itself around Dan, the man at the door stood easily in a sleeveless undershirt, greasy pants held up with suspenders, and stockinged feet. At least two days growth of beard surrounded yellow teeth.

"I'm sure she has, but the police files are kind of a mess. They don't always get their notes written right away. I was hoping you or she could help me get the story correct," Kirk said.

The man paused a minute, then let him inside. Newspapers, dirty dishes, empty beer cans, and overflowing ashtrays littered the room. Dan sat on a tattered brown sofa dotted with food stains. The man sat across from him in what was obviously his chair; the ashtray and full beer bottle were within easy reach.

He said his name was Jerry. Jerry and his wife, Anna, were good friends of Robert and Eloise Gaines and often visited each other or went out together. Sometimes Mrs. Larson came along. Dan asked if they had all been out together the night Twyla was killed. He said—just a little too adamantly, Dan thought— that his wife had been home with him all night. He asked if Jerry knew any of Twyla's other friends, and he said he did not. He said his wife and Twyla weren't very close friends, they just worked together and sometimes rode home on the street car together and he only saw Twyla a couple of times. He thought she was stuck up, dressed too fancy, was too full of herself. Outside, Dan took several deep breaths, cleansing his nostrils of the musty, dirty smell of the house.

He picked his way through the slick, crowded streets to Carrier Tool and Die. The farther west he drove, the lighter the snowfall became until, by the time he arrived at the plant, only an occasional flake drifted onto the windshield. Shifts were changing as he arrived, a stream of fresh employees filing into the building to replace those who had been there all day. Searching through the sea of faces, he found Robert Gaines and signaled to him with an upraised arm. As Gaines politely stepped around his fellow workers, Dan decided against taking out his notebook. He had a sense that this man would talk more easily if his words weren't being recorded.

Robert Gaines stood about five feet eleven and had a slender build under his heavy winter coat. His lips curled upwards in the corner in a permanent smile and he spoke slowly, a bit patronizingly as though dealing with a child or an imbecile. His haircut, his mustache, his hands, his clothes were more that of a banker than an assembly line supervisor.

"Mr. Kirk, is it? What can I do for you?" Gaines said.

"I just had a few questions I wanted to clear up about your relationship with Mrs. Larson. Can you give me a minute?"

"Just a minute. My wife is expecting me home. And I'm not sure I understand what you mean when you say my relationship with Mrs. Larson. She just worked for me."

"You didn't socialize with her?"

"We went out as part of a group several times. That's all." Gaines nodded a greeting to someone over Dan's shoulder as he spoke.

"You told the police that the reason you were so sure about where you were the night that Mrs. Larson died was that it was your wife's birthday. But you also said you weren't home with your wife. Didn't that upset her, you leaving her alone on her birthday?"

"My wife had been upset for several days, which is why I ignored her birthday. You know how these things are. Are you married, Mr. Kirk?"

"No, I'm not. You told the police you went to several taverns that night. Which ones?"

Gaines paused. "Are you going to put this in the paper?"

"That depends on what you tell me."

Gaines took Dan by the elbow and led him away from the stream of workers still filing out of the door.

"Look, Mr. Kirk. My wife and I haven't been getting on. We've been married twelve years and have two kids. It seems we're always short of money or she's sick or there's some problem with the kids. I've been seeing someone."

"Who?"

"Do you have to know?"

"If you don't tell me the police will." He said it knowing that it wasn't likely they would.

"Mrs. Harlow. I've been seeing Anna." Having just seen Anna Harlow's husband, Dan at least understood why she looked elsewhere for companionship.

"Is that one of the women that was with you at the funeral home?" he asked.

"Yes. Twyla usually covered for us. The three of us would meet somewhere and have a drink or two, then Anna and I would leave. If Twyla had met someone wherever we were by then, she would stay. If not, she'd go looking somewhere else."

"So are you saying that Twyla liked to meet new men?"

"Don't put words in my mouth, Mr. Kirk. I never saw her do anything but talk and dance with the men she met." He paused a moment and stroked his mustache. "You know, the last couple of weeks there was some guy in a big maroon Packard that she talked to. I never saw the driver and she never said who it was, but a couple of times when she walked out of the club with us, I noticed her going over to that car and talking to the driver. Once, when I couldn't get my car started, we sat in the parking lot for a few minutes. I saw her get in the car and drive off, but the way she stormed around to the passenger side and slammed the door, I got the impression she wasn't happy about going."

Dan thanked Gaines for his time and drove back to his office, mulling over what he had heard. Di Grassi said he had bought a Packard with the money he got from Twyla. Was this the same Packard? Who was driving it? Back at the newsroom, he found a message from Stan and immediately dialed the sheriff's office number.

"I hope you haven't written your story for tomorrow's paper yet. You'll have to start over again if you have," the Lieutenant said.

"Why? What's going on?"

"Clifford Malin just tried to commit suicide. I'm booking him for the murder of Twyla Larson."

"Suicide? What for?"

"A lot of things didn't gel about that man. I just didn't like him, and there were too many odd things about how he behaved and what he said. He put an awful lot of effort into making us think this Di Grassi killed the Larson woman when there's no way he could have. Then we found the missing Packard in Malin's driveway. I brought him in for a lie detector test and he failed miserably. When I told him he hadn't passed, I asked him to explain himself. He asked for a pen and some paper and said he would write out his story. We left him alone in one of the interrogation rooms. He must have suspected we were closing in on him, because he brought a razor blade with him and used it to slash his wrists. I figure innocent men don't try to commit suicide, so we booked him."

"How is he?" Dan asked, scribbling madly in his notebook.

"He'll live, much to his dismay, I imagine. He's at the hospital under guard."

Dan's story about Malin's suicide attempt ran that afternoon, complete with a photograph of the former cop in his hospital bed and another dredged from the files of Detroit Police Department of Malin in his police lieutenant's uniform.

Dan had just settled into his desk chair with a fresh cup of coffee and a cruller the next morning when the receptionist called to say he had a visitor. He took a bite of the cruller, swallowed a gulp of coffee, grabbed a notepad and two pencils, and headed for the lobby. The woman who stood at the counter waiting for him was a pretty blonde in her late twenties, he guessed. Her blue eyes had a certain tenderness about them, her pale white skin luminescent and pink from the cold air. She spoke softly, choosing her words carefully, as though she didn't want to offend anyone. Clutching a copy of that day's edition in her gloved hand, she identified herself as Mary Bacon and said she and her parents had moved to Detroit several years ago from Flat River, Missouri in search of work at the automobile plants. They lived at the north end of the city near Three Mile Road.

"This man whose picture is in the paper here," she said, spreading the paper on the counter top between her and Dan and pointing to Clifford Malin. "Well, Mr. Kirk, my parents say they remember him from back home. I didn't know if they were right about him. They are in their sixties, you see, but they seemed so positive. I don't remember him, but then the last few years before we moved from Flat River, I was away at school. I was just home briefly between semesters. But my parents are very sure. I've worried about this all night and I thought the best thing to do would be to tell you about it and see if you can find out anything."

She paused and cleared her throat, shifting from one foot to another before looking straight into Dan's face. "You see, Mr. Kirk, my parents say that when they were still living in Flat River, this man in the paper, this Mr. Malin, well, they say he killed his wife."

# CHAPTER 5

▼

Dan Kirk blinked against the strong morning light reflecting off the snow as he stepped down from the bus at Flat River, Missouri. It seemed like another lifetime when he'd left Detroit aboard the Baltimore & Ohio headed first for Cincinnati then St. Louis then a three hour bus trip to Flat River. He was stiff and dirty and his lungs were full of stale air.

As soon as the young woman had left the building, Kirk had telephoned Stan Cunningham and told him about the conversation with her. He could hear the lieutenant puffing heavily at his pipe, a sign that his mind was working out what should happen next. When Dan finished talking, Stan said, "You got more travel money than I have. You see if your editor will send you to Missouri. I'll drive up to Port Huron and talk to Mrs. Larson's family and friends. Her husband is supposed to be home the end of the week. The poor bastard's going to miss her funeral."

"I'll go provided you don't tell any other reporter about this woman and her news about Malin. I want this scoop."

"You got it," Stan said and dropped the phone in its cradle.

For a change, Dan hadn't had to beg his editor, Ed Harris, for permission to make a trip. When Ed heard the story the young woman had told Dan, he said simply, "Get your ass down there." But Ed wasn't so profligate as to let his reporter book a sleeper car, so now, standing at the bus station in Flat River, he longed for a flat, soft surface to stretch out on. He knew better than to sleep this early in the day, though. He'd be up all night and this town didn't look like it had a night life. Despite the crisp temperature, the sun was warm and the air was still. A stroll around town would take the kinks out and brighten his mind. He dumped his suitcase in a locker at the station and headed out.

There wasn't much to see, he quickly realized. In fact, the most notable feature of Flat River, Missouri was that it had no notable feature. No well-kept grassy park with sparkling white gazebo marked the city center. No stone statue paid tribute to the town's father or its most famous soldier. No ornate church steeple pierced the sky over the town. Instead, boxy, gray-brown buildings hunkered along the chief thoroughfare unremarkably named Main Street, other roads bleeding out from it around hills and trees and buildings without design. The mossy brown river for which the town was named twisted through the surrounding foothills, hills once verdant with oak and maple, now viciously scarred by a network of railroad tracks leading from mines to refineries to town.

And it didn't seem to fit the description he often heard of America as a melting pot. It seemed more a schizophrenic society of French, German, Russian, Irish, and Hungarian cultures inhabiting the same town. He stopped at Willy's barbershop and heard only German conversations. At the French bakery where he purchased a small bread roll and some coffee, he was looked at askance when he spoke English. The knot of women standing outside the Hungarian café spoke their native tongue. After walking nearly an hour, he stopped at what appeared to be an American café, ordered breakfast.

Dan picked up a copy of the local newspaper, *The Flat River Daily Telegraph,* and noticed it was dated yesterday. He'd remember to look for today's issue this afternoon when it hit the streets. The lead story was about the Thanksgiving dinner the St. Joseph Lead Company would be hosting for its workers. The grinning face of the company president, Harold Booth, stared up at Dan as he ate. He couldn't help but notice that the reporters at *The Telegraph* had never heard of a stylebook. Breakfast over, he dropped a couple of dollars on the table and asked the waitress for directions to the newspaper office.

Dan glanced at his watch. Quarter to ten. Deadline should have just passed. Clark Phillips was listed as editor in chief and Dan asked for him at the front desk after identifying himself as a reporter from Detroit. He waited fifteen minutes before a short, scrawny, gray-haired man descended a staircase to the right of the lobby. He walked quickly over to Dan and gave him a firm handshake.

"Sorry to keep you waiting. I'm Clark Phillips. We don't get many visits from big city reporters. Must be something hot. I go for breakfast after we put the paper to bed. You wanna come along?"

"I just ate, but I could use more coffee. It was a long, rough trip down here."

Clark Phillips didn't bother with a coat, apparently comfortable in his shirt with sleeves rolled up to the elbows and a wool waistcoat. He offered Dan a cigarette and the two men walked back to the café Dan had just left, talking about weather, Dan's trip, and the approaching holidays. Once seated, Clark ordered two eggs, fried, sausage, grits, pancakes, juice, and coffee. He seemed unable to sit still, either smoking a cigarette, lighting one off the last one, pushing his glasses up on his nose, running his hand through his hair. Dan figured he'd be hard to work for; all that nervous energy would translate into demands on his reporters for ever more stories, even if the tiny paper couldn't hold them. The men's conversation was frequently interrupted by people stopping at the table to speak or just calling across the room to the editor.

"Sorry about the interruptions," he said. "You get to be a big fish in a small pond when you run a small newspaper. And I been running this one for over thirty years." He stopped to light a new cigarette, offering one to Dan which he declined. "So what brings you to this neck of the woods?"

Dan pulled an envelope from his inside coat pocket and extracted a photograph, pushing it across to Clark. "You know this man?"

"Looks a little familiar. Who is it?"

"Cliff Malin."

"Ah, Cliff Malin. What's he got himself into now?"

"You mean he has a history?"

"Everyone has a history, son. It's just some are more interesting than others. Cliff, here, he ranks up with the interesting ones. What you got on him?"

Dan gave the editor a rough outline of what he knew about Malin, Twyla Larson's death. When Dan started to talk about the graft and corruption scandal that had rocked Detroit two years earlier, Clark stopped him. "I saw that when it moved on the wires. We carried a little bit of it. Are you telling me that our home town boy, Cliff Malin, was involved?"

"Involved up to his earlobes, it seems, although I haven't gotten into it yet. I covered a lot of that case, but I don't remember Malin. It was all handled through the grand jury, so a lot of it is sealed. I'll have to see what I can dig up when I get back."

"So what are you looking for down here? Just some background stuff?"

"A little more than that. I had a visit from a young woman the day before I left Detroit. She said she and her parents used to live here and that there had been a rumor that Malin killed his first wife down here."

Clark stopped moving for the first time since Dan had met him and looked straight into Dan's eyes. "How long you going to be here?"

"Long as it takes to find out what I need to know."

"Meet me at the newspaper office at three. We'll have dinner and I'll give you want I can."

Clark's car wound through the narrow streets of Flat River in the diminishing daylight as Dan gazed out the windows at the unremarkable buildings. On a quiet street a short distance from town, Clark stopped at the curb and pointed to a stately, two story house. "That's the Malin family home," he said. "Vera, the oldest daughter lives there now with her husband. She raised all her kids there. I'll tell you about the family." He put the car in gear and pulled away from the curb and began talking.

By the town's standards, the Malin family lived quite comfortably. While the average miner's home was little more than a hovel of three rooms with porches enclosed to make additional bedrooms as more babies arrived, the Malin family home was a tidy two-story building with an ample yard for the rompings of four daughters and a son. The house had been part of the reward Henry Malin received when he successfully sank Shaft No. 5 for the St. Joseph Lead Co. around 1915, a shaft that had confounded other miners and suffered several cave-ins. Henry also received a promotion to captain of the mine that came with a healthy pay raise. Each Friday, he handed his wife his total pay check—twenty-five dollars.

Though the son of German immigrants, Henry was considered American since no one had known his parents and he spoke without an accent. His large square jaw, thick dark hair, and broad shoulders made him much sought after as a young man. He had had his share of encounters with some of the more willing women of Flat River. He was happy to let them show their appreciation of his rugged masculinity in the hayloft or down by the river bank.

Henry never got past eighth grade in school. His parents died that year when their horse shied away from a snake and dragged their wagon on a wild ride through the forest. The wagon tipped on its side as the horse rounded a tree, dumping its passengers and landing on them. Henry took a job in the mines near Flat River to help his oldest sister, Hannah, raise their two younger siblings.

Henry married Etta Banks when they were both seventeen. She grew up in Flat River where her father ran the American hardware store. She had a couple of beaux before she met Henry, but they seemed to tire of her quickly. Sweet and charming one minute, she could burst into violent tantrums over almost nothing. Henry ducked many flying plates in the years since he married Etta. But he was smitten by her beauty, her wit, her sensuousness. She had skin like alabaster and moist pink lips that she licked frequently as she talked.

As Cliff was growing up, women in the Malin neighborhood gathered weekly at a different home to pare apples, quilt or husk corn as their children played in the yard or in front of the fire. They ate lunch together on these occasions, then put the children down for their naps wherever space could be found. The older women who had raised their children taught the younger women new recipes and quilt patterns. Etta Malin used to be invited regularly to these gatherings but, little by little, she was excluded. Some say it was having babies that made her the way she was, but others who grew up with her knew she had been that way since they could remember. Some said it was inherited from her mother who was sent to an asylum when she was twenty three. Etta's ravings about Armageddon, her running up and down the street at midnight in her nightgown, her tauntings of anyone who set foot on the Malin property—it all got to be too much for the neighbors and Etta was no longer asked to join the women in the afternoon.

Henry Malin bore his wife's actions quietly. He rescued her from the streets at midnight, wrapping his own coat around her and gently sliding a pair of shoes on her bare feet before leading her back home. "It's okay, Etta. It's time to come home," he would coo at her. His voice and big, warm arms acted like a sedative on her. She quieted down, became demure, let him lead her home. When she'd scream at someone who walked on their front lawn, he ran to the street and apologized for her.

Behind closed doors, he was just as solicitous of her, helping with meals if she didn't feel like cooking, making sure she got her bath every week, helping her choose her clothes. In his heart, though, he knew Etta was deteriorating. He had lost the Etta he had loved and he didn't know what else he could do but be there when she needed him.

Clifford was the fifth and last of the Malin children following Vera, Nina, Josephine, Catherine, and Cecilia. Since Cliff had been a little boy, his father talked of the day they would work side by side in the mines. Evenings they would join the other men at the Black Bear Saloon. As for Clifford, he could think of nothing less appealing than the damp, dark caverns beneath the Ozark foothills followed by guzzling cheap beer in a crowded, smelly, blue-aired bar. Clifford mirrored the disappointment of city founders LaMotte and Renault at the fate that dropped him in the midst of a remote town whose motto, Gateway to the Ozarks, meant to him Gateway to Oblivion. He felt smothered in the tiny burg and lived for the day when he could escape its dullness and predictability. Working in the mines for the rest of his life like his father, uncle, and neighbors held not the slightest allure. On soggy spring days, Clifford leafed through the Sears Roebuck catalog, studying the pages of handsome clothes, stylish furniture, modern graphophones, Edison records, and horseless buggies. Summers he climbed the hill in back of his parents' house and lay on his back hidden by the tall timothy, turning the clouds into beautiful women with long flowing gowns, lavish mansions, and bubbling bottles of champagne. Winters when the river froze over, he skated on its frozen crest past the edge of town and nearly to the neighboring town of DuBois, imagining he would never return. He might end up in New York or Los Angeles or even the wild Pacific Northwest with its untamed Indians. All that mattered was that he get out of Flat River.

After graduating from high school, Cliff had reluctantly taken a job in the mines figuring the good wages would allow him to build his get-away fund quickly. But Clifford had inherited his mother's pale Irish skin and after only a few weeks working in the ever-present grit and dust, his sensitive skin erupted in angry, red rashes. Try as he might to put up with the inconvenience and discomfort for the sake of the salary, he finally had to look for cleaner work. His father was mortified.

To make up for the loss of the high wages, Clifford was constantly on the prowl for work, accepting as many jobs as he could possibly fit into the day. He set pins at the bowling alley and sold tickets at the Dreamland Theater. He delivered oil for Mr. Gallagher, the local Standard Oil distributor, and he swept out the livery stable at the end of town and delivered newspapers.

Of all his jobs, though, it was the one at the Dreamland Theater that kept alive his fantasy of leaving town. Through the moving pictures, he tried on different lives, turning this way and that as if he were trying on a new suit, testing the lives for comfort. Aboard ships whose decks were piled high with treasure, he discovered uncharted islands. Leaping in front of speeding trains, he rescued Pauline from the perils of the railroad tracks. The head of a large corporation, he wielded power and authority as a captain of industry.

John Giessing, owner of the Dreamland, was a progressive, forward-thinking man and it excited Clifford just to be around him. As business improved, Giessing moved the Dreamland to larger quarters and replaced the gas picture machine with a brand new electric one, even though the theater needed to produce its own electricity to run it. "A businessman must have vision," Mr. Giessing was fond of saying.

Since Cliff had been a young boy working at his mother's side, he had felt at peace digging in a garden. He loved the way his family's home stood out from all the others around it, flounced as it was with rose-laden trellises, lush, brilliant azaleas, mums, iris, and violets. All summer long, the family dined on fresh beans, peas, corn, cucumbers, raspberries, and elderberries. Winters they continued the feast from the stores his mother had put up. As his mother's behavior became more erratic, Cliff took over complete charge of the flowers and vegetables in the yard. So accomplished a gardener had he become that he consistently won prizes at the county fairs and even won a blue ribbon at the state fair for the largest pumpkin. These days, he was growing much more than his family could consume, selling the rest to neighbors and adding to his nest egg. Occasionally, someone would buy some of his peonies, daffodils, or roses to decorate a table or take to a sick friend.

Clark stopped talking as he pulled into the driveway of a sprawling Victorian home. As they went through the front door, Clark called out, "Ruth, we're home." A woman emerged from a door at the end of the front hallway, wiping her hands on her apron. "Hi, dear," she said.

Clark introduced her as his wife then kissed her warmly on the cheek. Dan noticed her eyes glisten in response to the kiss. She was as thin as her husband but lacked his nervous gestures. "Can I fix you something to drink, Mr. Kirk? Clark always has a highball when he first gets home."

"A highball would be fine," Dan said, removing his hat and coat and placing them in her outstretched arms. The house was much like his mother's, though much larger. It was warm and the air was thick with the aroma of cleaning supplies and cooking. Clark led him into a room to the left of the front door that held a massive mahogany desk and shelves on every wall filled with books. The men sat opposite each other in two Queen Anne wingback chairs just as Ruth appeared with two highballs on a silver tray. "Dinner in about a half hour," she said as she left and closed the door.

"The newspaper business pays better in Flat River than it does in Detroit," Dan said, surveying the room.

"The newspaper business doesn't pay worth a damn anywhere," Clark grinned. "I inherited this place from my father who owned the Ford distributorship here. He also made a few bucks during Prohibition from the stills in the barn. Fortunately, he left enough money to maintain the place too, because I sure couldn't do it on my salary."

"So tell me about Flat River in general and anything else you might know about Cliff Malin," Dan said sipping from his drink.

"I can help you more with Flat River than I can with Cliff Malin personally. I've told you what I know about his family. His being desperate to get out of here everyone knew about because he was always looking for work. He was dependable and pretty much everybody hired him at one time or another. I lost track of him after he came home from the service, though. I remember there being some talk when he left town around 1920. I'll tell you what I can remember."

# CHAPTER 6

▼

Cliff's escape from Flat River came earlier than he had anticipated when the United States Congress declared war on Germany on April 6, 1917. When President Woodrow Wilson called for the conscription of all able-bodied men, Cliff enlisted in the Army immediately.

Though he was disappointed when he learned he would enter basic training at St. Louis, a mere sixty-five miles from home, Private Malin's spirits soared when he received orders to report with his unit to northern France. The fact he was going there to fight a war and could be hurt or even killed did not affect his elation. He had ten days to return to Flat River and say his goodbyes.

The first morning of his leave, Cliff rose early, unable to sleep much past sunrise after six weeks of rising before dawn at boot camp. He didn't want to sleep anyway. Sleep kept him from marking the passage of time until his departure, kept him from conjuring up images of France. Creeping downstairs into the kitchen so as not to waken his parents, he made a fresh pot of coffee then returned to his room and carefully dressed in his wool Army uniform. Despite an expected hot, sticky day so typical of July, he wanted to parade through town in his uniform, flaunting the fact that he was headed for high adventure while everyone else was stuck with their monotonous, single-dimension lives in Flat River.

Surveying himself in the large bureau mirror, he grinned at his reflection. Boot camp had toned and shaped his six-foot body to the stage where he could be called muscular and the shoulder pads in the uniform jacket enhanced his more brawny appearance. The doughboy cap smothered his unruly dark blond curls into submission, the uniform's brass buttons glistened, his boots shined like patent leather. He was ready to present himself to Flat River.

Downstairs, he found his parents sitting at the kitchen table sipping the coffee he had made. His mother seemed alert and calm this morning and his father sat peacefully in the chair across from her at the kitchen table. Clicking his heels together and standing as straight as he had been taught in boot camp, he said, "Private Clifford Malin reporting for duty." Relaxing his back slightly he smiled. "What do you think, Ma? Am I the handsomest devil you ever saw?"

Etta Malin grinned back. "My, my. You sure are a sight. Why, there isn't a girl in town wouldn't agree with me."

Clifford's father concurred. "You cut a mighty fine figure, lad." His disappointment in his son's failure to make it in the mines was assuaged at the sight of his son in uniform.

Etta left the room and Cliff heard the drawer in the dining room hutch open. She returned carefully holding her treasured Brownie camera. Since her husband presented the camera to her two Christmases earlier, no event in the Malin household went unrecorded on film.

"Get outside in the sunshine where I can get a nice picture, Clifford. Henry, you come along too. I want a picture of my two men."

The still, bright morning had not yet relieved the grass of its dew. The men stood in front of Etta's billowing yellow rose bush, their arms crossed at the wrists in front of them. Etta clicked off several shots, ending the roll of film.

"You'll have to take the camera into the post office later today," she said to no one in particular. "We'll send it off right away and get the new one back in time for the ice cream social at the church."

The trio streamed back into the kitchen. "Sit down, both of you. I'll make you a nice breakfast."

"Not now, Ma," Cliff said. "I'm going into town and look up some of the guys. See you later." He dropped a kiss on his mother's cheek as he brushed past her. "Bye, Pa," he called over his shoulder. The screen door banged shut behind him.

Walking the few short blocks from his home to Main Street, Clifford nodded to Cappy, the old Italian who sold coal door to door, then to Mrs. Milligan, tending her garden. Mr. Anderson, who sold ice in Flat River, called to women whose homes he was passing in his horse-drawn cart. "Miller! Ice!" At the next house "Watson! Ice!" then "LeBlanc! Ice!" The two summers Cliff had worked for Mr. Anderson he learned not to depend on the card in the window that was supposed to announce the household's need for ice. Far too often, he or Mr. Anderson had chipped off a ten-pound block, slung it on his back atop two layers of burlap and lugged it around the back of the house only to discover the woman of the house had forgotten to remove the card for her previous order. Back he would carry the ice to the cart, by now dripping as it melted. He would have to chip off a smaller piece at the next stop that wanted ten pounds in order to make up for what had melted.

Arriving at the railroad depot perched atop a hill overlooking town, he stopped and looked down at the bleak little buildings lying in the small valley below him. Not even the bright summer sun could penetrate the shadow of gloom Cliff imagined hung over the town, but it didn't matter to him anymore. In ten days, he would be gone. Forever, he hoped. His gaze fell upon a group of about a dozen men gathered outside the American barbershop, the American one. Loud, angry voices drifted toward him but he was too far away to hear what they were saying. As he drew closer, though, he caught a few words. "Foreigners." they were saying. Then he heard "garlic breath" and "real Americans".

Once in front of the barbershop, he realized he had seen only a portion of the group that had gathered. At least twice as many were packed inside. Through the open door, he saw Nate O'Hare, a man known around town as a loud-mouth malcontent, four years Clifford's senior. The sun bounced off the glistening mirror at the back of the shop, the row of customers' shaving mugs lined neatly on the shelf like a row of uniformed soldiers. John White, owner of the shop, and his barber, Oliver Ott, stood behind one chair, their eyes focused on Nate standing behind the second.

Nate was barking at the men gathered in front of him. Face grimy with dust, miner's lamp still fastened to his forehead, a barber chair for his rostrum O'Hare ranted on.

"Last night was finally it," he raved. "I been trying to forget it, but I just can't. Me and the missus and Jack here" he gestured to someone at the front edge of the crowd, "and his missus and a whole bunch of us. We was just trying to have a nice evening out, enjoying the pictures and all. But how can you have a good time when the stink of garlic is everywhere? Americans don't eat garlic! I just couldn't take it. First it was them taking jobs that belong to Americans. Then they start selling all that damn weird food. Next thing you know, they're going to be marrying our daughters. We gotta do something."

Cliff saw Warren Gladstone, a man who worked for his father, standing in front of him. Tapping Warren on the shoulder, he whispered, "What's going on? What happened last night?"

"Boy, you shoulda been at the Dreamland. They was some real going ons," Gladstone whispered back. Men standing nearby shushed them quiet, and Gladstone took Clifford's elbow and led him away from the crowd.

"We was all at the Dreamland last night, us Americans downstairs and the foreigners upstairs, just like usual. The movie just started when Nate there stands up and says real loud 'The smell of garlic in this place makes me sick. I don't know how any of you can stand it.'

"Tell the truth, I couldn't smell any garlic down where I was, but Nate, maybe he had a snoutful. And I hear his sister Mary Frances run off with one of them German fellas last week. But you know how Nate is. Gits hisself all riled up and everyone else, too. 'Fore you know, all the Americans was stompin' outta the Dreamland. Then someone upstairs, one of the foreigners yells 'Go ahead! Leave, you Yankee! And go to war while you're at it! We'll take care of your jobs for you. Your women, too!'

"I thought things was gonna get rough there for a few minutes, cuz the men started to sendin' their womenfolk home but nothing happened. They just all went down to the Black Bear and drank theirselves stupid. The foreigners just stayed and watched the movie. Next thing I hear is this morning. I come in for a haircut and Melvin was cuttin' the mayor's hair. Nate comes charging in like a wild man sayin' we got to do something about the foreigners. Men stopped to hear what he was saying, and that's where you come in."

Cliff turned back to hear Nate shouting "I say we get rid of them now! Today! We'll be sorry if we let this go any further." Suddenly, Nate burst through the crowd and into the street where his horse stood. Pulling a rifle from his saddlebag he called, "Are you with me?"

The men roared their reply, racing to their own horses and buckboards to retrieve their firearms. Nate led the crowd on foot through the streets to the edge of town then out to the Doe Run Lead Company's Shaft No. 1 where he demanded to see the foreman. Spellbound, Clifford followed at a safe distance.

"We don't mean no harm, sir," O'Hare told the foreman, Ed Wallace, in a voice surprisingly placid and polite. "It's the foreigners we're after. Just send them all up here and we'll go away."

"Now, Nate," Wallace said in a voice he might use with a recalcitrant child. "Don't go getting yourself all riled up like you do. Your Pa won't want to be hearing about this."

"I mean it, Mr. Wallace. We all do. We ain't taking anymore guff from these smelly foreigners. They want our jobs and our women. If they was real Americans, they'd be fighting in the war same as your son. Just send them up and there won't be any trouble."

"What do you intend doing with them?" Wallace asked.

"We ain't going to hurt nobody. We just want them out of town."

Glancing over the crowd of men in back of O'Hare, Wallace wasn't inclined to argue. He knew some of these men to be real hotheads. With guns in their hands, who knew what might happen. He climbed in the cage that took him to the bottom of the shaft and sent the immigrants he had working for him to the surface, riding in the first car himself to try to keep peace. It took nearly an hour to empty the mine of the wanted men. Nate and his band of followers stood quietly as the elevator graunched up and down the shaft. As the miners surfaced, they were surrounded and corralled in the midst of the Americans. Except for a few barked orders to the immigrants, no one spoke.

When the mine superintendent assured the Americans no more foreigners were left below, the march began. First, Nate headed them to the company paymaster, demanding the men's final paychecks be drawn immediately. Harvey Johnson, the paymaster, was a nervous little man with red hair that was graying. He was a man of routine, not easily adaptable to changes in his schedule and pay day was still two days away. He shook as he looked at the angry faces and threatening rifles but somehow managed to keep a steady hand as he calculated time sheets and wages. He enlisted the aid of the head bookkeeper in getting the checks issued.

Nate passed the checks to the immigrants as each one was completed and when all stood clutching one, he and his men surrounded them again and marched them to the bank to cash their checks. Trembling and confused, the kidnapped men then permitted themselves to be shepherded to the railroad station. The three fifteen to St. Louis was just easing away from the platform, a belch of steam pouring from its smokestack when the men arrived. Nate was the first to step in front of it, but several others stepped in behind him. The train screeched to a halt only a few feet in front of the knot of men. Nate and his men forced their captives into the few remaining seats, ordering the stationmaster at gunpoint to pull a freight car from the siding to accommodate those who did not get seats.

Serge Janklowicz, a short, middle-aged Hungarian who was among the men pulled from the mine, managed to separate himself from the crowd for a moment. Eyes round with fear, he approached Cliff who was standing at the end of the platform and spoke quickly.

"Please, sir," he mumbled through a thick mustache. "I know I can trust a man in uniform. Soldiers have great honor. Please, take this and give it to my family. Tell my wife what happened and I will send for her. Please," he said as he pressed nearly his entire paycheck into Cliff's palm. Glancing around to see if anyone was watching, Cliff wrapped his fingers around the crisp bills.

"Yeah, sure," he said. "Where does she live?"

Just then, Nate spotted Janklowicz and strode across the platform, grabbing the miner by his shirt collar. "Out in Number 6 town," Janklowicz called as he was dragged away. Number 6 town was the Hungarian settlement nestled in the trees south of Number 6 shaft. "Ask for Bertha," he called as the hands of half a dozen men stuffed him through the door of the freight car as the train began to move forward. Cliff counted the dollar bills in his hand. There were eight. He stuffed them in his pants pocket.

Word of the day's events—the *Flat River Daily Telegraph* called it a riot—spread quickly through town. That night, most of the men who had been involved gathered again, this time at the Black Bear Saloon bragging of their bravery and patriotism in running out the unwanted foreigners. Some thought the wives and children of the men who'd been forced out of town should receive the same treatment. Others opted for more violent steps. In the end, they decided to reconvene at the barbershop the next morning before moving on to other mines and expelling the rest of the men with accents.

St. Francois County Sheriff Charles Adams was a cautious man. He tried to stay out of local politics except for his own election and just enforce the law as he interpreted it. No one would have known he hated the foreigners as much as Nate and his men did. He had no intention of trying to stop the men if they decided to run more of the Hungarians and Italians and Germans out of town. He was just going to see to it that no one got hurt, no property got damaged.

All night long, he pounded on doors around town, looking for men he felt he could trust to take orders from him and not get involved in the dispute, men who were good shots just in case things got out of hand. By the time Nate O'Hare's men gathered in front of the barbershop at dawn, Sheriff Adams had deputized fifty-three men. He gave them orders to patrol in front of the local shops, keeping Nate's men away from plate glass windows and shop doors. The deputies' second priority was to see that no one got hurt. If shooting started, they were to attempt to disarm the shooter first. If they were unsuccessful, they were to shoot to kill.

The first of Nate's men to arrive behaved like children caught by their mothers stealing from the cookie jar. Conversations were hushed, heads were slightly bowed, boot toes poked into the dirt in the road. The men barely acknowledged each other. As the crowd grew, though, their bravado grew. Backs stiffened and heads sprung up. The din of the men's talk grew louder, more assured. Guns were held proudly and cigarettes and chewing tobacco passed around amicably.

Nearly four hundred men crowded in the street in front of the barbershop. Nate O'Hare appointed squad captains who then chose among the others for members of their squads. Sheriff Adams forced his horse among the crowd, urging them to abandon their plans and go home. When he realized no one was listening, he instructed his deputies to follow the squads if they left town, then headed back to his office and called the governor. He asked for the National Guard.

Throughout the day, barely any words were uttered and no shots were fired as the squads moved from the gaping mouth of one mine to another, the squad leader demanding the presence of all immigrants, the mine captains quietly complying. By sunset, nearly six hundred miners had been herded onto railway cars. Crying children and their frightened mothers carried clothes and toys and food hastily wrapped in blankets tucked under their arms as they joined the banished men. Bank tellers scrambled to cash paychecks. Shop owners scurried about filling orders for the unwilling travelers.

Edward Simmons, publisher of the *Flat River Daily Telegraph*, wrote that night "You are no man if you had consented to have done any different than help run the foreigners out." When a *Chicago Tribune* reporter criticized the action of the men and the tacit approval of the town's leaders, he was knocked unconscious, dumped on the train and run out of town with the rest of the foreigners.

At Number 6 town, it was not the respected man in uniform entrusted with a few dollars who told Mrs. Janklowicz that her husband would not be coming home. That news came from Mrs. Czarnecki who lived two doors away and had been in town at the bakery when the men were forced on the train. By then, Cliff Malin's bank account was eight dollars fatter. In a few days he left for France.

Clark Phillips and Dan Kirk had long since finished their meal and adjourned to the library by the time Clark had finished his story. A crystal decanter of port stood on the walnut smoking stand between them, and the air was thick with their cigarette smoke. Dan had been assiduously taking notes while Clark talked. Images of a two-page feature story flashed in his brain as he scribbled notes. The hook would be how a small town boy from a hard-working family came to be involved in graft, corruption, and murder. Could there be a Pulitzer in his future?

He drained his glass of port and Clark re-filled it as Dan sat back in his chair.

"What can you tell me about Cliff Malin's wife?"

"Not much. I seem to recall she died shortly after they were married, just a few months, and he quickly left town. I remember some talk about his having some insurance money from her death. She was from Desloge or Iron City, as I recall, so I wouldn't know her family."

"Did she die under suspicious circumstances?"

"Seems to me there was talk about that but, hell, it was over twenty years ago. You are welcome to come down and go through our morgue anytime. We have a copy of every paper we ever published. And Mrs. LaFleur down at the Hall of Records has practically a photographic memory. She's about a hundred and seven and knows everything about everybody. She'd be a big help. She can get you Mrs. Malin's death certificate as well."

Clark drove Dan back to the hotel in downtown Flat River and suggested another drink at the hotel bar. Dan was tired, having managed only a catnap before meeting Clark that afternoon, but he couldn't help but hope that some other tidbit of information might be forthcoming. After three more highballs, though, he realized Clark Phillips had nothing more to reveal that would help the story. They talked about dictatorial publishers, ad reps who thought every one of their customers deserved a sixteen-inch story, and the pathetic state of newly graduated journalists whose skill with the language was minimal and who had no idea how to research a story. It was nearly midnight before Dan collapsed in bed and slept as though he'd been drugged.

# CHAPTER 7

▼

The Hall of Records was a sparkling but old building that smelled of old paper and new floor wax. Mrs. LaFleur presided over the activities of the Hall from behind a wooden desk that stood a few feet away from the customer counter. A nameplate on the front edge of the desk identified her. Dan had assumed that Clark was exaggerating when he said Mrs. LaFleur was about a hundred and seven, but now he wasn't so sure. She stood about five feet tall with a girth of nearly equal size. Thick glasses squeezed against her fleshy face and her thin, gray hair was neatly pinned to the crown of her head.

"Excuse me," he said after standing at the counter a few moments and not being noticed.

Mrs. LaFleur looked up. "Oh, dear. I'm sorry. I didn't hear you. What can I do for you?" She continued opening envelopes and glancing at their contents as Dan spoke.

"My name is Dan Kirk. I'm a reporter with the *Detroit Free Press.*"

Mrs. La Fleur dropped the envelope she was holding and stood up. "A reporter? All the way down here from Detroit? What can I help you with, Mr. Kirk?"

She walked up to the counter limping as though her shoes hurt.

"Mr. Phillips over at the newspaper tells me you can help me with a story I'm working on. Did you know a Mr. Cliff Malin who grew up here in Flat River?"

Mrs. LaFleur's eyes narrowed and she spoke quietly. "Yes, sir. I knew the man."

"What can you tell me about the gentleman?"

"Well, sir, I can tell you he was no gentleman. He was married to my niece, Alicia, so I think I have the right to say so."

Dan reached into his coat pocket for his notebook asking, "Do you mind if I take some notes?"

"That would be fine, young man. I want you to get your facts straight. Why don't you come around to my desk where we can be comfortable? Would you like a cup of tea?"

Dan loathed tea, but he accepted for the sake of appearing friendly to this woman who was about to help him. With two steaming cups of milked and sugared tea in dainty teacups before them, Mrs. LaFleur began to talk.

"May I ask what Clifford has done that warrants a story about him in the newspaper?"

"He's accused of killing a woman near Detroit."

Mrs. LaFleur averted Dan's gaze by concentrating on blowing on her tea to cool it. She finally took a sip and set the cup back in its saucer.

"All I can tell you...Mr. Kirk, is it?...Is that I don't believe that is the first time he has done so. Was he married to this woman?"

"No, he wasn't."

"Well, something made him desperate enough to do it. I'm sure you have experienced in your line of work, just as I have in mine, that people kill when they think there is no other resolution to their problem. I think when you get to the bottom of this you'll find that's the case."

Dan Kirk nodded solemnly. As long as he he'd been at the newspaper covering murders, he hadn't given much thought to the deeper motive behind such crimes. He had written just the surface facts as he discovered them. People were killed by jealous spouses, during the commission of another crime, for revenge, or in territorial disputes. He had to admit Mrs. LaFleur was right. Killing was the desperate act of a desperate person.

"Mr. Phillips gave me a brief history lesson on Flat River and the Malin family, but he didn't know much about your niece or their marriage. I was hoping maybe you could fill me in."

"I can tell you plenty," Mrs. LaFleur said, "but I don't want you hurting Alicia's family. They are good people, and she was a lovely girl."

"I'm not interested in hurting anybody. I'm just trying to get a feel for what kind of man Clifford Malin is and what would have driven him to murder. Can you tell me how Clifford and Alicia first met?"

"I can indeed. They met at a picnic back in 1918. I remember it specifically because that was the year my dear husband Ivan moved us into the house on Elm Street."

It was a glorious day for the Red Cross July Fourth parade and picnic. Sun puddles dappled the school playing field where the rising sun's rays broke through the tangle of tree branches. Already the warm, homey smells of hot coffee, freshly baked bread, and frying chicken wafted across the grounds on the early morning breeze.

Dozens of men and women who had volunteered and children who had been conscripted bustled about the grounds, shouting directions to one another, setting up tables and chairs, building booths for the sale of lemonade and homemade baked goods. Saws ground through wood, hammers banged against nails, and planks clattered against planks. In one corner of the meadow, teenage boys argued as they measured out the site for the three-legged races. Another corner of the field had been chalked out as a baseball diamond where the Centralia, Illinois Tigers and the Flat River Panthers would meet in friendly combat. The women of the Methodist Church draped red, white, and blue bunting around the bandstand where Mayor Rinke would auction off a flag donated by the governor himself. Later, the Red Hot Jazzers, a first-rate band hired from St. Louis especially for the occasion, would take over the bandstand and play as long as folks would dance.

Across town in the main yard of the St. Joseph Lead Company, parade participants brushed horses' manes, pinned flowers in each other's hair, and made last minute adjustments to costumes. Ralph McNabb, director of the school band, led his musicians through a particularly difficult phrase of the national anthem while a contingent of twenty-seven brothers of the Benevolent and Protective Order of the Elks rehearsed a flag drill.

Promptly at nine o'clock, the school band led the parade on its march north up River Road then west down Main Street. The first entry behind the band was a hay wagon drawn by six roan horses. On board was Miss Lila Erickson, the school nurse, portraying Clara Barton, founder of the Red Cross, dressing wounds of soldiers. Behind the wagon rode Sheriff Charles Adams and his deputies in full dress uniform followed by another team of six horses pulling a flower-bedecked wagon bearing four veterans of the Spanish-American War in ill-fitting uniforms. Dozens of citizens with no particular affiliation who simply wanted to take part in the spectacle followed the floats or walked along beside them. They dressed as Uncle Sam, as confederate soldiers, as clowns, and as dancing bears, throwing candy and small toys to the children along the parade route.

Everywhere American flags fluttered in the breeze. Flags hung from shop windows and from lampposts while others were tied to baby carriages and buckboards. Old folks and children waved small flags on tiny sticks and a giant flag, hand stitched by the Episcopalian Women's Auxiliary, was draped across the church façade at the end of Main Street.

Just behind the Elks Flag Drill Team at the end of the parade came the town's proudest entry. Flat River's one and only automobile, a handsome Model T, was chauffeured by its owner, Mr. Joseph Corbett, president of the Federal Mine Company. In the back seat rode Mayor Henry Rinke and Private First Class Clifford Malin, Flat River's courageous hero of the Great War. Private Malin's return home was just the serendipitous touch that was needed to round out the parade and bring donations pouring in.

Military life had not been at all what Cliff had anticipated. He had imagined himself fighting bravely in hand-to-hand combat, slaying the dreaded Jerries, defending the honor of beautiful French women. Instead, he found mud, cold, illness, injury, and death. There was no hand-to-hand combat either. The new machine gun with its deadly efficiency allowed soldiers to kill each other from long distances, mowing down unseen men as a farmer would mow down his hay.

And every day was filled with palpable fear, thick as the mud they slogged through, knuckle-whitening, mind-numbing, paralyzing fear that hung over the troops like a fog. He saw it in every man's eyes, watched it crawl up their backs, felt it in their cold hands.

The fear began the last night at sea before they had set foot on French soil as Cliff roamed the decks of the luxury-liner-turned-troop transport. Others were on deck as well, some alone, some in small knots talking quietly. Leaning against the railing near the port stern, he watched a soldier produce a gnarled candy bar that had obviously been packed away for some time. He broke it into pieces and shared it out among those standing near him.

"Way I figure it," he was saying, "when your number's up, it's up. Nothing you can do about it. It's just a big bingo game. When they call your number, that's it."

The men—young boys, really—spoke bravely of how they would stand up to any enemy, but even in the dim light, Cliff saw the fear in their eyes. He had never thought about death before, his own or anyone else's. But that night, fear of death began to nibble at his insides, gnawing at his stomach, sticking in his throat, crawling on his skin. He tried to rationalize the fear away. Lots of men fought in wars and came back alive, lots. There was obviously a way to survive. He'd just have to find it.

Toward morning he was back on deck, watching the ship put in at Brest in northern France, the damp, brisk wind whistling through his clothes. In the distance he could hear the dull thud of mortar fire. Puffs of gray smoke, outlined in red by the rising sun, hovered over the skyline. Later, filing off the ship, he was keenly aware that the wild cheers of joy that rang through the ship on its departure from New York had given way to a quiet hum of only the most necessary conversation.

On shore, the men stood and stared at buildings punctured with holes from ammunition, rubble piled at their bases. Burned hulks that once were trees stood like giant exclamation points pushing against the sky. Cliff was struck by the irony of a few bright yellow daffodils that poked up through the ashes of destruction, a life-renewing force amid such death. The faint smell of burning wood and brush drifted through the air. At one end of the pier stood a large white tent laced up tight. The Americans watched as British soldiers unlaced the tent flaps and flung them open, revealing corpses of English soldiers stacked three deep, waiting for shipment home and burial.

By noon, the Americans had marched to within a mile of the front line, meeting up with more experienced soldiers who offered the new men their first real tips on surviving on the battlefield. Basic training covered marching in formation, cleaning a rifle, climbing ropes, and cooking in the field, but what they really needed to know was how to move quickly from trench to trench while keeping their heads down, how to move through sucking mud, how to see through the dark and the haze that hung over the smoke-shrouded battlefields.

The new men squeezed into the trenches beside those already there and were told to count off. Every third man was a sentry whose responsibility it was to poke his head up periodically to see what was happening on the field. But only for a second, they were told. You had to see everything you could in one second.

Back in boot camp, everyone had talked about what fun France would be. Beautiful, lusty women, cheap wine, ancient palaces filled with tapestries of brocade and silk and hung with famous art pieces. That was what they would find here. No one talked about the realities of the battlefield, about standing next to a man as he gave out a loud scream and fell over backwards, dead. About the piles of stinking carcasses-animal and human—they had to step over every day. About the clouds of arms and eyes and heads that rained on them after every explosion. About constantly burying bodies in hurriedly dug trenches that weren't deep enough to be graves, stuffing a hand or a foot back in as it came unburied like putting to sleep under a blanket that was too small. No one had told them about the millions of flies covering the bodies and the graves, so thick they formed a black funeral shroud, about dysentery and flu. starvation and gangrene, lice and maggots.

Nor had anyone mentioned the fear that was everywhere. It was etched in the faces of the French women, children, and old men as their homes and towns were demolished and their families separated or killed. It crawled through the guts of the horses, not trained for the noise and heat of battle and being ridden by soldiers who barely knew how to mount them.

When the fighting and the noise and the death stopped for a little while and he could sleep, Cliff woke surprised and afraid to be alive. Two men who had been part of his squad were returned home suffering from what was being called shellshock. They simply buckled under the constant barrage of booming explosives and whistling bullets, shaking uncontrollably from head to toe. Many of the remaining men grew more fearful everyday as their ranks thinned out. Three weeks after their arrival in France, only seven men from Cliff's original company were still in battle.

And they feared it would never end, that the war would last a lifetime until everyone was killed or wounded or died of starvation or disease or froze to death. They feared no one would see Baltimore or New York or Emporia or Sandusky or Flat River ever again and eat cherry pie or drink corn whiskey or swim in the ocean or slide down snowy hillsides.

Cliff had been in France nearly a year when a mine went off a few dozen feet from him. He felt a strange mixture of more fear and relief. Two men and a packhorse were blown across the field by the mine. Shrapnel sunk into Cliff's right arm and leg, shredding his clothes and his skin and he couldn't hear. But the explosion—and he knew this almost as soon as it happened—meant he was going home.

Now, as Mr. Corbett drove the Mayor and the War Hero into the schoolyard, the band struck up an enthusiastic if slightly off-key rendition of "Battle Hymn of the Republic," while everyone cheered and waved flags. Leaning out the side windows of the shining Model T, the two guests of honor waved and smiled, calling to people they recognized. Suddenly, the car jolted to a stop and the passengers were roughly flung forward. A small boy had darted in front of the moving vehicle, closely followed by a young woman in her early twenties. She swept the boy off his feet and deposited him at the edge of the crowd, out of harm's way. Cliff watched as she dropped to one knee, wagging her finger in the child's face, obviously scolding him for not watching where he was going.

She was a pretty girl, Cliff thought, her hair pinned to the top of her head, a few errant curls dropping out of the pins and falling gently on her neck. Her simple calico dress with lace at the neck and hem revealed a trim, softly curved figure.

"Who's that?" Cliff asked the Mayor.

"Oh, you wouldn't have met her," the Mayor replied. The two men continued smiling and waving out the windows as Mr. Corbett resumed driving into the field. "She's the new school teacher. Name's Alicia Walters. She's from Iron City. Came here last school term."

"Is that her little boy?"

"No, she's a single lady." The Mayor turned toward Cliff, a leering sparkle in his eye. "Say, would you like to meet her? I could introduce you."

Cliff blushed. "Maybe later," he said then called to a schoolmate he saw in the crowd. He had little experience with women, the most recent being a clumsy, over-zealous few minutes with a young French girl before he had been injured. It had been a complete disaster. He climaxed almost immediately as she took hold of him, making a mess down the front of her clothes. The second time a few minutes later, he did manage to get inside her first, but he had no staying power. She quickly pulled up her panties, straightened her dress and stormed out of the barn where they had found refuge. He couldn't understand what she was muttering as she left and he figured it was just as well. He'd have to think about whether he wanted to meet Miss Walters.

When the car finally stopped at the center of the field, the Mayor and Private Malin climbed out to wild cheers from the crowd. Icy glasses of lemonade were pressed into their hands as they were escorted through the crowd to a table reserved for them. Mayor Rinke sat at the table only a few minutes before he was called away to attend to some official duty or other. Cliff remained at the table entertaining any who asked about the tales of his exploits overseas. He never mentioned the fear, the smell, and the death and some of the more daring exploits he recounted really belonged to other soldiers, but who would know? The people at the picnic wanted a hero and he would be happy to be one. Before long, someone replaced his lemonade with hard cider that had an effect on the stories he told. With each sip, he became a bit more courageous, a tad more daring as he fought his way across France. He talked of spectacular French wine and passionate French women, though he saved the latter for just the ears of the men.

Mr. Johnston, the school principal, threaded his way through the crowd surrounding Cliff and reached out to shake his hand. "Clifford, my boy, good to see you."

Cliff stood up, a bit unsteady on his feet. "Hello, Mr. Johnston. Good to be home."

Taking Cliff by the elbow, Johnston steered him away from the table. "Why don't you come with me?" he said. "The baseball game is about to begin."

Glad to have a chance to clear his head a bit, Cliff let the principal lead him across the field. Though Cliff usually paid little attention to sports, he found himself watching the game with interest, particularly when he saw Alicia Walters was there. First, the Flat River Panthers led the scoring then the Centralia Tigers took the lead, losing it back to the Panthers in the fourth inning. At the end of seven innings, the Tigers claimed victory and posed for a team photograph with the War Hero. Afterward, they all headed to the bandstand to watch the auction of the ladies' box lunches.

The auction was one of the most popular and successful fundraisers every year. Every unmarried lady in the town and in the surrounding hillsides was expected to prepare a homemade lunch adequate for two people to be auctioned off to one of the area's eligible bachelors. The successful bidder was to share the lunch with the young lady who had prepared it. Besides good food, the auction also provided a source of gossip and speculation for weeks to come.

Bidding was active, and Cliff watched as his sister, Verna, the one closest to him in age, headed for the shade of a tree with Mike Townsend who had won her picnic lunch. It was no secret that she and Mike hoped to marry next spring. Elna Miller's lunch complete with her famous pecan pie went to Frank Harvey. Catherine Varney, her fried chicken and Arthur Nordyke drifted off to a table at the edge of the field. When the auctioneer introduced Miss Alicia Walters, heads turned as Mayor Rinke called from the back of the crowd.

"No need to auction this young lady's picnic, Sam," he called. "You just put this in the kitty, and I'll take care of her."

Sam Wachowski, the auctioneer, gawked at the five-dollar bill the Mayor pressed into his hand. The highest bid for any lunch so far had been two dollars and fifty cents, and that had been for Edna Waterbury's pork roast lunch, which included the company of the lovely and wealthy Miss Waterbury. The audience watched as the Mayor led Miss Walters off to the side where Private Malin stood. "Miss Walters, I would like you to meet Private Clifford Malin, our war hero. Private Malin, Miss Walters." The crowd applauded its approval.

If Cliff's hair could have turned red, it would have, he blushed so deeply. He simply nodded, unable to get his mouth to move. The Mayor stood beaming at the couple. "Now, off you two go," he said, pushing them away from the crowd. "Enjoy your lunch."

Alicia handed the box lunch to Cliff and led the way to a blanket she had spread beneath a tree overlooking the river.

"It won't be as comfortable as Mr. Corbett's Model T," she smiled apologetically. Her voice was so smooth, he thought, like cool silk on sunburned skin. He was sure he was about to make an enormous fool of himself. He offered her his hand as she stepped on the blanket and floated to the ground.

"Maybe not, but it's a far sight better than those trenches in France," he smiled back. A faint waft of lilac water drifted toward him as she moved. Nervous and excited, he sat cross-legged on the blanket and reached for the picnic hamper she had prepared. "What have we here?" he said a little too loudly.

"I'm not really much of a cook." That voice again. "Mrs. Moorehead, my landlady, did the fried chicken, but I made the chocolate cake."

The rest of the afternoon the two never left each other's side. They talked of Flat River and Iron City, where Alicia's family lived, of war and peace, of friends and family. Alicia listened intently as Cliff spoke of his desire to find a life outside Flat River. She asked him questions about what he wanted to do, where he wanted to live. He felt completely at ease talking to her, as though they had been friends for years. She laughed when he told her about some of the movies he had seen at the Dreamland and said Lillian Gish was her favorite actress. He laughed when she told him of some of the pranks her students pulled on her. The schoolyard grew dark as the sun set behind the foothills. Other picnickers who had fallen asleep beneath the trees began to stir as the Red Hot Jazzers tuned their instruments for their evening performance. Mothers dragged protesting children off to bed, and men dug under blankets in their buckboards for fresh jugs of cider. Young couples wandered along the riverside in the cool evening breezes, the boys trying to steal a kiss, the girls letting them, though not too easily.

Cliff and Alicia were among the last to leave when the band finished playing at ten o'clock. They walked to Mrs. Moorehouse's boarding house where Alicia lived and sat on the porch for nearly an hour talking of nothing and everything. As he was leaving, Cliff asked if he could walk her to church on Sunday, and she agreed. On Monday, they went boating, Tuesday to the movies, and Wednesday they took a picnic lunch up the river. When Alicia indicated an interest in museums, Cliff suggested a day trip to St. Louis to see an art exhibit there. Aboard the 7:15 train that morning, they chose seats in a nearly deserted car. Cliff busied himself opening several windows to let in the sweet morning air, air that did not bear the scent of death, he couldn't help but notice.

The train screeched slowly out of the station only a few minutes late and headed east a short distance before making a wide swing to the north. It was a slow train with many stops along the way, but neither Alicia nor Cliff cared how long the trip would take. As they approached Desloge, the first stop out of Flat River, Cliff leaned across Alicia and pointed out the window.

"Look at that fellow there." He indicated a farmer standing in his hay field, leaning on a shovel, watching the train pass by. Cliff smiled and leaned back in his seat. "He wishes he was on this train."

"You think so?" Alicia asked, watching as the farmer faded out of sight.

"I know so," Cliff said confidently. "You just watch on this trip and see how many people stop working in the fields or hanging out the laundry to watch the train go past. They want to be on it. They're tired of their lives, just like I was when I was growing up in Flat River. They want to go to beautiful places and do exciting things."

Alicia smiled demurely, but then a little cloud passed over her face and she frowned. "I don't know. I don't think everybody's tired of their lives. My father has never wanted to do anything but run the family farm. It has been in his family for three generations. He says he can't imagine living somewhere where he couldn't dig in the soil and raise his animals."

"Well, that's okay for some people but not for me. I'm for the city where things are going on all the time. People really know how to live in the city."

"What would you do in a big city you can't do in Flat River?"

"Lots of stuff. Get me a job in one of those factories maybe. Henry Ford pays his people five dollars a day, and they only work forty hours a week. Saturdays and Sundays off to do anything you please. Just think of it. You could go to the movies and see all the museums you wanted. Almost everybody has a car in the city. Up north, like in Detroit, they got roads all over the place. Paved roads. No getting stuck in the mud when you're out on a Sunday drive with your girl. That's the life for me."

"Is that where you want to go? To Detroit, I mean?"

"It's one of the places I've thought of. Don't know for sure just where I'll wind up. I'll bet you could get a good job there. With all those people moving in, there's bound to be a need for schoolteachers. You ought to think about it. You might like it up north."

She turned toward the window and let the breeze blow across her face as she digested what he had been saying. The city was so big and loud with all those people around. Even St. Louis frightened her, and she figured Detroit was even bigger, noisier, more crowded. She could just imagine what it was like with the sound of hundreds of automobiles in the streets. You couldn't hear the birds, and you'd have to scream to be heard when you were talking to your neighbor over the fence. Still, Clifford's enthusiasm was infectious, and if he really wanted her to go with him, well, she'd have to give it some thought. After all, she was nearly twenty-three with no prospects of marriage. She couldn't afford to fuss over small things like the noise of cars.

Squeaking brakes drowned out any further conversation as the train pulled into Desloge. The empty seats in the car quickly filled up, and Cliff and Alicia were silent for the rest of the trip, each with their own thoughts.

Cliff had never been to a museum before, and he found some of the paintings interesting, but they spent far more time in the building than he would have preferred. He didn't say anything, though, since Alicia was enjoying herself. Later, they walked around St. Louis, stopped for ice cream, road the trolley across town and had dinner at the Russell Hotel. It all made him feel very cosmopolitan, a man of the world. It made Alicia a little frightened, but she was comforted when she took Cliff's arm.

Riding home on the last train, Alicia drifted off to sleep, falling against Cliff's shoulder, her lilac water, now very faint, drifting up to him. It had been a pleasant day with Alicia, he thought. She was pretty in a folksy kind of way, not like the glamorous women he had seen in magazines and would meet when he got to the city. She was smart and listened to him when he talked, but his thoughts of her extended no further. In two days, he would return to the service, and that would be the end of it. He would have been surprised to learn that the day after the trip to St. Louis Alicia visited her mother in Iron City and told her that she and Clifford had discussed where they might live after the wedding.

# CHAPTER 8

▼

The smell of strong coffee drifted into the tiny bedroom, teasing Clifford awake. Peeling off the thick quilts that warmed him against the cold December night, he pulled on his trousers and boots and in two strides, was across the small room. As he stood peering into the mirror over the bureau, he reached out absently to his right, picked up the pitcher of water, tilted it over the wash basin. Nothing came out.

"Damn," he muttered. A thin veneer of ice had crusted on the water overnight. Stuffing his hand inside the pitcher, he punched a hole in the ice then filled the wash basin half full. He drew a sharp breath when the near-freezing water hit his face. As he dried himself, he stepped around the corner into the kitchen and in front of a roaring fire. Alicia was moving easily around the small room preparing breakfast and quietly humming.

"Good morning, Darling. Sleep well?" she said brightly.

"Like a bear," he said, dropping the towel on the kitchen table. Although marriage had not originally figured in his life plan, he had become quite comfortable with domestic life in the six months since he had made Alicia his bride. There was a sort of warmth and security about it he had not thought he needed.

After Cliff returned to active duty only a few months before the war ended, Alicia wrote long, cheerful letters to him almost weekly. He began to realize the importance of having someone in his life. When she started writing about wedding plans, he didn't protest. He would talk to her when he got home and tell her that he enjoyed her company and her letters, but he wasn't hanging around Flat River. By then, however, her mother had made her wedding gown, and the First Methodist Church was booked. He didn't feel inclined toward making a fuss. He hadn't thought about it before, but it might be more fun to have someone with him when he moved from Flat River. On July 19, 1919 they were married under a brilliant sun, surrounded by friends and family.

Their wedding night hadn't been much of an improvement over some of Cliff's encounters with French girls, but Alicia, with no experience herself, didn't comment on his clumsiness. In fact, she didn't show much interest in his attentions. Maybe she didn't know that women were supposed to move during lovemaking. He didn't know how to broach the subject, and they fell into a simple routine. He kissed her, spread her legs and rolled over on top of her. When he finished, he kissed her again, and she lay against his chest till she fell asleep. In the six months since their wedding, the routine had not varied.

"Something smells mighty good," he said this morning. He glanced over her head through the frosted window to see a few light snowflakes fluttering to the ground in the early morning light.

"I decided to make you flapjacks today," she said, moving from stove to table, "with fresh maple syrup from Aunt Hattie in Vermont."

"And to what do I owe this honor?" he asked, stabbing at the stack of pancakes she put in front of him.

"I was just thinking that I don't really have time to fix you a proper breakfast when school is in. Now that we're on Christmas vacation, I thought I would spoil my husband."

"Well, your husband very much appreciates it. You sure you aren't just fattening me up for the kill? You probably have some job you want me to do."

Alicia pulled out a chair and sat across from Cliff. She avoided his eyes, busying herself smarming butter on her pancakes and pouring syrup over them. "Now that you mention it, there is something I wanted to talk to you about," she finally said.

"Shoot," he said. "I'm very pliable when I'm well fed." He shoveled another forkful of food into his mouth.

She took a bite of her breakfast then chewed slowly before she spoke. "I don't want to be a nagging wife," she began hesitantly, "but I would like to know what your plans are about getting a job."

He dropped his fork and let out a big sigh. "I have a job," he said, exasperated at the emergence of this same old conversation.

"I mean a steady job, not just selling newspapers and Christmas trees. Something that pays decent money. You haven't had a real job since you came home from the service. If it wasn't for my teacher's pay, we wouldn't be able to get along." A sharpness crept into her voice.

"I'm working on some things," he said sullenly.

"What kind of things?"

"I don't want to talk about it. It's a jinx to talk about your plans too much. They never work out when you talk about them." He pushed his empty plate away.

"It can't be a jinx to talk to your wife. Just give me some kind of idea."

Cliff sat brooding, staring at the table. Suddenly, he pushed back his chair, leapt up and disappeared into the bedroom. Alicia could hear a drawer open then slam shut. When he returned, Cliff dumped the contents of a large envelope on the table, a half grin tugging at the corner of his mouth.

"I wasn't going to tell you just yet. I wanted to save it for Christmas." He spread the pieces of paper on the table.

Alicia picked one up. "What's all this?" she asked. She looked at the paper in her hand, a clipping from a newspaper. "Ford Announces Plans for Giant Plant" she read. Skimming the article she read that Henry Ford had purchased acres of marshland on which he intended to build the world's largest manufacturing facility near the mouth of the River Rouge in Detroit.

"What does all this mean?" Alicia asked.

"That's an old one," Clifford told her excitedly, snatching the paper from her hand. Rooting through the other clippings on the table, he handed her another one. Without giving her a chance to read it he said, "The plant is built now, and they figure they can build fifty thousand cars a year there. Just think of it!"

"Think of what? What does this have to do with you? That's clear up in Detroit."

"Remember everything I told you about how I want to get out of this town? How I wanted to go places and see things? Get a job that pays good money?" He ignored the frown on her face and continued talking rapidly. "I reckon now is as good a time as any to go."

"Now?"

"Well, not right now. When school gets out for the summer. We could leave right afterwards. That's why I haven't gotten a good job. There's no point in taking a job when I know I'm going to quit in a few months. You could take the whole summer to find you a new teaching job, and I'll go to work at Ford's."

"Oh, Clifford," Alicia sighed, getting up from the table. She carried their dirty plates to the sink and began washing them. After a minute she said, "Well, that certainly is a surprise."

"You can't be that surprised," he said to her back. "I've told you all along that I wasn't going to stay in this town."

"I know. It's just that, well, I guess I thought it was just a dream. Something left over from your childhood. Everyone has dreams, but that doesn't mean you can just give up life for them."

"Following dreams isn't giving up life. It is life." His face turned red as he held back his anger. Gathering the papers from the table, he stuffed them back into the envelope. "There's nothing keeping me here."

"Well, thanks a lot, Clifford Malin. I guess I'm nothing."

He crossed over to her and stood at her back, wrapping his arms around her shoulders, kissing the top of her head. "I didn't mean that. You're not nothing. You're coming with me. Think of all the things we can do in Detroit. We could go to the pictures every night, and there's museums and loads of dress shops You'd love it there. I know you would."

"How do you know I would?" she sniffed. "Have you ever been to Detroit?"

He turned her around to face him. "No," he said, pushing her hair away from her face. "No, I haven't, but I know you. I know you can't stay smothered in this little hole of a town any more than I can. You're an intelligent woman. You like to go nice places. Flat River just isn't our kind of place."

"I'm not so sure I want to leave my job and my family, Clifford. It all sounded very exciting when we talked about it before, but I'm not a city girl at heart. There's crime in the cities, and I'd be afraid. It's just a different world." She buried her face in his shoulder and took a deep breath. "Besides, I'd like to be near Mama when the baby is born."

Clifford didn't speak or move.

"Did you hear what I said, Clifford?" she asked quietly, speaking into his chest, afraid to look at him. Abruptly he dropped his arm, spun away from her, grabbed his overcoat from a peg on the wall and left the house, the door slamming shut behind him. Alicia watched through her tears as he emerged from the barn leading his horse. He gave a tug at the saddle straps before swinging up and galloping off toward the edge of town.

Two hours later, Clifford returned home to find Alicia, red eyed and puffy faced, napping in the bedroom. Out in the kitchen, he brewed a pot of coffee, poured two cups, and carried them into the bedroom where he set them on the small table next to Alicia. Leaning over, he kissed her then watched as she turned and blinked awake.

"I'm sorry, Darling," he said. "I didn't know about your condition. I guess I was just surprised, is all. I never really thought about myself as a father."

"Are you mad at me?" she asked, afraid she knew the answer.

"Of course not. I think it's wonderful. I can't wait to tell the guys at the Black Bear. And your mother and my mother. They'll be excited."

"I love you," she said, sitting up and wrapping her arms around his neck. He pulled her arms away. Reaching for the cups on the table he said, "Here. I made us some nice fresh coffee. You'll feel much better when you drink it."

They sat in silence for a few minutes sipping their coffee. Alicia broke the silence. "You were right," she said. "I do feel better." She set the cup on the table and leaned back against the pillows. "Are you sure you're not angry with me?"

"I'm sure," he said standing up and reaching for her cup. "Now why don't you wash your face and come on out to the front room. We'll talk."

When Alicia joined Clifford in the front room, she looked refreshed, her hair brushed and repinned to the top of her head. She perched on his knee and kissed his cheek.

"Why don't you run over to your mother's, and see if she has any of last summer's apples left in her cellar," she said softly. "I'll make you an apple pie for supper tonight."

"Yum," Clifford smiled back at her. "Great idea." He stood up so quickly Alicia nearly fell to the floor. She watched out the window as he mounted the horse he had left tethered to the front porch. A light dusting of snow had covered the front porch steps while Alicia was napping, and she went out to sweep it away. Suddenly, she felt a tightness in her throat. She coughed but was unable to catch her breath. Stomach cramps doubled her over, and she leaned on the broom for support. She turned to go back in the house but keeled over and fell down the steps.

Evelyn Bell had been sweeping her own porch across the street and saw Alicia fall. She called through the front door to her husband then raced across the street to Alicia's side. Dropping to her knees, she picked up the young woman's head and cradled it in her lap. Alicia was gasping for breath, her lips a cold blue.

"Help me get her inside," she said to her husband, who had just arrived at the steps. Once Alicia was inside, he left to find Doctor Ellsworth. When the men returned, they found Evelyn sitting in the front room, a kerosene lamp lit, its light turned down low.

"How is she?" Doctor Ellsworth asked, pulling his wool overcoat off. Evelyn shook her head. "She's gone."

"What happened?" the doctor asked.

"I don't know really. She just fell over while she was sweeping the front porch. When me and Ira got here, she was all blue and couldn't catch her breath."

"I better take a look," the doctor said and disappeared into the bedroom.

A few minutes later, the doctor re-appeared and dropped his bag on the davenport next to his coat. The Bells watched silently as he removed his glasses, slowly polished them, then repositioned them on his nose.

"What is it, Doc?" Ira finally said. "It's not the flu again, is it?" Ira's mother and youngest daughter had died in the previous year's flu epidemic.

"No, it's not flu," the doctor said.

The front door opened and a blast of cold air blew through the room accompanied by Clifford. He looked at the people standing in his front room. "Hi," he said hesitantly. "Where's Alicia?" His eyes darted around the room.

No one moved for a moment. No one found the right words. At last, Doctor Ellsworth walked over to Clifford and laid his hand on the young man's shoulder. "You'd better sit down, Son."

Mrs. LaFleur reached up the left sleeve of her dress and extracted a hankie. She blew her nose delicately, refolded the hankie, and returned it to her sleeve.

"That was December 19, 1919, exactly six months from the day Alicia and Clifford were married. We buried her three days later. As you can imagine, it wasn't a very happy Christmas in our family. In fact, Christmas has never been the same since then. We always remember that horrible time, even though we don't speak about it much anymore."

The sadness in her voice made Dan look up from his jottings. He dropped his notebook and pencil in his lap. When Mrs. LaFleur seemed ready to go on he asked, "What did the doctor say was the cause of her death?"

"I'll get you the death certificate," she said, rising slowly from her chair. She disappeared into a room behind her desk and was gone only a few minutes before returning with an official looking document. She stood next to Dan and placed it on the desk in front of him. He glanced over the document, Alicia Malin's death certificate. Near the bottom he saw a single word: asphyxiation.

"Was there any kind of investigation into her death?" he asked.

"No, sir, there wasn't. Alicia's parents were too devastated to think of such things. The doctor should have insisted on one, I think. We didn't have an official coroner here in those days. We depended on the doctors to do the right thing. I don't know why he didn't do anything about it. Maybe you can see that something is done."

"I doubt I can do anything, Mrs. LaFleur, except bring this situation to light. I don't really have any influence down here."

"Well, thank you for listening, Mr. Kirk. Alicia was a beautiful child and a lovely young woman. It just doesn't seem right that something like this could happen to her and no one does anything about it."

"Just one more question, Mrs. LaFleur. Do you know if there was any kind of insurance on Mrs. Malin's life?"

"Her mother told me that Clifford had taken out a fifteen hundred dollar policy on her a few months after they were married."

# CHAPTER 9

▼

Dan decided to file one story with his newspaper before making the arduous trip back home. It wouldn't be the big feature piece he had in mind. He would save that for when he had more time to put it together. He wanted to see what Lieutenant Cunningham had discovered in Port Huron. Maybe the story of Twyla Larson could be packaged with that of Cliff Malin.

He had one more stop to make before leaving Flat River. He wanted to try to talk to a member of the Malin family. Clark Phillips had said only one sister was still living in town. Since the editor would be off deadline by now, Dan decided to elicit his help. Clark said he would be glad to drive Dan over to the house again but said not to expect too much cooperation.

"Folks here don't trust people from big cities," he said by way of explanation.

He handed Dan a fresh copy of *The Daily Telegraph*. The lead story told of Cliff Malin's arrest for murder. Clark had pulled it off the wires. That would ensure a lack of cooperation from his family. No one in a small, close-knit community wanted to be in the limelight as the result of being related to a criminal. But, you never know, Dan thought.

Snow had been falling lightly all morning and Clark drove gingerly through the streets. The men picked their way up the front sidewalk and stamped the snow from their feet. Clark rang the doorbell and stood shuffling and smoking in front of the door. Though once considered grand, the house was in need of a lot of attention. Paint peeled and the wood frame around the door showed signs of a shoddy replacement. Dan could hear footsteps inside and a key turned in the lock, then the door opened just a few inches.

"You get off my porch, Clark Phillips. I got nothing to say to you." The woman who spoke pushed the door shut hard and turned the key.

"I guess that's a 'no comment'." Clark said.

The two newspapermen returned to Dan's hotel and spent the afternoon downing highballs and talking, mostly about stories they had covered, until long past dark. They ate in the hotel dining room, Dan picking up the tab, and drank for several more hours. By the time Dan boarded the bus to head back to St. Louis the next morning, his head felt like a herd of elephants was stampeding inside it.

Back in Detroit, Dan dropped into his office on the way home from the train station to pick up any messages. There were a number of them but only one got his attention. Lieutenant Cunningham was back from Port Huron. "Call me," was all the note said. Dan left a note on his editor's desk that he was back and would be in late the next day. It wasn't that he planned to sleep late; he was going to the Oakland County Sheriff's office bright and early. Stan Cunningham was much easier to talk to early in the day.

There had obviously been a heavy snowfall while Dan was in Missouri. Piles of blackened snow etched the sides of the streets and the number of parking places at the Sheriff's Office was reduced by half because of snow piles. The sun was bright the next morning, though, promising wet, muddy ground for days, unless there was another snowfall. Splashes as cars drove through the puddles on the street made Dan think he was on the river.

Stan Cunningham greeted him with the usual curt acknowledgement and a wave, directing Dan to clean off a chair. A sergeant appeared at the door with two cups of coffee, but Dan always let his get cold. He was never sure where those coffee cups came from or when they had last seen soap and water.

"How was the trip?" the Lieutenant asked.

"Illuminating," Dan said as he draped his coat over a stack of files on a chair. "Clifford Malin has some background. Did you learn anything up in Port Huron?"

"Not much. Probably stuff you can use more than me. You know, stuff for one of those human interest stories. Mrs. Larson came from a working-class family and so did her husband. I can't find any kind of connection with any criminal element."

"Did you take notes? Can I see them?"

"I took a few, but, like I said, there isn't anything there. I met her husband. He's coming down here in a couple of days, and he can give you what you need for your sob story about the victim. Piecing all this stuff together, though, I'm not so sure he has a clear picture of his wife, at least not the woman she was since she came to Detroit. You probably won't want to bother with the twin sister, Theresa. She hasn't stopped crying since she heard about her sister. Now, tell me what you got."

"In a minute. Did you talk to the family in Port Huron?"

"A little. They're pretty upset, as you can imagine. Mrs. Larson's father said she was a handful when she was growing up, but she never got into any serious trouble. She didn't finish her last year of school, but he didn't say why. My guess is the usual, a baby. Like I said, her husband is going to be here in the next day or so. He can fill you in. They started dating in high school, her father said."

"You know anything about him?"

"I didn't look into him much. His family lives outside of town. They call that part of town the Campau. You probably already know when Joseph Campau got tired of developing land here, he went up there. Laid out a development on the west side of town. The locals refer to it as 'out on the Campau.' He came from a big family, Catholic, I gather. The Department didn't have anything on either Mr. or Mrs. Larson or anyone in their family. Now, tell me what you found out."

Dan detailed what he had learned in Flat River, at least the portion he thought a cop would be interested in. Stan showed particular interest in the death of Alicia Malin, taking notes and saying he would follow up with the police department in Flat River. Dan asked the lieutenant for the names of any friends of Malin's he had turned up, hoping there would be one or two who could piece together a picture of the man since he arrived in Detroit. When Stan mentioned Big Bill Navin, Dan knew immediately that he would be able to get the details he needed. He'd spent a lot of time in Navin's Pool Hall when he was going to school, and he knew the proprietor to be loquacious and accurate about his information. Dan offered to buy Stan lunch, but the Lieutenant said he had too much work to do. Dan was just as glad as he was anxious to get to Big Bill.

The pool hall was nearly empty at that hour of the day. One man practiced shots by himself, and an old, black man was sweeping and emptying wastebaskets. The smell of old cigarettes and beer hadn't changed since Dan was last in the place. Big Bill sat at a booth near the back, his ledgers spread open in front of him, a stack of cash, presumably the previous day's take, sat in front of him. Dan ordered a beer from the bartender and carried it to Bill's booth.

"Mr. Navin?" he said and sipped from the beer.

"Big Bill. I ain't Mr. Navin to no one." He didn't look up as he spoke.

"My name's Dan Kirk. I'm with the *Detroit Free Press.*"

"I don't need no ads. Business is good."

"No, I'm a reporter."

Navin stopped writing in the ledger and squinted up at Dan. "I know you, don't I? You used to play pool in here years back. Where you been?"

"I don't have the time I used to have when I was in school. I work crazy hours."

"Well, take a load off," Bill said, gesturing to the seat across from him. Due to Bill's paunch, he had pushed the table away from him. If Dan had weighed ten pounds more, he wouldn't have been able to squeeze into the seat.

"What can I do for you?" Bill asked.

Dan told him about the story he was working on. He talked about Cliff's arrest and Bill said, yes, he had seen it in the papers. "Don't know if it was your paper, Son. I don't pay much attention to which paper I read."

Yes, he said, he did know Cliff Malin, had known him since shortly after he'd come to town from Missouri. Kind of showed him the ropes, he said. He wouldn't mind talking about it if Dan didn't mind riding with him on his rounds to the bank and various suppliers. Dan didn't mind.

Bill's Buick was as clean as his bar. He told Dan he had it washed and swept out every day. "Can't stand to live in filth," he said. He drove slowly through the streets, paying particular attention to pedestrians, trying to avoid splashing them with the mucky melting snow.

"How old are you, Son?" he asked after the stop at the bank.

"In my thirties."

"Well, you mighta been old enough to know some of this. Maybe picked up some of it in your line of work. I hope you'll forgive an old man for telling you things you may already know."

In 1920, in a country full of Monday morning towns, Detroit was Saturday night. Descending the steps from the 5:05 from St. Louis, Clifford Malin felt like he was entering the grandest, most amazing party of his life.

He couldn't help grinning as he strolled through the busy railway station, watching so many fashionably dressed people scurrying about at what he imagined to be very important errands. That man there in the fedora—a doctor rushing to present a paper at an important conference. Those two women, the hem of their dresses swishing tantalizingly at their calves, their high heels clicking as they seemed to dance across the marble floor, were important socialites off to rescue some poor orphans. That family standing at the ticket booth was taking the train to New York City where they would cross the Atlantic Ocean for an extended trip through Europe. Or so he imagined. Certainly no one in this important city could be doing anything as mundane as the people back in Flat River, Missouri did.

Outside, the air was filled with the music of a bustling city going about its business. Raucous automobile engines played bass to the alto and soprano conversations of pedestrians. The screeching AA-OO-GAH of the automobile horns rose in loud crescendos above the choir of city sounds. And the lights. How Malin marveled at the lights. Brilliant green, red and amber ones blinked at street corners. Bright white lights paraded down sides of the streets like chandeliers in a palace ballroom, piercing the bleak January Michigan dusk. Blinking yellow and blue ones bickered across the street at each other, advertising nightclubs, hotels, restaurants.

Woodward Avenue was the widest street Cliff had ever seen. It, too, looked like it was ready for a party. Shop windows lavishly displayed the latest in fashions: silks, and taffetas in colors he had never seen for women, rich woolen suits and handmade leather shoes for men. At J.L. Hudon's Department Store, a red carpet stretched from the curb to the front door and uniformed doormen escorted ladies in heavy fur coats inside. On both sides of the street, Cliff stared through shop windows at an enormous array of smart clothes, stylish furniture, imported china, silver, and jewelry. Even at S.S. Kresge's and Wilson's, where more frugal shoppers pored over goods he found trinkets and geegaws in colors and sizes and quantities beyond his wildest imagination.

But above all, Detroit was the home of the automobile. Long ones, short ones, green ones, and black ones plied the city streets at all hours of day and night. The car had become the most treasured possession and the most obvious, most flaunted sign of prosperity. It was poetry, passion, magic, and freedom. Housewives would skip meals before they would go without gas in their cars. Businessmen saw the car as a hallmark of their success, their chariot amongst the little people.

With nearly two thousand dollars in his battered suitcase, proceeds from a life insurance policy on Alicia and their savings account, Cliff hoped to make a fresh start on a new, more thrilling life than that of his family and neighbors in Missouri. Nice clothes, his own apartment, maybe even a car after he got a job, that was his future. For now, though, he just needed to find a place to stay for the night. Much as he wanted to, he couldn't keep wandering the streets like some Ozark hick. He stopped at the Roosevelt Hotel, an imposing stone building with giant marble lions guarding its entry, and, without asking the price, booked a room. He tried not to be embarrassed when the bellman in his fancy uniform picked up the beaten leather suitcase and led him to the elevators.

The room was a little smaller than he thought it would be, but the French Provincial furniture gave it a sophisticated, regal air. The single window behind heavy green velvet drapes looked directly into a chipped brick wall of a grimy building. He didn't care. He wasn't here to sit and look out the window. He pulled the drapes closed.

It was nearly seven o'clock by the time he finished unpacking his meager wardrobe and he was starving, having devoured the ham sandwich and lemonade his mother had given him for the train ride hours earlier. Besides, he was anxious to begin sampling the fares of the city's best restaurants, but where to begin. The bellman suggested the Blue Orchid, two blocks up the street from the hotel.

"You can get anything you want there," the bellman said with a wink.

Cliff stepped outside and was hit by a blast of icy wind. He pulled his coat collar up around his neck, pushed his hat down tighter on his head and headed for the Blue Orchid. He found it beneath pale blue lights with a doorman who greeted him and opened the door before he could get to it. Inside, the steamy smells of fresh bread, grilled fish, and steaks mingled with aromas of perfume and cigarettes. A small dance floor spread in the middle of the room before a bandstand on which a six-piece band was tuning up for the evening's performance.

"Good evening, sir," a tuxedo-clad man with pomaded hair said. "Will you be dining alone this evening, or will someone be joining you."

"No, I'll be alone," Malin said. "I'm new in town."

"Ah, well, welcome to Detroit and the Blue Orchid, sir. Come this way."

The tuxedoed man, noticing Cliff's out-of-date brown suit and scuffed shoes, seated him against a side wall at a small table draped in crisp white linen. A more sophisticated man might have protested sitting so near the waiters' workstation, but Cliff was happy to be inconspicuous. He shifted in his seat nervously as he read the menu. He had never heard of Bernaise sauce or cabernet sauvignon. He wasn't even going to try to pronounce them. Glancing around the room, he noticed cocktail and wine glasses on nearly every table. He wondered what might be in them since only a few days earlier, selling and consumption of alcoholic beverages was made illegal. When the waiter arrived, he ordered a steak and a martini, half expecting the waiter to refuse to serve the drink. Instead, the officious little man simply scribbled on a note pad, said, "Very good, sir" and disappeared.

His dinner was the best steak he ever ate, or so it seemed, Given his state of mind, though, it could have been an old boot, and he wouldn't have noticed.

When he'd finished eating, he sat back in his chair, ordered his third martini and watched the dancers. The band played the new jazz music as women decorated in glistening jewelry and rustling fabrics snuggled against their partners on the dance floor or bared a knee as they spun around. Handsome men in black bow ties and starched shirts whispered things to women that made them laugh.

Despite the howling winter winds outside, he ambled back to his hotel room after supper, glowing from the evening's experience, and from the three martinis he downed in two hours. Tomorrow, he'd go shopping for clothes like the ones he'd seen tonight. This was his town and he was going to fit in, maybe even become well known on the social scene. Yes, he thought has he slunk down under the crisp sheets that night, moving to Detroit had been the right thing to do.

# CHAPTER 10

▼

Cliff Malin had been in Detroit a week when he decided it was time to look for a job. Two new suits with matching shoes and hats, meals in restaurants, and hotel bills had already nibbled away at the cash he had brought with him. He bought a copy of the *Detroit Free Press* and headed for Navin's Pool Hall, a hangout he found on his third day in town. It was noisy and warm, the food was good and cheap and Big Bill Navin, the proprietor, had made him feel welcome, answering his questions about the city. Bill told him what parts of town to avoid, either because they were too rough or too expensive. He also told Cliff how people in the city did things such as where they shopped, what they ordered at restaurants, which newspaper to read. He never made Cliff feel like an ignorant country cousin.

The *Free Press* listed page after page of jobs in almost every industry imaginable: foundries, construction, the docks, the automobile factories, as well as more gentlemanly jobs like clerking and bookkeeping. The latter jobs looked appealing for being clean work, but their salaries were pitiful. He didn't come to Detroit to stay poor. He circled a few that sounded appealing and went on a few interviews. Everywhere he went, long lines of men interspersed with a few women waited to be interviewed for the same jobs. Some wore clean but shabby clothes and carried a suitcase as battered as his own. Others had obviously not seen a bathtub or a razor in days. At the automobile factories he saw signs that read "To apply for work you must have $35 in your pocket and an address."

"What's that all about," he asked the man in line in front of him.

"Where you from?" the man asked.

"Missouri."

"It's folks like you that make them put them signs up. You guys come draggin' your families up here thinkin' there's jobs aplenty for everyone. Ya got no place to live and ya figure these companies're just goin' to hand you a job. But there ain't that many jobs. So ya wind up living in the parking lot cuz you got no money for a hotel room or even a boardin' house. Ya's wanna use the factory bathrooms and when they won't let ya, ya shit and piss in the street. And ya think someone's goin' to come along and feed your snot-nosed brats cuz you can't afford to. 'Sides, you got no place decent to sleep at night, you're not right in the head in the morning. You make trouble on the job."

The man turned his back on Cliff and lit a cigarette. Cliff got out of line and went back to his hotel room, too depressed about having to stand in line next to this guy for God knows how long

Late one afternoon a few days later, after spending hours riding buses and filling out forms, Cliff hunched over a newspaper in a booth near the back of the pool hall reading more classified ads. He'd been looking for a job for four days and nothing seemed too promising. Big Bill finished polishing the bar top then carefully folded his towel and announced to his customers he was closing for a few hours.

"Gotta lay in some provisions," he said.

Cliff downed the last of his beer and buttoned his overcoat against the outside chill as Navin rounded the bar, pulling on his own heavy coat.

"Cliff, my boy," he said, jerking his head toward the back of the room. "I think it's time you see the other side of Detroit."

Cliff shrugged and followed Bill outside. He sat shivering in Navin's Model T as the corpulent man gave a couple of feeble tugs at the crank handle on the front of the vehicle. Afraid the man would injure himself or worse, Cliff climbed out of the car and offered his assistance. After several strong cranks, the car wheezed to life. He got back inside next to Bill and hoped the excitement of being in a car for only the second time in his life did not show on his face.

Neither man spoke as Bill eased the car along Grand River Avenue, the slush of melted snow and ice splashing across the windshield. At Griswold Street, Navin turned right, heading toward the Detroit River. Another right on River Road and the men were headed south, the city's skyline disappearing behind them. Navin's shoulders slumped slightly and he relaxed his grip on the steering wheel once he was away from the city traffic. He lit a cigarette then offered one to Cliff who took it.

"Aren't you curious about where we're going?" Bill asked.

"Yeah, sure, but I figure you'll tell me when you're ready, Mr. Navin."

"Bill. Call me Bill." He took a deep pull on his cigarette. "We're off to get some supplies. I got a big party at the place this weekend and my customers have come to expect certain things from me. We're going downriver to pick up some scotch and bourbon. Then we'll come back and get it ready to sell."

In only the few short weeks since he'd arrived in Detroit, Cliff had discovered that the Volstead Act and Prohibition might have been written in the sand for all the weight they carried. It seemed as easy to get a drink anywhere in town as it had been before federal legislators outlawed it. But he still wasn't used to the cavalier attitude these people had about breaking the law. In Flat River, no one even spit on the sidewalk.

The men rode in silence a few minutes then Bill said, "You ever use a gun?"

"Just in the service," Cliff said, shifting uncomfortably on the hard seat of the Model T.

"That'll do," Bill said. "Reach under your seat."

Cliff pulled out a small briefcase which Bill told him to open. Inside was a .22 revolver. Cliff stared at it.

Bill said he had the gun in case he came across the go-through gangs, guys that would go through anything to get the booze or cash others had on them. He told Cliff the gang could be one or two men or it could be a dozen. If the gang was more than two men, Cliff was not to resist them. Otherwise, Bill said, shoot to kill. Cliff's heart pounded as a chill ran up his spine. He wasn't sure if he was excited or scared.

"The worst thing that can happen is to run into the Gray Ghost. That son of a bitch don't care about nothing. He dresses all in gray like some kind of goddam actor or something. Even painted his Tommy gun gray and wears a gray cape. And he has no fear. He holds up the little guys and the big operators. He don't care. He's good, but he ain't going to last long," Bill said.

Cliff stared out the window at the dormant farm fields as the car bumped along the rough dirt road. Everything was happening so fast he didn't think he could stop it if he wanted to. And he wasn't sure he wanted to. Bill chattered casually for the rest of the trip as though he had just told his passenger about a night out with the boys or his family's last Christmas not about guns and illegal alcohol. He talked about his wife, his five kids and two grand kids, and his parents. His mother and father had come from Frankfurt, Germany he said and their name had been Nevenhoven.

"Hell's kitchen. When I opened the pool hall I couldn't afford a sign big enough to put that name on so I shortened it. That was twenty-five years ago," he said, patting his ample belly. "Before they could call me Big Bill."

They had been bumping along under the leaden Michigan sky over the frozen dirt furrows for nearly an hour when they arrived at Ecorse, a small town huddled beside the Detroit River. It was a humble little town, rundown in some respects but with a few signs of recent care. The mercantile had a new sign and looked as though its outside walls had been painted last summer. Outside the post office were new benches. Inside Maggie's Café where Navin stopped Cliff smelled fresh paint mixed with that of fried onions and fresh coffee.

The men headed toward the back of the room and sat at a small table in the corner. When a waitress appeared, they ordered coffee and sandwiches and Navin asked to see Maggie. The sandwiches and coffee had just been set on the table when a small woman appeared in the kitchen door. Wiping her hands on a towel, she walked briskly across the restaurant, speaking to customers as she moved. At Navin's table, she pulled out a chair and sat sideways in it.

"How ya doing, Bill?" though she spoke to Navin her eyes were on Malin. "Who's your friend?"

"Meet Cliff Malin. He's from Missouri or some damn place. I brought him out to give me a hand."

Maggie tipped her head slightly at Malin, acknowledging the introduction but did not smile. Cliff returned the nod. He noticed Maggie was past middle age, though it was difficult to say how far past. Her short, gray hair curled softly around her face, but her skin was smooth and clear. Her green eyes were bright and alert. She wore a blue work shirt open at the neck over a white turtleneck sweater, a beige skirt that was a fashionable six inches above her ankles, and an immaculate white apron. Despite her brusque manner, there was an air of gentleness and gentility about her.

Bill told Maggie he needed three cases of scotch and three of bourbon. Maggie said she had the scotch, but the bourbon wouldn't be in for about an hour.

"We'll wait," Bill said. "Meantime, I'll tell my friend here about the import business."

Maggie looked at Cliff through narrowed eyes. "So long as we aren't training the competition," she said and left the table. She picked up a stack of dirty dishes off a nearby table before disappearing back into the kitchen.

"Isn't she something?" Bill said chuckling and shaking his head. The wattle under his chin trembled. "You know she's sixty-four years old? Works every day here at the café, runs a regular route over to Canada for her customers, and dances her fool head off every Saturday night at the church hall. She's sure got some spunk. I wouldn't want to cross her, though. She can outshoot any man I know."

Bill ordered a beer and slid his chair away from the table. He told Cliff he could remember when the town of Ecorse was just a wide spot in the road. Most everyone was a farmer and in the winter, when there were no crops to tend, they chopped ice for the icehouses in Detroit. Prohibition had gone into effect in Michigan a year before the rest of the country. In that time things had really picked up for the sleepy little village of Ecorse. Because it was so far from Detroit, the police and border patrol rarely came out. Less than a mile separated Michigan from Amhertsberg, Canada, making it a perfect staging place for rumrunners. Bill said they had learned early how to deal with the occasional officer that did show up.

"Those poor bastards only make about fifteen hundred dollars a year. Hell's kitchen, I can make that on a good Saturday night. You give them a bottle of scotch or a couple cases of beer when their daughter gets married, or you cross their palms with a little jingle, and they just go away. Come down here of a Sunday afternoon and it's worth your life to be out on the river. In the winter, folks just drive across the ice, pick up their goods and git. In the summer, every boat in the county is on that river. You stand more chance of getting run over than you do of getting arrested."

Bill talked about getting the scotch and bourbon ready for sale. Maggie would pay four dollars for a quart of either drink and sell it to him for fourteen. Back at the pool hall, he would cut it with water making three quarts out of each one and sell each one for fourteen dollars. Sold by the shot, each cut quart would bring twenty-eight dollars.

Cliff whistled. "I suppose you'd have to have a club or pool hall or something to get your customers. I mean if you wanted to tap into that kind of business."

"Christ, no," Bill said. "Every dry cleaner and baker and milkman carries some of this stuff for their regular customers. So do half the housewives in town. I can never figure out if everybody's selling the stuff, who's buying it. Somebody is, that's for sure. Seems like there's never enough to go around."

When they had finished eating and talking, the two men sauntered around to the alley in back of the café and watched two scrawny black teenagers scuttling between the building and cars. Four vehicles besides Navin's were being loaded. Each bottle was removed from its wooden crate, wrapped in rags and tucked under the seat cushions or behind the liner of the doors. Maggie soon joined them in the yard.

"You can pay me for that load now and we'll settle up on the bourbon when it gets here," she told Bill. He peeled off five crisp one hundred dollar bills from a roll in his pocket.

"That's five hundred and four dollars," she said, wiggling her fingers.

"God damn you, woman," he laughed. "You think I'm going to cheat you?"

"I know you aren't going to cheat me, Bill Navin, cuz I'm not going to let you."

He fished in his pants pocket, pulled out another roll of bills and counted off four singles. "We'll be back in a little while," he said and headed across the yard to his car. Cliff tailed along behind. Navin headed the car farther south along River Road to just outside the city limits, stopping at a deserted beach. He took out his pocket watch.

"Hell's kitchen," he said, squinting and passing the watch to Malin. "Can you read that?"

"Five forty," Cliff said.

"Good. It should be dark before long."

They sat in silence till just after six o'clock then Bill pointed across the river at a light flickering on the opposite shore in Canada.

"There she goes," he said. "You'll be seeing some action soon."

More lights dotted the shore, not burning steadily but flashing in irregular rhythms. Dots of blue, yellow, and white lights lit the river bank like dozens of fireflies dancing an unchoreographed ballet. Suddenly a red light, larger than the rest, seemed to explode on the shore and the other lights went out.

"Damn," Bill muttered, pounding his knee. He scoured the frozen river and the bank on both sides. Cliff looked also, not knowing what he was looking for. They sat in silence nearly a half hour when the lights began twinkling again.

"Here we go," Navin said smiling.

"I don't get it," Cliff said.

"Over there is Canada. I told you how these guys go across and get their hootch. Well, they got this system with the lights worked out. That's how they find their contacts in the dark. All along the shore over there is different guys waiting for their American customers to come over. They set up some kind of signal with each other so they don't get to the wrong place. Those guys can be mighty touchy about strangers stumbling into their operations. Every one of them has a red light. If they see anyone they don't know or if John Law shows up, they hit the red light and every one stays where they are till the red light goes out."

"Sounds pretty organized," Cliff said. "I think I'd be a little nervous driving out on that river though."

"You have to be careful, that's for sure. At the beginning and end of winter when the ice starts getting thin, they lose a car here and there. The other problem is the ice fisherman. There's a lot of those, and you can fall in the holes they chop in the ice. Some of the drivers use their headlights, but the new guys who are worried about the cops seeing those lights send someone out on foot ahead of them. They lose some of those guys too. I know I could make more money if I made my own contacts in Canada, but I'm too old and fat to be worrying about all that. Maggie treats me right and if a load of booze gets lost, it's her loss, not mine." He pointed across the river. "Here they come now. You watch. They'll be across the river in two minutes and forty seconds."

Cliff watched as headlights began to appear from the far side of Fighting Island. There must have been close to two dozen cars. He squirmed in his seat, a smile beginning to creep across his face, his eyes bright with astonishment at the sheer audacity of it all.

"I can't believe what I'm seeing," he said.

"Well, you better believe it, boy. There's more hard-earned cash represented by those cars than Mr. Henry Ford himself put in the bank last week," Bill said.

Back in his room that night, Cliff could not sleep. He kept going over the events of the day and making calculations. If he used the money he had to buy liquor and resold it, then invested the proceeds into more purchases, he'd be a wealthy man in no time. He'd have to do it right, though. He couldn't afford to lose his nest egg. Maybe he could buy into Maggie's operation. She seemed to know what she was doing, and he figured every business owner could use an infusion of cash. With his help, she might be able to expand her business.

The next time Cliff went to Ecorse with Bill he found Maggie more hospitable than she had been on the first visit. The cafe was virtually empty and she was relaxed and talkative. He decided to broach the subject.

"Maggie, why don't you let me come to work for you?"

"Doing what?" she asked.

"I don't know, anything that needs doing. I'm a good worker and I'll work long hours."

"Do you drive?"

Cliff's face reddened. "No, but I can learn."

"How will you get out here to work until you can drive?"

"I'll get a place out here. There's nothing keeping me in Detroit."

"You got any money?"

"A little."

"You planning to learn the ropes from me then go into business for yourself?" She looked straight into his eyes when she asked.

"I'm no fool, Maggie. Bill told me how you can shoot." He laughed but Maggie just stared. More solemnly he added, "I'm new in town. I just need a job. I might be willing to invest in your business, if you need a partner."

Maggie lit a cigarette and stared at Cliff. She wasn't really sure about him, something about his eyes made her uneasy. Business was picking up, though, and she needed some extra help. Besides, Big Bill seemed to like him. She'd just have to keep her eye on him.

"I got an apartment over the garage I'll rent to you for twenty dollars a month. It's not much, but it's warm and dry. Till you learn to drive, you can ride back and forth with me," she said. "We'll talk about a partnership later."

She found Cliff was right when he said he would do whatever needed doing. From loading and unloading the trucks at any hour of day or night to shoveling the parking lot, even doing dishes in the cafe, he was willing to work. Maggie began to relax around him a little. She even had her foreman, Red Polanski, teach him to drive. But after a couple of months she started to notice unexplained absences. Cliff's lunch or supper break began to take longer and longer. Sometimes he didn't ride home after work with her. Her old suspicions began to return and deepened one afternoon when she saw him walking along on the ice near the shore, dragging something behind him. The river bank obscured what he was towing.

Eileen Sullivan, a regular customer, was lingering over a cup of coffee. Maggie asked her to watch the cafe and wrapped herself in a heavy overcoat. Outside, she walked along the street a short distance behind Cliff. At Third Street, she turned into a small park that stood between the street and the river and climbed up on a stone bench to get a better view. She saw that Cliff was pulling a large sled loaded with something covered with a tarp.

"I was right about that kid from the start," she muttered.

Back at the café she wondered what to do. Fire him? Confront him? Buy him off? Threaten him? She decided to work him till he couldn't move. He wouldn't have time or energy to work his own gig till she could find out what he was up to. When he returned to the café an hour later, she told him she was going to raise his pay ten percent—and double his hours. Cliff didn't even wince. For the next week, he was never out of Maggie's sight except when he went to his apartment. Then one afternoon he told her he was coming down with a cold and wanted to go home and go to bed. She had no choice but to let him.

Just before sunset, Red Polanski burst into the kitchen and grabbed Maggie's coat. Thrusting it at her with one hand and pulling her out the door with the other, he said, "Maggie, you have to see this. It's the goddamnest thing you ever saw. That new guy you hired? I been watching him. He's a sly one. When he started disappearing for a long time, I started following him. I figured he was trying to get his own action going. When I saw where he went—down to that old boathouse by the pier—I was sure something was up. I went inside to have a little talk with him, and I couldn't believe what I found. I can't believe none of us thought of this before. The kid's got a head on his shoulders, all right. When he saw me, he told me to come and get you."

Red led Maggie down to the park where she had spied on Cliff a few days earlier and lifted her up on the stone bench. Looking up and down the river, he stuck two fingers in his mouth and gave out a loud whistle. From behind the pier to their right, Maggie and Red saw a triangle of white fabric appear, fastened to a large pole like a flag. It began to move along the pier toward the center of the river slowly, until it cleared the pier's pilings, then turned and headed north. When it came into full view, Maggie saw it was an iceboat with Cliff at the helm.

"Hey, Maggie, watch this," Cliff called.

Deftly, he maneuvered the boat back and forth in front of her, first sailing with the wind then turning and tacking back into it. Around in circles, even in a giant figure eight, he sailed the craft then turned and headed back to shore. Wading through knee-deep snow, he made his way to Red and Maggie.

"What do you think?" Maggie was annoyed that Cliff addressed the question to Red.

"Pretty slick," Red said, clapping Cliff on the shoulder. "What made you think of it?"

"We played with ice boats all the time at home. It just seemed like the perfect thing for the job. They're lighter than cars, so you can use them when the ice isn't thick enough for cars. And once they get going, there isn't anything that can catch them."

"What are you going to do with it?" Maggie cut in, a sharp edge to her voice.

"We can use them in the business."

"We?"

"Yeah, you didn't think I was doing this for myself. Listen, Maggie. Let's get something straight. I'm not going into business on my own for a whole lot of reasons, but that doesn't mean I can't think of things to help your business out. And make some extra bucks for myself in the process, of course."

"What is this little baby going to cost me?"

"Nothing. I'll put up enough money to build three more iceboats for fifty percent of the take."

"Fifty percent? You're out of your rabbit ass mind. I spent a lot of time and money building this business. I'm not just going to hand over fifty percent."

"I have to be honest with you, Maggie. I told you I wasn't going to take your customers and I won't, but I got an idea here that someone can use. If you aren't interested, I'll find someone who is. I'll take it to some of the other operators, and they'll see what they pay me will be made up in the shipments they don't lose through the ice or to the other gangs."

"I don't lose fifty percent of my shipments," Maggie said.

"But with the best delivery system going, you'll be able to pick up some big customers, because you can guarantee delivery when no one else can."

Maggie jumped down from the bench and started walking back to the café. Digging in her coat pocket, she pulled out a lace hankie and wiped her nose. Turning to Cliff she said, "Twenty-five percent."

"Thirty-five," he said.

"Thirty."

He nodded. He told her he could pick up some old row boats at the boat livery, rebuild them, and have them ready in two weeks. She insisted they be kept completely out of sight until they were ready, that he not talk to anyone about the boats, not even to Bill Navin. Their greatest advantage lay in being the first one on the river with the boats. She started walking back to the café then turned back to Cliff.

"And one other thing, Cliff. It's up to you to get out to those customers we don't have and tell them about guaranteed delivery. I don't want you sitting around collecting thirty percent off the work I already have. If my business doesn't pick up in a month, the deal's off."

# CHAPTER 11

▼

It was several weeks before iceboats operated by other rumrunners began appearing on the river. By then, Cliff and Maggie had managed to woo away a substantial number of clients from other operators. Speakeasy owners eager to quench their customers' thirst, businessmen who had special clients in town, family men preparing for a big party or wedding were placing orders with Cliff because he said he could guarantee delivery. And he did. Not a single load was lost to go-through gangs on the river or to thin ice and fishing holes. But customers who switched suppliers soon found that the theory of open market competition was lost on their previous suppliers. Roy James had his left arm broken, Frank McGeary had to replace all the glass in his bar and Claude Sonowski's daughter's wedding was utter chaos as a result of their switching allegiance to Maggie and Cliff.

As for Maggie and Cliff, their actions could not be ignored. Filching from another bootlegger was as bad as cattle rustling had been fifty years earlier, even if it was a woman doing the filching. And it called for the same immediate action.

Late one night, a dozen armed men broke into Maggie's warehouse. The cases of liquor they couldn't pack in their own trucks were broken, the contents oozing out the door and down the alley. Two of the dock workers were badly beaten. Two more quit.

One dirty Monday morning as Cliff walked to the café from the river under a pewter sky, he saw a familiar blue stocking cap in a ditch along the road. He climbed down and picked it up. It was Red Polanski's. Thirty feet farther along the ditch, he found Red's frozen body. All his fingers had been pulverized. His face looked like raw steak. All but two of Maggie's men quit when they heard about Red. In order to meet the few deliveries they still had, Cliff was going to have to make a run across to Amherstberg himself.

The iceboats had one disadvantage over trucks and cars. The best time to use them was during daylight hours when winds were at their most brisk. That made the boat more visible than Cliff would have liked, particularly now that so many men were watching for him. He decided to make his run on Wednesday when traffic was lighter. Days were warming up a bit as winter edged out of the sky and the ice would be a little soft, slowing down the boat. But the thinning ice may just deter those smugglers still using cars. At least Cliff hoped so. Sitting at Maggie's Café, Cliff sipped coffee and watched a small flag he had impaled into the riverbank. Marine weather forecasters were calling for fifteen knots today, strong enough to overcome the mush ice and outrun any pursuers, he figured. When the distended flag remained outstretch for a steady ten minutes, it was time to go.

Cliff pulled three blankets off a stack Maggie kept in the warehouse and piled them in the back of Red Polanski's old Ford. He laid a .12 gauge shotgun on the floor, careful not to let Maggie see he was arming himself. She would only worry. He was finishing a cigarette when Maggie appeared in the doorway.

"You sure you want to do this?" she asked.

"I don't see as I have any choice. We got orders," Cliff said.

"I think this better be the last one. We made more money off this than we ever thought we would, and now people are getting hurt. Let's just call it quits," Maggie said.

"Yeah, I guess you're probably right." In fact, Cliff had been having similar thoughts since he found Red lying by the side of the road, but he felt an obligation to Maggie to continue as long as she wanted.

"Got a deal on some nice porterhouse this morning. One's got your name on it," she said.

"Fried onions and mashed potatoes come with that?"

"Probably."

"You better start peeling potatoes, because I'm going to be mighty hungry when I get back.:

"Cliff." She reached into her apron pocket and pulled out a .38 revolver. "You better take this."

Cliff stared at it. "Thanks," he said, stuffing the gun in his coat pocket. He leaned over and planted a kiss on the top of her head. "Don't worry. I'll be fine."

The trip to Canada was uneventful. Cliff encountered only one group of ice fisherman packing up to leave for home and a small band of boys playing hockey instead of going to school. The cold air shocked his lungs, but the bright sun warmed his face. The sun hadn't yet softened the surface of the ice, and Cliff's boat moved quickly. By this late in the season there were few holes left behind by ice fisherman, and Cliff adroitly avoided them. At the distillery docks outside Amherstberg, he helped the men load his boat leaving a small clearing at the stern where he would sit and a narrow slot under the starboard gunwale so he could reach the shotgun. Pushing away from the dock, he winced as the bitter wind bit into his face.

Raising the sails, he watched them grow taut in the grip of the wind then turned the boat upriver toward Ecorse. As he guided the boat up the Canadian shore, he kept a careful lookout for any signs of trouble—other rumrunners, border patrol, and police. Except for two cars moving along the road on the riverbank to his right, he could have been the last man on earth.

Cliff's boat had just rounded the northern edge of Fighting Island in the middle of the Detroit River headed into American territory when a car that had been huddled in the shadow of overhanging trees pulled away from the shore of the island directly ahead of him. Behind the first car, another drove into his path then a third. Despite the icy wind enveloping him, his palms began to sweat. He eased the boom slightly to starboard to allow the sails to catch more wind. A sudden gust shot him a hundred yards ahead of the cars but off course for his dock. He would have to turn and tack back into the wind to get home which would cut is speed in half as he headed back toward the cars. Continuing his track north, he considered his options. A quick glance over his shoulder revealed that the cars had stopped, and two men stood next to each one brandishing a weapon. They knew they didn't need to chase him. He would have to get past them to get to the dock.

Cliff looked back around just in time to avoid a huge hole an ice fisherman had cut. A thin sheet of ice had formed over the water in the hole, but not enough to hold any weight. He had an idea.

Maneuvering the boat around, he tacked back south, heading toward the cars and noticing that, as he had feared, his speed was cut by almost half. This would have to work the first time. Just before he got within shooting range of any of the weapons the men might have, he steered the boat in a giant arc heading north again. He grinned as he looked over his shoulder and saw the men scrambling into their cars. As he figured, the stupid bastards had grown impatient waiting for him. They weren't going to pass up the opportunity for a good chase.

As he angled toward the Canadian shore, the cars turned to follow, one in back of the other. The wind roared in his ears and bit at his dry, chafed face. A bullet ripped through the sail just above his head and he pulled the .12 gauge from under the gunwale and lay it on his lap. He steered the boat toward the yawning hole in the ice he had narrowly missed earlier. A quarter mile past it, he turned the boat back south. The cars slowed and turned to follow him, sliding sideways before returning to their ducks-in-a-row parade.

The first car hit the hole like an eight ball in the side pocket. The second driver slammed on his brakes and slid sideways into the first car, pushing it nearly out of sight beneath the ice. Two down. The third car fishtailed across the ice as the driver tried to avert crashing into the pile of metal ahead of him. He regained control of the car and headed after Cliff.

Tacking into the wind, Cliff headed for home, certain he was out of range of the guns he could hear popping in the distance. Suddenly, a bullet ripped through the sail near the mast. Cliff's head spun around. The car must have come across snow on the ice that allowed it to gain traction and pick up speed. It was closing on him fast. He would never reach the dock in time. With a flick of his finger, he removed the safety from the shotgun. The car was behind him and to his port side and getting closer. The pulse of his heart pounded heavily in his ears as he tightened his grip on the lines. When the car was less than fifty feet away, Cliff gave the line a jerk, spinning the boat around and sending it headed directly for the car. Tucking the lines between his knees, he raised the shotgun with both hands and blasted both barrels through the windshield of the lumbering black Buick. A scream from inside the car told him he had hit someone, and he watched as the car slid sideways and rolled on its side.

Dropping the shotgun at his side, he steered the boat in a full circle around the car and watched a man push the passenger door up and climb out. Ducking behind the overturned car, he began firing a volley of shots at Cliff, bullets thudding into the side of the boat or skipping over the ice. When the shooter paused to reload, Cliff whipped the boat around in back of the car, pulling the revolver from his coat pocket and emptied it at the shooter. The stubby little man lurched forward and fell face down on the ice.

As Cliff eased the boat into the slip at Maggie's dock, he realized he had gripped the boat lines so tightly that his left hand had cramped. Dropping the lines, he rubbed the back of his hands against his hip. He couldn't feel his fingertips or the end of his nose or his feet. He just sat in the boat staring. Ike and Purvis, Maggie's two remaining dock workers, stepped into the boat, hooked their arms through Cliff's and set him on the dock like another case of whiskey. Ike jerked his chin toward Cliff.

"You better get that looked at, Mr. Malin." Cliff looked down and saw blood soaking through his overcoat just above his right elbow. Suddenly, he felt whoozy.

Standing at the window of the café, Maggie watched as Cliff crossed the street.

"Oh, my God," she said when she saw the blood-stained sleeve. "Eileen, call Doc White," she called as she grabbed her coat from a hook next to the door.

Cliff's heavy clothing had absorbed much of the momentum of the bullet, causing only a minor injury to his arm. In the days following his encounter on the ice, he relived leading the two cars into the hole in the ice and the shattering of the windshield with his shotgun. He began to feel invincible. Although he had promised Maggie there would be no more iceboat runs to Canada, a drop in temperatures promised at least another week of strong ice. He repainted the boat navy blue and fitted it with a blue-and-white-striped sail, hoping no one would link him to the new boat in the few short weeks before spring thaw.

The night before he was to make another run across to Amherstberg, he returned from making a delivery in Detroit to find Maggie's restaurant deserted, an unusual condition at suppertime.

"Maggie?" he called. "Anyone here?" No one replied. A sharp, putrid smell hung in the air, and he followed it toward the kitchen. Something on the other side of the door kept it from opening all the way. Squeezing through the narrow opening, he peered behind the door. His lunch bubbled up in his throat and spewed out.

Maggie's gaunt, gray face stared back at him, her mouth open, a stream of spittle down her chin. She was impaled on the coat hook where her coat normally hung. Her blouse and camisole were torn open, the small amount of flesh remaining on her torso blackened. Smoke from the grill drew Cliff's attention. Crossing the kitchen, he looked down at the rest of Maggie's skin burned into the hot surface.

The next day, Cliff paid off the two remaining warehousemen, burned the iceboat and gave away the remaining inventory of liquor to passersby on the street. He kept the restaurant open until he decided what to do next, but he needn't have bothered. The story of Maggie's gruesome death spread quickly through Ecorse. Not enough customers showed up to pay the electric bill. Unable to locate any of Maggie's relatives, Cliff sold off her possessions, depositing the money in his own account.

In the few short months since his arrival in Michigan, he had turned his two thousand dollars into more than fifty-three thousand.

# CHAPTER  12

▼

When Cliff returned to Detroit from Ecorse, Bill Navin had already heard what had happened at Maggie's and advised Cliff to leave Detroit at least for a while. He gave Cliff the name of a family who owned a turkey farm out near Pontiac, said he should stay there till tempers eased.

The Blumenthals, Esther and Melvin, were in their late fifties and had been married thirty-eight years. The farm had been Esther's dowry. Every day of those thirty-eight years showed in their faces and hands. Esther stood five foot nine inches tall, nearly the height of her husband. There was nothing superfluous about her. She had not an ounce of flesh she didn't need to cover her bones and hard muscles. Her hair was pulled straight back from her face and pinned into a tidy bun at the top of her head. No matter how hard she worked, no single strand of hair pulled loose from its pinnings. She wore no makeup, but years in the elements gave her face the color of coffeed milk. Her lips were naturally the color of a faded Pink Cushion begonia. Her only adornment was her wedding ring, a narrow gold band scratched and pock marked from years of manual labor by its wearer.

Melvin was much the same as his wife, tall, spare frame, simple, short haircut, always dressed in denim overalls over a plaid shirt, the sleeves and neck buttoned up regardless of the weather. His one concession to style was a gold pocket watch fastened to a loop inside his left overall pocket. His wife sewed the loop in each of the two pair of overalls he purchased every year from the Sears Roebuck catalog. The watch had belonged to his grandfather then his father. Cliff figured the watch was as much a practical item as it was an heirloom; Melvin was never late for lunch exactly at noon or at supper exactly at four-thirty.

Cliff assumed there were no young Blumenthals since none were ever mentioned, and there were no pictures in the plain, immaculate house. One lone photograph stood on an end table next to the faded brown serge sofa. It had been taken the day Esther and Melvin were married. Cliff looked at the photograph frequently during his stay trying to decipher his inscrutable hosts. He thought he saw a glint in Esther's eyes in the picture, perhaps reflective of her hopes for the future. There was no glint in her eyes now, just weariness.

The Blumenthals' conversation was as economical as their appearance. During meals they spoke about work that needed doing on the farm, the cost of feed. and what neighboring workers of the land were doing. After supper, they generally sat in front of the radio, catching up on the news of the day, the weather forecast. and the changes in crop prices. Esther mended or knitted while she listened; Melvin fixed his gaze on something in the room and remained motionless till he turned the radio off. When he was ready to go to bed, Esther put down her work and followed him upstairs. It was never later than eight thirty when they turned in.

There seemed to be nothing half way about spring that year. A skein of soggy, gray days were followed by brilliant, cloudless ones. Rain, sunshine, rain, sunshine through March, April, May. Temperatures were either warm enough to work outside in an undershirt or required thick coats.

The Blumenthals main occupation was raising turkeys, but there was also a vegetable garden, larger than was necessary to feed the two of them, planted in a corner of the yard. Cliff figured Esther sold the vegetables they didn't use either to the neighbors or to the green grocer in town.

One bright morning in mid April, Cliff awoke to the sound of chopping in the back yard. From his bedroom window, he could see Esther hacking at the refuse from last year's garden in preparation for the compost heap. The sun was still low in the eastern sky and the trees were still. He threw open the window and breathed deeply the damp, fresh smell of spring, so clean and inviting. He was tempted to call down to Esther, but it seemed somehow impossible to speak loudly in this household. He dressed quickly and pounded down the stairs, filled a coffee cup with fresh brew that had been left on the stove, and strode across the back yard to Esther.

"Could you use a little help? I was a pretty fair gardener back home," he said.

Esther looked up against the morning sun and squinted at the tall man looming over her then shrugged. "If you like," she said simply. She had had other house guests from the city like Cliff who thought they were going to sweat away their troubles on the farm. Most didn't last till lunch the first day. Cliff probably wouldn't be any different, but she'd take any help she could get.

"What's the plan?" he asked.

That was impressive, she thought. He was willing to take direction and not tell her how to manage her garden.

"First, we have to get last year's stuff out of here, but not everything comes out. How well do you know plants?"

"Pretty well. I assume you have some foxglove and camomile in here somewhere that you'll want to keep. Do you want to rotate herbs this season?"

Esther pulled her lips into a straight line that Cliff figured would have to pass for a smile. "I guess you do know something about gardening."

"I know enough to know that every garden and every gardener is different. I don't know your soil here, so you'll have to tell me how you want things."

He'll be alright, Esther thought. Maybe with this help, I can get the flower garden back in shape this year.

Over lunch Cliff and Esther had more conversation than they had had all the time he had been staying at the farm. They discussed whether the beans should be next to the onions, where the tomatoes do best, and what to do about aphids. Esther said the garden was plagued with snails and Cliff suggested planting garlic to deter them.

"Tried it," Esther said. "Must be Italian snails. Ate them right down to the ground."

Cliff asked about other animals that were attracted to the garden like deer and rabbits. Esther just shrugged. "If you got a garden, you got deer and rabbits. Simple as that. I figure the Lord is just making it easier for us to have rabbit stew and venison."

Cliff spent virtually every daylight hour when it wasn't raining digging, hoeing, and planting. He carefully followed the planting design Esther had sketched out for him, occasionally making suggestions, some of which she took. He loved the aroma of freshly turned earth as it exhaled its life-giving minerals and warmth into the air. The work felt good after the weeks of lounging around the house; it gave him a reason to get out of bed every morning. He noticed Esther had withdrawn from the vegetable garden and was pruning the pear and the apple trees, moving the fuchsias, and tying up the climbing rose to a trellis she had persuaded Melvin to build for the side of the barn.

Periodically throughout the summer, other guests appeared at the Blumenthals, sometimes singly, sometimes in pairs. Mostly they were men with hats pulled low over their eyes who spoke in hushed tones and came in the house only if the weather was inclement. When they entered the house, Esther quietly left them alone, regardless of what she was doing at the time. Twice Cliff noticed that a woman remained in the car in the driveway while the men conducted whatever business they had. Melvin generally pocketed a thick envelope during these visits and, quite often, another houseguest appeared the next day, taking one of the upstairs bedrooms down the hall from Cliff. Those houseguests were as reticent about themselves as their hosts and usually stayed only a few days. Cliff wondered if Big Bill had sent a thick envelope for his stay.

By the end of May, the roads had dried enough to make the drive back to Detroit relatively without hazard. Though the country air and physical labor was invigorating, Cliff was anxious to return to the bright lights and promises of the city. Life at the Blumenthals was what he had left Flat River to escape. He was getting restless and anxious to return to the action he had come to Michigan for. He telephoned Big Bill who assured him that what had happened in Ecorse was a dim and distant memory; it would be safe to come back.

Cliff had sent Big Bill money to purchase a new six-cylinder, four door Maxwell Special he had seen advertised in the newspapers. Bill let out a long, low whistle when he saw the twelve hundred dollars the car would cost. That flashy car would make Cliff stand out wherever he went. Bill had advised against it, suggesting a quiet, unobtrusive black Chevy instead, but Cliff was insistent. He felt the Maxwell would make him look prosperous, more trustworthy at whatever endeavor he would pursue. Bill drove the car out to the Blumenthal farm barely driving fifteen miles an hour, afraid the powerful car would get away from him and send him to his death on a lonely stretch of road.

Cliff drove back to town, pushing the car much faster than Bill had, even on the rutted country roads. With all the windows open, the warm, fresh smell of a Michigan spring surrounding him, his spirits were buoyed as he looked forward to a fresh start. Big Bill nattered as they drove along, telling Cliff the latest events in town.

Now that the Detroit River was free of ice, rumrunners were using boats to bring whiskey in from Canada, he said. Residents of St. Clair Shores who lived on the river were paying the various smugglers handsome fees to stay off their property, afraid that their families might get caught in a fiery gun battle, he said. The Coast Guard still had only two lumbering forty horsepower boats to try to interrupt the flow of booze from across the border. On some days, Bill said, those two boats tried to chase down over fifty high-speed Chrysler-powered boats used by the gangs.

"Hell's kitchen," Bill said, releasing his raspy laugh. "They might as well flush the cost of those boats down the crapper for all the good they're doing."

Bill told Cliff the organization of the gangs in town had changed. Abe, Isadore, and Ray Bernstein had consolidated the Hastings Street gang with the Oakland Sugar House Gang and Sammy "Purple" Cohen's outfit. Although Abe Bernstein was the brains of the new organization, they had taken the name of the Purple Gang. Their influence reached far outside Detroit, Bill said.

"He's been shipping liquor from Canada to some guy in Chicago named Capone. I guess this Capone fella cuts it and ships it all over the Mid West," Bill said.

Bill said the Bernsteins were loud, garish little Jews with no taste and an appetite for brutality. Their activities had grown to include insurance fraud, contract murders, kidnappings, drugs, and gambling. Cliff remembered hearing about the Bernsteins when he worked for Maggie. They had started out as a bunch of roughneck kids on the east side of Detroit, extorting money from merchants, stealing from old women, beating up anyone who stood in their way. When making liquor became illegal, they expanded into that trade. But rather than invest in a fleet of boats or cars of their own, they merely showed up on the shore of the Detroit River and appropriated what others had bought and paid for. Anyone who resisted was badly beaten or simply shot.

"You sure want to give them a wide berth," Navin concluded.

When the new Maxwell finally reached paved roads, Cliff pressed the accelerator to the floor, inching closer to its advertised limit of fifty miles an hour and causing Bill to blanch. Laughing like a child on its first carousel ride, Cliff threw his hat in the back seat and loosened his tie as Bill hunkered lower in the passenger seat.

Once back in town, Cliff headed straight to Bill's Pool Hall where he guzzled down two ice-cold beers—the Blumenthals didn't permit drinking in their home—and caught up with old friends. Later, he booked a room at the Roosevelt Hotel where he had stayed when he first arrived in Detroit. The next day he went on the most lavish shopping spree of his life: three dress shirts with nine collars, three seersucker suits—white, beige and pale blue—a straw boater, his first pair of spats, and a wristwatch. An equally extravagant dinner at the Blue Orchid followed. His experience with alcohol was limited to hard liquor so he bought his first bottle of wine based solely on price. Eight dollars and he wasn't sure if it was any good. Sleepy from his shopping and heavy meal, he decided not to look for a nightclub and returned to his hotel.

As the doorman at the Roosevelt helped him unload the packages, he told Cliff a man had been waiting for him for several hours. Inside, the desk clerk directed him to a tall, burly man dozing in an overstuffed leather chair. Cliff was hesitant to wake him. He didn't know the man and wasn't sure he wanted to, but he laid his hand on the man's shoulder. He had to shake him several times before the sleeping hulk roused.

"You looking for me?" Cliff asked, stepping back out of the man's reach.

"You Cliff Malin?" the man asked, rubbing sleep from his eyes and yawning.

"Who wants to know?"

"Mr. Bernstein wants to see you."

Cliff's throat went dry. In light of what Bill had told him, he wasn't sure this was good news.

"What for?" he asked.

"I don't ask Mr. Bernstein his business. I just do what I'm told."

"Well, I'm not sure I want to see Mr. Bernstein."

The man rose from the chair and clamped his massive hand around Cliff's elbow. He stood easily six inches taller than Cliff with shoulders like a bear. His face had met more than one fist.

"I don't see as how you got anything to say about it." He spun Cliff around and pushed him toward the door. Outside, a green and black Cadillac zoomed up in front of the two men and screeched to a stop. Someone inside flung open the back door, Cliff was pushed roughly inside and the bear sunk into the seat beside him. The car leaped forward and onto Woodward Avenue.

Cliff didn't pay attention to where they were going, keeping his eyes on the hands of the men sitting on either side of him, expecting to see a gun emerge from a jacket pocket or a shoulder holster. After a drive that seemed an eternity up side streets and through alleys, the car stopped abruptly in back of a gray stone building that bore no identification. Cliff was pulled from the back seat, shoved through a wide delivery door and loaded into a freight elevator like so many pounds of potatoes. One of his escorts punched a button for the tenth floor and the car groaned slowly upward. When it stopped, Cliff was pushed through the door, but neither of the two men who rode up with him followed. Straightening his jacket and hat, he looked around. He was in a wide hallway, bright with yellow walls and gold carpet, the ceiling dotted with bright crystal chandeliers that lit the halls like midday. A door opened at the far end of the hallway and a man in a butler's uniform stepped out, signaling Cliff to go inside.

Cliff's hands became clammy and the air seemed to be sucked out of the room as he walked toward the door, but he tried to appear unconcerned. Standing in the doorway, Cliff surveyed the room he had been ushered into. An ornate carved mahogany desk occupied nearly one whole side of the room with the remainder jammed with too many chairs and tables. It reminded Cliff of the furniture department at J.L. Hudson's. None of the pieces matched. It was as though someone bought everything they saw that they liked without regard to whether it went with anything else. And it was gaudy. Heavy gold brocade curtains hung at the windows, held back by red satin ropes. The carpet was a shade of green he was sure never appeared in nature. The walls were expensive mahogany paneling. Behind the desk, a massive leather chair was turned backwards. Above it, a plume of blue cigar smoke rose in wispy curls. Cliff heard a voice from behind the chair. The man talking was obviously angry.

"Listen, I don't need your bullshit," the man was saying. "You either take care of it for me or I'll get someone who will. I pay you plenty to see this kind of thing don't happen." The man paused to listen a moment then yelled, "I don't give a good goddam who caused it! Fix it!"

The chair spun around, the man clicked the earpiece of the telephone into the hook so hard the phone fell over. "Shit," he muttered, righting the phone. He looked up at Cliff. He was so short his chest barely cleared the top of the desk. He had a square bulldog head with squinty eyes of indeterminate color. His silk shirt and wool suit looked custom tailored and, from the style, Cliff figured this guy was the one who decorated the room. The suit jacket was a raucous blue and gray plaid and the shirt was pink. A red silk handkerchief spilled out of the breast pocket. Soft, pink hands that had recently been manicured drummed on the desk.

"Excuse my language," he smiled, puffing on his cigar. "My brother says I got a toilet for a mouth." He stubbed the cigar out in a lead crystal ashtray and pulled another one from the teak cigar box on his desk.

"I take it you're Mr. Malin."

Cliff had remained standing in the doorway in order to survey the room before entering it. He leaned against the door jamb in an effort to appear unconcerned about this visit. In truth, he hoped the door frame would hide the fact he was shaking.

"And I take it you're Abe Bernstein," he said.

"You take it right. Sit down, take a load off." Bernstein smiled broadly as he gestured to one of the chairs crammed in front of the desk. Cliff pulled the chair back and sat down.

"You know, Clifford my boy, you're a very clever fellow. I hear from my sources you're the one that started using those iceboats. That's good thinking. I like a man that thinks."

Cliff sat motionless, unsure of where all this was leading. Was he listening to his own eulogy?

"Trouble is, you didn't think far enough ahead. You got into something you didn't understand, and you made trouble for a lot of people, me included. I lost a lot of lettuce over you. Course I got it back now, but you hurt me for a while there."

Cliff fidgeted in his seat.

"Relax, son. I ain't going to hurt you. Sure, I was real sore for a while, but I get over things. Business is good again. In fact, it's better than ever."

"So what is it you want with me?"

"You got moxie. I like that. I want you to come to work for me. You and me, we could be a good team. I got lots of guys working for me who will do whatever I tell them. I got an enemy, they take care of it. I got a collection problem, they take care of that, too. I even got judges working for me who will take care of my parking tickets. What I need is someone who's a thinker. Someone who can help my little business get ahead. Not a Mr. Smarty Pants, mind you, but I think you learned it don't pay to be a Mr. Smarty Pants. Whadda ya say? Pay's pretty good."

Cliff was stunned and relieved. A job offer was the last thing he expected to hear. "What did you have in mind for me to do?"

"I didn't have anything specific in mind. I thought once you saw my operation you'd have some ideas about how we could work better. You know, improve our profits, lower our overhead like old Henry Ford is always trying to figure out."

Cliff and Abe talked late into the night. By morning Cliff had a new job.

# CHAPTER 13

▼

Over the next few months, Cliff floated around the various Bernstein enterprises watching operations, getting to know key people and absorbing the technicalities of running brothels and policy houses, making collections, and getting booze from Canada to warehouses sprinkled around town. At a whorehouse on Brush Street, he belted back the best gin in town as Ella McPherson, a black madam, explained where she got her girls (she paid juvenile probation officers for references) and how she dealt with obstreperous patrons (Whitey, a gorilla of a man who guarded the front door, threw them down stairs). At the Golden Door Salon, he watched Alberta Stern tally slips from the bookmaking operation she ran in a room just a few feet from where some of Detroit's most prestigious women had their hair bobbed and permed. On a balmy June night, under cover of a band of thick clouds that blocked the new moon and promised rain by morning, he rode in the stern of a large cabin cruiser, its Chrysler engine powering it quickly the half mile across the Detroit River, first to Windsor then back to St. Clair Shores. Aboard were twenty-seven cases of the best Canadian whiskey to be had. He couldn't help but think of that wintry day just a few months earlier when he wasn't sure he would actually complete a similar route in his iceboat.

One of the men on board, a short, solid, ebony man whose knuckles looked as though he dragged them across a cheese grater once a day, told Cliff that the last run he had made for the Purples had met with disaster. Officers from the U.S. Border Patrol had recently obtained a boat with a Chrysler engine of the same size that the rumrunners were using. They had managed to overtake the Purples boat on the trip back to Detroit and boarded her. As the dock workers watched helplessly, the officers threw nearly fifty cases of booze over the side, creating a flurry of white foam as the wooden boxes sunk below the surface.

"There was some pretty shit-faced walleyes and pikes in the river that night, I can tell you," the man laughed.

"What did the Boss say when you showed up empty handed?" Cliff wanted to know.

"Well, we didn't show up right away. We was all drug downtown to the police station and booked. The Purples is good to us, though. They bailed us out. But we only get bailed out twice, then they figure we is jinxed and they fire us. At least that's how they treat us colored guys."

The story of the liquor lost overboard gave Cliff an idea. Before the next run to Amhertsberg, At one of the Bernstein's distilleries, he picked up three dozen oak barrels that had not yet been coated to make them waterproof and purchased two hundred pounds of salt. He drove the supplies to the dock and ordered them loaded on the boats headed to Canada. When the whiskey was paid for at the distillery, Cliff directed the workers to take the bottles out of the wooden crates and stand them in the bottom of the barrels. He had them pour a layer of salt in around the bottles then add more bottles and more salt.

Cliff hadn't expected that his idea would be tested on the first run, but it was. When they were fifty feet from shore, the Border Patrol boat pulled away from shore, siren blaring and lights flashing. Cliff ordered the barrels thrown overboard. The cops had a smug, satisfied look on their faces as they watched hundreds of dollars of booze sink to the bottom of the river, but decided not to arrest anyone. Cliff waited twelve hours then took up a position on the shore across from the site of dumping. With him were three workers, a boat moored at the shore, and enough food to last a week, if that's how long it took. It was only aother twelve more hours, though, before the salt in the barrels dissolved, and the barrels began popping to the surface like dead fish. The workers scooped them up, loaded them in the boat and headed home, their cargo safe.

Abe was ecstatic.

"God damn you boy," he laughed, slapping Cliff on the back and forcing drinks in his hand. "For a country boy, you are pretty damn smart. You gotta think of something I can do for you. There must be something you really want, money, women, drugs. You just name it, you got it."

"I don't know, Mr. Bernstein. I'll have to think about it."

"Abe. Call me Abe."

He thought about several things he could have asked for: diamond cuff links, an open account at Hammond's Haberdashery, maybe a trip to Florida. But Cliff didn't want his employers knowing about any secret desires he had. He felt the less they knew about his private life, the less they could control him. Abe, impatient for Cliff to suggest a bonus for saving the shipment of liquor, finally passed five crisp hundred dollar bills into Cliff's hand.

While Cliff went to great lengths to keep his own life secret from his employers, he made it his business to know about everyone else's. He had begun accumulating a secret file on every key man in the operation, a file he did not share with his employers. He kept it wrapped in heavy oilcloth buried in his bucket of potting soil. The file contained any information he thought might be useful at some indeterminate date in the future. He knew Frankie at the Southern Michigan Insurance Company was a collector for the Purples, that he had two kids, a cranky wife, heavy debt, and loved blondes with names like Daisy and Tootsie. He knew that Andrew Strong, a lawyer who defended drug cases for the Bernsteins, was sleeping with Cecilia, his receptionist, who had been diagnosed with syphilis last year. Volcano, so named for his hulk and his explosive temper, was a devout Catholic, rarely missing Mass. To see him with one of his seven children, you'd never guess he had killed or maimed more than a dozen men with a single blow. He never dallied with other women, was fastidious about his manicure, and could drink a quart of full-strength whiskey in an evening, drive home without weaving, sleep soundly for four hours, and wake without a hangover. The amount of food he consumed was legendary.

Cliff never mentioned this file to his employers. He would use the information he had accumulated to keep the Bernsteins' employees in line and to persuade those who did not work for them that they should. The Bernsteins made available to him a squad of goons to break windows, cause accidents, break arms, or otherwise convince people to do the Bernsteins' bidding, but Cliff didn't like violence. He felt more subtle styles of compelling obedience were just as effective and far less messy. Besides, he reasoned, injured or dead people could not contribute to the Purples' fortunes. When he needed assistance on a project, he could count on someone with something to hide to be all too eager help. Sometimes all he wanted from them was additional details to add to the files he already had. Other times, they would be called on to house someone on the lam, much as the Blumenthals had housed him, or carry an envelope of cash or a packet of betting slips across town. Volcano need only show up at someone's door or stop them on the street and deliver a verbal message in order to pull a recalcitrant gambler or numbers runner into line.

Over lunch with his brothers on a rainy summer day, Abe bragged to his brothers, Izzie and Ray, for his brilliance in hiring Cliff Malin. The young man was resourceful, careful and analytical, he said. He didn't rush into anything without a thorough understanding of an operation, and then his suggestions were almost always good ones. When bartenders began floating from one speakeasy to the next in search of an extra dollar a week—often taking with them the secrets of who the distributors were and what kind of money their bosses earned—Cliff created loyalty among the Purples' bartenders by raising their pay to seventy-five dollars a week plus whatever tips they could pick up. Not only did they stop looking for other work, but the extra pay cut down on the number of bartenders selling information to cops about the locations of speakeasies.

Abe also bragged to his brothers that Cliff had established a line of communication with local precinct officers who kept him informed of intended raids. Many of the customers at the Bernsteins drinking and gambling establishments were the upper echelon of Detroit society who feared their photograph on the front page of the newspaper as much as they loved it on the society page. When Cliff learned of a raid from one of the policemen on his payroll, he ordered the customers out of the speakeasy, replacing them with men and women from the streets hired specifically so they could be arrested. When they had been hauled into the precinct, the customers returned to their festivities, comfortable that they would be in their own beds that night, rather than a stinking, frightening jail cell. For many of those who did get arrested, it would be the only time that week they had a hot shower, solid food and a bed to sleep in.

"I got a great idea for this Clifford," Abe told his brothers. "I just wanted to run it past you first, get your ideas."

The three brothers discussed Abe's idea briefly. Ralph and Ira told Abe to go ahead, and the three split up to attend to their various enterprises.

Abe met with Cliff that evening in the gaudy offices from which he ruled Detroit's underworld. The office was overly warm, but Cliff was still chilled from the damp night air and accepted the glass of sherry Abe offered, concentrating more on the warming effect than on the harsh taste of the cheap stuff his boss kept on hand. Abe thought drinking sherry gave him an air of elegance but, though he could afford better, he only bought brands made in the U.S., eschewing the better French brands because of loyalty to his country.

This evening, Cliff watched his boss pace from his desk to the window and back, great clouds of gray smoke puffing from his lips as he smoked his cigar. Abe finally stopped and stood at the window, silently gazing down to the street below.

Cliff could hear the metallic hum of cars down in the street even through the closed windows. A horn bleated harshly as Abe took a deep breath and began to speak, still looking out the window. Something was obviously on Abe's mind, but Cliff knew from experience there was no point trying to rush him into speaking.

"Clifford, my boy," he said. Cliff hated being called that. He would be twenty-three in a few days. "This is a bad business we're in. Brother fights brother, friend betrays friend. It's bad. It makes me tired to always be arguing with someone. It breaks my heart when a man I have loved and trusted for many years stabs me in the back."

Cliff held his breath. He had been expecting that someday he would be asked to rough up someone who had crossed the Bernsteins. Rough them up or worse. He wasn't sure how he would respond if asked. Abe continued.

"You know Judge Mazza over at municipal court?"

"I've heard of him, but I haven't had the pleasure."

"He has been my friend for twenty years. Our children played together, or wives go to the same garden club. He's a wonderful man. When my mother, God rest her soul, was sick and lying in the hospital, Frank Mazza went by to see her every single day. Every day! She was so happy to see him, 'Abe,' she would say to me. 'Frankie is such a busy man. Tell him he don't have to come to see a sick old lady. He has better things to do.' But always she smiled when she said it. She loved to have him visit. He was standing at the foot of her bed when she took her last breath."

Abe walked across the room and sat in the chair behind his desk. He downed the last of his sherry in one gulp then slammed the glass on the desktop so hard he broke off the stem. Cliff jumped in his seat.

"And now you know what that son of a bitch does to me?" he shouted. "I'll tell you what he does. He tells me that he ain't gonna fix any more cases for me unless I double my payments to him. Him telling me what to do! Him who wouldn't even be a judge if it wasn't for his old friend Abraham Bernstein. Who does he think he is? I give the orders around here, not no goddam judge. Just because he's got Miss Fancy Pants set up there in her own apartment don't mean I gotta support her. He thinks he's so goddam smart telling me to pay up. I'll show him how friends treat friends. He'll be sorry he talked to me like he did."

Cliff sat looking at Abe not knowing whether to speak or not. This was it, he thought. Abe was going to ask him to dispose of the Judge. He took a sip from the glass of sherry he held, not noticing its bitterness. Dropping his voice, Abe waved his hand in the air. "That's not your problem, Clifford. I got big boys for that job." Cliff let out a surreptitious sigh.

"It's happening everywhere, Clifford. Everyone thinks I am made of money. Used to be I could give a cop a case of whiskey at Christmas, maybe arrange a little something for his daughter's wedding, and he would take care of me and my friends. Now they all got their hand out. Always they want money and each time they ask for more. If I don't pay, they don't give me no information. Sometimes even if I do pay, they find out I pay someone else more, they don't give me no information. It's so you can't even trust a cop anymore."

Abe took a new glass from a mahogany liquor cabinet that covered one wall of his office, poured another drink, then sat in the gold brocade chair next to Cliff. He leaned forward and laid his hand on Cliff's arm.

"Clifford, my boy, it's not like me to trust people, especially so soon, but I have to say I trust you. Since you been working for me, I figure you cut my losses nearly twenty percent. That just about makes up for what I lost to you and your goddam iceboat. I been thinking about something. A way you can really help me out."

"What's that, Abe?"

"Here's my plan. Instead of trying to make these cops see my side and hope they don't rat me out later, why don't I just put someone on the force I know I can trust. Someone I don't have to wonder is he my friend or ain't he, someone who won't keep digging in my pockets trying to get my last nickel."

"Sounds reasonable," Cliff nodded as he lit a cigarette.

"Who would that be? I ask myself. Who am I sure will take care of Abe Bernstein when I need him? You know who?" Abe beamed broadly, leaning back in his chair. "You, that's who."

Cliff sat speechless. After a moment, he shook his head. "I don't know, Abe. I never figured myself for being a cop."

"There's nothing to think about, Clifford. You just do it. I'll take good care of you. You get an extra paycheck and it isn't like you'd be a real cop. You'd have to make it like you are, but all you gotta do is what I tell you. You don't like it, you quit, simple as that."

"I'll have to think about it. I'll let you know."

The next day, Cliff worked in his garden, trimming his prized peonies and turning over a new bed for a row of hybrid tea roses he had in mind. The house he bought not long after coming back to Detroit had a small, unkempt yard, which was precisely what attracted Cliff to it. Since early spring he used every spare daylight hour weeding, trimming, and digging. On rainy days he sketched ideas for the yard. The peonies were the first things he planted and they were as special to him as a first born child. Digging in his garden was not work to him, it was relaxing. It gave him a chance to think about things. He had some of his best ideas while turning the rich, fragrant earth.

Today as he worked, he considered Abe's suggestion that he join the police force. He realized as he dug that it was probably not a suggestion at all; Abe was used to having things the way he wanted. He wondered how this would all work out. Would being on the police force be like being back on the battlefield? Cops carried guns. These days it seemed as though there were frequent shoot outs on the streets between cops and bootleggers and bank robbers. The idea of being in the midst of whizzing bullets again was not appealing. Abe had said he'd have to act like a cop, but would there be some kind of special protection for a man Abe Bernstein had hand picked? Most of the cops in the neighborhood knew he worked for the Purples and accepted payoffs from him. Would Abe cut their payoffs once he was on the force? Going to a precinct where no one knew him wouldn't do Abe any good, so that was out of the question. But the extra money was attractive. Cops only made twelve dollars and fifty cents a week, but, on top of the hundred dollars a week Abe was paying him, he could do well. He had been investing in the stock market, starting slowly at first. He now had almost all the money he had earned with Maggie in the market. He could invest his cop's pay and continue to build his portfolio. He finally decided he had nothing to lose by accepting Abe's proposal.

On a crisp February afternoon in the conference room on the third floor of City Hall, Cliff Malin and eleven other men were sworn in as officers on the Detroit Police force. Their few weeks of training refreshed his firearm training and taught him to fill out paperwork. He also learned that police officers pretty much made up their own rules about law enforcement and treatment of prisoners.

He was assigned to the Bethune Precinct which encompassed the Bernsteins' territory. He had decided that, if he ran into any of the cops he had dealt with as a Bernstein employee, it wouldn't be any problem. If they knew who he was, they were already on the pad and wouldn't dare say anything. If they weren't on the pad, they wouldn't know of his connection with the Purples.

Cliff's first partner was Fred Vogel, a thirty-three-year old from Royal Oak who had been on the force for ten years. He was already developing a fleshy paunch above his belt and a small wattle under his chin. His pasty complexion made his hazel eyes all the darker, and his pink scalp was beginning to show through his thinning hair.

Taciturn at first, as the two men drove the city streets together, Fred eventually started talking about his career and his exploits as an officer, exploits that had little to do with law enforcement. He talked of finding politicians in compromising situations, of wives running numbers for a little extra butter and egg money, of famous athletes who had to be driven home from a raucous party. He seemed to take a particular interest in the streetwalkers on his beat. Part of the beat Cliff and Fred drove regularly was Brush Street, populated by women in short, tight skirts, fish net stockings, and plunging necklines, offering their bodies for rent.

One warm August night when the sticky humidity of the day had evaporated into a still, close night, the two cops drove slowly down Brush Street watching as the women stopped under a street light to show their wares when a car drove past. The women pushed their breasts forward or leaned over and shook them, hiked up their skirts to mid thigh, whistled, and made cat calls till a car stopped and one of them was beckoned over.

The car in which Fred and Cliff rode was one of the first to be recently outfitted with a radio. The monstrosity stood whirring and crackling on the floor between the two men. Cliff, riding in the passenger seat, could only sit rigidly with his feet straight out in front of him, the thing took up so much space. Considering that half the time they used it they were unable to understand what the dispatcher at the station was saying, the radio seemed more an inconvenience than an advancement in communication.

Fred stopped the cruiser in the middle of the block, between streetlights. He rolled down the window and called to the woman strutting a few feet away. She turned and smiled. "Hey, Baby," she said as she sashayed toward the cruiser. Cliff noticed several inches of cleavage peering over the top of her tight blouse, her long, shapely legs accented by the tight silk skirt she wore. Her milk chocolate skin and full, red lips glistened with beads of sweat.

"Hey, Ruby," Fred said, making guttural sounds. "How's my favorite street walker?" They both laughed. When Ruby reached the driver's side of the car, she leaned over and kissed Fred. He reached out and sunk his hand between her breasts, massaging first one then the other. "This here is my new partner, Cliff. I want you to be real nice to him, Ruby. He's okay people." His hand pressed deeper inside her bra.

"Sure, Fred, anything you say."

Cliff watched as Fred's fingers roughly stroked Ruby's nipples. "Cliff, this is Ruby. She's good people, too, no matter what she does for a living. She knows how to take care of cops, and she expects cops to take care of her. You need anything, you go to Ruby."

Cliff thought he recognized Ruby from one of the brothels where he had picked up envelopes of money for the Bernsteins. He couldn't be sure, though. He hadn't paid a lot of attention to the working girls.

This trip down Brush Street was just the latest in Cliff's orientation of the beat in the months since his induction. Fred took the new recruit to the White Horse Inn where he introduced Cliff to George Gates, a man who could make the worst bathtub gin into a half-decent martini. Gates was an affable man with a Texas drawl and a rolling gait. Fred said he had come north when his wife and two kids died in the flu epidemic in 1917. He liked the ladies, but didn't stay with one too long, Fred told Cliff before they went inside the Inn.

On another day the cops stopped at Richard's Barber Shop for a haircut on the house. Cliff noticed Fred slide a thick envelope under his jacket as they left. When they were back in the squad car, Fred said the envelope was in consideration of ignoring the poker games in the back room on Fridays and Saturdays.

At Smuggler's Cove, they had one of the best prime rib dinners Cliff had ever had—again at no cost to them—washing it down with a bottle of cabernet sauvignon, then had a quick shot of whiskey before heading back on patrol. Cliff tipped the waitress, but Fred said that even that wasn't necessary.

After only a few weeks on the job, Cliff realized that very little of a policeman's duties involved real law enforcement. Cuffing a young boy who had pinched a penny candy or intervening between a drunk husband and his bloodied wife were about all the peacekeeping the officers were involved in. Fred seemed to have created a social circle of is beat, talking with the shop keepers, gathering cash from those who sought protection from neighborhood gangs, and visiting a string of women.

On a rainy Monday afternoon, Cliff and Fred were called to 2156 East Jefferson, known simply as 2156 to policemen. They pulled up in front of a large Victorian home that Fred explained had become a hangout for some of the richer, better known and more debauched of Detroit's citizens. Wild, drunken parties went on there for days, Fred said, often requiring a visit, sometimes several, from the police. Neighbors complained of loud music, broken bottles on the streets and sidewalks, and people fighting in the yard in the dead of night. Officers arriving on the scene might find a drunken judge dressed in women's lingerie, an overzealous lover bound by handcuffs, or a neurotic sculptor wearing nothing at all.

Fred introduced Cliff to Viola Peterson, owner of the house. Cliff noticed that Viola had been well into adulthood at the turn of the century. Her face was landscaped with more than just laugh lines and her eyes were weary, without mirth, although she laughed constantly. She was dressed in the latest flapper style, a lavender satin dress bedecked with deep purple fringe that brushed her knee caps and the new flesh-colored stockings. Her hair had been bobbed and permed into deep waves and held a large, curled feather at the left temple. A wrap that looked like a tapestry she had pulled off the wall clung to her shoulders. She was clearly wearing one of those new brassieres instead of a full corset, since Cliff could see her abdomen pushed out against the fabric of her dress. The only time she stopped talking was to puff on a cigarette clamped into an ebony, ten-inch cigarette holder.

Viola was said to be a patron of the arts, but just what the output was of the people she called artists was nebulous at best. She seemed to prefer pretty or famous people around her regardless of what they might produce in return for her support. As usual, Viola had only a vague notion of why the officers had been called.

"Something's going on upstairs, I'm not sure just what," she said. "Take care of it, will you, before they damage my beautiful house."

Fred and Cliff strolled leisurely up the stairs in the direction of the yelling they could hear.

"You miserable son of a bitch," they heard as they reached the top. Something crashed to the floor and shattered. "You told me you never got any from your wife. Then how did she get pregnant? Tell me that. You think someone else is poking her? I don't. I think you're two timing me and I don't want to see your ugly face again."

Fred and Cliff arrived at the door of the bedroom in time to see a man's shoe hurled at a large mirror and shining shards falling to the floor. A bewildered, frightened man stood in a corner trying to pull on his pants while dodging the next shoe hurled at his head. The woman stood to their left, looking around helplessly for something else to throw, her Oriental robe open in front, her bare breasts swinging as she heaved a vase at the cowering man. Fred stepped behind her and pinned her arms at her side while Cliff crossed over to the terrified man. He recognized him as a member of the City Council.

"Let's get you out of here," Cliff said. The man had managed to get into his pants and pull his suspenders up over his shoulders. He grabbed his shirt, jacket, and shoes and raced out the door, never looking back, not uttering a word.

Cliff turned to see the woman struggling to free herself from Fred's hold. Fred picked her up and threw her on the bed, telling Cliff he'd meet him downstairs. The City Councilman dressed hurriedly at the bottom of the stairs and dashed out into the rain not waiting to open the umbrella he carried. When Fred came down ten minutes later, they both raced out into the rain and back to their car.

"God damn, a mad woman is a good lay," Fred said, sliding in behind the driver's wheel.

Cliff was earning more money in a week than his father saw in a year, and he became a student of what to do with his new-found wealth. It started with clothes. Under the tutelage of the Bernsteins' tailor, he bought the latest style in double-breasted suits, silk shirts and ties, and felt hats, black, brown, and gray. The tailor said he was happy to learn that the Bernsteins' taste in clothes hadn't rubbed off on their employee. After visiting several furniture stores and J.L. Hudson's to study the latest styles, he hired an interior decorator to furnish his home, directing her to use the top brands and latest fabrics. He traded the Maxwell in for a Cadillac.

He had become a student of the stock market since his first investment shortly after returning from the Blumenthals, learning the language and techniques of investors. He was cautious though. Before he made a buy he practiced investing, making a list of stocks he thought were good buys and watching them over the coming months then "selling" them when he thought they had reached their peaks. He learned about selling short, options, and margins. Twice, he even sent twenty dollars to Evangeline Adams, a New York psychic who said she could pick winners and see market trends. She counted Mary Pickford and Charles Schwab among her clients, so Cliff thought she was a good resource. After her advice proved fruitful, he began subscribing to her monthly newsletter. It certainly seemed more beneficial than the Sunspot or Oyster Theories or any other method touted for helping investors pick the right stock. On Evangeline's advice he purchased American Telephone and Telegraph, Pennsylvania Railroad, and, of course, Ford Motor Company. He could not have faced his friend Harry Bennett, the man regarded as Henry Ford's second in command, had he not held some of that stock. By the end of the year, his portfolio was valued at nearly a hundred thousand dollars.

# CHAPTER 14

▼

Cliff and Harry Bennett had become quick friends, if men like these could be said to have friends. The work they did for their respective employers was remarkably similar. "Fixing things" they called it. As the head of the Ford Service Department, Harry was responsible for carrying out Henry Ford's every whim and appeasing his every paranoia. Though knowing little about the design and manufacture of automobiles, Harry was the highest-ranking company official after Henry and his son, Edsel. No one dared antagonize Harry.

Abe Bernstein called Cliff at the police station early one morning and told him to see Harry about an urgent matter relating to Henry Ford. Cliff was to wear his police uniform. Following the directions of the guard at the gate to the plant everyone called The Rouge, Cliff parked in the underground garage and headed into the building. The guard had said Harry's office was in the basement which left Cliff wondering just how important a man this could be. He had heard the stories, that Harry had the ear of Henry Ford when no one else could get it, but why would such an important person be closeted in the basement? Following the arrows on the wall that directed him to the Service Department, Cliff walked down a long, narrow hallway, elbowing his way past thick-necked, square-bodied men who said nothing but watched his every step. Making his way down the hall, he felt like the baton in a relay race, being handed off from one man to the next. Nearing the door at the end of the hallway, he heard a tinny thud then the ring of a bell. A bulky, grim-faced man stood with his arms crossed at the wrists in front of the door, prohibiting entry without having to say a word.

"Cliff, uh, Officer Malin to see Mr. Bennett."

The man reached behind him and pressed a button that emitted a low buzz on the other side of the door. A responding clink apparently unlocked the door, and the guard turned slightly to open it and admit Cliff. Inside he heard the metallic thud and the bell again but saw nothing but a secretary and her office furnishings.

"Officer Malin to see Mr. Bennett," he told her.

"Good morning, Officer Malin. Mr. Bennett is expecting you." She pulled her glasses from the bridge of her bony nose and took two steps to a door behind her.

"Officer Malin, Mr. Bennett." Again the clink-and-bell sound.

A hearty voice called out, "Come in, Officer. Come in."

Stepping inside the office, Cliff saw immediately what had been causing the indiscernible sound he had heard clear down the hallway. Affixed to the side of Harry's metal filing cabinet was a paper target. In his hand was an air gun. By way of demonstration, he fired it once again. When he hit the bull's eye, a bell went off.

"Quite a marksman," Cliff said.

"The only question Mr. Ford ever asked me when he interviewed me for this job was whether I could shoot. I assume he needs me to shoot well, just like he expects everyone else around him to be the best."

Harry dropped the gun on his desk and stood up, holding out his hand to Cliff. He wasn't a very imposing man, only about five foot six, Cliff guessed, but he was taut and muscular, obviously the product of regular workouts, just like the men standing guard in the hallway. He was well-dressed in a brown suit, a crisp white shirt and a plaid bow tie. Cliff had heard about the bow ties. Harry wore them not because they were particularly fashionable, but because they couldn't be used to strangle him in a fight. He had warm blue eyes, perfectly trimmed brown hair that bore just a tint of red and a bright smile that revealed perfect white teeth,.

"Sit down, take a load off," he gestured to his guest. "I have to admit I'm a little surprised to see a uniform. I understood that Abe was sending one of his best men."

"Well, it's nice to hear he thinks so highly of me," Cliff grinned slightly as he dropped into the hard chair in front of Harry's desk.

"But you're on the force?"

"Yes, for just the last few months."

Harry shook his head and put his hand to his chin. "Well, that old son of a bitch. He's got everything covered. You want some coffee?"

"No, I'm fine. Abe said you had something you wanted to discuss."

"I guess you probably know that it's my job to take care of Mr. Ford and his family. Mr. Ford is very concerned about the safety of his family. All this shooting in the street and the activity on the river is making him nervous. I figure the Bernsteins have their hand in just about everything and they'd be the ones to go to."

Cliff began to protest, but Harry held his hand up. "Let's don't quibble about things we know are facts. The Bernsteins are involved in every illegal operation they can think of. And they like making their money the easy way—hijacking other people's whiskey shipments and kidnapping rich people's kids. Mr. Ford isn't so worried for himself. I pick him up at his home almost every morning and many nights I take him home. He's fine with me around. It's the rest of the family he's worried about, his son, Edsel, and Edsel's wife and kids as well as Mrs. Ford."

"And you want our help."

"That's right. I want the Bernsteins to promise they will leave the Ford family alone. Pick on someone else. And I want their promise that, if anyone else kidnaps any member of the family, they will deal with it. I don't expect this to come free. I need someone to provide lunches for our employees. There's good money in it, good, clean money where you don't have to worry about competition or hijackings or shootings. And, if you want to cover a few bets while you're at it, long as Mr. Ford doesn't find out about it, well, you pick up a little extra. Whaddya think?"

"I don't know. We've never been in the food service business."

"It wouldn't do any good if you owned half the restaurants in Detroit. Mr. Ford is very particular about his employees eating healthy. He has a list of foods that he wants them to eat and ones they are to avoid. You don't need to know a banana from a squash, just fix the lunches he sets up. We'll set you up with everything you need. Once the people supplying us with lunches now lose this contract, they'll fold like a house of cards. We'll pick up their facilities and employees for a song. You'll just have to put one of your people in to manage it. Like I said, good, clean, easy money."

Cliff knew he had the authority to speak for the Bernsteins, but he didn't like to act impulsively. "I'll have to give it some thought," he said.

"Fine. Fine. Let's take a walk around the plant. I'll show you our little operation here while you think about it. When you see what you stand to make, it'll be an easy decision."

Harry pushed back his chair and grabbed a hat hanging on a rack in the corner.

"We're going for a walk, Mrs. Miller," he said to the woman in the outer office. "Be back shortly."

Cliff and Harry walked back down the long hallway past the pugilistic-looking young men, Harry exchanging nods or muttered greetings to them. In the garage, Harry led Cliff to a cage standing in the corner. Cliff was amazed to see a fully grown tiger stretched out on a thick rug inside. Harry pulled a leash from a hook on the front of the cage and opened the door. The tiger opened its eyes into mere slits when it heard the clank of the cage door then raised its head as Harry approached. Harry snapped the leash on a collar around the tiger's neck and gave it a gentle tug. The tiger heaved itself to its feet and followed Harry out of the cage, as placid as a house cat.

"What the hell are you doing with that?" Cliff said, following Harry at what he hoped was a safe distance.

"This? This is my little pussy cat. His name is Corkie, after County Cork in Ireland where Mr. Ford's family is from. He wouldn't hurt a fly, but he sure gets plenty of attention when we go for a stroll."

Harry, Cliff, and Corkie left the garage and headed into the assembly plant where the whir and bang and clunk and whine of metal and machines produced an unending stream of Model Ts. Long conveyor belts carried chassis or transmissions or car bodies as a flurry of hands fastened, ground, drilled, and cut, each performing the same task repeatedly, never moving, never stopping to adjust or fit. Harry told Cliff it was this process, this assembly line, that had been Mr. Ford's brain child, allowing him to produce more cars with fewer employees in less time than any other manufacturer. The Olds brothers, the Buicks and the Dodges eventually copied his methods, Harry pointed out, but it was Mr. Ford's idea.

The noise was deafening; Cliff could only hear Harry if his ear was nearly at Harry's lips. But he noticed the building was immaculate, the air somehow scrubbed clean of the fumes of the engines that made the assembly lines move. No one seemed to notice the two men and the tiger strolling past them. Cliff figured it wasn't the first time Corkie had been in the plant.

At the far end of the building, Harry led Cliff to a lunch counter. On the wall behind the counter was a blackboard on which was scrawled "Turkey sandwich, apple, banana, chocolate cake."

"That's what lunch is today. You just have to make one meal every day. They eat what we fix or they go hungry. We charge them twenty-five cents for each lunch and just take it out of their paychecks. No muss, no fuss. That way, they can eat even if they drank their whole paycheck. We try to see they don't do that, but we can't be everywhere."

"So we get the twenty-five cents or do you get a cut of that?"

"You'll get fifty cents for every lunch you serve. And we have over fourteen thousand employees. I told you, I don't expect you to protect the Ford family for nothing."

Cliff did some quick math in his head. "I think we can do business, Mr. Bennett."

"I was hoping you would see it that way, and call me Harry."

Corkie was fully awake from his nap and smelled the food behind the counter, letting out a growl to announce his hunger. Harry handed Cliff the leash and slid behind the counter, disappearing for a moment then re-appearing with a whole chicken which he held in front of the tiger. It disappeared in one gulp and the crunch of bones made Cliff wonder what those powerful jaws would do to a human arm or leg. When the cat had digested the chicken, Harry led him out to the parking lot where he strode to an area marked "Visitors." Opening the back door of a sleek black Cadillac, Harry tugged the leash, leading the tiger inside then closed the door behind it.

"Whoever owns that car will have a shit fit when he looks in the mirror and sees old Corkie having a nap back here," Harry seemed unable to contain his laughter. He turned to Cliff.

"One other thing I want to mention to you. We got some trouble makers around here talking about unions. They got a list of complaints you wouldn't believe. They don't seem to realize they got the best goddam job with the best goddam company in the country. I was wondering, if we needed a little muscle from time to time to straighten these guys around, can we count on you?"

"You can count on us," Cliff said, shaking hands with his host.

# CHAPTER 15

▼

In early September 1927, long before the first rays of light appeared in the sky, the Ford Airport in Dearborn already bustled with activity. The rustle of heavy silk and the thump of large wicker baskets punctuated the otherwise quiet morning. The air was fragrant with a mixture of exhaust from the gas trucks and cooking from the concession stands. Strolling around the field, Cliff heard hushed voices giving directions and asking questions. Michigan had been enjoying a string of Indian Summer days, and today promised to be another one. Crisp brown and red and yellow leaves lay motionless on the ground.

Fifteen gas balloons from eight countries had gathered in Dearborn for the sixteenth running of the Gordon Bennett Cup, one of aviation's most prestigious competitions. Aviation had been capturing more attention by the public since Detroit's own Charles Lindbergh had flown alone across the Atlantic Ocean and landed at Le Bourget airport near Paris just last May. But the Gordon Bennett Balloon Race was one of long standing. Named for the eccentric newspaper owner, the race had been pitting balloon pilots against each other in a distance race for twenty-two years. Whichever pilot won the race would host the one the following year. American Ward Orman would be defending his win of last year, when he flew eight hundred sixty-four kilometers from Antwerp to Solvesborg, Sweden in seventeen hours. Promoters of the event thought holding it in Lindbergh's hometown this year and inviting him to be the guest balloonmeister would be a monumental tribute to the daring aviator. Not to mention that an opportunity to meet the famous airplane pilot would draw in paying spectators.

Cliff picked his way in the dark across long gas-filled hoses stretched across the field from trucks to balloons. With Cliff was Elmer O'Rourke, a cop for only a few months. Cliff was a sergeant now, due in part to so many officers being gunned down or simply quitting under pressure. Pressure came from two sources: wives who didn't want to lose their husbands and fellow officers who were on the pad and expected their partners to follow suit. An officer who didn't take money from racketeers couldn't be trusted to keep his mouth shut. No one wanted him for a partner.

Cliff and Elmer were part of a team of ten officers assigned to keep traffic moving and prevent disturbances as the airport filled with spectators for the balloon race. It was the kind of an assignment Cliff could have easily avoided, but he was there for more than just his official duties. Frank Lejewski, one of the Bernstein's best bookies, was making book on the race and Cliff had placed half a dozen trucks around the field to dispense whiskey and gin to thirsty patrons. He had also asked Belle LaTour to send some of her best girls around to visit the pilots the night before to give them a royal Detroit send off.

"What the hell time is it, anyway?" Cliff asked the man at his side.

Elmer pulled his pocket watch out and maneuvered it around till light from the headlights of a nearby truck fell on the clock's face.

"Five forty-five," he said.

Cliff grumbled. "Christ. God's not up yet."

He pulled a cigarette from a gold case, but Elmer intercepted it before it reached Cliff's mouth.

"Good God. You want to blow us to kingdom come?" he almost shouted. "That's hydrogen in those hoses."

A half hour later, the sun exploded over the horizon, adding color and shape to the bodies and equipment that littered the airport. Piles of silk and huge nets began rising slowly from the ground like giant mushrooms as gas was pumped into them. Cliff and Elmer watched as crew chiefs blew whistles and called out "Down one diamond" signaling workers positioned around the balloons to lower heavy sand bags to new positions on the net.

"You suppose they think this is a good time?" Cliff asked his partner.

"Beats me. Maybe they're getting paid. They have some pretty big bucks riding on this. It's kind of interesting to watch, but you sure as hell couldn't get me up in one of those things."

The two cops ambled across the field, dodging gawking spectators and busy crew members as they headed to the west side of the field and the row of concession stands. They bought cups of coffee and crullers then continued their saunter around the field. At the north edge of the airport, spectators streamed from their cars onto the field, some stopping for a cup of coffee, others heading straight to the balloons. Young women in bright dresses clung to the arms of young men in stylish seersucker suits. Old men in their Sunday best steered silver-haired women through the crowd and mothers herded children along in front of them.

By noon, several of the balloons were fully inflated, anchored to the ground by the circle of sandbags hung from the nets. Pilots huddled over large maps and studied the few wispy clouds that drifted overhead in hopes of determining their flight paths. Completely at the mercy of the winds, the pilots would maneuver to different altitudes, hoping to find the wind that would take them the greatest distance.

The sun was nearly directly overhead when Cliff and Elmer lounged at a table in front of the food booths having finished a lunch of cold chicken, potato salad, and lemonade, Cliff's spiked with a splash of whiskey. Inflating the balloons took much longer than anyone thought. The few people who had arrived before dawn had almost all left, replaced by spectators who only wanted to see the lift off. Cliff checked in periodically with Frank and at the vehicles carrying liquor. They were having a wonderful day, adding substantially to the Bernsteins' fortune. Cliff pulled a flask from his inside coat pocket and passed it to Elmer.

"No thanks," the younger cop said. "I don't drink."

Cliff shrugged and took a couple gulps before returning it to his pocket. The September sun was warm and Cliff was considering slipping off to the squad car for a nap when he saw a tall, graceful brunette woman heading in his direction. As she drew closer, Cliff recognized her as a woman he had seen at one of Abe's parties.

She was the kind of woman you almost didn't notice, pretty but not stunning. Her chestnut locks fell loosely around her shoulders, a small barn red hat holding back a few loose curls at her forehead. She wore a tailored suit the color of toast, the hem brushing her mid calf. Her long, slow stride moved her easily through the crowd. Cliff raised an arm in greeting but almost immediately realized she wasn't crossing the field to see him. She headed for the young police officer standing next to him.

"Hi," she said. "I was hoping you wouldn't be too hard to find. She gave no indication she had ever seen Cliff before.

"You been out here long?" Elmer asked.

"Fifteen or twenty minutes. This looks pretty exciting. Have you been watching what's going on?"

"Some. We've been here since before sunup, and it's gotten to be kind of boring."

Cliff shifted in his chair hoping to get Elmer's attention.

"I'm sorry. Cliff…Sergeant, this is my baby sister, Helen."

Helen turned toward Cliff, her eyes widening slightly as she recognized him from their previous meeting. He was flattered she remembered, despite the fact they had not spent much time together that night, fifteen minutes or so, one drink's worth of time. She had been pleasant, and he had been just about to ask if he could call her when Sammy Campanetto showed up at her side and steered her away. Sammy ran the Oakland Sugar House, a distillery the Bernsteins owned. He had been having trouble with hijackings of his deliveries and looked as though he had just got a chewing out from his bosses. He and Helen had left the party almost immediately.

"We've met," Cliff told Elmer, looking at Helen. "I thought you had a Polish name."

"That's my ex-husband's name." She turned back to her brother. "Can I see you a minute?"

Elmer left the table and let Helen lead him away, her arm looped through his. When they were out of Cliff's earshot, they turned to each other in animated conversation. Cliff hoped they were talking about family business and not about the encounter at Abe's party. When Elmer returned to the table, Helen was not with him. The subject of their conversation was not a mystery for long.

"I didn't know you knew Abe Bernstein," Elmer said, dropping back into his chair.

"You meet all kinds of people in this job," Cliff said.

Elmer picked at the remainder of the chicken in front of him then turned to look at the people milling around. After some time, he spoke.

"Do you work for the Purples?" he finally asked.

"I'm a cop."

"Lots of cops have a side income. Do you work for the Purples?"

"No, I don't work for the Purples."

Elmer stared at Cliff for several seconds before speaking again.

"Helen said she met you at one of Abe Bernstein's parties. She got the impression you were pretty important to them."

"Does Helen work for the Bernsteins?"

"No, she was there as a guest of someone. She doesn't know that kind of people. She's a good kid. The divorce was pretty rough on her. She really loved Warren, but he regularly took out his frustrations on her face. She had to leave him. I guess she's just trying different things out right now. She's confused. That man you saw her with at the party, she didn't know he sold booze till they had been going out for a while. She wouldn't associate with someone like that. One of those bastards sold some of their coffin varnish to my father, and it blinded him. Dad was never the same after that. He was a teacher, an English teacher. He loved to read, and he would read to us all the time, at dinner, at breakfast, on picnics. He always had a book with him, and when he came across a passage he thought had a message or was beautifully written, he would read out loud to us. When we were kids, we thought it was pretty hokey, and we were always embarrassed when he would read to us in front of our friends. Now, I'd give anything to listen to him read, right in the middle of Grand Circus with everyone I know around. He's become a bitter, heart-broken man. He lost the one thing that meant the most to him. He just sits in the dark living room now. Helen and I go over and read to him when we can, but it isn't the same. That wonderful man is only a shell now, and it's the fault of people like the Bernsteins."

"Your father didn't have to drink the stuff. It is illegal."

"That doesn't give these guys the right to sell poison. Do you know how many lives they have ruined? People going blind, dying from that stuff they sell, and at top dollar besides."

Cliff stood up. "We better take another stroll around the field," he said. Helen may have told her brother she wasn't seeing Sammy any more, but it was only two weeks ago that Cliff had seen her at the party with Sammy.

Just before sunset, Helen found her brother again. She stood with the officers and watched as, one by one, the balloons lifted off in the gentle evening breeze. Pilots waved and the crowd cheered, the western sun spotlighting the glistening sand cascading from the baskets as it was jettisoned a handful at a time to make the crafts rise. The balloons drifted northeast from the field, and the spectators watched till the aerostats were mere motes in the eye of the sky.

"Are you going to take me home?" Helen asked her brother.

"I can't. Edna expects me home. Her parents are over for dinner, and it's going to be bad enough I'm not there now."

"Can I drop you somewhere?" Cliff asked.

Helen hesitated a moment then accepted. It was better than joining the throngs of people trying to get on buses, she thought. Neither spoke for the first few minutes of the drive, then Cliff said he had to stop at the precinct station to change clothes. Helen waited in the lobby of the station while Cliff disappeared down a hallway. He returned wearing a brown serge suit with stylish wide lapels over a crisp white shirt. A brown fedora shaded his deep-set eyes from view. Helen smiled. "You have excellent taste, Sergeant, for a cop."

"Call me Cliff, and thank you. Clothes are my weakness. One of them anyway."

He escorted her to his shiny Cadillac and held the door as she slid into the passenger seat. Again they drove in silence for some minutes before he asked if she minded if they made a stop.

"I got no place to go, and the rest of my life to get there," she said.

They stopped at 2156, the Victorian home famed for its colorful guests. Cliff introduced Helen to Art Jaegger, an artist known as much for his lavish costume parties as for his work, who was currently taking advantage of Mrs. Peterson's generosity while he was between shows. Cliff disappeared up the massive carved mahogany staircase that wound up from the entry foyer while Art poured two gin and tonics, offering one to Helen. She declined. Carrying both drinks, he showed her around the lower floor of the ornate mansion with its carved ceiling, marble floors, and massive rooms. She noticed that the furniture was worn and dust accumulated on all but the most used pieces. As they returned to the foyer, Cliff appeared at the top of the stairs, his arm buried under the arm of a silver-haired man. They inched their way down the stairs, Cliff steadying the old man to keep him from pitching headlong to the bottom. When they reached the foot of the stairs, Helen recognized the man as a municipal judge. Fresh vomit clung to the front of his expensive shirt, his tie hung askew, and his fly was open. She inhaled the stench of alcohol and vomit and curled her nose against it, stepping back to avoid the staggering pair. Cliff fumbled in the man's coat pocket and extracted a key.

"We gotta drop him off at home," he said to her. "It wouldn't be so good for his career if his constituents found out he was here."

Outside, the man vomited again, mashing the bed of the fading pansies beneath his feet.

"Do you drive?" Cliff asked Helen.

When she said she did, Cliff handed her the judge's keys and said, "Follow me." He eased the judge into the back seat of his own car, took a towel from the trunk, and tucked it under the judge's chin. Cliff drove carefully through the streets to St. Clair Shores, watching in his rear view mirror to make sure Helen was behind him. When the man was safely deposited at home, Cliff asked Helen if she wanted to stop for a drink. She said that she didn't drink but would keep him company, and he drove to the Blue Orchid.

Angelo, the maitre d', greeted Cliff by name and escorted him to his usual table at the edge of the dance floor. Strains of "The St. Louis Blues" drifted across the heads of the diners, barely masking the conversations around the room. Cliff ordered a whiskey and water and Helen asked for coffee, then both turned to watch the band. When Cliff recognized the first bars of "Girl of My Dreams", he asked Helen to dance. She was stiff at first, following him easily around the floor but kept him at a stiff-armed distance. They stayed on the floor for the next three tunes. With each one, she relaxed a little more until she was dancing close enough that her hair occasionally brushed his shoulder. When he led her back to their table, they were both laughing and talking comfortably. He ordered another whiskey and water and offered her a cigarette, which she accepted.

"I been wondering about something for a long time," he said. "Maybe you can tell me how these guys do it."

"How what guys do what?"

"The guys like the Bernsteins and the ones who go to their parties. Here's a bunch of dumpy old guys with loud suits and greasy hair, but they got dames like you hanging all over them, beautiful women that can't seem to get enough of their fat little bodies or their fat little checkbooks or something. How do they do that? What do you women see in them? You could have any man you wanted, but you go out with guys like Sammy Campanetta. I wouldn't say he was any Rudolph Valentino, if you don't mind my saying so. You're a pretty woman. What gives?"

"I don't know. Maybe we're desperate."

"You? Desperate? I doubt it."

"I don't mean desperate for someone to go out with. There are plenty of guys to go out with. But these guys treat you right, at least in the beginning. They don't scrimp on dinner or nightclubs. They always have money in their pocket. Sammy would sometimes just hand me a twenty dollar bill and tell me to pick up a new outfit for our next date. Not every woman is looking for someone to keep her at home and pump a baby into her every year."

"There's guys all over that would treat you right. Take you to the clubs and to New York. They come from the nice families. They're younger and better look-ing than these thugs."

"You mean those Grosse Pointe snobs? They're a bore. They think a rousing game of croquet is a hot date. That's if you can break into their crowd in the first place, which you can't unless you're born into it. Sammy and his friends, well, maybe they know how to have fun like I like to have fun. Parties that last for a week, dancing till the wee small hours. Maybe girls like me are just desperate to live a little."

Something about what she was saying rang hollow. Party for a week? It was only ten-thirty and she could barely hold her eyes open. It took her a long time to relax when they first got to the club. Party girls were perpetually relaxed.

"Are you sure that's all you want from these guys, a good time?" He reached across the table and covered her hand with his, putting a little extra pressure on it. She pulled her hand away, sat back in her chair, and lit a cigarette.

"What do you mean am I sure that's all I want? What else could I want? I sure don't want to marry the guy."

"I think you know exactly what I mean." He stared directly into her eyes.

Ever since he had re-met Helen today at the airport he had been putting pieces of conversations and events together. The Bernsteins had been having deliveries hijacked for several months. They coincided with the period of time Sammy Campanetta had been seeing Helen. Helen's father had been blinded by bad liquor. Her brother is a cop. The connection seemed clear to Cliff.

Helen finished her cigarette and pushed it out in the ash tray.

"It's getting late. Would you take me home now?"

He called for the bill and they sat without speaking while they waited. Cliff drove Helen to her apartment on Frontenac Street and stopped at the curb. She started to get out of the car, and he asked if she had any coffee.

"I don't think Sammy would be too happy about you coming into my place," she said.

"I also don't think Sammy would be too happy if he were to know that you have a brother on the police force. A brother that everyone knows can't be bought off, something about his father going blind from bad gin. A real crusader, that Officer O'Rourke is. Probably gets some help from his sister, information about delivery routes and stuff."

Helen stopped, half in, half out of the car.

"You're a cop. Maybe he figures you're the one pulling the raids."

"He knows me better than that. I report straight to the top. I got references. Who you got references from?"

Helen stared at the misty halo around the street lamp in front of the neighboring apartment building.

"You still want that cup of coffee?" she asked.

When Cliff let himself out of Helen's apartment, the sun was just beginning to peer through leafless trees. Rain from an early morning shower puddled in the streets and speckled his shiny car. A man in a gray suit emerged from a house across the street, slid into a black Buick, and drove away. Cliff sat at the wheel of his own car and lit a cigarette, thinking through his next move. There was no question in his mind that it was Helen who was tipping the cops about liquor shipments, resulting in raids and lost booze. He would have to take care of it. Volcano could handle the assignment in a few minutes. He drove across town to the big man's house and sat in his car until Volcano emerged. Cliff followed him to a diner where Volcano routinely ate breakfast and slid on the stool next to him. Few words passed between the two men. When the waitress left with Cliff's order he slid a piece of paper to Volcano that bore Helen's address and said, "Quiet and quick." Volcano stuffed the paper into his coat pocket and nodded curtly.

"When?" Volcano asked.

"Soon. And deliver the package here." He pressed another piece of paper into Volcano's fist. It bore Elmer O'Rourke's address.

They ate in silence, Cliff leaving the diner first. When Volcano finished his four eggs, half a pound of bacon, biscuits and gravy, and three cups of coffee, he returned to his car. Only then did he look at the address. It wasn't one he recognized, and it was an apartment which would make things a little more difficult. With people coming and going at the other apartments, he ran a greater risk of being seen. The slip of paper Cliff had given him included the name of the person he was to take care of. He didn't like doing women. They required different handling because of their propensity for screaming. At night would be better, when she was asleep. He could get into her apartment quietly and have it over with before she knew he was there. The only thing to do was make sure he got the right woman. He drove to the nearest flower shop and bought a dozen yellow roses. At Helen's apartment, on the ground floor, second from the front door, he stood holding them while she signed a phony invoice he had dummied up in the car. He looked at her carefully, making sure he knew her face. He glanced at the lock on the door; he could pop it with one twist of his wrist and he noticed there was no chain inside.

The next night he drove to within two blocks of the apartment house, parking behind a warehouse where his car would not be noticed by anyone passing by. He had dressed in nondescript dark clothes, ducking from shadow to shadow to minimize the chance of being spotted. The window in Helen's living room was lit and periodically, he saw her silhouette against the shade as she moved around the room, apparently home alone for the evening. At last she turned off the light and went into what Volcano expected was the bedroom. When that light went out, he waited another hour, hunkered in the shadow of a tall Italian cypress that hid him from view. No one had entered the building in the hour he waited, and no other lights burned in any of the apartments on the front of the building.

Volcano quickly stepped from his hiding place behind the cypress tree and into the front door of the building. The door was unlocked, requiring no one to let him in. He moved stealthily toward her door, creeping along the edge of the hall way where the boards were less likely to creak. With a flick of the jimmy he had brought, the door was open and he was inside, easing the door shut behind him. He paused a moment listening for any motion. He heard nothing and in a few steps was inside the bedroom. Helen lay with her back to the door. In one move Volcano's huge mitt covered her mouth, his other hand on the back of her head. Another flick of his wrist and her neck was broken with the ease he had opened the front door of the apartment.

He lay the bedspread on the floor and placed Helen's body on top, rolling the fabric around her like he was bundling a baby against the cold. He lifted her and headed for the living room. Voices in the hallway made him stop before opening the door to the hall. The voices and footsteps of a man and a woman passed the door. Volcano cracked the door open just enough to see out, watching the couple in front of the apartment next door. They kissed, his hand running down her hip and then her leg. She pushed his hand away, and he tried again. Volcano hoped she would let her date inside so he didn't have to wait for the man to disappear before he could take Helen outside. He didn't have to wait long before getting his wish.

Outside the building, he tucked Helen's body under some bushes near where he had watched her apartment and headed back to his car. With the lights out, he stopped in front of the building, retrieved the bundle from the bushes, put it in the trunk and drove slowly away, not turning the lights on till he was several blocks away.

Elmer O'Rourke was reading the evening paper in his front room, having gotten off the late shift at the precinct, when he heard a car stop in front of the house. The sound of traffic on his street at this hour of night was unusual, but he was too tired to get up and look out. A moment later he heard pounding on the door then the sound of retreating footsteps followed by the car pulling away. He got to the front door too late to see the car but stumbled over a large bundle wrapped in a flowered bedspread. He pulled back the edge of the blanket and screamed when he saw Helen's pale, cold face.

Bill Navin parked his car behind his pool hall and he and Dan Kirk entered the building through the back door.

"All this talking has left me thirsty," Bill said as he sidled behind the bar. "How about you?"

"A beer sure would hit the spot," Dan said, pulling a money clip from his pocket.

Bill waved the money off. "On me," he said. "I don't get to blather on like this very much. I hadn't thought about this stuff in years. You gonna put my name in the paper?"

"Do you mind if I do?" Dan asked.

"Naw. Might be good for business." He picked up his own beer and raised the glass to Dan. "Take you time over that beer, Son. I got work to do. Nice meeting you."

Dan downed his beer quickly and glanced at his watch. He'd better check in at the newsroom before his editor thought he'd left town again. He picked up a pastrami sandwich from the deli next door to the newspaper office and dropped it on his desk on his way to the city editor's office.

"Hey, Ed," he said, leaning against the door jamb of Ed Harris' office. "What's new?"

"You tell me. Where the hell you been? You ever hear of deadline?"

"I'm still working on this story. I want to do a double truck on the murdered and the murderer. These aren't just a couple more thugs who got crosswise with each other. These people could have lived next door to you or me when they were growing up, but something happened to them. I think I have what I need on Cliff Malin. Twyla Larson's husband is supposed to be here tomorrow or the next day, and I'll get her story from him. I'll have this ready for Sunday's paper."

"You working on anything else or is this the only crime in Detroit?"

"I'll get down to the station and see what's been happening."

"See that you do."

At his desk, Dan worked his way through his sandwich as he returned phone calls and made notes, but he was unable to concentrate on much besides the Larson woman and her murderer. He lit a cigarette and sat back in his chair, suddenly realizing there was someone who could tie the stories of the two people together, and he was sitting downtown in jail. He glanced at his watch. He could probably persuade Stan Cunningham to give him clearance to talk to Vincent Di Grassi and he called the lieutenant. Stan said he would make the phone call if Dan would pass along any information he picked up. Dan said he would then left the office. He would have time to look through police reports for any newsworthy items while he waited for Stan to make the necessary call. He found reports on two small robberies at businesses on Woodward Avenue, a suicide at a flophouse, and an automobile accident with two fatalities. He scribbled details of the robbery and the accident, leaving the suicide to his anonymity, and phoned a story in to the paper. That should keep Harris off his back for a while.

Snow had been falling most of the day and the roads were slick making the trip over to the Detroit City Jail a slow one. Dan found a parking spot near the door and signed his name in the visitor's log inside the front door.

"How ya doin'?" The officer at the front door asked. Dan recognized him from previous visits but needed to glance at his name tag to recall his name.

"Freezing my ass off, Tom. How about you?"

"Just dandy. They just told me to expect you. Cunningham from out in Pontiac called. You're here to see Vince Di Grassi, I understand."

"Yes, I am. Has he had many visitors?"

"Just his sister. You got here just in time, too. She put up bail, and he's out of here tomorrow."

The officer led Dan into an interrogation room that was furnished with a plain wooden table mottled with cigarette burns and etched with initials and two battered chairs. In a few minutes a second officer escorted Vincent Di Grassi into the room and he sat opposite Dan. Dan offered him a cigarette, which he accepted.

"I guess they told you who I am," Dan said. "I'm trying to put things together here, and I think you can help me. Do you mind?"

Vince shrugged. "It's either talk to you or hang out in my cell listening to men fart. Makes no difference to me."

"Cliff Malin tried to push the murder of Twyla Larson off on you. Why do you suppose he did that?"

"That's what guilty people do. They try to frame someone else."

"But why you?"

"We had a run in a year or so ago. I guess my name was the first one he thought of."

"What kind of a run in?"

"I owed Twyla Larson some money, and she used him to try to get it back."

"Back up a minute. Why don't you tell me about yourself. I understand you live in New York now. Are you originally from Detroit?"

"Yeah. I grew up on the east side."

# CHAPTER 16

▼

Angelo Di Grassi had been out of work for most of 1929, like hundreds of other men, because The Rouge had been closed to retool for the new Model A. Henry Ford had resisted the change until long after all the other manufacturers and modernized their cars to meet the demands of a more sophisticated car-buying public. Spluttering Tin Lizzies were no longer acceptable when a six-cylinder Oldsmobile that virtually purred could be had for nearly the same price. Car owners wanted style and comfort, and when the new A eventually came off the assembly lines, it would more than meet their demands: hydraulic shock absorbers, electrical starter, strong and simple gears with a stick shift and balloon tires. Until the factory re-opened, six thousand men including Angelo were trying to hang on.

After fourteen years as a die maker at Ford's, Angelo had been living comfortably before the shut down, despite an occasional bout of Ford Stomach. Others hadn't stayed at the factory as long as he had; the constant pressure to work faster and build more cars took its toll on workers' digestive systems. But Angelo figured, what's a little discomfort when a man could count on a regular paycheck to feed his family?

While they were unemployed, some of Angelo's friends had resorted to making bathtub gin or beer to take care of their families. It was quick money, but Angelo would have none of it.

"The good Lord brought me to this country to raise a family. I don't take no chance to cross the good Lord," he would say when someone tried to persuade him to join them in their illegal activities. He did come close one time. Jake Dowd knuckled under to the pressure of quick money and decided to brew up a batch of gin in his basement. He said he would only do it once. By the time he had made and sold it, he would find a job, he was sure. He asked Angelo to help finance the venture. Angelo was becoming worried about his dwindling savings and thought if Jake was going to do one batch and quit, that would be okay. But at the last minute, he just couldn't do it. A week later he was at Jake's funeral; the still in the basement had blown up and taken Jake and two of his children.

Angelo knew that it was the men who brought the whiskey in from Canada who had the most money and who had jobs to offer. He decided to visit his old friend Chet La Mare. Chet had moved from New York to Detroit a couple of years earlier when he heard that the Bernsteins' organization was in disarray. He made no secret of the fact that he intended to take over. He told everyone he was Sicilian, but Angelo didn't believe it. His color was all wrong and besides, what kind of Sicilian name is La Mare?

Chet had been buying cigars at The Wooden Indian on Plum Street one day and overheard Angelo speaking Italian with some other men. Chet introduced himself and offered to buy the men a round of drinks. Although they would never travel in the same social circles, every few months, when Chet seemed to want to surround himself with the kind of people he grew up with, he picked up Angelo and some of his friends and took them to the Indian. It was a simple place that reeked of stale beer, cigarettes, and the sweat of the assembly line workers who frequented it. Chet was always overdressed for the occasion in his silk shirts and cashmere overcoat, causing other customers to stare and whisper. But Angelo rarely introduced him to anyone outside his own close circle. Chet, Angelo, Angelo's friends, and Chet's bodyguards sat in the back of the room drinking, smoking and laughing loudly until one of the bodyguards whispered something, and Chet said he had to go. He always paid the bill and left a little extra so that Angelo and his friends could drink all night.

And now, with a house full of hungry mouths to feed, Angelo was going to visit Chet on his own turf. Chet owned Crescent City Motors out in Hamtramck, a gift from Harry Bennett. Harry could see the writing on the wall: the Bernsteins were losing control of their operations, and Chet La Mare was the likely successor. Keeping his deal in tact with Cliff and the Bernsteins, Harry gave Chet the dealership as payment for his promise not to touch the Fords and to take retribution on anyone who did.

Angelo took the bus out to the dealership and found the boss in. He explained his situation: no job, dwindling savings, a family to feed, and no idea when The Rouge would re-open. He told Chet he would do anything that wouldn't get him arrested. Chet put him to work washing cars, fetching sandwiches, picking up dry cleaning, and generally catering to the needs of La Mare and his executives. Angelo kept his head down and his eyes and ears closed. He didn't want to know anything that the police could beat out of him and betray his employer.

On a crisp October morning, Angelo reported to work as usua, standing before Chet's desk as he did every morning, waiting for his day's assignments. Chet told him another employee was home sick, and Angelo would have to do his work that day.

"Fine, fine," Angelo smiled. He didn't recognize the name of the employee who was ill.

Handing a set of car keys across the desk to Angelo, Chet said, "I need you to run a little errand for me, Angelo. Just pick up some envelopes from some of my managers and bring them back to me. Nothing to it."

Angelo held the keys gingerly. "I don't know, Mr. La Mare. I don't want to get mixed up in anything. I got a wife and five kids to think about."

"You're not getting mixed up in anything. It's just some envelopes full of papers. What can be wrong with envelopes full of papers? You go to a candy store, a dry cleaners, maybe a beauty parlor, and you take the envelope they give you and bring them all back here to me. What could be simpler?"

"I don't know, Mr. La Mare. I'm real grateful you gave me this job and all, but what if I get stopped by the police? What if I wind up in jail?" Angelo frowned, his thick eyebrows knitting into one furry piece across his forehead.

"Look, Angelo," La Mare said impatiently. "I'm in a real bind here. Don't worry about the police. They won't stop you if you're driving my car." He reached into his pocket and withdrew a thick wad of bills. Thumbing through it, he extracted a twenty-dollar bill and passed it to Angelo. "You will probably need to stop for lunch."

Angelo just stared. Twenty dollars was nearly a week's pay at The Rouge. He took the bill quietly and said, "Where do you want me to go?"

La Mare directed him down a hallway that led to the back of the building. He was to ask for Ollie Priestas. When Angelo opened the door to the room, he was at once overpowered by the din of dozens of adding machines crunching away. Three rows of desks ran the length of the room with men and women sitting at them. As they thumbed through small pieces of paper or ran a finger down long columns, their fingers flew over the machines, punching numbers. Although there was a long row of windows on one side of the room, overhead lights blazed since Chet La Mare required that the blinds on the windows be kept closed.

Angelo knew Ollie from having washed his car and occasionally bringing him lunch. He spotted him at the far end of the room and picked his way around the desks till he stood before the accountant. Ollie Priestas was a cherub-faced man with appley cheeks and pale pink skin. He had a thick head of blond hair that he was constantly pushing back away from his forehead and wore wire-rimmed glasses that seemed to absorb the grease from his complexion. His fingers reminded Angelo of raw sausages and his hands were too soft for a man. When Angelo told him why he was there, Ollie pulled open the top right hand desk drawer and extracted a file folder. Flipping it open, he pulled out a sheet of paper with a list of names and addresses, glanced briefly at it then handed it to Angelo.

"Just follow this list and be back here by one thirty," he said. Angelo was always surprised at how deep a voice came from such a waif of a man. He glanced at the list then at his watch. It was only nine thirty, but some of he addresses were in unfamiliar parts of town.

"What happens if I'm late?"

"Big trouble, that's what. Just don't be late." Ollie dropped the file folder back in the desk and slammed the drawer shut. He put his head back down and picked up his pencil, ending the conversation. Angelo started to leave the room when Ollie called him back and handed him twenty dollars.

"You might need this."

"Mr. La Mare already gave me some money."

"That's okay. Take this." Ollie thought the extra money would assuage the old man's discomfort at having to do this job, but the extra money made Angelo nervous. Why were they paying him so much if the job wasn't dangerous? He took the crisp bill Ollie handed him figuring if anything happened, his family could use it.

He found the boss's bright new Cadillac in the parking lot behind the building and slid behind the wheel. Wouldn't Emma be surprised to see him in command of such a machine? He glanced at his watch. If he were quick about it, he would have time to drive past the house to show her the car and still make his runs on time. He inched the car out into the traffic. The Cadillac was big and bulky, and Angelo's driving experience was limited. He sat up as tall as he could to make sure he could see the front corners of the car and not scrape them against anything. Horns blared around him as he drove slowly at first, never going fast enough to reach third gear lest the car go out of control. In front of his house, he honked the horn as he pulled to a stop. Mrs. Perkins from next door was mulching her garden against the coming winter. She stood up straight to get a better look at the strange car stopping in front of the Di Grassis' house.

"Morning, Mrs. Perkins." Angelo waved as he strode proudly up the front walk. Opening the front door of his house, he called to his wife who came running from upstairs. He took her by the hand and led her to the curb where the Cadillac glistened in the morning sun.

"Oh Angelo? What have you done? We can't afford this."

"It's okay, Emma. I didn't buy it. It's Mr. La Mare's. He gave it to me to run some errands for him. Come and sit in it." He opened the passenger door and held her hand as she eased onto the thick gray upholstery.

"Oh, Angelo. It's beautiful."

Vinnie, their fourteen-year-old son exploded out the front door and down the porch steps. Walking around the car, his eyes wide, Vinnie whistled and ran his hand over the sleek exterior. Cupping his hands around his eyes, he peered into the back window then the driver's window. He pulled open the driver's door and crawled in behind the steering wheel.

"Where'd you get the car, Dad? Jeez, it's a Cadillac. Is it ours? Can I go for a ride?"

Angelo tried to resist his son's pleas, but then he got to thinking. If he were making his rounds with his son, it would keep him from looking too suspicious to the police. He'd be just another man out with his son. They could drift into a candy store or a barbershop without looking out of place. Angelo told his son to run back inside and put his shoes on.

Father and son headed north on Jefferson Avenue past the Belle Isle Bridge then along the shores of Lake St. Clair. The deep blue water was dotted with stiff white caps, whipped up by the strong breeze that seemed constantly to blow down the river and made it the favorite of sailors. A few sailboats were scattered around the lake, and occasionally, Angelo could see a powerboat rising then disappearing in the swells.

At Cadieux Avenue Angelo turned left and made the first pickup at Mrs. Schober's Candy Store. Vinnie strolled lazily around the store, his glance roving casually from one case to another. Angelo gave his son a nickel and told him to pick out what he wanted but cautioned he was not to eat it in Mr. La Mare's car. The next stop was at Sal Silverstein's Tailor Shop on Warren Road, then Anne and Bill's Bakery, and Betty Harper's Beauty Parlor, both on Moross. With each stop, Angelo grew more nervous, afraid someone might be following him, afraid of what was really in the envelopes. He had been thinking about what Mr. La Mare said, that the police wouldn't stop him while he was driving the Cadillac, but then he began to worry about who else might be interested in the car and its contents. Maybe one of the people that didn't like Chet La Mare would force him off the road, or someone might think that anyone in such a car had lots of money and would try to pull a robbery. He was always reading in the papers about some rich man's wife or children being kidnapped. He pulled over to the curb, removed the envelopes he had been piling on the back seat and locked them in the trunk.

Vinnie chattered incessantly. He was seeing parts of town he had never seen, watching the freighters making their way up the river, gazing at the tall houses with expansive front yards. He had the same question about everything new he saw. "How much do you think that costs, Dad?"

. Angelo hadn't bothered to stop for lunch, and he realized now it was just as well because it was one o'clock. He would just make his deadline of one thirty back at Crescent Motors if he didn't take the time to drop Vinnie off at home. Angelo heaved a big sigh as he dropped the bundles on Ollie's desk, relieved to be rid of them then went down the hall to Chet's office to return the car keys. He introduced Vinnie to his boss.

"What do you think of the car, Vinnie?"

"It sure is swell, Mr. La Mare. I've never seen a Cadillac before except in the magazines. How much did it cost?"

"Vinnie," Angelo said, smacking him on the arm.

"I don't know how much it cost. My accountant takes care of that," La Mare said. He pulled a dollar bill from his pocket and handed it to the boy. "Why don't you run next door and get yourself a soda while your papa and I finish up some business?"

Vinnie's eyes expanded to their fullest as he reached for the dollar bill. "But...but Mr. La Mare, a soda don't cost this much."

"It's okay Vinnie. You just keep that money. You helped your papa on his rounds today, didn't you? A boy shouldn't work for free."

"Gee, thanks, Mr. La Mare. I'll be downstairs, Dad." He stuffed the money into his pants pocket and raced out of the room.

Angelo and his boss talked for a few minutes about the run Angelo had made that day. Chet pressed another twenty-dollar bill into Angelo's sweaty hand and said anytime he wanted to earn extra money, he could. Angelo looked at the bill in his hand and hesitated before stuffing it in his pants pocket. Tempting as that kind of money was, he would not make any more runs for Mr. La Mare.

When The Rouge opened two months later, Angelo took up his position on the Number Four line fitting wheel rims on the passenger side of every Model A that left the plant.

Angelo's return to The Rouge left a vacancy at Crescent Motors that Vinnie was happy to fill. Working after school and on weekends, he ran to delis for lunch, washed cars, picked up suits at the dry cleaners, and anything else the men around Mr. La Mare would let a boy do. He told his parents he had two paper routes to explain the sudden appearance of money in his pocket, for he knew they would not approve of his working for Chet La Mare. Unlike his father, though, he didn't try to avoid the other activities the men were involved in. He was disappointed when they would quit talking or lapse into Italian when he came in with their lunch. He never let on he could speak Italian, thanks to his mother, and when he had been working at the dealership for several month, he realized that La Mare and his captains had serious problems on their hands.

Vinnie learned La Mare had come from New York to take over the Bernsteins' operations and, while his own operations were going well in Hamtramck, he had not made much of an inroad into rackets in other parts of town. Then in early summer Sam Catalonotte, who ran the East side of Detroit, was stricken with pneumonia and died. Angelo Melli stepped into the breach upon his boss's death, but he knew he was no match for the vicious ambition of Chet La Mare. He contacted La Mare and suggested a conference to agree on who would run which operations in what parts of town. La Mare agreed and set a date for the conference to be held at a fish market on Vernor Avenue. Vinnie overheard plans for the conference. He also overheard plans for a double cross.

The morning after the conference Vinnie came down to breakfast to hushed conversations between his parents. Angelo sat at the kitchen table as his wife leaned over his shoulder, studying the front page of the *Detroit News*. Vinnie's mother shook her head and clucked her tongue as Angelo read quietly. Vinnie stood in the doorway out of their sight and listened.

"Witnesses said they saw two men run from the building and jump in a large black sedan that had been kept running at the curb," Angelo read.

He folded the paper and pushed it across the table as his wife went back to the stove.

"I just know this has something to do with Mr. La Mare," he said quietly. "I'm so glad I got out of there when I did. He was good to me and some of my friends, but he is not a nice man in his heart. He has evil in his heart."

Vinnie's mother put a plate of eggs, ham, fried potatoes, and toast in front of her husband. She returned to the stove to get coffee.

"It was nice that he helped us out when The Rouge was closed, but I am glad you aren't there any more. I was always nervous about what he might make you get into," she said pouring steaming coffee into his cup.

Vinnie stood quietly another minute so they wouldn't think he might have overheard anything then entered the kitchen and sat in the chair at his father's right. His mother served him the same breakfast his father ate, and they ate in silence. When his mother left to walk her husband to the front door, Vinnie snatched up the newspaper and read quickly. "TWO GUNNED DOWN IN VERNOR AVENUE FISH MARKET" read the headline.

"In what police believe was intended to be a peace conference, two men known to have connections with east side gambling and prostitution operations were viciously gunned down.

"Gasper Scibilia and Sam Parina, who have been associated with both the Sam Catalonette and the Chester La Mare gangs were identified as the two men shot. Witnesses said they saw two men run from the building and jump in a large black sedan that had been kept running at the curb."

Vinnie put the paper back down when he heard his mother approaching. She didn't like her son knowing about such goings on. He gulped down the rest of his breakfast, grabbed up his schoolbooks, brushed his mother's cheek with a kiss, and ran down the front steps to the curb.

"Do well on your math test," he barely heard his mother call. He had no intention of going to school today, though. He had to know what happened at the fish market. As he rode the bus to Crescent City Motors, he recalled the conversation he had overheard a few days earlier as the conference was being planned. Each mobster was to send his best *capos,* men who would speak for their bosses and who were empowered to work out details of splitting territories and operations. But instead of sending his top lieutenants, La Mare planned to send his best shooters. They were to arrive several hours before the planned conference and hide somewhere in the market where they had a good view of the conference table that the owners of the fish market had set up. When Melli's men showed up, they were to be gunned down in their seats. But something had gone wrong. Only two men showed up as representatives of Melli, according to the newspaper. Vinnie had gotten the impression from the bits of conversation he had heard that there would be many more. When he arrived at the dealership, he quickly busied himself emptying wastebaskets and ash trays in the office. His boss and the two men with him spoke in Italian.

"Your plan was a good one, Boss, but who could have guessed they would pull a goddam trick like this?" one man was saying as he paced the floor in front of the desk. The other man sat but fidgeted constantly and chain smoked.

"Start from the beginning and tell me what happened," Chet said. Vinnie had never seen him so strained, the veins on his forehead and thick neck protruding like welts.

"We was all set to do just what you said," the seated man said. "We went to the market three hours before anyone was supposed to show up and hid, just like you told us. We had time to look around the joint and make sure we could see everything, but they couldn't see us. We had our Tommy guns, just like you told us. When Angelo's men showed up, we were going to gun 'em all down." He stopped to light a new cigarette.

"Jesus God, we couldn't believe it when we saw who showed up. Scibilia and Parina, of all people. What the hell was that all about? None of the real *capos* was there, just these two guys. We didn't know what to do. We like those guys, even if they do work for Sammy. They're good people. I guess we just panicked and we gunned 'em down. We figure you wanted to send a message, and no matter who got killed it would be the same message."

"You coupla morons,' Chet snarled. "You damn betcha they were good people. They were about the only ones no one had to worry were they honest guys. Shit. It's going to be goddam ugly now."

La Mare turned to the young boy working in the corner.

"Ain't you supposed to be in school today?" he said irritably. He spoke in English.

"No, sir. We got a day off." Vinnie lied.

"Well, go find something else to do," and waved him out the door.

Cliff Malin—now Lieutenant Malin—had gone straight to Abe Bernstein's office as soon as he read the morning's headlines. Abe's brothers Ray and Izzie sat in chairs in front of the window, the morning sun behind them shading their faces.

"Those goddam assholes! They had no business! They want to kill someone did something to them, that's a different matter, but they kill two such decent guys, guys never did nothing to them, they gotta answer. You gotta make this right, Cliff. You gotta make this right." Abe ran his hand through his hair, his jowls shaking, the corners of his mouth filling with spittle as he ranted.

"You gotta do something, Cliff. We can't have another mess like last year with the Cleaners and Dyers. We lost a lot of good men in that war. I start up something with La Mare, we're going to lose a lot more. But, if the police go after him, that's a different matter all together. You got the support of the press and the public behind you if you put this son of a bitch out of business. And you got my undying loyalty."

"I don't know what I can do, Abe. La Mare's operation is in Hamtramck. It's going to look mighty funny seeing Detroit officers over there. I have to think how I can work this out." Cliff lit a cigarette and breathed its heat deep into his lungs. His years with the Bernsteins and their confidence in him gave him leave to speak further. "I warned you about these guys like La Mare coming into town. They're after your action. They want your territory. You got runners and hookers and God-knows-who going to the highest bidder. La Mare is paying good money to find out about your shipments. He's big buddies with Capone over in Chicago and he wants Capone's action."

"Capone is my man," Abe raved. "He'll never deal with no goddam fat guy says he's Italian but can't prove it."

"You've been spreading yourself too thin, Abe. You buddy up with Bugsy Moran in New York and Capone in Chicago thinking you'll be part of some giant operation with action everywhere. This isn't General Motors trying to sell cars all over the country. These guys are going to protect their territory till they die. They aren't about to share with you or Chet La Mare or anyone else."

Ray spoke up. "Share? Who's talking about sharing? These guys need us more than we need them. Detroit's where all the whiskey comes in from Canada. We are their pipeline. We dry up, they're in trouble. Share? We'll be running them before long. But first we gotta clean up our own back yard. We gotta shut down La Mare."

"What do you want to do that for? You're making plenty of money for all three of you and a lot of people who work for you. You go after La Mare, you'll have a bigger bloodbath than you can ever imagine."

"It's a matter of protecting ourselves. We let him get away with this, every two-bit gun with ambition is going to show up in Detroit thinking they can have a piece of me. We gotta send a message."

Cliff headed over to the fish market on Vernor Avenue where dozens of blue uniforms crawled around the neighborhood like ants, knocking on every door, speaking to every merchant, climbing the stairs to second and third and fourth floor apartments and knocking on more doors, asking more questions. By the end of the day, they had been able to obtain a clear description of the men who dashed from the fish market after the gunshots: they were short men, maybe six feet tall, big and burly, probably weighing a hundred forty pounds, in their late twenties with gray hair, and driving a maroon, black, brown, blue Chevy, Ford, Buick. No arrests were made.

It was no surprise to anyone when more deaths followed. Two men who worked for La Mare were gunned down as they ate in a restaurant on Jefferson Avenue. Another one died in a hail of bullets as he stooped to pick up the newspaper in his front yard. A policy house that had once belonged to Sammy Catalonette was raided, and a bookie and two secretaries died at their desks. Detroiters avoided going out after dark if they possibly could, trembling in fear that they may be caught in the crossfire.

By the time the trees upholstered the earth with hues of scarlet and gold, The Purples had had six loads of whiskey hijacked, two speakeasies busted up, and four numbers runners shot while Cher La Mare lost three *capos,* a distillery, and six numbers runners.

# CHAPTER 17

▼

Flint, Michigan was little more than an assemblage of buildings in the midst of expanses of corn and wheat sixty-five miles northwest of Detroit when Billy Durant first purchased the Coldwater Cart Road Company in 1886. Hitching posts outlined Saginaw Street, the main thoroughfare through town, which wasn't much wider than a cow path. Every Saturday, the hitching posts restrained horses and carriages huddled against buildings as farmers who tilled the soil for miles around, their wives and families streamed into town for weekly shopping and socializing, sometimes staying over to attend church services the next day.

Twenty years after Durant purchased the carriage marker, James Whiting who built Buick automobiles in Detroit, approached him for help in promoting his own car. Their association would lead to the creation of General Motors, breathing prosperity into the little country village and changing forever its physical and social structure.

Charles Mott had once owned Weston-Mott, an axle manufacturer that supplied Buick, Oakland, and Olds auto manufacturers. Durant's General Motors eventually swallowed up Weston-Mott and Charles put his new-found wealth into a more gentlemanly business, a bank. His board of directors elected him chairman of the board. He asked his friend, Billy, to invest in his Union Industrial Bank, but Billy didn't trust little banks. He had heard far too many tales of tellers at small banks making off with depositors' funds.

Mr. Mott had no trouble attracting depositors, despite the lack of support from the man who made Flint what it was. Jolan Slezsak, a pretty fifteen year old, amassed four hundred dollars slyly driving her baby sister around town in a baby carriage, its false bottom holding home-brewed gin. She entrusted her fortune, what she thought of as her dowry, to Union Industrial. Homer Dowdy's carefully garnered dollars were being kept safe at Union Industrial for his children. Mrs. McGrath on Elm Street had faithfully deposited two or three dollars at Union Industrial every week since it opened, proceeds from doing laundry for people too busy and too rich to do it for themselves. Mott's business acquaintances such as Irving Cassidy who owned the hardware store, Martin Boyle who had a thriving accounting practice and Jack Moseley, proprietor of the lumber mill, moved their companies' accounts to the Union Industrial. By 1929, the bank was the center of commerce in Flint.

Mott became Flint's most beloved citizen, thanks to his generosity in supporting civic programs and his frequent bequests that received lavish coverage by the *Flint Journal.* His courtship of Dee Van Balkom Furey, a beautiful divorcee and a journalist many years his junior, was not nearly as well covered by the press until the two were married on March 1, 1929.

The Motts' wedding was small and simple followed by a luncheon for the few guests before the couple flew to their ranch in Arizona for a honeymoon. Mrs. Mott did not like the bumpy flight in the small tri-motor and wasted no time in expressing her displeasure. Over Indiana, the plane encountered a storm, causing the pilot to lose sight of any landmarks. He flew lower in an effort to establish his location and was pushed into a plowed field. The distraught but unhurt bride stumbled to a nearby farmhouse where she called her attorney.

Mrs. Mott preferred being in Detroit and, since her husband was on the board of directors of General Motors, the couple spent most of their time there.. He didn't mind leaving his bank since he had a solid group of men running it for him, and business was booming, thanks in large part to the incredible success of investors in the stock market. An occasional phone call to his staff was all that was necessary to keep things running smoothly, he believed.

On the surface, Union Industrial's president, vice presidents, cashiers, and tellers did appear to be honest and trustworthy. The men were mostly family men and the women, whether single or married, were of the most respectable families. Nearly everyone spent Sunday mornings in church. Troubles brewed beneath that tranquil façade, though.

Frank Montague, a vice president, was diligent and company minded, not approving of any frivolous behavior or conversation, but his growing family was putting increasing strain on his finances. At thirty-nine, another vice president, Milton Pollock, had a family and a sick wife whose medical bills continued to mount during her long, slow recovery. Ivan Christensen was the assistant cashier at the bank. His wife, Betty, loved the country club life and belonged to three.

She dressed well, as did her husband, and they were having a seventy-five-thousand-dollar mansion built, far more than his three hundred seventy-five dollar monthly salary could maintain. John De Camp was the bank's senior vice president and looked the part in his expensive suits, a solid gold watch fob tucked in his vest pocket. He, too, had his eye on a luxurious home that befitted his station as a deacon of the church and a pillar of the community. And Robert Brown, the twenty-eight-year-old son of the bank's president, Grant Brown, who was expected to one day take over his father's position, was a leading member of his church.

James Barron, Mark Kelly, David McGregor, George Woodhouse, and a handful of other employees were responsible for the day-to-day operations as well as the long-term investment of their customers' hard-earned funds. As a group they referred to themselves as the League of Gentlemen.

Emboldened by the absence of Charles Mott, the trusted bank employees began systematically raiding their accounts in a variety of ways in order to feed their expensive lifestyles. They wrote loans in the names of prominent citizens, using the proceeds of those loans to invest in the stock market or to cover margin calls. Share certificates intended to be forwarded to another bank made their way into the Gentlemen's hands and were used as collateral for the loans.

On March 14, 1929 President Herbert Hoover held a press conference cautioning against the excesses of the stock market. Three days later, the League of Gentlemen in Flint purchased shares of Radio Corporation of America. Three days after the purchase, the stock dropped. When they finally sold, they had lost nearly fifteen percent of their investment.

On a sunny May morning, Grant Brown, president of Union Industrial Bank, made his customary morning tour of the bank, excited about the imminent move to new, stately headquarters in the center of Flint. Himself a new bridegroom, he had sent a note to his boss, Charles Mott, saying he was "deliciously happy" with his new wife and hoped the Motts were the same. "Things have never been better," he wrote to Mott. There was no need for Mr. Mott to leave Detroit to attend to the bank.

The morning's tour revealed that his deputy, John de Camp, had followed orders and had the brass bars around the tellers' cages polished. Miss Boughner, his secretary, was working quietly and efficiently at her desk just outside his office, raising her head only briefly to greet her boss. He sunk into the large leather chair behind the mammoth, gleaming mahogany desk and looked across the room through the sparkling glass and into the bank. Tellers were busily checking the cash in their drawers, organizing stacks of small papers they would use throughout the day, and opening stamp pads in front of their windows. Brown had particularly chosen that location for his office to give him a view of the entire work space. He hummed quietly as he watched his industrious employees going about their business, the leather chair creaking as he leaned deeply into it and puffed on his cigar.

Promptly at nine o'clock, the bank doors opened and customers began streaming through. Brown was suffused with a warm feeling as he watched people clutching their pay envelopes and their deposit slips, lining up at the tellers' cages. He unrolled the blueprint for the new building and began studying, making notes on a crisp white sheet of paper about things he wanted to discuss with Mr. Mott and with the architects. At noon he left for lunch at home, a lunch that normally lasted nearly three hours.

After the bank closed that day, The Gentlemen met in the conference room to assess their investments and debt. Ivan Christensen's face was pale, and he struggled to bring moisture to his mouth as he announced that they had redirected a total of two million dollars of customers' funds to their own use.

Two weeks later, Grant Brown was back in Detroit and The Gentlemen added, subtracted, and signed away unfettered by the chance that he would ask to see the ledgers that revealed their activities. On Wednesday, with rain clattering against the smoggy windows, the men shuffled quietly into the conference room. Chairs scraped against the wooden floor as they took their seats, eyes avoiding each other. The room was quiet as a funeral service as Frank Montague opened a portfolio and spread some papers out before him. His face wan from lack of sleep, he strummed the table with his right hand waiting for the last two seats to be filled When all were seated he stood at the end of the table.

"Gentlemen, we have gone too far. We seem to be losing more than we are making. It is only a matter of time before someone stumbles on to what we have been doing. We must stop and we must stop now." He surveyed the men seated around the table as he sat down.

Ivan Christensen leaned forward, his arms splayed on the rich mahogany table in front of him, the overhead light shining off his pale forehead.

"Now, Frank. I think you're over reacting. There's no question we are in deeper than we ever have been, but I see no cause for alarm. The market is already doing better today, and I have a direct line to two brokers in New York. With careful monitoring, we can turn this thing around. It would be one thing if we were all acting separately, but we are in this together. We can watch out for each other. With all our eyes and ears open around the bank, we'll know if anyone is suspicious of anything."

For fifteen minutes, the men debated whether to continue. In the end, they felt they had no choice; no one had the wherewithal to replace what they had taken.

A few days later the men met again in the conference room. Again, Montague expressed his concern. Again, Christensen assuaged his fears.

"I haven't heard a single word uttered from any employee of the bank questioning anything we have done," he said. "But I'll tell you what we do need to worry about is the bank examiners. They can drop in at any time, and we could be caught in a very uncomfortable position. Does anyone have any suggestions about how to handle that eventuality?"

The examiners were based in Lansing, nearly half a day's trip away by car. They would leave their offices early in the morning and arrive in Flint in time for lunch. There was some talk of bribing an employee in the Lansing office to alert the Union Industrial staff when examiners were headed to Flint. The plan was scuttled, though, since no one had any contacts in Lansing they could depend on.

George Woodhouse spoke up. "We may not know anyone in Lansing, but we all know people around here, waiters and waitresses and bellhops at the hotels where the examiners stay. Why don't we enlist their assistance?"

"Wonderful," Christensen said. "We can provide them with names and descriptions of the men who usually come. When one of them shows up, our friends can let us know in plenty of time to come up with a plan for keeping them out of our books."

And one day the phone call came. A bellhop at the Durant Hotel called Frank Montague saying that a man matching one of the descriptions on the list was lunching at the Hotel. Word passed quickly among the embezzlers and, in the two hours before the examiners appeared at the bank's door, De Camp and Christensen had prepared themselves for the inevitable questions.As they worked with the examiners, eyes from around the bank lobby surreptitiously bored into their backs as the other men looked for any sign of what was transpiring between the auditors and the bank employees. But they needn't have worried. Each time a question came up, DeCamp and Christensen managed to evade it or sufficiently obfuscate the answer to appease the auditors. So pleased were they with their performance, they took the auditors to dinner after the bank closed.

The Gentlemen continued what they called "borrowing money without approval" over the next couple of months. Some investments did very well, and they were able to recoup the losses they had suffered with Radio Corporation of America. Aviation and automobile stocks were paying off handsomely, garnering The Gentlemen a $200,000 profit in just a few days. They earned even more when their investments in food companies were buoyed by J.P. Morgan's purchase of the same companies' stocks. Frank Montague's color returned and the lines around his face relaxed for the first time in weeks. George Woodhouse whistled as he strode behind the tellers' cages collecting stacks of paper from each of them. Ivan Christensen took a lunch break for the first time in a month.

Weekly, they met in the conference room when their president was absent to discuss and plan their next moves. Emotions surged as they added up numbers and realized they would soon be able to repay all they had borrowed. They didn't know it, but they had managed to conceal the longest-running fraud in American banking history.

Although Mrs. Mott consulted her attorney about leaving her husband following the plane crash, her husband had managed to mollify her with lavish gifts and promises of trips. In June they announced they were leaving for a delayed honeymoon to Europe.

Grant Brown decided to attend a bankers' conference in San Francisco where he hoped to meet the famed A. P. Giannini, director of what was becoming a behemoth in banking circles, Bank of America. He hoped, also, to hear what other bankers were doing about the increased incidence of employees embezzling, not that he had anything to worry about he was sure.

Frank Montague was relieved to hear that both the Chairman of the Board and the President would be absent for some period of time. With judicious planning, The Gentlemen would be able to replace the money they had been borrowing before they were found out. The market had turned on them again, and signs of strain were increasing in Montague. He was losing weight, gaunt lines appeared in his face, and small hives erupted on his skin. He had been tempted to confess what he had been doing to his wife but thought better of it when he realized that the police would make her suffer along with him. Even Ivan Christensen and John de Camp, the most optimistic of the lot, were beginning to show signs of the pressure.

By August, Charles Mott knew his marriage to Dee Furey had been a big mistake. He decided to return to Flint and his bank and bury himself in work. He arrived unannounced on a weekend and visited his friends at the country club where he learned that one of his employees, Ivan Christensen, was building a home that seemed to be beyond his means. He determined to find out about the house when he reached the bank on Monday.

Frank Montague's face reddened, and he could barely catch a breath when he saw Mott stride through the front door that Monday. He was sure that the Chairman was at the bank because he had learned of the embezzlement. The market had been inching up in recent weeks, and they were so close to squaring the books. It would be an ignominious end if their deception were unveiled at this stage.

Mott strode briskly past all the employees, nodding curtly to anyone who spoke to him, ignoring the rest. He unlocked his office door and placed his hat carefully on a hall tree inside the door. He turned and again strode briskly across the floor of the bank lobby, stopping at Ivan Christensen's desk. He spoke quietly.

"Mr. Christensen, I wish to see you in my office immediately."

Christensen stood without speaking and followed his boss across the lobby, the stare of more than two dozen eyes boring into his back.

"Close the door," Mott said as he sat in his massive leather chair. "Sit down." He gestured to a smaller leather chair across from him.

"It has come to my attention, Mr. Christensen, that you are building quite a substantial home near the country club. A home which, I might say, I would be hard pressed to afford. Can you explain to me where the funds for that house originated?"

"Yes, sir, I can. You know that Mrs. Christensen likes to live well. She has had her heart set on a beautiful home since we were first married. We have had quite a few words about it, I might add. I told her that I simply could not afford the kind of luxury she wanted on my salary. Not that my salary is inadequate, Mr. Mott, quite the contrary. You pay me very well for my services. But Mrs. Christensen was determined to have her house, and she set her hat to it. She began researching investments, particularly the stock market and, I might add, she has done remarkably well. I was very impressed with her financial acumen. She seems to know just what to buy and when to buy it, and she is equally astute as to how long to hold it. It's her money that we are spending on the house, sir." He could feel warm, wet circles creeping out from under his arms. He folded his hands in front of him to keep them from shaking.

Mott sat puffing his cigar a moment. "Well, I'm happy to hear that, Mr. Christensen. I wish my own wife took such an interest in financial matters. She seems only to know how to spend money. You are a very lucky man. That'll be all."

Christensen returned to his desk, his head high, a smile big as a Chesire cat's. He could almost hear a sigh of relief spread around the lobby.

The market turned again in the next few days. Stocks that once held the promise of getting The Gentlemen out of debt dipping below their purchase prices. Through August, perhaps unable to face each other in view of their tremendous losses, the League of Gentlemen was no longer holding weekly meetings. Montague, Pollock, and Robert Brown peppered the heavens with prayers every night, hoping to find a way out of their dilemma.

In Detroit, Cliff Malin clung to the words of the psychic Evangeline Adams in her monthly newsletter as he, along with thousands of other Detroiters, watched their investments surge ahead then drop. "The Dow Jones could climb to Heaven," Miss Adams had declared. Given her previous successes, most recently seeing the slight downward trend in May, Evangeline's clients, Cliff included, were loath to act contrary to her advice. Cliff held tight, able to meet his margin calls so far, thanks to his two salaries.

By Labor Day, the League of Gentlemen and virtually every investor in the country breathed easily as the market seemed to stabilize. Over the holiday weekend, business magnates, housewives, and shoe shine boys relaxed over their morning coffee, reading newspapers filled with good news: the Graf Zeppelin completed its circumnavigation of the globe, the much loved Fiorella La Guardia predicted he would handily win the mayoral race in New York City; clothing manufacturers introduced the fall's fashions, an even flatter, more boyish look than the previous year's. On the day the market opened following the three-day holiday, it went volcanic, just as Miss Adams had predicted. Buyers and sellers made deals quickly and moved on to the next transaction. Radio Corporation of America soared, Anaconda led copper stocks up, American Telephone and Telegraph, U.S. Steel, and New York Central, all up over a hundred dollars. The Dow Jones Average stood at 381.17 on the sale of nearly four and a half million shares. A collective sigh of relief found its way skyward from Wall Street and from the Union Industrial Bank in Flint.

Jolan Slezsak's boyfriend, Steve Vargo, finally proposed to her, showing off a wad of cash he had saved from his work at "the Buick" as she made her daily rounds with her sister in the baby carriage atop a cache of homemade gin. He was headed for Union Industrial where he would deposit his hard-earned funds to keep them safe. That money plus what Jolan had saved would be their stake in a new life somewhere away from the drudgery of Flint.

By mid-September the market dropped again, wiping out many of the profits that had been earned two weeks earlier. The League of Gentlemen hastily resumed their meetings after non-participants in their scheme had left for the day. The phone had been ringing nearly continuously in Flint as three New York brokerages demanded cash to cover margin calls. Ivan Christensen and John de Camp found a $100,000 of customers' funds to cover the calls, the brokers unaware that the bankers were not investing for their customers.

Frank Montague was about to unravel. His eczema kept him from sleeping, his temper was short, and he still had not divulged that he had "borrowed" $50,000 without the knowledge of his compatriots. He had planned to take the profits from the investment to repay some of the debt; instead, he lost it all. Unable to withhold that information any longer, he confessed to his best friend and co-conspirator, Milton Pollock. Pollock promised to pray for his friend. Montague grew despondent.

Robert Brown grew more concerned that his father, the bank's president, would stumble on their endeavor, and he applied pressure to his colleagues to balance the books. They were fighting a war, he said and they "had to break out of their positions or perish." But, as the market continued its slide, they were unable to meet his demands. In just the month of September, a million and a half dollars had slipped through their fingers.

Nervous customers began demanding that the money they had entrusted to the bank for investment be recalled from New York, except their money had never made it to New York, at least not under their own names. The fifteen Gentlemen were forced to become ever more creative in juggling the books to meet their customers' demands.

Meantime, Bank President Grant Brown spent his days on a mission of his own. His competitors were making a concerted effort to topple the mighty Union Industrial Bank. After a cursory inspection of the bank each morning, Mr. Brown called on businessmen around the city, assuring them his bank was the safest and most trusted in Michigan. Part of his plan was a large direct mail campaign that would include sworn statements from bank employees confirming the bank's solvency. To ensure his statements were accurate, he would audit the bank's books himself.

The Gentlemen went into quiet panic when their boss announced his plan. John de Camp offered to perform the audit for the president, but Grant refused. The tellers held their breath as the first ledger was carried to the president's desk in the corner of the room. He spent some time poring over it then called for the second. To the relief of the tellers, Christensen sprang into action. He marched up to the president's desk.

"Sir, the market is slipping. We've got our hands full with margin calls. I need to keep the ledgers by me to make sure our customers have enough cash to meet the calls. We've got to look after our customers," he said.

The president agreed, even thanking the young man for being so diligent in protection of the bank's customers. Grant Brown soon left the bank for his usual three-hour lunch and none too soon. The market continued to slip. Even the blue chips the group had invested in were down an average $7. By two o'clock that afternoon, with another call from a broker demanding cash to cover a margin call, Christensen bellowed, "It's over." He knew they could no longer cover their deeds.

In New York, banks were pooling their resources to buoy up key stocks such as General Electric and U.S. Steel. Within an hour of Christensen's pronouncement, The Gentlemen gulped with relief as the descent of their stocks' value was arrested.

In Detroit, Cliff Malin as well as thousands of other investors clustered in front of stock market tickers and fell silent as they watched the slide: Westinghouse, down $11; Allied Chemical, $10.75; Columbia Carbon, $17.25. Nervous as he was, he was tempted to sell everything and quit, but Harry Bennett persuaded Cliff to hedge his bets and just sell some of the stocks to cover other margin calls. He took Harry's advice, hanging on to Radio Corporation of America, American Tel and Tel and a couple of airline stocks.

September 27: Westinghouse lost $11, General Electric, $13, Columbia Carbon just over $17, the Flint embezzlers, $100,000. They had heard the phrase "organized buying support" from the New York brokers and clung to it with the fervor of a penitent to her rosary. There may still be a way out if the big money in New York was successful in shoring up the market.

October 4, the *New York Times*: "Year's Worst Break Hits Stock Market." Buyers struck quickly and the market surged the next day. Margin calls were down, and A. P. Giannini of Bank of America declared the market was healthy. After twenty-five years running his bank, he should know, everyone thought. Searching for good news, reporters told of a valet, a nurse, and a cattleman, all of whom were rolling in new-found wealth. They were "fixed for life," the readers were told.

October 18: Jolan and her brother, Michael, took a break from their home brewing to visit the Union Industrial. Jolan and Steve would be married in a few days and Michael wanted some of his money to buy his sister a wedding present. Redolent with the peculiar smells of gin mills, the pair sauntered up to Russell Runyon's cage and asked to withdraw funds. He disappeared for a few moments and, when he returned, told them they couldn't have their money until the following week. Indignant, they stormed off, assuring the teller they would return.

As Steve and Jolan repeated their wedding vows, events in New York were shaping their future. Otis Elevators, down $5; General Electric, down $8, Auburn Auto, down $15. The men to whom the newlyweds had entrusted their savings virtually fell to their knees seeking deliverance.

October 21: nearly fifty years since Thomas Alva Edison, former resident of Port Huron and now close friend of Henry Ford, had unveiled his light bulb, his good friend, Henry, was holding a special celebration. As he dedicated his "American Village" in Dearborn, a panoply of Detroit's history as Henry saw it, he would unveil a re-creation of Edison's laboratory in New Jersey where the light bulb had first cursed the darkness. He even transported an acre of New Jersey clay on which the tableau would stand. The climax of the day's events would be Edison re-enacting the first lighting of that first bulb. President Herbert Hoover, Will Rogers, Madame Curie, Orville Wright, and Albert Einstein would witness this momentous occasion.

Harry Bennett was worried that his boss, Mr. Ford, would be the target of assassins or kidnappers during the event and spent frantic hours for weeks ahead of time anticipating every possible security breach. Barricades were raised to keep the crowds from Mr. Ford. Cliff arranged for an army of the Bernstein's biggest men to keep reporters and spectators at bay, and Harry added to their legion with his beloved football players who normally worked at The Rouge.

The event was a welcome relief from the stresses of market watching as Henry Ford provided the usual spectacle with his off-beat views and pronouncements. As reporters followed him through the displays of Abraham Lincoln's Illinois law office, Longfellow's blacksmith shop from Massachusetts, and Stephen Foster's birthplace, Ford regaled them with his plans for building car bodies out of soybeans and his views on reincarnation. Ford had once believed he was Leonardo da Vinci re-incarnate, but now was of the opinion he was King Midas in a former life with more than a modest knowledge of the god Bacchus, the god of intoxicating beverages, although he no longer drank strong beverages, he assured the throngs.

In answer to reporters' questions, President Hoover declined to comment on the slipping stock market until its close. By then, it had rallied.

At 7:30 p.m., in rooms lit only by candlelight at the suggestion of radio commentator Graham McNamee, thousands listened to NBC as Thomas Edison pressed two wires together in his reconstructed laboratory in Dearborn. The country held its breath as McNamee built the drama. "Will it light? Will it burn?" he pondered. "Or will it flicker and die, as so many previous lamps had died?" and then, "It lights!" and millions of lights flickered on in offices and living rooms and bedrooms around the country.

October 22: Western Union, up $18; Hershey Chocolate, up over $10; Columbia Carbon, up nearly $17.

October 23: the president of the New York Stock Exchange was on his honeymoon, and his deputy took the day off to visit the horse track. Westinghouse dropped $35, General Electric lost $20 and Adams Express fell an incredible $96.

October 24: 6:30 a.m. Frank Montague slipped from his bed in Flint, fumbled for his clothes, and left the room without waking his wife. A blizzard had downed the long distance telephone lines the day before, and Montague was at wit's end having only radio reports to rely on for the day's events in New York.

Not all The Gentlemen had telephones in their homes, but those who did called each other repeatedly as reports of falling stocks, particularly the auto stocks, streamed in unabated. Still hoping to stem the tide of their losses, the League had invested heavily in General Motors.

Now, in the cold kitchen, sipping steaming coffee, Montague debated with himself about continuing in what he thought of as a quagmire or simply quitting, persuading the others to do likewise. But quitting would reveal their activities, their horrendous losses. The thought of what that revelation would do to his wife and children, not to mention his fellow parishioners who viewed him as a pillar of Christianity, was too much to bear. He would continue embezzling.

He felt certain he wouldn't be alone in his decision. Ivan Christensen would not be able to face his wife's retributions when her friends at the country clubs learned of his thievery. Milton Pollock's wife was still quite ill, and medical bills mounted. Robert Brown would continue out of fear that his father would learn of his actions over the past year and a half. What the others would be inclined toward doing was a mystery, but Montague was certain the strength of these men would be sufficient to persuade the others as to their continued course of action. When his wife joined him in the kitchen, he was listening to the early broadcasts from New York. He told her he would be home late and not to hold dinner.

The market opened warily that morning, but, just after ten o'clock New York time, trading became brisk and prices rose dramatically: Kennecott Copper up $11, Sinclair Oil, 50 cents, Standard Brands 40 cents. And they were big transactions: fifteen and twenty thousand shares at a pop. But margin calls continued on other stocks, and more and more sell orders were issued. By eleven o'clock, Charles Mott, a member of the board of directors at General Motors and chairman of the board of Union Industrial Bank in Flint, received a phone call from an automobile stock analyst who specialized in General Motors stocks. There seemed to be nothing that would prevent GM from plummeting, he said. Mott called the other executives into emergency session.

Just before lunch time, Ivan Christensen told his fellow investors that a wave of selling was coursing through the market, swallowing up any buying that was happening. The ticker was running fifty-five minutes late as a result of the heavy trading. By mid afternoon, Frank Montague calculated The Gentlemen were down $2 million. The men flocked to Ivan's desk, oblivious to stares and comments from other workers and customers. Their chief concern was the market's activities. The ticker was now two hours late, and the news was dismal. Montague suggested they get out of the market, and his colleagues laughed. He fainted. When he recovered, he learned Elton Graham had diverted an additional $350,000 to cover margin calls. A slight rally in the afternoon's trading spurred hopes. John de Camp assured Frank that the bank couldn't afford the publicity of having so many of its key staff members arrested; they may be found out, but they wouldn't be jailed.

At 7:08 p.m. the ticker finally caught up with the day's activities. A record twelve million shares had changed hands. The morning's $6 billion loss had been cut to just three. Representatives of thirty-five of the largest wire houses in Wall Street issued a joint statement saying the market was "fundamentally sound." The message ended, "The worst has passed."

In Detroit, Cliff Malin and Harry Bennett attempted to reach Evangeline Adams for a current reading, but she was no longer giving personal consultations. Hundreds of investors gathered in Carnegie Hall for advice from the woman who had given them such good advice in recent months and not just about the stock market. She had foretold Charles Lindbergh's successful trans-Atlantic flight, Rudolf Valentino's death, and the 1928 Tokyo earthquake, all within minutes of their happening. Small investors and large wanted to know what the next day's market would do. Should they sell or try to meet their margin calls?

Evangeline felt the investors wanted reassurance more than they wanted truth, and she gave it to them. She said "spheres of influence over susceptible groups" would result in good times. That was enough for her followers. They continued to buy or meet margin calls.

When the last of her clients left that evening, Evangeline's broker told her she had lost $100,000. Despite the advice to her clients, she told the broker to sell everything the next day.

October 25: Charles Schwab supported the views Evangeline Adams gave her public. He saw no reason that prosperity should not continue, he said. Alfred Sloan, chairman of General Motors, announced that the previous day's events were healthy. Not everyone was persuaded by the robust statements, however, and money was recalled from Wall Street.

October 28: Sightseers trailed through the financial district as gawkers eyed the place where so many millions had been lost the previous week. U.S. Steel opened down $1.25; General Electric, down $7.25; other blue chips fell. The ticker lagged a half hour, an hour, two hours. Even after the market closed, sell orders piled in.

Tuesday, October 29: One stock price after another fell at dizzying rates with no end in sight. Allied Chemical, Radio Corporation, U.S. Steel, American Can, General Motors, General Electric. None seemed immune to devastation.

In Flint, Jolan and Steve Vargo were among dozens streaming up the streets to their Union Industrial, the safest place to keep their money, they had thought, to withdraw the funds they had sought last week just before their wedding. But, from some distance, they could see the bank's doors closed, although it was at least an hour before normal closing time.

The fifteen Gentlemen of Flint spread themselves between the telephone lines and the ticker tapes. Just after lunch, Frank Montague estimated they owed the bank $3 million. In fact, it was closer to $3.5 million. Unable to keep his silence any longer and feeling he had been duped by the others, he marched stridently to the desk of Grant Brown, the bank's president, and requested a private conversation. In the very same conference room the men had used to plot their deceptions and thefts, he began to confess. The president stopped him the moment he realized what he was about to hear, He returned to the bank lobby and announced loudly that the bank would be closing early. Stunned customers moved slowly toward the doors, glancing back, hoping to hear from Mr. Brown the reason for the closing. He said nothing as he stood stiffly in the center of the lobby watching it empty, his head pounding. When all the customers were out in the streets, he locked the doors firmly behind them.

He turned to face his employees, cleared his throat and said loudly, "Anyone who was involved in Mr. Montague's transactions is to come to the conference room immediately." He strode across the quiet lobby, eyes fastened firmly on him until he disappeared. The employees of the bank turned first to the person nearest them then to those farther away. Who could Mr. Brown be referring to? many of them wondered.

A chair scraped against the wooden floor as Ivan Christensen pushed away from his desk and walked toward the conference room, his head down, his right hand tucked into his coat pocket. George Woodhouse stepped away from his teller cage and reached for his suit coat hanging on a peg nearby. He put it on as he started off behind Christensen. Milton Pollock, Russell Runyon, Elton Graham, and the rest of the League quickly trailed behind, their heads low, looking neither right nor left.

Grant Brown sat at the head of the vast table in the conference room, staring straight ahead, acknowledging no one as they entered. His perfectly manicured hands were splayed in front him as if in resignation. Most of the seats at the table were filled, and he opened his mouth to speak when a last knock came at the door.

"Enter," he said then blanched to see his son's shape filling the door frame. "My God," was all he could muster the strength to say.

The elder Brown rose from his chair and stepped to Miss Boughner's desk, handing her the key to the front door, and telling her to unlock the doors before rejoining the men in the conference room, confident that the worst that could happen to his bank had already happened, sure he could reverse its fortunes and salvage its reputation.

For nearly an hour, the men told him details of their involvement in the actions of the last few months as he made notes. At three o'clock, he left the room and telephoned Charles Mott in Detroit telling him of the embezzlement. Mott said he would leave for Flint immediately.

At the close of business on Wall Street that day $10 billion had been lost on sales of just over16 million shares.

Mott arrived in Flint and drove directly to Union Industrial. Throughout the night and well into the next morning, the men detailed their activities. Ledgers were pulled out and reviewed and, with each revelation, Mott felt himself grow warmer and warmer. By five thirty on the morning of October 30, he felt drained, exhausted, beleaguered. How could this have happened to his bank? These men whom he had so trusted, whom he represented to his friends and to the community as the most trustworthy in the community, had decimated all he had worked for. His reputation would be tarnished along with theirs. Could he ever hold his head up again in Flint? In Michigan?

The embezzlement was only part of what caused his world to crumble. The bank was finished and so was his marriage. He had received divorce papers the previous week and wrote a press release announcing the divorce with orders for it to be released October 29. There was nothing left for him.

He demanded resignations from each of the so-called Gentlemen and went home to his empty mansion. He rested briefly then telephoned the city prosecutor, Charles Beagle, asking that the attorney come to his home. After a long meeting behind closed doors, Mott returned to Detroit, withdrew $3,592,000 from his personal accounts and had it loaded into three armored cars. The caravan drove to Flint and placed the funds on display. His bank was, indeed, the safest place to have your money, he announced.

In Detroit mayhem ruled. At Bill Navin's pool hall, the only subject discussed was the crash of the stock market. Cliff Malin received a frantic call from his friend Harry Bennett at The Rouge. Workers no longer stood at their assembly line positions but thronged outside the company's offices demanding to know if their jobs were safe. Had Mr. Ford lost everything in the markets as so many other wealthy people had? they wanted to know. Harry told Cliff to bring officers to augment his own Service Department thugs, but The Rouge was in Dearborn and out of Cliff's jurisdiction.

In his own precinct, investors who had lost everything lined up at their banks, anxious to find out if the events in Flint were being repeated in Detroit. The demand for withdrawals far exceeded the banks' cash on hand, and the doors were usually locked by noon, leaving angry depositors empty handed. Windows were broken first then, as the anger grew, cars turned over and burned. Two men who had lost their entire fortunes in the stock market jumped to their deaths from the top of the J.L. Hudson's building.

# CHAPTER 18

▼

A soft winter rain fell on the street outside the Fort Street Railroad Station late one night in 1931 as a broad-shouldered man with a thick neck threaded his way past other passengers and outside, sidestepping puddles that glistened in the light from the station. The front door of a brown Buick sedan standing at the curb swung open for him, and he disappeared inside. Two other men who followed him at a short distance climbed into a Chevrolet standing behind the Buick. The cars disappeared into the gathering mist, headed for downtown.

The men—Herman "Hymie" Paul, Joe "Nigger Joe" Lebowitz, and Joe "Izzy" Sutker—had come in from Chicago at the behest of their boss, Al Capone. Capone had long been ordering his whiskey from the Bernsteins and the men had become friends, of sorts. But the Bernsteins were becoming sloppy, losing too many shipments to hijackings, and Capone decided to take matters into his own hands. He sent the men to Detroit, telling them to report to the distillery on Oakland Street. They were to escort deliveries back to Chicago.

But the three had plans of their own. They were aware that the Bernsteins—La Kosher Nostra, as they called them—were having trouble. When Capone ordered them to report to the Oakland Sugar House, they began hatching a plan to go into business for themselves.

On the way into town from the railroad station, the driver cruised down Brush Street looking for women. Surveying the available hookers, each man chose the one he thought would give him satisfaction, and the cars sped off. Ruby sat snuggled against Izzy in the front seat of the Buick while he pulled a bottle of whiskey from the glove compartment, took a swig, and handed it to Ruby. After she had downed a gulp, she passed it to the back seat to the two lumps of men who were serving as body guards. A bottle was passed around in the Chevrolet, as well.

By the time the vehicles reached the Cadillac Hotel, their occupants were buzzed and laughing. The bellman led them to the eighth floor and into a sprawling suite furnished lavishly with the latest in walnut, brocade, and tapestry. The women poked into each room, whistling and oo-ing at everything they saw. Pearl, whom Joe had chosen, flopped on one of the beds and wriggled into its soft chenille bedspread.

"Now, this is the life," she said. "I could get real used to this."

Izzy told the bellman to send up glasses, ice, and soda to go with the whiskey they had brought with them, tipped the man, and closed the door behind him. All that night and well into the next day the men and women drank, ate, had sex, played cards, and laughed. Twice the manager knocked on the door to tell them they were disturbing their neighbors. Tongues loosened as the bottles of whiskey were consumed and replaced. Ruby confessed to having a daughter living with her mother in Traverse City. Pearl said she had once partied with the Mayor for an entire weekend, while his wife was in the hospital giving birth to their third child.

The women asked the men what they were doing in town and, in the early hours of their partying, the men were vague. They were there on business, they said, the import business. The women knew what that meant and didn't press for details. The more they drank, however, the more they talked until Hymie revealed their plans for taking over the Purples' operations. Pearl and Opal laughed when he first mentioned it.

"You gotta be crazy," Opal said, pouring whiskey into Hymie's glass. "You don't know what mean is till you start messing with them boys."

And at first Ruby didn't pay much attention to their ramblings. These weren't the first men she had partied with who had grandiose plans for horning in on the Bernsteins' business. They were usually young, smart asses who thought they had the world by the balls but soon realized they had taken on formidable opponents. If they lived, they were crippled or blind or missing a hand or a foot.

The way these men were talking about their plans made Ruby take notice, though. They worked for Al Capone they said, and she had heard about the ambitious head of crime in Chicago. These men would have learned at the master's knee about how to muscle in on someone. Ruby knew that meant blood running in the streets. She had lost her brother during just such a skirmish for power. He was just waiting on Woodward Avenue for a bus when a stray bullet pierced his heart. He was dead before he hit the ground. She didn't want to see that grief visited on other families.

Back on Brush Street, she was plagued with what she had heard at the Cadillac Hotel. She remembered that police officer Fred had introduced her to. Cliff, she thought his name was. She had seen him around a few times after that first meeting, but he seemed to be avoiding her. He spoke to some of the other girls more than he did to her. At first, it had troubled her. She was used to attention from men. She had thought maybe he was one of those clean cops who wouldn't let her off a shoplifting charge in exchange for free sex. From the first, she'd had a feeling she had seen him somewhere before, but it took some time for her to remember. It was actually Opal who figured it out. She remembered him from one night when they had been called out to a party in St. Clair Shores given by Rube Goldberg whom she knew worked for the Bernsteins. This Cliff had been arranging things, she remembered. He made sure there was always food and drinks on the table, made sure no man spent time alone unless he wanted to. She thought at first that night that he didn't like women because he seemed oblivious to the half-naked bodies that littered the room. but then late into the evening, when it seemed everyone's needs were satisfied, Ruby saw him slip into a back bedroom with Louise. Ruby figured he was now avoiding her lest she connect him to that party and the Bernsteins.

Once Ruby realized that the men from Chicago were serious about moving in on the Purples' operations, she figured she could sell the information for enough money to allow her to abandon the streets and take her daughter someplace clean and safe, maybe up north on the lake. She knew she couldn't just walk up to one of the Bernsteins with some outlandish story about danger to their empire. She didn't even know where to find the Bernsteins, but she did know Cliff, even if just slightly. Maybe she could persuade him of the imminent danger to his employers.

For the next week she kept a sharp eye for the black squad car. Although he was a lieutenant now, he seemed to enjoy being on the streets. She expected he was of more service to the Bernsteins there than stuck behind a desk. Early on a Saturday night, a week after partying with the men from Chicago, she saw him. He had parked the squad car up the street and walked the beat, rattling doorknobs and peering in windows. He was alone.

Ruby hung back when the other girls sidled up to him, running their hands up his sides and over his face, offering five minutes of happiness in the alley. Fred, the cop who had introduced Cliff around, had pretty much trained the girls that if they kept police officers happy, they wouldn't have to worry about arrests. Fred had been true to his word and, so far, Cliff had as well. He'd been a tough nut to crack, but he eventually had taken advantage of the women's friendliness.

He smiled and chatted with the girls patting a butt or cupping a breast for a little squeeze. Cliff didn't seem to be in need of their services, though, and they eventually drifted away as paying customers appeared. Cliff continued down the sidewalk, his long legs gobbling up distance easily. Ruby stepped away from the lamppost where she had been standing and intercepted him.

"How ya doin', Officer?"

"Not bad," he said, glancing sideways and slowing his gait slightly. "Ruby, isn't it?"

"That's right, Sugar."

She walked beside him in silence for a minute, modifying her hooker's walk to keep pace with him. Unlike the other girls, she didn't touch him. She was close enough, though, that he could smell the cheap perfume she lavished on herself.

"Ya know, I think we met before. I got a pretty good eye for faces," she said.

"I'm not so good with faces," he said. "Where did we meet?"

"At a party last summer down on the river. I think it was at Mr. Goldberg's. You remember that party? Lots of great food and liquor."

"I imagine all the parties on the river have lots of great food and liquor. I'm not sure I remember that party."

"Ooo, that's a shame, Lieutenant Malin. It was a mighty fine party. I bet under that quiet face you put on, you can do some real partyin'."

"Oh, I don't know. I like to have a good time, for sure, but I guess what I think of as having fun isn't the same as what you think of."

"There's certain kinds of partyin' everyone likes to do. I bet you can show a woman some good times."

Cliff didn't speak. He doubted that either Alicia or that girl in France would agree with Ruby, but he hoped in the intervening years he had picked up some skills in that department. But he did remember the party at Rube's. Ruby was right, it was a good party.

"I was at another party last week, was a lot of fun. Guys talked too much, though. Normally, I don't mind so much. I get paid the same no matter what they do. But these guys, they was different. They was talking about some creepy things. Course, ya never know when to believe a guy, and when he's talking out his ass."

"I can't imagine what anyone would say that makes you feel creepy. I would guess you've seen just about everything."

"I seen a lot, that's for damn sure. Enough to know I don't think these guys was talking out their ass."

"Is their conversation something you think I should know about it?" Cliff stopped and turned toward Ruby. The light from the nearby lamppost cast a shadow across his face giving Ruby no opportunity to figure out what he might be thinking.

She looked at him a moment then down at the ground, tugging at her tight skirt.

"You might find what I heard interesting, maybe even real helpful. You think a girl can earn a few bucks if she had some good information?"

"Could be," he said. "Depends how important this information is."

"Well, if these guys mean what they say, Detroit could get real bloody before long."

"Why don't you tell me what you heard and I'll see if it's worth anything." He took a pack of cigarettes from his inside jacket pocket and offered her one.

"Well, it wouldn't be worth much to a cop. I figure you guys would be just as happy if all these hoodlums killed each other off. Make your job a lot easier, I figure. That is unless you in bed with these guys. You know, making a little extra on the side, buy your wife a fur coat or something. Now, if that's the case, you might want to know if anything is going to upset your little apple cart."

"Why don't you tell me what you heard, Ruby? I'm sure it's worth a few bucks." He lit both cigarettes.

Ruby could only tell Cliff the first names of the men she had partied with, but she could describe them, and she remembered they came from Chicago. Cliff peeled a fifty dollar bill off a roll of cash and handed it to her. She turned up her lip.

"I thought what I had to tell you would be worth a lot more than that."

"It just might be. Let me check it out, and I'll see what shakes."

Ruby rolled up the bill and pushed it deep inside her cleavage, gave him a long smile and turned to go back to her corner. She could go home early tonight if she wanted to.

Cliff finished his shift at six the next morning. After showering and downing a quick breakfast at the Five and Diner, he headed for the Cadillac Hotel where Ruby said the men from Chicago were headquartered. Flashing his police badge at the desk clerk, he gave the names of the men Ruby had told him, demanding to know their room number. Scared what would happen if he revealed the names, just as scared if he didn't, the clerk turned the registration ledger around so Cliff could read it and simply pointed to the names. Cliff asked if the men were still in their rooms, and the clerk started to nod then stopped. He pointed across the lobby. Cliff turned and watched three men crossing from the elevator to the front door where a uniformed bellman opened the door and spoke to them as they left.

"That them?" Cliff asked the clerk. The clerk nodded as he turned the registration ledge back to face him.

Cliff walked quickly across the lobby arriving on the sidewalk just as the three men were getting in a cab. He headed to the car he had left parked on the sidewalk and eased into traffic behind the cab. He could see the men through the rear window laughing and talking, unaware they were being followed. When the cab dropped them at Rossi's, a popular coffee shop on Jefferson, Cliff drove past and headed for Abe's.

Abe did not arrive at his office before noon as a rule, but there were always men milling around, toting up the figures from the previous night, making assignments for the day's activities or just lounging on the plush furniture, maybe sleeping off a hangover before going home. Cliff called Abe at home who was in the midst of his first cup of coffee and said they had to talk immediately. They agreed to meet in an hour. Abe picked Cliff up just off Grand Circus, and they headed to the river. Cliff told Abe what he had learned from Ruby. Abe said he knew that Al Capone had become nervous about his shipments in recent months. Abe's friend Bugs Moran in New York thought Capone was crazy, taking wild chances, killing far too many, far too easily. Moran wanted to take over Chicago and get rid of Capone.

"Capone probably figures since me and Bugs are friends, I'm going to stiff him on one of the deliveries or something. He's been telling me I'm getting sloppy and loosing too much of his shipments. Bugs is right. Capone is going crazy. I heard he got the clap from one of his hookers, and he's going off his rocker. He probably put these three yahoos up to moving in on me, thinking he's protecting hisself. I'll show the son of a bitch who he has to protect hisself from."

As they headed back to town, Abe and Cliff speculated as to where the three might strike. Back at Grand Circus, Cliff walked Abe over to his own car and stood on the sidewalk as Abe leaned out the back window of his Cadillac.

"You're a good boy, finding this out, Clifford, and so soon after they arrived in town. There'll be a little extra something for you this week."

Cliff lit a cigarette thinking he would give part of his bonus to Ruby.

Abe gave him a broad wink and said, "You keep your ear to the ground and keep me informed."

Cliff watched the big car move into traffic and finished his cigarette before returning to his own car. The streets were quiet this Sunday morning with wide spaces between the few cars that moved around Grand Circus. It was actually quiet enough to hear a few birds chirping from the windowsills overlooking the street. The sun peeked between two buildings, reflecting brightly off the chrome of parked cars.

This wasn't the first time someone had threatened to move in on the Purples' operations, but Cliff had an uneasy feeling about this one. If Abe was right and Al Capone was behind it, they wouldn't care what they did to make inroads into Detroit operations. Capone and the Bernsteins were all known for their brutality and vindictiveness. It could be a long, hot summer.

Abe and Cliff had decided that taking over liquor runs or distilleries was likely to be the first area of the Bernsteins' business that the men from Chicago would go after. It was the most lucrative and would affect Capone's business most quickly. Cliff headed for the Oakland Sugar House, the biggest distillery the Purples owned.

Hal Fleischman, the foreman, leaned over an open ledger at his desk, the sleeves of his white shirt rolled up to his elbows, thin wisps of graying hair pasted across the top of his head. He looked up when Cliff came in then leaned back in his chair. Cliff told him about the men from Chicago and Hal's chin dropped slightly though his mouth didn't open.

"Oh, God," Hal said. "I may have hired these guys. They're going to ride shotgun on the trucks tonight."

"You know where I can find these guys right now?"

"Not for sure. I heard they been hanging out with the Third Avenue Navy, but I don't know nothing for sure."

"And you don't know that I was here, do you?"

"No, sir. I don't know nothing."

The Third Avenue Navy had once been allies of the Bernsteins, but lately they had become trouble. There were unwritten rules and codes among Detroit's gangs, but the bunch at the Third Avenue Navy didn't care. They hijacked from anyone, ignored territorial boundaries, and double-crossed even their best friends. They would be a natural ally for the three men from Chicago. Cliff headed over to the railroad yards between Third and Fourth Avenue where they were headquartered. Vince Fratelli was in the warehouse talking to one of the laborers but turned and watched Cliff cross the warehouse floor.

"Yeah, whaddya want?"

"More to the point, what do you want?"

"Who the hell are you? I got work to do here."

"You know who I am, Vince. And I'm pretty sure you know why I'm here. You got some new boys working for you. I hear they want to make trouble for the Bernstein brothers. You know better than anyone that isn't a very good idea for anyone who wants to see their children grow up. You maybe want to pass that word on to those new boys."

"I don't know what you're talking about. I got some new guys poking around here, but no one wants to make trouble."

"That's bullshit, Fratelli, and you know it. You don't do anything but make trouble around town. I'm warning you and I'm warning them. Stay out of our business and out of our territory, or you'll have more trouble than you can deal with. Am I making myself clear?"

"Very clear."

Driving back home, Cliff thought about Fratelli. He was too stupid to take seriously the warning Cliff had given him. There would be trouble.

Di Grassi asked Dan Kirk for another cigarette then stretched out in his chair. His muscles ached from sitting still too long, but he knew if he tried to stand the guard would force him back into his chair.

"I guess I don't have to tell you about the Collingwood Massacre and the Battle of the Overpass out at The Rouge. You maybe even covered them. Malin had his hand in those things too. He wasn't at the Collingwood, but, anything Ray Bernstein was involved in, he knew about. And I'm pretty sure some of the goons there were at The Rouge that day were there because Malin sent them."

He finished his cigarette as Dan continued writing. When Dan finished he stood up and signaled the guard.

"Thanks for your time, Mr. Di Grassi."

"Like I said, it's either talk to you or..."

"Yeah, I know."

Driving back to the newspaper office, he recalled the two events Di Grassi referred to, two very bloody events that he had covered, as Di Grassi guessed. He also remembered Janet McDonald and the fallout from her death.

# CHAPTER 19

▼

Spring was late in coming. Dwindling mounds of snow crusted black from splashing mud stood piled in the shadows of buildings out of reach of the sun's melting rays. The earth stood soggy, withholding fresh shoots of grass and daffodil heads as though begrudging the city a fresh new year. A solid fabric of thick clouds hung low in the sky more days than usual. The windows at J.L. Hudson's were filled with stylish new frocks in fresh spring colors, but no one seemed in the mood for them. The streets remained populated with men and women in the drab grays and browns of winter.

Solly Levine paced in front of Lieutenant Malin's desk, lighting one cigarette from another before stubbing the spent one in the ashtray on the desk. The Lieutenant leaned back in his chair and watched silently. Solly was a good guy but could be downright stupid at times. Loyal to his friends, he sometimes picked the wrong ones then didn't know how to get out of a fix he'd gotten himself in. Cliff figured when Solly finally talked he would relate a similar situation.

"How's the family, Solly?"

"Fine, fine." Solly kept his glance downward as he paced and smoked and frowned. "They're just fine."

"You want a drink, Solly?"

Solly looked up for the first time since he had entered the office and his face eased a bit. "Yeah, that would be great. You got something?"

"Course I do." Cliff pulled two glasses and a bottle from the bottom drawer of his desk and half filled the glasses. Solly snatched one before Cliff had a chance to offer it to him and downed it in one gulp.

"Why don't you sit, Solly. You're making me nervous."

Solly dragged a chair sitting in front of the desk back away from the Lieutenant and sat on the edge. He finished his cigarette and didn't light another one meaning he was ready to talk.

"I need a real big favor, Mr. Malin. I don't even know if you can help me."

"Why don't you try me?"

Solly had befriended Hymie, Nigger Joe, and Izzy when they first came to town, he said, met them at the Blue Orchid. They seemed like nice guys, and they were away from home in a strange city. He was just trying to be friendly. He just wanted to have a few drinks and a few laughs with them. But then they started this bookie operation. Solly was a bookie himself and, in the past, hadn't been all that interested in seeing anyone else set up a book, but things had been pretty busy lately. Solly couldn't always handle all the action that came his way, so he thought his three new friends could use a little extra dough, he said. Things went along fine for the first few months, but now there was trouble.

"I just don't know anyone else to turn to, Mr. Malin."

"What is it you need?"

"It's not me, exactly. It's these other guys. It's just that they're kind of working under my name, you know. These guys get into some trouble, it could come back on me."

Solly told Cliff that the new bookies had taken a bet they couldn't cover, and the people they owed the money to were some Italians from the East Side, mean guys who weren't about to take an IOU for what was owed to them. And it was a lot of money, Solly said, two hundred grand.

Cliff whistled. "These guys got some balls laying down that kind of action. Are they out of their minds? I heard Izzy got kicked out of his apartment for not paying the rent. Is that right?"

Solly was on his feet again, pacing and smoking. "Yeah, it's true. And that's not all. They all three lost those big fancy cars they been cruising around in. Can't pay those bills either."

"Well, I'm not sure what I can do. What did you have in mind?"

"Well, they was thinking maybe if you could get the Purples to make them a deal on some whiskey, they could sell it off and raise the cash they need to pay off the bet."

"I don't know. We don't like to deal with stupid people, and these guys sound pretty stupid to me. If they can't pay their rent, how are they going to pay for the booze?"

"They figure if you could carry them for a few days till they sell it, they can pay you and raise enough to pay off the debt."

Cliff leaned forward resting his arms on the desk. "You think we can trust these guys or are they going to make off with our money?"

"Oh, no Mr. Malin. I'll see to that. In fact, I'll give you my personal guarantee. If they don't pay you, I will."

Cliff said he would talk to the Bernsteins and let him know what their answer was. In fact, Cliff didn't need to ask the Bernsteins permission to make the deal, but he wanted to give it some thought. It didn't make a lot of sense to finance the men who had announced they were going to take over the Purples' operation. On the other hand, maybe if the Bernsteins bailed them out of this trouble, they would abandon their plans out of loyalty. If not, at least Cliff would find it easier to keep track of what they were doing, because he was going to insist on knowing how to get in touch with them at all times.

At five thirty the next evening, a large van pulled up in front of Solly's policy house and fifty-seven cases of fresh Canadian whiskey were unloaded. The driver handed Solly an invoice to sign and disappeared without a word.

But Solly underestimated his new friends. To pay the Italians off before trouble started, they needed to sell the whiskey Solly had obtained for them in a hurry. They decided to cut the whiskey, cut the price below what anyone else was selling it at, and sell it fast. And they decided to do it on the East side, the realm of the Bernsteins. For three days, the Purples whiskey sat untouched in the warehouse, their regular customers buying the cheaper booze from Solly's friends.

Even though the three men from Chicago paid the Bernsteins for the liquor they had bought, Abe was furious. In a bold move of disregard for consequences, he stormed into the Bethune Precinct Police office and threw open Cliff's office door.

"Is it true what I hear? Are you the one that sold our good liquor to these no good assholes? Liquor they turned into nothing but water and sold it for nothing? What in God's name were you thinking? I told you to watch these guys, not get in bed with them."

He dropped into the chair in front of the desk, the very one from which Solly had made his appeal to Cliff. He seemed to deflate from the effort of his tirade.

"You want a drink, Abe?" Cliff asked. He pulled open the bottom desk drawer.

"No I don't want no goddam drink. I want answers. What the hell were you thinking?"

Cliff poured himself a drink and took a big swallow.

"I was thinking two things. First, I figured we could make some money on their stupidity but, most important, I wanted to keep track of them. I wanted to know about their operations. I figured the best way to know what they were up to was to help them out. And they did pay us back, Abe."

"Big goddam deal. They paid us back with money that belonged to us. They sold that shit they made to our customers. We still come out on the short end. I'm disappointed in you, Cliff. I thought you had better sense than this."

Cliff sat looking at Abe and didn't speak. He had learned that was the easiest way to get Abe to calm down. And he did calm down. He stood up and reached for the half-full glass in front of Cliff. Downing it in one swallow, he left the office without another word.

Late that summer, breweries and distilleries around Detroit worked long hours in preparation for an American Legion conference scheduled for the fall. Thousands of Legionnaires were due in the city for one of their infamous week-long gatherings. These patriots would saturate the city with money and their demands for women, food, and drink would be nearly insatiable.

News of the Legionnaires' conference was the first good news in Detroit since the stock market crash three years earlier, Times had been very difficult for everyone from Henry Ford to the Bernsteins to Solly Levine. Men left unemployed by massive layoffs around the country didn't buy automobiles. To make ends meet they began making gin in their basements and bathtubs, creating more competition for the Bernsteins. Solly did better when layoffs first started; men tried to make the most of their last few dollars by betting them on boxers or horses but, eventually, even his book suffered. Tired women stood on street corners in any weather hawking pencils, apples, cast-off clothing or themselves to feed the tattered children clinging to their skirts. Long lines formed in front of buildings where free soup and a blanket could be had, much of it supplied by the Bernsteins at the request of elected officials. It wasn't necessarily altruism that prompted their magnanimous gestures. They figured by making those officials look good to the voters, the re-election of men who would cast a blind eye to the Bernsteins' activities would be assured.

But soon the Legionnaires would fill the hotels, gorge themselves in the restaurants and speakeasies, and spend lavishly in what remained of the retail shops. These were men who had managed to hold on to their jobs and had even prospered enough to be able to afford attendance at the conference. Spirits brightened as chefs freshened their menus with new recipes, shopkeepers painted the front of their buildings, magicians practiced new acts, and hookers bought new shoes. Everyone was sure to profit from this conference.

Outside of their business, the Bernsteins themselves had never fought in armed combat, but they had been welcomed as members of the American Legion. They could always be counted on when funds were needed for the various Legion projects. Consequently, the Legionnaires could be counted on for regular purchases of whiskey and women. This year's conference would be a windfall for the Bernsteins.

Cliff had kept an eye on the three men from Chicago and was satisfied they were never going to be able to pull off the takeover they had planned. They were just small-time operators, taking a few small bets, pimping for a few women, and occasionally selling a crate of beer or whiskey. They were never going to be a serious threat, he decided. Still they bore watching. He knew that Al Capone was still behind them and could augment their forces at any time.

Late in August, Solly came to Cliff's office at the Bethune Precinct again, making the same plea for his friends that he had in the spring. Once again, he said, these idiots had taken a bet they couldn't cover on a "boat race" as it was called, a fixed horse race. Again, they needed thousands of dollars and they needed it in a hurry. Cliff wasn't going to get into this again. He told Solly he'd have to talk to the Bernsteins himself.

Cliff was surprised two days later when Solly said Ray Bernstein would honor the request. Once again, the three men from Chicago watered down the whiskey beyond what had become standard, severely cut the price, and sold it to the men who had arrived early for the Legionnaires' conference. This time, however, they did not reimburse Ray Bernstein for his advance. They sent their friend Solly, who seemed to have all the right connections, to ask for more time. By the time the Legionnaires' conference was over, they would have Ray's money, Solly promised Ray.

The whole time Solly was giving explanations and assurances, Ray sat placidly at his desk, his perpetual scowl growing deeper, his eyebrows pulled closer together. Every inch the gentleman his brother was not, Ray was not given to angry outbursts but his physiognomy betrayed his emotion. Solly paced and smoked as he spoke trying to ignore the growing storm in Ray's face.

"I'll tell you what I'm going to do," Ray finally said quietly. "Me and my brothers are tired, and we can't keep up with everything anymore. Maybe we should let your new friends in on some of the action. We have plenty of money to take care of our families. I know your friends have been having a difficult time financially. In these difficult times, we should be thinking of how we can help out."

Solly stopped pacing and turned to face the man who held his future and that of his friends in his hands. Solly didn't trust what Ray was saying, but he had no choice but to accept at face value what Ray was saying.

"What I want you to do is set up a meeting with the boys. Once the bill is paid off, we're going to let you boys handle the horse bets and the alcohol."

Solly grew increasingly agitated under that cold blue gaze. Why would the Bernsteins' want to give up such lucrative aspects of their operations? It was true they were losing control but to just give over control was something entirely out of character, but Solly said he would arrange the peace conference.

The three men from Chicago were elated when they heard of the plans for a meeting. They had won, they had made the inroads into the Purples' operations they had planned to, and they had done it without bloodshed and with the Bernsteins' own money. Izzy gave one of his henchman a roll of bills and told him to drive up to Port Huron to pick up Virginia White, his eighteen-year-old girlfriend who had gone there for a last few days in the sun before the chill of a Michigan autumn settled in. She arrived back in Detroit just in time for dinner. They headed for a speakeasy where they ate and drank till the morning hours.

Hymie Paul was equally relieved that their troubles were over and the Bernsteins seemed to have no retribution planned. He went home and went to bed early. No need to worry about tomorrow. Ray Bernstein was coming to them with his tail between his legs, ready to share the city with them. Lebowitz partied all night, drinking himself into a horrendous hangover.

The peace conference was scheduled to be held in two days, September 16 at three o'clock at the Collingwood Apartments, Number 211. It was just a few blocks from where Solly and his friends made book, so they worked till two forty-five, leaving their guns behind. This was a peace conference, after all. They wanted to show good faith.

Apartment 211 was at the back of the building, overlooking a shabby alley. When Hymie knocked, Ray Bernstein himself opened the door. Hymie was impressed, the Boss himself opening the door for the men to whom he was giving a sizable portion of his operations. Ray Bernstein was slim, well dressed in a custom-tailored brown wool suit and a brown felt hat perched at a jaunty angle on his head. From behind him, Hymie heard the strains of "Stardust" being scratched out on a Victrola. As the guests entered the apartment, someone turned the machine off, not bothering to raise the needle from the record.

Ray stepped back ushering the guests into the tiny apartment. Izzy looked around a bit surprised. When Mr. Capone proposed a conference, it was always held at a luxurious hotel in a large room with a tantalizing array of food and drink. This was just a cramped little apartment, a worn burgundy davenport standing against one wall, two mismatched chairs pushed into opposite corners. Instead of the heady aroma of a lavish meal, the air was redolent with the fragrance of the opened bucket of green paint standing in the doorway to the next room. He had heard the Bernsteins had no class, but this was a surprise.

Ray Bernstein had brought three men with him and introduced them. Harry Keywell was a smooth-faced, innocent looking man whose name Joe recognized. He was said to be been one of the men dressed in police uniforms who had gunned down men in a Chicago warehouse, the killing that the newspapers were calling the St. Valentine's Day Massacre. His soft exterior hid a bitter, hardened man who would has soon beat someone with his own fists as have a steak dinner.

Izzy was surprised to see Harry Fleisher whom he had worked for briefly. Word on the street had it that the feds were after Fleisher, and he had left for Kansas City. Twenty-nine years old and small of build, he was as eager to beat someone as Keywell was. The feds wanted him for kidnapping and receiving stolen property. Izzy didn't recognize the third man whom Ray introduced as Irving Milberg.

The four guests shook hands as they were all introduced. Hymie and Nigger Joe sat on the couch, Izzy perched on its arm. Milberg passed a box of cigars around, and the guests helped themselves. Solly stood nervously at the door refusing a cigar. After a few moments, conversation fell of,f and Fleisher looked across the room at his boss.

"Where is that guy with the books?" he asked.

"What guy is that?" Izzy wanted to know.

"The accountant," Ray said. "He was supposed to be here by now to help us with the details of splitting things up. I'll go down to the street and see if I can see him." Bernstein left the apartment leaving the door standing open behind him.

Hymie leaned deep into the sofa, inhaling the strong taste of the cigar, tilting his head back to blow smoke toward the ceiling. Leibowitz rubbed his forehead where it throbbed from the dozens of drinks he had downed the night before. Solly paced in front of the window, watching Ray Bernstein slide behind the wheel of a black Chrysler parked in the alley. What was he doing? Solly wondered. He was supposed to be out front watching for the accountant. He heard the engine of the Chrysler race and blanched. In the same instant, he heard the click of a trigger and the roar of a gun being discharged. He dropped to the floor as a bullet barely missed the end of his nose and thunked into Nigger Joe's chest. More bullets tore through the air and into the three men on the couch. Eight sunk into Hymie Paul who slumped where he sat on the couch, his cigar clenched in his hand. Lebowitz had attempted to make it into the next room but only made it as far as the tiny hallway where a hail of gunfire sent him to the floor. Izzy got as far as the next bedroom, but Fleisher found him, planting two bullets not more than an inch apart in his forehead.

Fleisher returned to the living room and looked at Solly.

"You okay?" he asked, dragging the terrified man to his feet. Solly could barely manage a nod but realized he remained unscathed as the three shooters stood together a moment in front of the open door. One of them said, "Let's go" then all three dropped their guns in the open bucket of paint and darted out of the apartment, forcing Solly ahead of them, Arriving at the curb where the Chrysler stood idling, Ray Bernstein at the wheel, Solly realized Fleisher was not with them. Bernstein raced the engine nervously as he saw the last of the shooters emerge from the building. Sliding into the back seat Fleisher muttered, "Nigger Joe was still living a bit."

Bernstein stomped on the accelerator, heaving the Chrysler into the street, barely avoiding a woman pushing a baby carriage on the sidewalk. The car squealed around corners and past curious onlookers for only a few minutes before Ray pulled into another alleyway and all but the driver's door popped open. Ray pulled a roll of bills from his vest pocket and pushed it into Solly's hands. "I'm your pal, Solly," he said then pushed his pal from the car. Solly stood amazed and motionless, trying to absorb the events of the last few minutes as he watched the Chrysler disappear up the street.

Ray Bernstein was his pal. He had said so himself. He had to do something to protect his protector. He had an idea.

Word of the killings at the Collingwood spread quickly with the building superintendent and residents of other apartments freely granting interviews to the police and reporters. Descriptions of the men seen leaving the apartment and the car they drove were detailed and fairly accurate. Knowing he would be picked up soon anyway, Solly presented himself to Lieutenant Malin at the Bethune Precinct whom he told reporters had been his friend for some years. He said he and his three friends were on their way to visit a mutual friend, Harry Klein who owned a deli. They had been busy and hadn't had lunch yet, he said. The deli was close to their office so they decided to walk. From nowhere, some number of men, he wasn't sure how many, jumped the men and forced them into a Buick then drove them to the Collingwood apartment. The kidnappers forced them into the apartment and, without explanation, opened fire. Solly managed to escape death by feigning being mortally wounded. When he was sure they were gone, he crawled out of the apartment and away from the building.

Ray Bernstein had already telephoned Cliff Malin before Solly appeared at the precinct station. Without going into detail, Ray told his police officer that Solly was actually the shooter at the Collingwood. Nothing Solly said was to be believed, Ray said, which wasn't all that difficult since Solly never told his story the same way twice. He had been spirited away first in a Packard, then a Buick then a Chrysler. At first, he was unable to say how many men had kidnapped him and his friends. By the time he talked to the *Detroit Times* reporter, however, he was sure there had been five men, though he was unable to say what they looked like. In one telling of the story they were headed to the deli for lunch, but later they were going to see Harry Klein about a debt he owed.

Malin went through the motions of an investigation, unable to ignore three such visible murders, though he knew ahead of time what the outcome was to be. He doubted that Solly actually did the shootings as Ray told him, but Solly was to go to prison for the deaths nonetheless.

Wayne County Prosecutor Harry Toy had other ideas, however. Blood in the streets was becoming far too common, especially with elections coming up soon. No precinct lieutenant was going to handle such a public case. He called Malin and told him to leave the case alone; Toy would take things from here. He called a press conference to announce he had enough of bloodshed and the Purple Gang. He distributed a long list of names whom he either knew or suspected were members of the Purples. A city-wide dragnet he was initiating that day was designed to pull in those men on the list and any others that might result from tips received at police headquarters. "I want these men dead or alive," he said.

Cliff quickly called Ray Bernstein with the news, advising him to leave town quickly.

Phones at all police precincts rang non-stop as tips poured in about where the men on the list could be found. Following Cliff Malin's phone call, Ray Bernstein threw a few personal items and two guns into a small suitcase and flew out the door, headed for his friend, Charlie "The Professor" Auerbach who later told police he was a jewelry salesman. Charlie was a fairly new compatriot of the Purples, and, since he had never been arrested, Ray figured the police wouldn't think to look there for him. He underestimated the will of his enemies to see him out of business. Acting on an anonymous tip, Charlie's apartment was surrounded by a platoon of heavily armed officers. Inside, in addition to Charlie and Ray, they found Charlie's wife and a young cabaret singer named Elsie Carroll. Between them, the women had nine thousand dollars. The apartment also housed a cache of tear gas and guns fit for a small barrage of defense. Angry but defeated, Ray left quietly with the police.

Within forty-eight hours of Ray's arrest, the rest of the gunmen from the Collingwood Massacre, as reporters dubbed it, were under arrest.

# CHAPTER 20

▼

Cliff stamped his feet against the cold on the metal grating of the overpass that tied the parking lot to Ford's River Rouge plant across Miller Road on a damp March morning in 1932 Next to him, Harry Bennett pulled his collar up and clapped his kidskin gloved hands together as he surveyed the scene on the street below. Hundreds of workers milled around in the cold March air, many under-dressed for the spring chill. Harry recognized many of them as employees who should have been at their positions on the lines amid the roaring and chunking of the factory machines inside. George Schmidt should be installing right taillights. Herbert Hale should be fastening inside door handles on front doors. Sam Booker belonged on Line 4 sinking spark plugs into their chambers.

Mingled among the unworking workers were men who had been fired for a variety of infringements. Allen McGrath had been overheard calling Mr. Ford a son of a bitch. Fred Frederickson was clocked spending eighteen minutes in the bathroom in one day. And still others in the crowd had been turned down for jobs at Ford because they looked feeble or didn't stand on the hiring side of the line or couldn't produce the required thirty-five dollars and an address. Even from the overpass suspended twenty-five feet in the air, Harry could see those men's faces gaunt with fear and desperation. He didn't care. From time to time, one of the men would shout up at Harry and shake his fist or a sign he was carry-ing, but Harry didn't respond. The signs called for a six-hour day or free medical care. Red banners flew in the morning breeze, which both Cliff and Harry knew meant that the American Communist Party had a hand in this demonstration, if not having completely engineered it from the outset.

"These sons of bitches," Harry muttered to Cliff. "They're lucky they even have a god damn job the way things have been these last few years. There's plenty of men would be happy to have a paycheck at all."

Cliff said nothing, thinking about the call he had received before sunrise from Harry, sounding yet another alarm about threats to Mr. Ford, the plant, and himself. Cliff nearly hadn't responded, so immune had he become to these phone calls. Besides, The Rouge was in Dearborn, outside Cliff's jurisdiction, but he was off duty today and he thought, what the hell, Harry's a friend.

Harry saw Walter Reuther working his way through the crowd of men below, hoisting signs up, patting men on the back, urging them to stand their ground. Reuther was a pink-cheeked twenty-year old when he showed up at the River Rouge plant in 1927 looking for a job as a tool and die maker. He had to persuade the guard at the gate that so young a man could have the skills necessary for so prestigious a job, insisting on being tested to determine his qualifications. Though his skills turned out to be minimal, the supervisor had been sufficiently impressed with the kid's answers to technical questions that he gave him a job for a dollar five an hour.

During the first few weeks of his employment at The Rouge, Walt had been impressed. The work areas were bright and fastidiously clean with fresh air circulating throughout the factory. Daily, an army of 5,000 men repaired, painted and cleaned everything in sight. A special suction mechanism siphoned iron dust away from the area where piston rings were made. Concessionaires who brought lunches into the plant were required to meet strict nutritional standards and calorie limits. He couldn't know all these measures were a result of Henry's obsession with cleanliness, not his wish to create a pleasant, safe working environment for his employees. Whatever the motivation, it was a far different world from the steamy steel mills where men were frequently injured or maimed that Walt had left behind in West Virginia.

Like so many others, he had come to Detroit on the promise of good pay, steady work, and a safe working environment. And like so many others, he learned the myth of the highly touted Henry Ford and how he handled his employees. The Five Dollar Day, much ballyhooed in 1914 when it was introduced, was only available to men who met a string of conditions such as age and length of employment. Ford's Security Department made the private lives of Ford employees their business, watching for marital infidelity, drunkenness, and any other moral turpitude. By the time Walter Reuther became employed, a condition called Ford Stomach was rampant. Conveyor belts were speeded up by just a few seconds in an effort to get men working faster. The constant fear of being discovered in what could be considered a suspicious situation—in the company of a woman who wasn't your wife, home Sunday morning instead of at church, failing to pay a debt—created an ever-present anxiety that showed up as digestive distress. Walter Reuther could sit quietly no longer as he watched fellow workers dismissed for petty reasons or not hired because of their appearance. Reuther appealed to various trade unions but was rebuffed by union officials who thought turning nuts and bolts on an assembly line did not require sufficient skill to warrant union membership. Eventually fired from Ford's for his rabble rousing and blacklisted at all other factories, Reuther moved to Russia. He was back now, working under an assumed name, but Harry Bennett never forgot a face.

Reuther returned to Detroit with an increased fervor to right the wrongs he saw in the factories. He came back armed with the knowledge that, although the American unions were not interested in his problems, the American Communist Party most certainly was. Today was the day selected to let Henry Ford and the world know that the employees had the power to bring the great machine of industry to a grinding halt. The event was timed to gain the maximum attention and assert the maximum influence. All the world's eyes were on Henry Ford; on April 1 he was to unveil his new V-8 engine that was expected to catapult the company light years ahead of other automobile manufacturers. Reporters from around the world had been arriving in Detroit for weeks in an effort to ferret out any detail of the new engine in order to get the story ahead of their colleagues.

Responding to the call by the Communist Party to assert their rights and power, Ford employees were calling their event a Hunger March. They had marched in the bitter spring chill from Detroit to Dearborn where Chief of Police Carl Brooks asked Walter Reuther for his permit to stage a parade. He admitted he had failed to obtain one and was ordered to disperse the crowd. Reuther milled among the men telling them about the Chief's orders but not telling them to go home. When the Chief, a former member of Harry Bennett's Service Department, realized his orders were being ignored, he began to bellow.

"Reuther or whatever you call yourself these days, I told you to get your men out of here. They can either go back to work or they can go home, but they can't stay here. You don't have a permit."

Cliff and Harry watched from the bridge as the men began responding to Chief Brooks, not by leaving but by bellowing back. Fists rose in the air, picket signs were shaken in officers' faces and the decibel level began to rise. A loud metallic clunk on the street somewhere deep in the crowd made Harry and Cliff turn suddenly. Tear gas spewed from a can in the midst of the marchers. Then another was lobbed and another. The gas spread upward and out as men choked and coughed and daubed at their eyes. As the marchers scattered to escape the fog of gas, dropping their banners and signs, the police headed after them, clubbing any they could reach. Cliff and Harry heard the cries of the men and watched as they fell to their knees or on their backs, the crunch of club against bone reaching them up on the overpass.

The workers replied to the officers' blows with a hail of rocks and clubbings with fence posts that had been ripped from the ground. Chief Brooks dodged clubs as he made his way across the yard to nearby fire trucks, intending to have them train their hoses on the men. Several of the Hunger Marchers anticipated his move and arrived at the trucks first. They hauled firemen down from the trucks, pushing them onto the street as other marchers scrambled up the trucks to incapacitate them.

"I've had enough of this shit," Harry yelled at Cliff over the roar of the marchers below. He turned and headed back into the plant, reappearing a few moments later at the door of the plant on the street. Cliff could see him waving his arms and pointing at the men who worked for him positioned around the perimeter of the crowd. Apparently following Harry's gesticulated orders, the men reached into metal cabinets on the side of the building and extracted their own thick fire hoses. Icy blasts of water sprayed over the already freezing marchers. Harry pushed his way into the midst of the melee, shouting and shoving.

Nineteen-year-old Joseph York, a member of the Young Communist League, recognized Harry and approached him. Both stood screaming at each other unable to hear above the din of the crowd. Suddenly, a lump of slag sailed through the air, landing on the side of Harry's head. Harry, his face scarlet, blood streaming from his wound, grabbed the young man and wrestled him to the ground. The two rolled around still shouting and landing a few easy punches on each other until the young man had managed to pull free of Harry. He had barely staggered to his feet when the stutter of machine gun fire rang out over the cacophony of the fighting men. The order from Chief Brooks had been to fire over the heads of the marchers, but someone's aim had been poor. A bullet sunk into the back of Joseph York's head, killing him instantly. His corpse collapsed on top of Harry as three other men were struck by machine gun fire.

The men in the parking lot, officers and marchers alike, fell silent. Fists dropped to their sides in mid-punch, feet about to land on a kneecap fell to the ground. Officers lowered their clubs, fence posts clunked to the pavement, men locked in combat on the ground rose to their feet. Not a word was spoken.

Cliff turned and headed down to the crowd as reporters and photographers scrambled away from the scene, as anxious to return to their radio stations and newspapers with the story as they were concerned about their own safety. Cliff forced his way through the crowd to Harry's side and dragged him inside the safety of the building. As Cliff pulled, Harry continued yelling and landing punches in the face or on the back of the marchers.

"This wouldn't have happened if you assholes had stayed on the job instead of making trouble," he bellowed. His was the only voice that could be heard.

Inside the building, Harry straightened his tie and tucked his shirt back in his pants. Cliff saw no fear in his eyes, only vile hatred. He stood back to avoid the flying spittle Harry sprayed as he continued yelling.

"Those bastards. Who do they think they're fucking with? I ain't no goddam yahoo from Apple Alley, Kentucky for crissakes. I'll teach the fuckers to mess with me."

Four days later, fifteen thousand mourners packed the streets for the funerals of Joseph York and the three others, now deemed martyrs, who had died in what the press called the Battle of the Overpass. Harry Bennett ordered his Servicemen to circulate among the mourners, writing down names or taking photographs of men they recognized as Ford employees. Over the next few weeks, those men found their time cards missing when they checked out at the end of their shift, their final paycheck at the paymaster's window.

Harry and Cliff laughed over their scotches one day after Harry had claimed retribution for his injuries and for the riot. Splayed on the wall of his office were photographs taken at the funerals and Harry would point to men in them.

"That was the first one to get his walking papers," he laughed. "That son of a bitch has been with us for twelve years, but he's gone now." Pulling his air gun from his desk drawer, he fired at the target on the file cabinet. "I always get my man," he said, striking the target dead center and ringing the bell.

# CHAPTER 21

▼

Janet McDonald grew up in Ireland and married her husband, Ian, when she was eighteen. Ian farmed his family's meager allotment, scraping out a bare existence by working bone-wearying long days in all kinds of weather. Janet's sister had moved to Michigan and sent frequent letters about the relatively easy life there. Jobs were plentiful, everyone owned a car, and weekends were free to go to the lake or spend with your family in the park, she wrote Ian and Janet left their native land to get their share of the good life.

But life in America had not been what Janet has expected. The paychecks were bigger than any either of them had ever seen, but Ian usually took it straight to the bar. If Janet wasn't working, she would meet him at the bar and extract enough from his pay envelope to meet the week's bills, but often, she worked late at her own job, a string of waitressing, cleaning, and ironing jobs that often kept her late into the night.

Two years after arriving in Detroit, the couple had their first child, a beautiful little girl whom Janet named Pearl. Janet begged Ian to move to the country where the air was clean and Pearl could grow up with the same country values her parents had, but Ian refused. He was staying in the city where he could support his family on only five days work a week, sometimes as little as eight hours a day.

Ian's charming good looks and ready smile made it easy for him to get hired. He worked in foundries and at first one auto manufacturer after another as his employers soon tired of his surly nature when he showed up drunk or hung over. Argumentative and prone to throwing a punch at anyone who disagreed with him, male or female, Ian was regularly handed a couple of dollars and sent home in the middle of the afternoon to avoid an impending fight. He would be unemployed for days at a time before he would tell Janet he had lost his job. By then, the pittance he had been paid had found its way to any one of a dozen bars in the neighborhood.

As much as she could, Janet hid her meager earnings from her husband, spending them on food and paying the rent before he got his hands on it. When he demanded her wages with kicks and punches, she often had to quit her job till she recovered from her injuries.

Four years after arriving in Detroit, on a clear, sunny day in May, Ian lay on the couch, bloated and nearly unconscious after drinking non-stop for two weeks. Janet came home from work and found him cold and blue, an empty whiskey bottle overturned on the floor beside him. Janet borrowed enough money from her employer to buy a cheap casket and had her husband buried at Sacred Heart Catholic church.

She was able to work steadily after that, feeding and clothing herself and her daughter and nibbling away at the four-thousand-dollar debt her husband had left her. Selling what few possessions had any value, Janet moved herself and her daughter into a rooming house run by Mr. and Mrs. John Hall. The Halls liked Janet and Pearl and often invited them to Sunday dinner. Afterwards, Janet would play the piano and Pearl would sing. By 1939, Pearl was nine years old and barely remembered the days when her father came home drunk and mean, or she had to go to bed hungry for lack of money.

Janet longed for a better job than those she had had while Ian was alive. She wanted to dress nicely and meet nice people, maybe even find a husband to take care of her and Pearl, but she didn't know where to look. One Sunday afternoon in 1939 as they sipped iced tea in the back yard after dinner, Janet told her land-lady of her wish for a good job in an office. Mrs. Hall said she didn't know any-thing about finding jobs since she had never worked herself, but her son had a friend who seemed to be able to help out with everything. His name was Cliff Malin and, if Janet wanted, she would ask her son to speak to Mr. Malin. Janet said she would take whatever assistance she could get.

A few days later Cliff appeared on the Hall's front porch and introduced him-self. He and Janet talked for a while in the front room and Cliff promised to pick her up Saturday morning and introduce her to someone who would give her a job in an office. The job paid fifty cents an hour and Janet could be home in time to meet Pearl after school every day. Janet was elated.

On Saturday, Janet was up early and fussed over her appearance. She was a square-faced woman with wide shoulders and not much of a waist. Her fine red hair curled at its own will and her nose spread gracelessly across her face. Mr.

Malin made it sound as though she already had the job, but she wanted to make a good impression nonetheless. She finally decided to push her hair on top of her head and cover it with a navy blue hat that matched the suit she had borrowed from one of the women she worked with.

The sign on the front of the building where Cliff took Janet said "Great Lakes Development Co." and Janet wasn't sure what that meant, but she didn't want to show her ignorance by asking. Inside, Cliff introduced her to Bill McBride, a burly Irishman with thick red hair as unruly as her own. His green eyes looked her up and down in what she thought was an approving manner. She felt instantly at ease with him when she heard his brogue, probably from Dublin.

Janet's job, he told her, was to work with numbers. Was she any good with numbers? he asked her.

"My mother always told me I should do something that involved ciphering. She said she never saw anyone who could work numbers like me."

Bill explained that all over the city were people collecting bets for the Great Lakes Development Co. People would bet on everything from horse races to when—and if—Howard Hughes would complete his flight form Los Angeles to New York. Runners would bring the money and the betting slips in, and it was up to Janet and the other workers to keep track of everything. He led Janet into a large rectangular room that was stripped of anything but the barest working necessities. The morning sun streamed through dirty windows over the heads of the workers. The room was filled with the clacking of calculating machines and typewriters as men and women tabulated and sorted a variety of betting slips and collection sheets. Bill led his new employee through the long room to two offices more plushly furnished than the main room. He said one was his and the other was his partner's, Art Thatcher. Each man had large mahogany desks with two upholstered chairs in front. Black leather chairs stood behind the desks. He stood in the doorway of his office and called out to someone. In a few minutes, a lanky, bald man who looked impatient appeared in the office. He was introduced as Edgar and told he would teach Janet what she needed to know for her new job.

Janet was originally apprehensive about the job when she found out what she would be doing. Gambling was illegal. What if she got arrested? What would become of Pearl? How would she pay for lawyers? But she reasoned getting arrested couldn't be much of a threat. This office was right on a busy street and people came and went openly. And, after all, it was a police officer who had brought her here in the first place.

Janet was immediately smitten by Bill McBride. When one of the other girls in the office said he was divorced, Janet used every excuse to bump into him or talk to him. Three weeks after she started work at the Great Lakes Development Co., Bill took Janet to dinner at the Blue Orchid then over to Luigi's Café to hear Mezz Mezzrow play jazz. When he dropped her off at her boarding house, he walked her to the front door and kissed her gruffly on the mouth then strode down the sidewalk and jumped over the picket fence that bordered the yard. Despite the fact it was three in the morning, he honked loudly as he drove away.

Janet and Bill dated regularly after that first night. Janet's sister took Pearl when Janet thought she would be out all night. She had never been so in love, nor had anyone ever paid so much attention to her. Bill took her to all the fashionable restaurants and nightclubs she had only read about in the newspaper's society pages. Money she should have spent on paying off Ian's debts sometimes went for a new dress or a pair of shoes befitting the places Bill took her. He introduced her to many of his friends who took them sailing on the river or drove them to the theater in long limousines. Janet tried not to notice the thick envelopes that passed between McBride and many of the men they met. Often, she wasn't introduced to the other people, but she recognized their faces from the newspaper. A city councilman, a police lieutenant Bill called Mac and one time, even the mayor received these envelopes. She asked no questions.

A twang of conscience pulled at Janet when Pearl occasionally complained of her mother's absences, but her feelings for Bill and the life he was showing her soon assuaged her maternal misgivings. It helped that Bill often brought little presents for Pearl, a doll or combs for her hair.

And Janet's original misgivings about the job evaporated as she fell more deeply in love with Bill. Bill had given her two raises in the six months she had been working for him and, just as Cliff had promised, she was home to meet Pearl when she came home from school.

On an especially sticky August afternoon, Janet stepped down the steps of the bus and walked the two blocks home, her feet aching and her back sore. Pearl had piano lessons today and wouldn't be home for nearly an hour, time enough for a long soak in the tub. She let herself in the front door and started upstairs when Mrs. Hall appeared from the kitchen at the back of the house and said Janet had a guest in the front room. Puzzled and annoyed, Janet turned and headed into the living room. The woman waiting there was in her late twenties, tall and blonde and fashionably dressed in a pale blue suit, no perspiration on her face, despite the humid day. She was smoking and pacing nervously when Janet walked in the room. She introduced herself as Virginia McBride, Bill's wife.

A crease formed across Janet's forehead. "I thought he was divorced," she said.

"Well, he ain't," Virginia said. She had a nasal twang Janet had never heard before. "We was going to get divorced but never did. And now, we're getting back together, and I want you to stay away from him, see."

"He hasn't said anything to me about getting back together with you."

"Well, I'm saying something to you. Stay away from Bill, Sister, if you know what's good for you."

Pivoting on her heel, Virginia stamped out of the house, slamming the front door as she left. Janet dropped into the nearest chair. How could this be? Bill loved her. He wouldn't go back to his wife. But the next morning when she confronted him in his office, he admitted that is just what he had done.

"I was going to tell you, Janet. I didn't mean to hurt you, Kid, but Virginia and I, we're just meant for each other. We're two of a kind. Sure, we fight all the time, but we belong together."

Janet returned to her desk in a daze. Unable to concentrate on her work, she left early. Pearl was still at the school and the Halls were nowhere to be seen. Janet paced the front room picking up a vase then a figurine then an ashtray, turning them over and looking but not seeing them through the tears that flooded from her eyes. How could Bill treat her in such a grand fashion for all those months if he hadn't loved her? She certainly hadn't done well with men, a drunken sot of a husband and now a miserable clout of a boyfriend. She raced up the stairs to her room, flinging herself across the bed. She had no idea how long she cried. The late afternoon sun was streaming through her window when she was finally able to stem the tide of tears and heard the Halls downstairs opening and closing doors and talking quietly.

She stared at the ceiling convinced there was only one way past this heartache.

The next morning Dan Kirk picked his way around two sheet-draped stretchers in front of a garage a block from the Halls' boarding house. At the entrance to the garage, he pushed his white Panama hat to the back of his head and peered in, pulling his notebook and pen from his inside jacket pocket.

"Morning, Pete," he nodded to the policeman standing next to a green Buick. A hose attached to the car's exhaust pipe stretched around to the driver's side door. Pete, Detective Pete Janik, held a stack of letters. Dan jotted down the details of the car including the license plate number before the cop cknowledged him.

"Looks like a murder suicide," the officer said. "Woman and a little girl."

"Any ID?"

"The woman's driver's license says Janet McDonald. She lived in the next block. Woman who owns the garage said this McDonald woman had a little girl named Pearl."

Scribbling as he talked and sniffing the air, Dan asked, "Is that exhaust fumes I smell?"

"Yeah, but you know we have to go through the autopsy before we can say for sure. But they were both blue and that hose was stuck in the driver's window. Doesn't take a genius to figure it out."

"Any note?"

"A whole passle of them."

"How many is a passle?"

"Six or so."

"What's in them?"

"All I can tell you is they're addressed to Bugas over at the FBI, Police Commissioner Pickert, the governor, and some guy named McBride. She didn't leave you guys out either. There's one for each of the newspapers."

"Can I see them?"

The detective's voice rose. "You kidding? I can't let you see them."

"How about just the one that's addressed to my paper?"

"No deal. Get it from your editor."

"How about if you let me hand deliver it to him."

"I might. Long as you don't ask me to see the other ones."

"This is me not asking."

Pete flashed a quick grin at the reporter then led him to the squad car at the curb. He reached inside and withdrew a stack of letters and started to thumb through them.

"Shit," he said. "I don't have time for this." He shoved the letters into Dan's chest. "Find the one for your paper and leave the others on the seat."

Dan waited till the cop was out of sight then opened the letters one by one. In the envelope addressed to his paper he read:

Dear Sirs:

On this night a girl has ended her life because of the mental cruelty caused by Racketeer William McBride, Great Lakes Numbers House operator. McBride is the go-between man for Lieutenant John McCarthy. He arranges the fix between our dutiful Lieutenant and the Racketeers.

Should you care to learn more of this story, get in touch with McBride through the book at 222 Lafayette Street West. Phone Clifford 1572.

He glories in telling lies so don't believe everything he tells you as I did.

Janet McDonald.

# CHAPTER 22

▼

Homer Ferguson stepped out on his front porch and took a deep breath. The air, freshened overnight by a soft spring rain, was sweet with the fragrance of his prize lilac bushes. Lawns, vibrant green with new growth, stretched along both sides of the street. Trees heavy with buds lined the street while across from his home, Mrs. Johnson's famous tulips flooded her yard with pools of reds and yellows and pinks.

Six feet tall and two hundred pounds with a shock of silvery hair receding from his forehead, Judge Ferguson was the image of sagacity and justice. Eleven years on the bench had sharpened his commitment to the law and to the citizens who had elected him. When the Michigan Supreme Court appointed him as a one-man grand jury to look into Janet McDonald's deathbed allegations, Detroiters were confident of a thorough, probing investigation.

Ferguson's appointment was born of public outrage at official responses to McDonald's allegations. Members of the City Council called on Mayor Richard Reading for an immediate investigation, but Mayor Reading said he didn't want to take any action until the city prosecutor and the police commissioner returned to town. City Council President Edward Jeffries requested that the Mayor demand the officials return home.

"I am no soldier but it seems to me when the enemy is at the gate, all leaves are canceled, but it appears several of your police officials have been out of the city during this investigation," he told the Mayor. "Two or three weeks have gone by. That's an awfully long getaway period."

The Mayor remained firm in his stance to let the men return in their own time.

When City Prosecutor Duncan McCrea finally did return to Detroit, he called a press conference. With the courthouse looming behind him, McCrea told reporters, "We have completed our investigation and find no reason to issue any indictments."

He had spent less than a week on the investigation.

Attempting to deflect attention from himself, Lieutenant John McCarthy ordered all precincts to step up raids on several small gambling houses. When the Police Superintendent Fred Frahm returned to town, he joined some of his men on a raid in which the total take was one adding machine and the princely sum of ten dollars and sixty-five cents.

This spring morning in 1940, Judge Ferguson picked up the newspaper from his lawn and, adjusting his wire-rimmed glasses, glanced at the front page as he walked to the car. A small item at the bottom of the page caught his attention.

### Target of Investigation Found Slain

A Detroit gambler who was being investigated by the Ferguson Grand Jury was found dead in Florida yesterday. William McBride, one-time operator of the Great Lakes Development Company, had been choked before his body was dumped in a ditch, according to the Florida State Police.

The Judge's heart sank. McBride had been the object of an intensive search since the beginning of this assignment, but now there was no hope of finding out what he knew about payoffs to police and city officials. It was just one more frustration piled on top of all the others in the investigation. The article said there were no suspects and no leads in the killing.

In the six months since Ferguson's appointment, he had known many frustrations. Lieutenant McCarthy had been the first person interviewed. McCarthy was head of a special police squad charged with finding and closing illegal gambling operations. The squad operated autonomously. Their record was less than sterling. In over a year, they had seized 12,000 rolls of adding machine tape, 126,000 policy pads and 1 million mutuel betting slips. But only $6,830 had been turned in from operations that generated millions of dollars a year. Still, McCarthy denied taking payoffs. Judge Ferguson had sentenced him to five days in jail for lying, but it did nothing to loosen McCarthy's tongue. Dozens of interviews revealed little information. Records couldn't be found and people disappeared. Ferguson and his assistant, the tireless Chester O'Hara, felt thwarted at every turn. And now Bill McBride was dead.

Driving up the street, Ferguson glanced as he always did at the gracious Victorian-style mansions and manicured yards in the neighborhood. He loved this old section of town. In a few more weeks, the ancient oak trees now standing naked along the streets would be lush with new leaves, forming a long arbor shading passing traffic. Today, though, the bright morning sun shone through the bare branches, casting intricate, lacy patterns on the pavement. He did not noticed the battered black Chevrolet that pulled away from the curb two houses away and was now following him.

At Jefferson Avenue, Ferguson turned right and headed into town along with hundreds of other commuters, the Chevy close behind. At Washington Boulevard, the Judge signaled to make a left turn and had just begun moving the car toward the center of the road when the Chevy raced around from behind and pulled up on his left. The man in the passenger seat rolled down the window.

"Hey, Your Honor," the man yelled. Ferguson thought he detected a New York accent, but it was difficult to tell over the sound of traffic. His mouth fell open as he saw the muzzle of a pistol appear at the windowsill. The man smiled slowly then said, "Pow!"

Ferguson ducked, his car swerving to the right as he tried to hide his head. Narrowly escaping a collision with the car next to him, he realized the man had not fired the gun. It was only a warning, and it was not the first. He and O'Hara had received anonymous phone calls at home even after they had their phone numbers changed. Threatening letters appeared from time to time, some handwritten, some with words cut from newspapers. While he found those things unsettling, he had not particularly worried about them. Today was different. Today was the first time a gun had been leveled at him.

Chet O'Hara was already at his desk when Ferguson arrived at the office. He was talking on the phone but looked up when the Judge came in. He abruptly ended his conversation when he saw the expression on Ferguson's face.

"Are you okay, sir?" he asked, crossing the room to the Judge's desk.

"Yeah, I'm fine, just a little shaken up." He told Chet about the black Chevrolet. "I think it's time we change our operation somewhat. We haven't really paid much attention to security, but there's more than ourselves to consider. There's our families and the other people on the staff."

"I'm glad to hear you say that, sir. I didn't want to let on, but these letters and phone calls are beginning to get to me. What do you think we should do?"

"My brother is a vice president over at Detroit Bank and Trust. He might have some empty back offices we could use. We won't tell anyone where we are and there'll be no sign on the door."

He also decided to call John Bugas at the FBI and ask for guards at the office and at his and Chet's homes.

Several weeks later, Ferguson leaned against a pillar at the Grand Trunk Western railway station on Fort Street looking up and down the platform. When Cliff Malin stepped out of the station, Ferguson strode over to him and handed him a ticket. Neither spoke as they stepped into the first class car and found their compartment. Ferguson gestured Cliff inside then looked into the compartments on either side before taking his own seat.

"Sorry about all the cloak and dagger stuff but I'm sure you understand," the Judge said.

The train began to move slowly to the sound of escaping steam and grinding metal. The men rode in silence for several minutes then Homer began asking questions. Who was paying off the police? Who was taking the payoffs? On and on throughout the trip to Muskegon and back, the Judge pummeled Cliff with questions which Cliff artfully dodged or answered vaguely. When they got off the train back in Detroit, Homer turned to Cliff.

"You know, my old dad used to say 'Even a blind hog will find an occasional acorn if he just keeps his nose down.' I'm keeping my nose down, Lieutenant, till I find everyone involved in this. You might as well make up your mind you haven't seen the last of me. You better be ready with some answers next time."

The next morning over coffee at the grill next to the police station, Cliff and John McCarthy discussed Ferguson, chain smoking as they talked.

"We have to do something, give the old dog a bone to chew on," Cliff said.

"I figured the old guy would be happy when the prosecutor's office cleared me, but I guess he thinks he's on to something. You got any ideas?" McCarthy raised his coffee cup toward the waitress asking for a refill.

"How about if we give him Boettcher? He's the one that was the most visible. He'll be easy to tie to the money since he was usually the bagman."

"God, Boettcher. I've known him since we were kids in Hamtramck. His old man will croak for sure."

"That's not our problem. We gotta get Ferguson off our backs."

Two days later, an anonymous letter arrived in Ferguson's mail box with the name of Inspector Raymond "Buddy" Boettcher spelled out in letters cut from a newspaper. It was the first time that name had cropped up in the investigation. Ferguson and O'Hara decided to enlist the aid of Boettcher's father, a retired cop whom Ferguson had known since he began practicing law, hoping family pride would force the inspector to talk. Chet drove out to the old man's house on the east side of town and found him trimming his roses. He introduced himself as

Frank Boettcher continued working on his flowers without speaking. When the old man finished one bush, he removed the glove from his right hand, revealing a thin hand badly gnarled with arthritis.

"Mr. O'Hara did you say?" He shook hands weakly then reached into his back pocket and pulled out a handkerchief.

"That's right," Chet said looking around the yard. "This must keep you awfully busy."

"What else have I got to do? Elsie died eight years ago. I'm too crippled to do much traveling. I thank God I got this yard to keep me busy." He blew his nose in a loud snort before asking "Would you like some iced tea, young fella?"

"Oh, don't go to any trouble, Mr. Boettcher."

"It ain't no trouble less you call walking up those goldang steps trouble. Tea's already made."

Chet walked slowly behind the bent, wizened man noticing the sharp protrusions where his shoulder blades pushed against his sweater and his trousers hanging loosely from his waist. Frank Boettcher led Chet around back to the kitchen door and inside to a small, tidy kitchen. The breakfast dishes stood drying in the sink and the table was set for lunch for one.

"Have a seat, son," Boettcher said, pointing to the kitchen table. "Elsie would skin me alive if she knew I was entertaining in the kitchen. You don't mind, do you? Now, what was it you wanted to see me about? One of my old cases come up?"

He poured two glasses of tea and shuffled to the table sitting across from O'Hare at the place set for lunch.

"No, not exactly, Mr. Boettcher, but there is a case we're having a little trouble breaking, and we thought you could help."

"You know when I was on the force, we was still using rubber hoses to get information. We had one fella, Sergeant Mitchell his name was. He really liked them hoses. We used to tell the suspects they were going to get a Mitchell Massage. Me? I never used them. Never had to. The guys used to say I coulda got Lot's wife to talk."

O'Hara grinned. "Yeah, I heard you were pretty good. This problem we're having needs someone like you. We can't get anyone to talk."

"Well, I'm your man, Sonny. I'll show you young fellas a thing or two. Who you trying to break?"

"Your son."

The smile dropped from Frank Boettcher's face. O'Hara waited. The old man got up, walked slowly across the room, picked up the pitcher of iced tea then set it back down with a thump. When he turned around, O'Hara saw tears in the corners of his eyes.

"All the time my boy was growing up, he talked about being a police officer just like his dad. We was so proud of him when he got his uniform. He worked hard, got his promotions. His mother used to keep his picture on top of the piano in the front room. Every time he got promoted, she got a new picture showing his new stripes. I thank the living God she's not here to see her son now."

"Maybe your son didn't know what was going on."

"You a cop, Mr. O'Hara?"

"No, I'm a lawyer."

Boettcher scoffed. "Lawyers. You don't know what goes on on the force. The Inspector knows everything that goes on in his precinct. He has to know if he's any good, and Buddy is a good cop."

Frank Boettcher said he would do what he could to help, and O'Hara returned to his office. Ferguson decided to interview Buddy Boettcher at the First Evangelical Church. It was only a few blocks from old Mr. Boettcher's home, and the Judge knew the pastor o f the church. Buddy Boettcher sat slumped in a chair in front of Ferguson and O'Hara, his face etched with sleepless nights. He had the same thin frame his father had but was taller and more muscular. He shifted nervously in his chair and smoked heavily. When he saw his father enter to the room he was first shocked then broke into hard sobs that shook his shoulders. Now, composed, he looked at the Judge.

"They suspended me this morning, you know. Called me at home. I'm the only one suspended. I'm getting smeared for a lot of things I never did."

Frank, who had been standing quietly at the back of the room, crossed to his son and lay his hand on his shoulder "It's okay, Buddy. I'm here."

Buddy began to cry again. His voice muffled by his handkerchief, he said, "I'll tell you what you want to know, but I'm not talking with him here."

O'Hara drove the old man back home while Ferguson began the questioning.

"Are we talking any deal here?" Boettcher asked.

"What sort of deal are you looking for?"

"The best I can get. Complete immunity. I'm going to need some protection, too, a lot of protection, in fact. You have no idea what kind of can of worms you're opening up here. This thing is so big, it'll take the rest of your career to sort it out."

Boettcher stood up, dug a pack of cigarettes from his pocket, withdrew one and dropped the pack on the desk in front of him. He lit the cigarette then poured a cup of coffee from the pot the minister's wife had brought it. He turned to the Judge.

"I'm scared," he said quietly. "I don't know the hell which way to turn. Can I get some kind of protection?"

"We'll give you all you want. We are aware of how dangerous this crowd is. We've had to protect ourselves from them"

"Where do you want to start?"

Boettcher said he took his first bribe in January of 1938 from Monk Watson, a numbers boss who operated in Boettcher's precinct. Monk paid the Inspector a $1,000 a month for himself and gave him more money to be passed on to Boettcher's superiors. The Inspector got a second grand a month from Eddie Hayes, another bookie. Boettcher told Ferguson that the person referred to in Janet McDonald's letters as Ryan was Elmer "Buff" Ryan, head of the Consolidated News Bureau and kingpin of the whole operation. Ryan used his wire services to link up to Moe Annenberg's bookie operation in upstate New York.

Chet O'Hara had returned from taking Frank Boettcher home and listened as Buddy unfolded a labyrinthine conspiracy. The investigators' frustration of the previous months dissipated over the next five hours as Boettcher couldn't stop talking.They continued to meet over the next few weeks, Boettcher providing names, dates, and dollar amounts. Every revelation left the Judge and his investigator speechless. Mayor Richard Reading received a $1,000 a month through Boettcher. The Mayor demanded another thousand for his son, earning him the nickname "Double Dip". Other bookies funneled an additional $4,000 a month through the mayor's office. Police Superintendent Fred Frahm got $2,000 a month, but Boettcher said he didn't know if he kept it all or passed it around.

Once Buddy Boettcher opened up, other witnesses began appearing. Sammy Block, a petty gambler, said he made payments as far back as 1935 to Harry Colburn, chief investigator in the city prosecutor's office. Colburn folded when he was interviewed. He said some of the money he got went to his boss, Chief Prosecutor Duncan McCrea. He knew McCrea was also getting money from John Roxborough, boxer Joe Louis's manager.

By the end of the Ferguson Grand Jury investigation in 1943, twenty-eight officers offered to cooperate in return for favorable treatment. They would quit the force but would not serve any prison time. The twenty-eight named an additional 150 of their fellow officers who were on the pad of various gamblers and underworld bosses.

Lieutenant Clifford Malin was one of the twenty-eight who talked and walked.

# CHAPTER 23

▼

Twyla Larson had been dead nearly two weeks when her husband, Captain Ernest Larson, arrived in Pontiac. He had learned of the death of his wife when his lieutenant, Doug Lawrence, showed him an article in the *Stars and Stripes*, the military newspaper. It had been a cold, wet day in St. Dizier, France. The war had ended and, little by little, companies were being returned home. Ernie was in charge of a unit that remained behind packaging U.S. equipment to be shipped back to the states. He had been writing a letter to Twyla and looking forward to the time when they would be together again, before Christmas, he hoped, when Doug came to his room.

Twyla's body had been discovered a week before her husband read of her death. By the time he obtained the necessary permission to return home, her family had buried her at Mt. Hope Cemetery in their home town. He spent two days at his mother's house then he and his brother, Barney, took the train to Pontiac where he hoped to learn the details of his wife's death.

Ernie and Barney checked into a hotel in the heart of Pontiac then walked to the Oakland County Sheriff's Office. Clouds scudded across the sky portending another winter storm, and the men hunched their shoulders against the cold. The desk sergeant lead them directly into Lieutenant Cunningham's office.

"Thanks for coming down. I know this is a difficult time for you," the lieutenant said. "Do you have any questions?"

"I don't really know anything about my wife's death. I know she was found in the river and that she had been shot. Do you have any idea who did this?"

"We have arrested a man, yes," Stan said.

"What's his name?"

"Clifford Malin. Did you wife every mention him in any of her letters?"

"No. I never heard of him. What's his connection to my wife?"

"We are still trying to piece that together. We know that they worked together at Carrier Tool and Die. He was a security officer. We have a report that he tried to help her collect some money that was owed her. Do you know anything about that?"

"No. I have been sending her money, and she was saving as much as she could out of her paycheck. We bought a piece of property on Black River in Port Huron before I went overseas, and I was going to build a house there when I got out of the service. How much money did this person owe her?"

"We're not really sure, but we found these." Stan handed Twyla's bank statements to Ernie.

Ernie leafed through them slowly. Stan had placed them in chronological order, the oldest first, and Ernie smiled as he saw the balances rise. The smile faded though when he saw withdrawals in the months before Twyla's death, large amounts. He was white when he saw the final statement that showed $1.67 remaining in the account. He looked up at Stan completely bewildered.

"Did this person take all of this money? There's $4,000 or more missing."

"We've talked to him and he said he can account for about half of the missing money. We don't know about the remainder."

Ernie sat clutching the statements, his hands in his lap and stared at Stan. His brother reached for the statements and thumbed through them quickly. "That bitch," he muttered.

"Captain Larson, can you tell us anything about your wife's activities while she lived in Detroit?"

"If you had asked me that two weeks ago, I would have said 'Yes.' Today, I have to say, 'No.' I don't know the woman I am hearing about."

"I have a friend who is a reporter at the *Detroit Free Press*. We've known each other since high school, and he's been a big help to me in the past. Would you mind talking to him? He'd like to do an article about your wife but only if you agree. And, I'm sure if there's something you tell him that you don't want published, he'll agree to that."

Ernie looked to his brother then back at the lieutenant. "I don't know what I can say that would shed any light on this, but I'll help any way I can."

Stan picked up the telephone and called Dan Kirk, setting up an appointment for the reporter and Ernie Larson to meet. Kirk said he would come to Pontiac first thing the next morning and meet Ernie at his hotel.

The skies seemed to have opened during the night and a heavy snow blanketed Detroit and Pontiac. Dan Kirk was nearly two hours late meeting Ernie Larson and apologized profusely. Ernie had been putting off having breakfast assuming the reporter had an expense account for interviews. They went into the hotel dining room and ordered before Dan took out his notebook.

"I know this is difficult for you, Captain Larson, and I appreciate your willingness to meet with me. I want you to know that what you say is on the record but, if there's something you would rather I not put in the article, let me know. I can't promise I'll leave it out, but we can talk about it."

Ernie began his story while they waited for the meal to be served.

Twyla Van Buren stood at the top of the steps leading to the sidewalk outside school and breathed deeply the fresh, moist air blowing over from Black River just across the street. Damn Charlemagne. And damn pi and Socrates and all the rest of it. What difference does it make what some stupid king did four hundred years ago? This was 1940 in Port Huron, Michigan. None of that stuff could possibly have any use to anyone now. Only two more weeks and it would be summer; one more year and she would have school behind her forever. She would find someone to take her to Manny's a coffee shop where the owners tolerated the raucous teenagers with their loud chatter, sly smoking and flirtatious hopping from table to table.

Twyla drifted through one knot of students after another, idly listening to their chatterings. That snob Rosemary Kwiatkowski was bragging again about how well her father was doing in business and their impending European vacation and Twyla breezed past. She stopped briefly to talk to Edna Barnes and Phyllis Atwell about their plans for the weekend without taking her eyes off her ultimate goal, Ernie Larson.

Twyla had been attracted to Ernie all through the school year. When he appeared in class that first day last September, she realized how he had grown and become more handsome over the summer. The few pimples he had last year were gone. He seemed less gangly and awkward and his shoulders were broader. A stylish new haircut made him look older and augmented those deep hazel eyes.

Twyla had spent most of the school year trying to get Ernie's attention, but he had seemed oblivious at first. Gradually, he began responding to her comments and laughing at her jokes until he finally asked her out three weeks ago. She envisioned this summer as an incessant series of parties, picnics at the beach and maybe even some intimate moments in the back of Ernie's father's Packard.

Ernie watched Twyla work her way through the crowd, stopping to speak to other students so as not to seem too eager to get to his side. He had learned that much about girls this last year, or at least about this girl. Being with her wasn't just about going to a movie and having milk shakes. It was like an ancient ritual dance passed down from generation to generation in which every gesture carried meaning. And he wasn't always sure what the meaning was. What he did know was that Twyla intrigued and enthralled him. He wanted to figure out the mysteries of women as he had never wanted to before.

Twyla was one of the most popular girls in school, more so with the boys than with the girls. He figured that was because she was more mature than the other girls. She understood a boy, while the other girls seemed to just giggle at everything.

When he had first seen Twyla, he hadn't really thought of her as pretty, but there was a magnetism about her he couldn't quite describe. Her individual features were nothing spectacular; her eyes were a little dull, her nose a little too wide, and her naturally curly brunette hair refused to be controlled. Still there was an aura about her. Maybe it was her bright smile or the way she made a fellow feel special. She was petite, just over five feet tall, and knew how to dress to cinch in her waist and accent her breasts. Ernie knew her family didn't have a lot of money, but she seemed to be able to accumulate a sizable wardrobe of well-made clothes. He learned after he started taking her out that she made them, and he was impressed. She moved with a grace that made men's heads turn whenever she moved. Perched on the edge of a chair, she looked like an elegant flamingo about to spring into flight. When she laughed, her head bobbed as though it was on springs. Her walk had a gentle sway, pressing at the fabric of her clothes like the sea lapping at the shore.

He continued talking with his friends while keeping Twyla in his peripheral vision as she casually made her way to his side.

"Hi, Ernie." Her voice was like a velvet glove.

"Hi, Princess. How'd your classes go?"

She winced. "I don't want to talk about school. What are you going to do this summer?"

"Work for my father, I suppose. He gets pretty busy remodeling houses during the summer, and he's always complaining he can't find good help."

"That all you going to do?" She turned sideways and lowered her eyes.

"That depends." He rubbed his hand across her shoulder. "What are you going to do?"

"Well, for now, how about going over to Manny's?"

He stretched out his left arm for her books then crooked his right elbow for her hand, and they followed a crowd headed up the block to the café. Inside, the prattle of the teenagers who had already arrived was punctuated by the clatter of dishes, scraping of chairs, and calls of waitresses to the cook. Tall mahogany booths with ornate carvings lined both walls with another row parading down the center. They were one of the reasons the café was so popular with the students; it was possible to repeat or create gossip without anyone in the next booth hearing. Shiny brass coat hooks hung at the end of each booth, some holding hats flung there by occupants. The hardwood floor glistened from the cleaning it had received after the lunch crowd departed. The air was redolent with years of steaks, chops, eggs, and baked goods that emanated from the kitchen. Ernie steered Twyla to a booth midway down the aisle and slid across the hard seat next to her. He gave her a quick kiss on the cheek just as Lloyd Webster and Catherine Emmett slid in the seat across the table.

"I saw that," Catherine winked at Twyla.

"Jealous?" Twyla smiled back.

"Not hardly," Catherine said, patting Lloyd's leg.

A waitress dropped four menus on the table on her way to delivering a tray full of food to another booth.

"Be right back," she called over her shoulder.

Twyla noticed Dave and Ed Degraw, brothers who lived across the street from the Van Burens, enter the café and head for the booth behind him, the only one vacant. The brothers were always hanging around the Van Buren front yard when they saw Theresa and Twyla outside. The twins considered them buffoons with their silly antics meant to attract the girls' attention.

"Ernie, quick. Grab the sugar jar from the booth before they get there," she said, poking his arm.

Ernie slid out of the booth and quickly grabbed the sugar jar from the empty booth then returned to his own seat. Unscrewing the lid, Twyla placed a paper napkin over it then turned it upside down, slid the napkin out, and balanced the lid on the upturned jar. When the Degraws ordered coffee, they realized there was no sugar on the table and Ed stepped over to the next booth

"You guys got any sugar?"

"Sure," Ernie said, not looking up. "Help yourself."

When Ed picked up the jar, its entire contents spilled across the table and on the floor. Ernie, Twyla, Lloyd, and Catherine howled as Ed stood sheepishly clutching an empty sugar jar.

"You're such an asshole, Larson, "he was finally able to say over the laughter.

"Don't blame me," Ernie said, trying to catch his breath. "I'm just an inno-cent bystander. You look like you just shit your pants."

The girls continued to giggle after Ed returned to his booth. "Geez, Twyla. You are such a stitch," Catherine said, wiping her eyes.

It was nearly five o'clock when Ernie dropped Twyla off in front of her house. Twyla's twin sister, Theresa, was setting the table for supper.

"You should have been at Manny's, Theresa. I got that clown Ed Degraw real good." She related the sugar jar incident.

"I don't think embarrassing people is particularly funny," was all her twin had to say.

Twyla dropped her books on the couch on her way through the living room.

"Mom just cleaned that room, Twyla. Could you put your books in our room?"

"Yeah, in a minute. You need help?"

"No, I'm nearly finished. Why don't you check on Anne Marie."

Twyla found her younger sister in the back yard spinning round and round with her arms extended, her head thrown back, and her eyes closed. Twyla called to her as the screen door banged shut and Anne Marie stopped, staggering from the dizziness of spinning. Twyla threw her arms around her sister whose difficult birth had left her unable to progress beyond the emotions and intelligence of a seven year old. Like others of that age, little beyond her own needs and interested touched her. Hers was a world of extremes that Twyla seemed to be able to coun-terbalance. At Woolworth's when Anne Marie was beset by giggles at the sight of an obese woman, overly made up and wearing an outlandish hat, Twyla quieted her. At the movies, when she cried hysterically after a dog was struck by a car in the show, Twyla consoled her.

Standing at the kitchen sink to watch her two siblings in the yard, Theresa wondered what would become of Anne Marie after Twyla left home. She didn't understand her identical twin. Twyla hated school, performed her household chores perfunctorily, and used any excuse to get out of going to church, but she doted on her younger sister, even occasionally canceling a date to take care of her. Twyla loved to fuss over the rather plain young girl, setting her hair, painting her fingernails, and making beautiful clothes for her with all the attention she gave her own appearance.

Theresa's thoughts were interrupted by the opening and closing of the front door. Edmund Van Buren's frame nearly filled the door, the sun behind him etching the shape of his broad shoulders and square torso out of the shadow of the porch. Eighteen years as a stevedore burnished his complexion to the color of highly polished mahogany. A year ago, he had been promoted to supervisor and already, the taut muscles were becoming flaccid, creating soft lumps beneath his shirt. Hands like bricks hung at his sides as he crossed the room to his favorite chair as the screen door banged shut behind him.

"Daddy! Daddy!" Anne Marie had come in from the yard moments earlier and ran to clutch him around the waist. Theresa and Twyla sauntered in behind her.

The twins had once run to their father as Anne Marie did, but years earlier they had become aware of how uncomfortable physical contact made him. Maybe it was because they were growing into young women, they thought. But lying awake in their room one night, they talked about how they had never seen him show any affection to their mother, no hand holding or quick kisses in the kitchen or even a hand on the shoulder. For a while, the twins undertook a spy mission, crawling down the hallway when they were supposed to be sleeping to see what their parents were doing in the living room. Even then, with no one around and the curtains drawn, they saw only their father reading or asleep in his chair, their mother mending clothes or writing letters, neither speaking.

Now, each night when he came home, one twin stood on each side of their father and dropped a kiss on opposite cheeks, then Theresa brought him a drink: a cold beer in the summer, a cup of tea in the winter.

Edmund Van Buren picked up the afternoon paper and fell heavily into his favorite chair. Anne Marie untied his boots and pulled them off then sat on the arm of the chair and leaned against his shoulder asking about the picture on the front page.

Shirley Van Buren stood in the archway between the living and dining rooms. "Hi, Dear. How was your day?" She wiped her hands on her apron.

"Fine, dear. What's for dinner?" He didn't look up from the paper.

"Meat loaf."

Her husband nodded, and she wondered if he'd heard her. She turned back to the kitchen.

Edmund noticed Twyla was unusually quiet at the dinner table. She scooped a large pile of mashed potatoes on her plate and helped herself to two pork chops, not a good sign. Generally she ate barely enough to please her mother, in too much of a hurry to get to whatever she had planned for the evening and too worried about her figure. The amount of food on her plate meant something was on her mind. Edmund would wait to see if it was something that a father should know about or if the situation called for a mother's counsel. He didn't wait long. He had just dipped into his own pile of mashed potatoes when Twyla spoke up.

"Daddy, do I have to go back to school next year?"

He had expected this conversation for sometime and was surprised only that it took her this long to broach the subject.

"Yes, you do, Twyla. All my kids are going to have as much education as I can afford."

"But, Daddy, what does a girl need an education for? You know I'm only going to get married eventually, and that doesn't take any brains." Twyla didn't notice her mother's eyebrows rise and her back straighten.

"How do you know you'll get married? Maybe you'll want to do something more substantial with your life than just stay home and keep house," he said. His wife dropped her napkin next to her plate and left the table. "Even if you do stay home with the kids, you'll be a better mother with an education. You can help the kids with their homework and teach them things they may not learn in school."

"But it's so boring, Daddy," Twyla groaned. "I can't take another day of it. We just sit and listen to teachers go on and on about stuff we'll never need to know except to pass the tests in school. I don't care what happened in Europe a thousand years ago and all that algebra and English. What am I ever going to do with it?"

"You'd be amazed how that stuff comes back to you in some useful way in later life. You'll just have to take my word for it."

"But, Daddy, I could get a job. Woolworth's is always hiring girls for their counters. I could make my own money, and that would help you and Mom. And when I'm not working, I could help with Anne Marie more. I wouldn't just lay around the house. I promise."

"You are not quitting school and that's final. There's only one more year left till you and your sister graduate, and it's not even a full year. You'll have fun this summer, then it's just nine months of school and it's over. Nine months isn't much when you think about it."

Twyla pushed her half-full plate away from her and propped her head up with her hand.

"Elbows off the table," her mother said.

Twyla's hands dropped into her lap and she sat quietly the rest of the meal.

# CHAPTER 24

▼

Summer arrived late that year. Spring showers stretched into early June, keeping Twyla penned up indoors. The dirty gray skies and sodden earth deepened her low spirits over having to return to school. She was just about convinced she would never get a tan this summer when the skies cleared and the sun blazed. With the warm days and balmy nights, parties abounded, and Twyla was happy again. The sewing machine hummed almost daily as she crafted new fashions for each new party or picnic. While most of the girls wore beige and brown and gray, Twyla garbed herself in scarlet red, sunshine yellow, and apple green. On one rare occasion, Theresa agreed to attend a party with her sister. Twyla copied her own sky blue dress for her sister but in a more sedate off white. Twyla suspected Theresa selected that color to please her boyfriend, Ralph, a nebbish little guy who had no more spark to him than Theresa did.

Except for the two weeks his family went to Ohio to visit his grandparents, Ernie and Twyla were virtually inseparable. Days of ripping out walls, painting, and laying tile continued to carve firm, strong muscles in his arms and chest. Twyla noticed, and she noticed the other girls noticed.

Twyla underwent her own changes. She grew a bit taller and her breasts pushed more firmly against her new clothes. Her tanned arms and face were accented by her choice of bright colors. Ernie noticed the changes and noticed the other boys noticed.

When Twyla first started seeing Ernie, Betty Gray had moaned, "Why him? He's so serious all the time. I'd think he'd be pretty boring."

Initially Twyla had thought so too, but the more she was with Ernie, the more she liked his intelligence. He was thoughtful and insightful without being stuffy or trying to show off. No one had ever considered Twyla bright, including herself, but Ernie was different. He didn't patronize her or, worse, ignore her, when he had something serious to say. He made her feel smart the way he talked to her. Maybe her father had been right about the importance of school. She started picking up the evening paper when her father finished it so she could understand what Ernie talked about. At least school had taught her where Germany and Czechoslovakia were.

One hot afternoon after he finished work, Ernie picked up Twyla, and they headed for a secluded spot on the shore they had found north of the public beach. Ernie was unusually quiet on the drive along Lakeshore Road, and Twyla decided she would wait for him to tell her what was on his mind. He pulled his shining black Buick into the shade of a stand of poplars, careful not to raise too much dust to mar the finish of the car he bought a month ago and washed every day. Ernie picked up the basket and blanket from the trunk and led Twyla by the hand to a spot where the sun was shielded by a leafy umbrella of tree branches. They loved this spot. From here they could see and not be seen, though few people ventured this far up the beach. Last time they were here, he had carved their initials into one of the white birch tree trunks. They held a blanket up for each other while they changed into their swim suits then stretched the blanket over top of a soft mound of fallen leaves, and he dug ham sandwiches and cold beer from the picnic basket.

Twyla had chattered throughout the drive up here, rambling from subject to subject. Ernie seemed to be only half listening and said very little. He still hadn't told her what had sent him into this taciturn mood. He was well into his second sandwich before he spoke.

"I'm thinking of joining the Army," he said flatly then took a swig of his beer.

"You're what?"

"I'm thinking of joining the Army."

They sat without speaking a few moments while Twyla digested his announcement. That meant he would be going away. How could he do that now that they were just getting to know each other? Now she'd have to start over with some other boy. Or would she? When Edna McBain's boyfriend decided to enlist, they ran off to Niagra Falls and got married. Was this what Ernie was proposing?

"Why do you want to do that?" she finally asked.

"I've been watching the papers about what's going on in Europe. That idiot Hitler is going to make trouble for everyone including us. Churchill has been trying to get us to help England, but Roosevelt doesn't seem to want to. Something's going to happen where we don't have any choice about getting involved. I can just feel it. I figure if I get in now, I might stand a better chance of getting the assignments I want. Now that I've graduated from high school, I might even be able to get into Officer's Candidate School."

"Don't officers have to go into battle?"

"Sometimes, but if there's a war, I don't want to be a desk jockey."

"It sounds dangerous."

"It could be."

Silence loomed between them again. He still hadn't said anything about her. Did he want her to wait for him or go with him? She suddenly realized how much he meant to her. She already felt a void in the pit of her stomach at just the thought of his not being around nearly every day. Was this love?

"When are you thinking of enlisting?" she asked quietly.

"I was thinking maybe just after the holidays, maybe the first of the year. By the time you finish school, I'll be through with basic training, and I'll know where I'm going to be stationed at least for a while. We could talk about whether you'd want to join me then."

Twyla looked deep into his eyes for a moment then turned to trace designs in the sand with a twig she had been playing with. He didn't say anything about marriage, but the thought of getting out of this boring little town was intriguing, even if he wasn't prepared to make an honest woman of her. Her mother would pitch a fit, of course, and so would her dad, but that didn't seem so important right now. Ernie wanted her with him. She wanted out of Port Huron. That alone would get her through this final school year.

She rose from the blanket wrapping a large white towel around her and strode to the beach, her feet sinking deep into the warm sand, her hair blowing to one side of her head. She waded into the water up to her knees.

Ernie lay back down on the blanket and stared at the graying clouds streaking across the sky behind the canopy of giant oak trees overhead, hoping the impending storm would cool the evening air. He watched as Twyla bent to scoop handfuls of water over her shoulders and chest. Was this someone he could spend the rest of his life with? he wondered. She was sweet and pretty, good company, and adoring. She could also be petulant and manipulative, but he figured that was just part of being female. He lay in the shade, not wanting to worry about the future just now.

He must have dozed off, because the next thing he saw was Twyla standing over him, wrapped in her bright white towel. He peered up through one eye.

"You look so pure and virginal in white," he grinned.

"I am. Pure as the driven slush," she said, kneeling next to him.

He unknotted the towel, letting it fall to the blanket around her as he slid one strap of her bathing suit from her shoulder.

"Come here you slush pile you," he said, pulling her down toward him. She covered his face with soft kisses and stroked his chest. He slid the other strap off her shoulder and drew the suit down to her waist. Her hair against his face tickled, and he rolled her onto her back, kissing the stripe where sun-darkened skin turned to milky white at the top of her breasts. Robins yodeled with all the enthusiasm of a starlet auditioning for her first Broadway play, melding with the moans and pants of the lovers beneath the trees.

Large, cold drops of rain roused them later, and they quickly scooped up their swimsuits and towels and dashed to the car, laughing as they dusted off dried sand and struggled into their clothes. They stopped for hamburgers and malted milks along the highway before Ernie dropped Twyla at home, long after dark.

Ernie tried for nearly two weeks to reach Twyla, but she hadn't returned any of his calls. He didn't understand. The last time they were together they had a terrific time. Bob Maxwell bought a new boat with his summer wages and invited Ernie, Twyla, and his girlfriend Opal, out for a day of skiing. After hours on the river, they moored in a little cove and ate the picnic the girls had prepared. At twilight, Bob and Opal disappeared ashore, while Ernie and Twyla stayed on the boat, talking and laughing as always. The gentle lapping of the water against the side of the boat lulled them asleep after their lovemaking. When he drove her home, they stopped up the block for a long, warm goodnight before he drove to her house and walked her to the front door. Everything had seemed fine, but now she wouldn't talk to him.

Frustrated by her freezing him out, Ernie decided to go to the Van Buren home to face her. He finished work, went home to clean up then drove over to Elm Street. All the while, he wondered just what to say to her and hoped she would say something, anything that would give him a clue about her behavior. Even if she had tired of him and found someone else, he needed to know. The porch light snapped on a moment after he knocked on the front door. Mr. Van Buren opened the door.

"What are you doing here?" he asked curtly. Ernie was surprised at the way he was greeted by this man who had just a few weeks ago seemed to like him.

"I came to see Twyla. I've been calling her, and she isn't returning my calls," Ernie said quietly.

"Well, you're not going to see her, you son of a bitch. Now get off my property." Mr. Van Buren slammed the door shut and snapped off the porch light.

Ernie was even more puzzled than before. What possibly could have happened to turn not only Twyla, but her father against him? He drove to a quiet spot on Black River, one of several he and Twyla had frequented. He watched as wispy fingers of clouds striated the watery lemon sliver of sun as it drifted lower in the sky, finally disappearing behind the stand of trees across the river. Every moment he and Twyla had spent together this past summer crept into his thoughts. If Twyla had grown bored with him, wouldn't she have said something? Did she say something that he hadn't caught on to? She could be so subtle about what she wanted from him. Maybe he had missed something. But how could that affect her father's attitude toward him? After he didn't know how many hours, he made his way home and lay awake in bed, sorting and resorting the events of the last few months, unable to comprehend the chasm that had developed between him and the girl he was sure he loved.

Fall cloaked the Michigan woods in a Jacob's coat of gold and scarlet, and Ernie joined his brothers for a week of deer hunting up near Alpena. Tramping through the woods in the morning mist beneath a gray flannel sky, he could only think of Twyla. The wind moaning through the ancient oaks sounded like her moans of pleasure as they pressed their bodies together. The rich aroma of fresh coffee over the campfire recalled those late nights in her mother's kitchen after an evening twirling her around the dance floor.

Two days after Thanksgiving, Ernie's father had suffered a heart attack and died before they could get him to the hospital. That left Ernie's mother with no source of income and four children still at home. Ernie, who was still living under his parents' roof along with his brothers, considered keeping the remodeling business open, but none of them particularly enjoyed the work. Besides, it had been a hit and miss proposition all along. They felt their mother needed more security now that she was alone, Roy, who still had another year before graduating from high school, decided to get a job working the freighters that plied the Great Lakes. That would mean one less mouth to feed and a regular paycheck, most of which he would send home to his mother. Fred was married now and had announced at Thanksgiving dinner that their first child was due in the summer. He had left the sea-going life in favor of a job at Detroit Edison that would keep him home. He said he would help where he could, but this job barely paid enough to support one family He could help out with work around the house but would not be able to contribute financially. Ernie took a job at the Chrysler plant in Marysville and remained living in his mother's house. That way, he could help with the expenses and with the younger kids.

Ernie worked the first shift from six in the morning to two in the afternoon. That allowed him time to get back up to Port Huron and pick up the kids at school. They attended St. Stephen's Catholic School as he had, across the street from the public school Twyla attended. Every afternoon he studied the faces of the students streaming from the high school, hoping to catch a glimpse of Twyla, maybe even talk to her. A couple of times he saw Theresa, but Twyla never appeared. One bright, still January afternoon he saw Theresa again and decided to see what he could find out. Dashing across the street, he wove his way through the throng and approached Theresa.

"Can I speak to you a minute?" he asked.

Theresa began to turn away, and he clutched her elbow. "Please?" He said it so quietly, so intently Theresa couldn't turn away. She let him guide her away from the other students. When she turned to look at him, she could see the ache in his eyes. She didn't know what she should say to him.

"Can you tell me where Twyla is? I have been looking for her after school, and I haven't seen her at all. Is she okay? Do you know why she won't talk to me?"

"Twyla didn't come back to school this year. She has a nervous condition," Theresa told him then turned to leave.

"Wait a minute. What do you mean a nervous condition? What kind of nervous condition?"

"I really can't say any more. She will have to explain things to you."

"But she won't talk to me. How can she explain anything?"

"I'm sorry." Theresa looked at him a long moment then turned and left.

His conversation with Theresa left Ernie even more puzzled than ever. A nervous condition? You could say a lot of things about Twyla but nervous wasn't one of them. She was a real cool cucumber in any situation he ever saw her in. What could Theresa be talking about?

Late that night, he sat at the kitchen table over a cup of coffee. The house was still except for the ticking of the clock on the sideboard in the dining room. The padding of feet on the linoleum roused him, and he turned to see his mother at the stove. She fixed herself a cup of coffee and sat across from her son. Neither spoke as she added sugar and milk. She had noticed a sadness about her son for several months, but she hadn't known how to approach him. She had never been the kind of mother her sons confided in, not because there was no deep feeling between them. The Larsons just weren't talkers. Mrs. Larson rarely talked about her own feelings even to her husband. She had never liked the kind of woman who unburdened every little thought and problem on her husband, and she didn't want to be one of them. But the years of keeping her thoughts and feelings to herself had left her unprepared for being available to her children when they needed to talk.

"Does this have to do with Twyla?" she finally said quietly. Ernie stared into his coffee cup and nodded.

"Do you want to tell me about it?"

"I have to ask a question, Ma. You know how women are. They say all kinds of things I can't figure out. What does it mean when a girl has a nervous condition?"

Mrs. Larson blushed. She had never been comfortable with such conversations with other women or even her own husband. She couldn't look at her son when she replied.

"It means she is having a baby."

Ernie raised his eyes to his mother's face. "Are you sure?"

"Yes, Dear. I'm sure."

She watched his eyes fill with tears till they welled up and spilled down his face. "My God," he whispered. Mrs. Larson took her cup to the sink, rinsed it and went back to bed. She didn't know how to comfort him. She hoped solitude would help.

# CHAPTER 25

▼

Twyla had put off telling her family about her pregnancy as long as she dared. She was a bit past three months when she decided she had better say something before she had to start making new clothes for herself. One afternoon when Theresa had gone to the beach with Ralph and Anne Marie was napping, she sat in the kitchen waiting for her mother to return from the market. Mrs. Van Buren came though the kitchen door carrying two big bags of groceries and set them carefully on the kitchen counter, glancing furtively at Twyla. Beyond greeting her daughter, she didn't speak, taking her hat off and setting it on top of the Frigidaire then putting on her apron. She was well into cleaning the vegetables she had bought and wrapping them in heavy white butcher's paper before she spoke again.

"Something on your mind, Daughter?"

Twyla had been fidgeting with a tea towel since before her mother arrived home, developing and rejecting a thousand ways of saying what she wanted to say. She still didn't know how to break the news.

"Mama—," she started and burst into tears. Mrs. Van Buren stepped to her daughter's side and pulled the sobbing girl toward her. "I know, Honey. It's okay. I've known for a long time. Shhhh. It's going to be okay."

Twyla buried her face deeper into her mother's abdomen and let the weeks of frustration and confusion flood through her eyes. When she could finally speak, she looked up at her mother's face, filled with tenderness and worry. "I'm so sorry, Mama. I'm so sorry."

"It's okay, Darling. Everything's going to be okay."

"Daddy is going to be so mad at me. He's going to throw me out in the streets."

"He'll do nothing of the kind," Mrs. Van Buren said soothingly. "You leave your father to me."

"And Theresa. She's going to sit there with her superior face and superior thoughts and tell me she warned me. I don't know if I can stand it, Mama."

"Your sister loves you and just wants the best for you. She'll be fine. You go in and take a nice long bath before everyone gets home, then put on your nicest nightie and get into bed. I'll bring you dinner later."

The tears started again as Twyla filled the tub then ebbed and flowed while she soaked. She hadn't realized how much she had been keeping her emotions in check since she realized she was pregnant. Telling her mother unfettered those pent up feelings. She felt less alone, but new thoughts crowded in where the initial worry had been. What should she do about this child? Would her parents make her marry Ernie? Would they want her to keep the baby and stay home with it for the rest of her life? What if they left all the decisions up to her? What if they didn't?

Twyla and Theresa's bedroom was just around the corner from the dining room. Twyla closed the door tight and crawled beneath the covers then got up again to open the door slightly. She figured, bad as it was going to be, she had better find out as soon as possible what her father's reaction was going to be. As if she didn't already know. Since she started dating, he had been telling her she shouldn't be going out with so many different boys. She should be more settled and ladylike like Theresa, he said, find a boy she liked and go out with him for a long time, so people wouldn't say she was loose. She tried to do what her father wanted, but he just didn't understand how she so quickly bored of the same boy. She might as well have stayed home and done her homework as to go out with the same boy more than a half dozen times. Ernie had been different, though. Her father was probably secretly happy that she dated the same boy all summer. Maybe that would assuage his anger about her condition.

The warm bath and freedom from the weight of carrying her secret left her drained, and she dozed off. The next thing she knew, she heard voices in the dining room and the dull thud of dishes being set on the cloth-covered table. The aroma of fried chicken reached Twyla, and she realized her mother was softening her father up for the conversation with his favorite meal. Along with the chicken would be creamy mashed potatoes, buttered peas, and buttermilk biscuits. If Twyla didn't miss her guess, one of her mother's fabulous apple pies was thawing on the kitchen counter, and Theresa was making ice cream.

Theresa asked where her twin sister was, and their mother said simply that Twyla wasn't feeling well and was lying down. Anne Marie wanted her sister as well, but she was instructed to let Twyla sleep. Her father came in from work to the usual squeals of delight from Anne Marie.

Twyla lay in the darkness listening to the clinking of dishes and idle conversation as food platters were passed and plates were filled. The room fell silent as her family began to eat then she could hear her mother's soft voice but couldn't distinguish the words. Suddenly she heard a pound on the table and dishes rattled. "Damn!" she heard her father yell then a chair scraped away from the table, the front closet door opened and closed followed by the front door. Her father had gone for a walk or a drive.

Her mother brought in a tray with dinner for Twyla, but it was untouched when Theresa came in some time later. She sat on the bed across from her twin sister, her hands in her lap, eyes fixed on Twyla's face.

"Why didn't you tell me?" she asked quietly.

"I just couldn't, Theresa. I knew what you'd think and what you'd say."

"And what is that."

"Actually, you probably won't say anything. You'll just give me that look you do when you disapprove of something I've done, like you're so superior and wise, and I'm just an idiot child. Then you'd rush in with all kinds of suggestions about what I should do."

Theresa crossed to her sister's bed and sat on the side, holding Twyla's hand.

"You have just never understood me, Twyla. I just want you to be happy and respectable. Ralph and I are so happy together. You don't have to be chasing different boys all the time to find love. I found it right off the bat. And Ralph would never ask me to do something that would get me in trouble. That's not love."

"Ralph may be fine for you, but I like fun and excitement, not just sitting around reading and going to the movies. I don't badger you about what you do. I just wish you'd let me make my own decisions without picking on me about it."

"Well, you've made a pretty good decision this time, haven't you?" Theresa took her nightgown and bathrobe and went down the hall to the bathroom.

Twyla was still lying awake in the dark when her father returned hours later. She held her breath waiting for him to come into her room yell, maybe even hit her. Instead, he just stood in the door of her bedroom as she lay motionless, afraid even to breathe.

"Twyla?" he whispered. She rolled over in her bed. "Yes, Daddy."

His bulk was framed by the light in the hallway, his shoulders slumped as he stood for several long minutes without speaking. The outburst Twyla had been dreading never materialized. She was sure she heard a sob escape from his lips before he turned and walked slowly to his bedroom.

Both Twyla's parents encouraged her to give the baby up for adoption, though she felt that her mother longed to keep her first grandchild near her. Twyla didn't need much encouragement to rid herself of that unwanted responsibility. She would be more careful in the future.

She had wanted to contact Ernie when she learned she was pregnant, but she didn't know what she would say to him, and she was afraid of his reaction to her news. Would he insist on marriage? Would he call her names and say it wasn't his? Would he want her to end it with one of those horrible doctors she heard about? Facing such uncertainty and confusion, she took the easiest way out she could think of. She said nothing to him. That way there would be no ugly scenes, no decisions to confront. A month after her mother made the announcement at the dinner table, Twyla's father asked his daughter if the baby's father was going to do the honorable thing by her. Twyla just shrugged.

Twyla thought she could manage the few months alone before the baby was born, but she missed Ernie terribly. When Theresa told her about Ernie appearing at school looking for her, she struggled for several days against an overwhelming urge to call him. He really did care about her if he went to all that trouble to talk to her. Maybe he would understand, but she couldn't take the chance, and she never called. After the baby was born, when she was ready to start going out again, she thought it best to make a fresh start and leave Ernie to history.

After the baby boy was adopted by a family in Lexington, Twyla entertained briefly the notion of returning to school. Ernie had engendered a curiosity in her that made sense of school, but she couldn't stand the idea of the way people would look at her, speculating as to why she was a year behind in school. Besides, giving birth made her feel older than everyone else her age. She thought about taking a job at Woolworth's or Kresge's, but she didn't think she had the patience to wait on whining customers. In the end, she took a job at Mueller Brass, an assembly plant that made various fittings for various mechanical devices. It was just the sort of mindless job she needed, putting elbow fittings together with washers and returning them to the conveyor belt for the next person to add something to before passing it on. No thinking, no decisions, just put metal parts together and pass them on. She was tired the first few weeks, but being tired made her sleep like she hadn't in months, the welcome sleep of no dreams.

Mr. Dowd, a kindly older man who had worked on Line Three for more than twelve years, was assigned to train Twyla, as he frequently was assigned to new employees owing to his limitless patience. An avuncular man whom Twyla guess was in his fifties, he seemed drawn to the younger workers, both male and female, more than those his own age. He enjoyed their stories of dances and parties, getting married, raising families, and buying houses. All the workers, regardless of age, knew him to be a ready ear when they needed to unburden themselves of personal or work problems, offering a soothing word or a piece of advice if he felt it appropriate, sitting quietly, and listening if not.

He was a short man, five foot five tops with pale skin, a rounded abdomen, and surprisingly soft hands given his line of work. His dumpling cheeks pinkened when he heard someone tell wild stories about vacations or the antics of their children. His voice was soft and warm as an old shirt.

Mr. Dowd never spoke of a family of his own, and, somehow, everyone knew better than to ask. He was a consummate gentleman, always referring to someone as Mr., Mrs. or Miss unless invited to use their first name. No one ever called him anything but Mr. Dowd.

He seemed to take particular interest in Twyla when she first started work. He sensed the wounded bird in her but never broached the subject. The first few days on the job she struggled, obviously unused to things mechanical. She regularly burst into tears from frustration. Mr. Dowd would pat her hand cooing. "There, there, Dear" until she calmed down and returned to work.

Twyla thought Mr. Dowd was being unduly harsh with her at first. No one could be expected to work as fast as he said she should. Toward the end of the first week, though, she looked at the other workers on the line and saw them working like automatons, fastening and hooking things together and accumulating the required number of parts by the end of their shift. And she realized it wasn't Mr. Dowd's fault the way he pushed her. He was just doing his job, and she didn't want to get him into trouble by not learning.

At first, just because he was the only one she knew, she had lunch with Mr. Dowd, but it took little time for her to actually enjoy his company. Often other workers would join them, and, gradually, she got to know other people from around the factory. She had decided that first day though, that she wasn't going to get too friendly with these people. They were too old and just not her type. Besides, this was only a temporary job until she decided what to do next. She had done pretty well keeping most of them at a distance, but with Mr. Dowd she was an open book. Without asking, he had learned about her family, her feeling about school, her favorite foods and movie stars, and that she water skied and ice skated. It was as though, in the effort to repress the story of her child, everything else spilled out the sides like trying to hold a lid on an overflowing pan of popcorn.

And one day the lid did come off. Twyla thought she had put all thoughts of her child and Ernie behind her, but one night she lay awake wondering if she had done the right thing, afraid she might have passed up all opportunity for a marriage. After all, she was damaged goods now. No one would want her. She wondered about her son. Suppose the couple who adopted her little boy died and left him an orphan at a young age. Maybe they would make him work like a slave on their farm, and he'd never get to know a real childhood. Would his parents tell him he was adopted? What if, deep in his heart, he knew he wasn't born to the couple that raised him, even if they didn't tell him he was adopted? He might go through his whole life wondering who his parents were and why they didn't love him enough to keep him. She didn't always agree with her parents, but she knew she was loved. What if her son never had the warm comfort of a parent's love?

And Ernie. Maybe she hadn't been fair to him. Every man deserves a son. Suppose ten or twelve years from now he was married but had only daughters. Would he feel an emptiness for lack of a son?

For days on end, these thoughts plagued her, and she became sullen bordering on morose. No one joined her and Mr. Dowd for lunch one day, and he ventured a question.

"Want to talk about it, Dear?"

Twyla tore off a piece of her sandwich and stuffed it in her mouth, staring at the table top.

"How do you know when you've done the right thing? You know, made the right decision about something?"

He chewed slowly as he pondered her question then said in his soothing way, "I guess you know because the decision you made leaves you satisfied."

"You mean if you've done the right thing, you don't keep wondering if you did?"

"No. It's perfectly natural to second guess ourselves. But I think if you've done the right thing you know it immediately. You feel comfortable about it as soon as you've done it. If it wasn't the right decision, you know immediately. You walk away from the decision feeling uneasy about it. It doesn't really matter what you think about it later, because later you have the benefit of hindsight. You can look back and start the if onlys because you see the results of the decision. But you may not have known, in fact probably didn't know, how things would turn out. You can only make the best decision you can, based on the facts and conditions you have at the time. And there's a difference between wishing you had made a different decision and wishing things had turned out differently."

"What do you mean?"

Mr. Dowd sat for some moments before speaking again. Twyla saw a tear sparkle in the corner of his eye.

"When I was just a little bit older than you, I was in love with the most beautiful, caring woman God ever put on earth. I didn't think she would take the time to even say hello to me. Angelina was her name. I thought I would end up marrying Carrie Richardson from across the street. Our parents wanted that. But one day I worked up the nerve to speak to Angelina, and she told me she was wondering why I hadn't spoken to her before. From then on, I never even thought about Carrie. When Angelina said she would marry me, I couldn't believe my good fortune. I had no real prospects and didn't know how I would support a family, but that didn't matter to her. We were only married three months when she got sick. It was the Influenza epidemic of 1917. Four days after she first developed a fever, she died in my arms.

"Carrie married Harvey Cruikshank, and they have four children. If I had married her, I would have a family today, but I married Angelina, and I don't regret it. I wish things had turned out differently with us, and there are times when I long for children and grandchildren to bounce on my knee, but our courtship and marriage made me deliriously happy. It was the best time of my life, and I'll treasure it always."

Neither Twyla nor Mr. Dowd spoke for some time then he reached across and patted her hand.

"Whatever it was, Dear, put it behind you. You probably can't change the decision and regretting it is futile. Remember what happened to Lot's wife when she looked back. If the good Lord intends for your decision to be changed, he'll give you a hand."

Twyla didn't care much about sports, but one sticky, idle June Saturday Eva McGuire from Line Two called Twyla and suggested going to the company baseball game. Chrysler was Mueller Brass's rival that day and it promised to be a good game, she said. The teams had already played each other this season and they stood evenly pitted at one win each.

Twyla and Eva sat with some of the other workers from Line Three including Mr. Dowd between first and second base. As they chattered and settled in their seats, Twyla caught a glimpse of a tall, muscular man in a Chrysler uniform. She grew warm and her heart pounded as she realized it was Ernie. She hadn't expected to have any kind of a reaction if she saw him again, but here she was all twittery the way she had been when she was dating him. She looked away, hoping he wouldn't notice her.

It was late afternoon when the first pitch was tossed. A humid summer breeze wafted across the grandstand as the spectators settled on their cushions, sipped on cool drinks and began cheering their teams on, even before any plays had taken place. Twyla could smell the slightly fishy, slightly oily aroma of St. Clair River from across the street and with it came memories of lying in Ernie's arms on the beach as he covered her with soft kisses from head to toe. She wondered if she would ever smell the river again without thinking of that wonderful summer with Ernie.

Mueller Brass got off to a bad start. By the end of the first inning, Chrysler had gotten six hits, two of which went home. Mueller wasn't on the scoreboard. Things tightened up a bit in the second inning, and Mueller scored twice. In the fourth inning, a fly to the left, over the head of the outfielder, put Chrylser ahead, three to two.

George Sommers was up next for Mueller's, the team's best hitter. He got a hit and went to first. The next hit put him on second but the third hit went to the infield and he was out at third.

Now it was Fred Carter up—not a great hitter but a terrific runner. He doubled, driving one home. Chrysler was a little slow getting the ball from the outfield to the infield. Three to three. Ernie Larson was up next. His hit put him on first and Carter on third. That was the end of it for Mueller for that inning for the next hitters were three up, three down.

The Mueller Brass team was known for being strong in the early part of the game and fading later due to their habit of having a beer or two when they weren't up. They began to fade. Gordon Newman hit a line drive down first and was out practically before he left home. Clark Houlihan fouled out and, though Allen Moody made it to second, he was out at third. The players took a break before starting the next inning, pouring water over each other to wash off the sweat, dust and bugs of the steamy summer night.

"We're going to do it," Ernie said, slapping pitcher Jim McDonald on the back. "You just keep at it. By this time of night, those guys couldn't hit a cow in the ass with a snow shovel."

Across the field, water from the canteens went over the Mueller Brass players' heads while they downed more beer. They talked strategy, but no one listened.

Top of the six, Chrysler is up. Randy Carver singled. Bud Krause bunted and Carver makes it to third. Joe Campbell singled to right field, and Carver made it home. Four to three. Sommers singled but was out at second. Carter popped out to left. Eddie Greene fouled out.

Mueller Brass was up. Newman doubled to center, Moody took first and Carver hit Newman home. All tied up.

Top of the seventh. Larson hit a single to right followed by Campbell who walked. An outfield fly ended with bases loaded. Stasenski popped out, and O'Reilly grounded out. Still bases loaded, four all. Eddie Clements was up. The league had agreed to no pinch hitters, but now everyone wished that wasn't the case. Eddie Clements insisted on playing but couldn't hit, couldn't run, hell could hardly see. They kept him on the team because he worked in the payroll department and covered for them when they came in late or had to leave early. He swung and missed. He swung again. Foul. On the next swing, the umpire called a bal,l and the pitcher took issue with the call. So did the first baseman and the catcher. So intent were they on arguing the point they didn't realize no one had called time out. Larson realized, though. He stole home bringing it to five to four. When Clements resumed the plate, he struck out. End of the game. Afterward, at the Rustler's Inn, Ernie was the hero.

"You old son of a bitch," Carter laughed, smacking him on the back. "No one can put anything over on you. We were all watching the ump and the pitcher go at it, and you sneak your little scrawny ass home. God damn. Lemme get you a beer."

Stasenski bought him a beer and so did Krause and Carver. Even Ev Rawlings, the pitcher who got into it with the umpire over Clements swing bought him one. At nine o'clock the band started playing. Their opening number was "Chattanooga Choo Choo" and Ernie reached out blindly pulling the woman behind him onto the dance floor. It was Twyla. They both stood still looking at each other a moment then danced till midnight.

Twyla wouldn't let Ernie drop her off in front of her house when he drove her home that night. She wasn't sure what her parents would say if they knew she had been with him. There wasn't much point in causing a scene until she knew for sure whether she wanted to see him again. Lying in bed that night, she wrapped her arms around her pillow as she tried to sort out her feelings. She could still smell Ernie's musky warmth and feel his strong arms around her as they danced. He had been a little awkward when he first realized it was Twyla he had pulled onto the dance floor. He stumbled more than danced the first few steps, and she followed him as though it was a new dance. Before long, though, they were laughing and talking as though they had never been apart. He told her he had abandoned his plans to enlist when his father died and talked about his job. She told him Theresa and Ralph were planning a fall wedding. He asked how her parents and little sister were. She asked about his mother and brothers. She listened intently as he spoke of more trouble in Europe and union matters at Chrysler. He listened while she talked about her job and the people she worked with. Neither spoke of their child.

Lying in bed, Twyla realized how much she had missed him all those months, his easy laugh, his gentleness, even his intellect, which she didn't always understand. She hadn't realized it before, but being with someone who was such a deep thinker made her feel smarter. Yes, Twyla decided, she was in love with Ernie.

Her parents wouldn't be happy if they knew she was seeing him again. That wasn't important. She would endure their wrath if it came to that. She loved Ernie and that was all that mattered.

Winter came early. Black River didn't usually freeze over thick enough to skate on till Thanksgiving weekend, but, by Halloween, the river was dotted with figure skaters and hockey players. Ernie called Twyla on a bright, crisp Saturday morning and suggested a snow picnic. They met downtown, skates slung over their shoulders, Twyla carrying a picnic basket, Ernie concealing a small flask in his coat pocket. They tied their skates on and piled their shoes behind a tree before heading north up the river beneath a sky the color of a baby blanket. They took turns carrying the picnic basket, finally sharing the load, the basket hanging between them. The sun warmed their faces and Twyla pushed her hat to hang on her back; Ernie tucked his stocking cap in his pocket. They skated easily, circumventing copses of young children learning to skate, two teams pushing a hockey puck back and forth between themselves, and teenagers showing off for each other with figure eights and flying camels. North of the paper mill they were alone and Ernie suggested they lighten their load by eating lunch. He spread his coat on a snow bank and held Twyla's hand as she eased down on it. They washed down the sandwiches and chocolate cake with a mouthful of lemonade and whiskey chasers. When Ernie finished a cigarette he bowed deeply and said, "Would madam care to dance?"

"We don't have any music, you nut," Twyla laughed.

"We make our own music," Ernie said bowing again and taking her hand.

She followed him out onto the ice blown clean by yesterday's wind and joined in as he hummed "Blue Danube". With as much grace as they had on the dance floor they twirled and spun to the off-key music, laughing when they didn't hum the same phrase. Out of breath, they returned to the snow bank, and Twyla sank down on the coat as Ernie lit another cigarette. Neither spoke for a few minutes as they caught their breath. Twyla gazed up at the bare branches of the ancient oak and elm trees stretching along the banks of the river. She loved how they bared themselves in the fall to admit the rare warm sun to the earth at its feet during the winter then dressed themselves in spring to provide cooling shade in the hot, sticky summers. Across the river she watched as a brilliant crimson cardinal punctuated the stark white snow stippled by ebony shadows cast by the bare branches. For all the aggravation of driving in it and dressing for it, snow made the world clean and pure, she thought, masking dead grass, muddy roads, and rusted hulks of automobiles and farm equipment, at least when it was fresh. She breathed deeply, pulling the sharp coldness into her lungs, holding it, and letting it out slowly. The sun had crossed the river and was warming her back now. She looked up at Ernie and saw him staring far behind her and chewing on his lower lip. He always did that when he wanted to say something but didn't know how to start.

"Penny for your thoughts," she said quietly.

He continued to stare a moment then looked into her eyes, still not speaking. His deep-set eyes were shaded, but Twyla could tell by the furrow on his forehead he had something serious on his mind.

"I'm glad you're back in my life," he said quietly.

She reached her gloved hand up to him, and he held it with both his. He bent and kissed it.

"I can't help feeling there is something ominous in the air. I keep reading about that little shit Hitler over in Germany, and it makes my skin crawl. I just know things are going to get worse before they get better. I am thinking about joining the Army. I wanted to go last year, but Dad dying kept me from going." He looked away, not ready to see what was in Twyla's eyes. She pulled her hand away.

"Well, that's quite a shock. How long have you been thinking about this?"

"A few weeks now. Actually, a few months off and on but more seriously these last few weeks. Things are under control for Ma now with Roy sending money home and only two kids left at home. I think it would actually be better if I was out of the house. One less person for her to take care of."

"Jeez, Ernie. This really takes me by surprise. We have been having such a great time, I never thought about it ending, at least not so soon."

"It doesn't have to end. Not if you'll marry me."

It was Twyla's turn to fall silent. Marriage had never been part of her thoughts, not like it was with other girls. She didn't dream about a wedding dress and a big church ceremony the way other girls at school did. She had no image of the perfect husband they way they did. She didn't wander through Sperry's china department picking out her favorite pattern as they did. But she was sure she loved Ernie. Those long, lonely months without him and the joy of his unexpected reappearance had convinced her of that. Maybe that was all that was necessary for a marriage.

"When were you thinking of going into the service?"

"I thought I'd go after the holidays, January, maybe."

"When were you thinking of getting married?"

"I was thinking December 6, 1941 has a nice ring to it."

# CHAPTER 26

▼

Twyla flung herself across her narrow bed and stared at the ceiling. What an absolute waste of an evening it had been. For all the fun she had had, she might as well have stayed in Port Huron. Moving to Detroit was supposed to be fun, exciting. People who lived in big cities were supposed to know how to live it up. But, in the two years she had been here, she couldn't tell much difference from Port Huron.

Tonight's party sounded like it would be great. Stella Nielsen from the plant had said her friends really knew how to have a good time. There would be food and drinks and a lot of people whom Stella said knew how to laugh. They laughed alright, at things Twyla thought were stupid: the antics of their kids, the cleverness of their animals, or some inane joke they had heard at church. They talked about last year's tomato crop, their mother's arthritis, and what to expect from the Detroit Tigers this year. After much cajoling, Twyla was able to persuade the hostess to put on a few records, but she kept the volume turned down low so as not to wake the children. Frustrated and bored, Twyla finally left at nine-thirty. Now, sprawled across her bed, she wished she had stopped in at Tommy's on the way home. She thought of going back out, but she didn't want to have to answer questions from her landlady about why she left the house so late.

Ernie and Twyla had spent the first weeks of their marriage in North Carolina as he waited to learn whether he had been accepted into Officers' Candidate School. Although Twyla thought the barracks they lived in were incredibly hideous, bereft of any sort of artistic touches, she loved the time she spent there. Whether Ernie went to OCS or overseas, he and Twyla would be separated, perhaps for several years. He seemed to want to crowd every moment of pleasure he could into the time they had together. There were parties, dinners at nice restaurants, nightclubbing, and dancing. Ernie denied her nothing he could afford, and she had several fashionable party dresses she had made herself with shoes and bags to match. When Ernie's orders finally did come for OCS, he learned he would take his training near San Francisco. He suggested that his wife go to Detroit and live with her twin sister.

Theresa and Ralph had married the summer before Twyla and Ernie did, and Ralph had a job as an office clerk at one of the war plants in Detroit, having been denied an opportunity to serve his country because of his poor vision. He had told Ernie and Twyla that women were working in the plants—Rosie the Riveter they were being called—filling the jobs left vacant by men called to war. It wasn't especially easy work. The women were required to wear slacks and a shirt and tie their hair up in a turban. They sometimes had to lift heavy objects and learned to operate power tools, but they made good money. Ralph had thought it would be a great opportunity for the newlyweds to build a nest egg. Twyla could work just until the war ended. By then they should have saved a tidy sum that would help them buy and furnish their first house. Both Twyla and Ernie thought it was a great idea but for different reasons. Ernie's thoughts focused on the nest egg; Twyla thought of all the new and exciting people she would meet.

Twyla stayed with Ralph and Theresa for a few weeks when she first arrived in Detroit, but everyone quickly realized it was not a workable living arrangement. Ralph would not hear of his wife working, since he was around to support her so she spent the day in domestic tasks. She cleaned and shined the few meager pieces of furniture they had managed to accumulate. She read recipes, trying to concoct tasty and inexpensive meals for her husband. She chatted with the neighbor ladies over coffee, washed clothes and hung them carefully on the line in the back yard, ironing even the socks, just to keep herself busy. It soon became evident that she resented Twyla's coming home from work and eating the meal that was already prepared, and heading off to her room or out with friends without so much as an offer of help with the dishes. Weekends Twyla was either working overtime, shopping, or gone somewhere with friends. Before she was asked to leave, Twyla found a room to rent from the Searle family in East Detroit. It was closer to her work, and Mrs. Searle did not expect any help with household chores.

Ella Montgomery had told Twyla that the Searles were looking for someone to rent out their back bedroom. Twyla couldn't remember how they knew each other, but Ella had said the Searles were very particular about who they chose as a boarder. They had a teenage daughter, Lillian, whom they both shielded from the evils of the world like jazz and novels. They weren't about to have anyone sully their household or unduly influence their daughter.

Twyla was immediately impressed with the modest, immaculate home the moment she was ushered inside. It was furnished sparely, but every piece of furniture was of the highest quality that could be expected in that neighborhood. Snowy white antimacassars protected the backs of the blue serge davenport and matching chair, and stiffly starched doilies protected shining wood surfaces from scratches. Unlike many homes where the occupants spoke with accents, the air inside the Searle home was fresh smelling, not redolent of boiled dinners and sweat. Twyla would learn that Mrs. Searle kept the home smelling fresh by throwing open all the doors and windows, regardless of the outside temperature, for what she called a Swiss airing.

Lillian, the Searles' daughter, was fifteen years old when Twyla first moved in with her family and was still wearing her hair in pigtails, but she soon sported a fashionable though conservative more adult coiffure, thanks to the urging of Twyla. Twyla and Lillian spent long hours together, looking at fashion magazines, shopping, and redoing each other's hair. Sometimes whole rainy Sunday afternoons would pass with neither of the girls having settled on just the right hair style for the coming week. Mrs. Searle was pleased her boarder took such an interest in Lillian. She wanted her daughter to be American but not like those wild young people she sometimes heard about with their crazy music and wild dancing. Her Lillian would be a proper young lady. Now at seventeen, Lillian was indeed the lady her mother had hoped she would be, much sought after by the boys in her class but discrete about who she went out with.

Mrs. Searle sometimes worried about the late hours Twyla kept. Sometimes her sleep would be disturbed late at night when Twyla crept in the back door thinking she was not disturbing the sleeping Searle family. A young lady, especially a married young lady, shouldn't be out late alone like that, Mrs. Searle thought. Only once did she speak of it to Twyla, asking if she wasn't tired after being out late at night then rising so early for her job. Twyla just shrugged and said, "It's all part of the war effort." Mrs. Searle never mentioned it again. She assumed her boarder was working overtime, helping with a victory garden or otherwise participating in efforts to help the boys overseas.

Now, following the party that had been such a waste of time, Twyla sat on the edge of her bed and peeled off her precious nylons which she had been saving for a special occasion. She draped them over the back of a chair to be washed the next day and hung her yellow linen suit carefully on a hanger. She wiped off her matching yellow pumps and lined them up carefully along with a dozen other pairs of assorted colors on the floor of the closet and took a soft pink nightgown from the drawer. Pulling it over her head, she mumbled again about what a waste of a Friday night that party had been, resolving not to take Ella's word about a party in the future.

The next day Twyla had a rare free Saturday, but it had begun raining long before sunrise. She flitted about the house, reading, helping Mrs. Searle hang laundry in the basement, and peeling apples for pies. Lillian begged her to go to a movie, but Twyla knew she wouldn't be able to sit still through a movie. Besides, she wanted to be with adults, fun adults who could dance and laugh and who weren't filled with stories about the war and death. At four o'clock Twyla ran a tub full of warm water, liberally sprinkling bath salts in till the suds rose above the rim of the tub like the whipped cream on a soda. She sank beneath the suds and soaked, trying to decide what to do. If she didn't get out of the house, she thought she would scream. There must be something to do and someone to do it with. But she could think of no one who was capable of lifting her from her mood as sullen as the day. She would go out by herself, she decided, wagging tongues be damned. She was old enough to be married, after all, she ought to be able to do what she wanted when she wanted to do it. She would go to Tommy's.

Tommy's was little more than a neighborhood bar, but Twyla called it a nightclub. It sounded more sophisticated and safer than calling it a bar. Tommy served decent food and always had a band on Fridays and Saturdays, a good one that could be counted on to know all the latest tunes. Twyla had brazenly stopped in there alone one night on the way home from work; it stood midway between the Searle home and the bus stop. That night she had been tired and every bone in her body ached from muscling around heavy metal objects at Carrier Tool and Die where she worked. She wanted to relax and talk to someone new, someone with something different to say than her co-workers or the Searle family or her sister. She found the place warm and inviting. The bartender, Bob, talked almost incessantly on any subject his patrons brought up, introducing those sitting at the bar to each other. Twyla didn't realize it that first night, but he was actually keeping an eye on her as he did with any woman who came in alone to make sure there was no trouble for them or for his customers. Since then, she dropped in periodically, often enough to be talked to, not often enough to be talked about. It was the perfect place to brighten her mood.

She wrapped herself in her chenille bathrobe and went to the kitchen to tell Mrs. Searle she would not be joining the family for dinner. In her room, she pulled several outfits from her closet and held them in front of her as she stood before the mirror. The red crepe was beautiful but probably too much for

Tommy's. The pale pink suit looked best when she had a tan. Brown was too depressing on a rainy night. She finally decided on the navy blue suit with the white shawl collar. She pushed her hair to the top of her head and pinned a silk white peony to hold it there. Pirouetting in front of the mirror, she decided she looked great. Swell was what Ernie would have said.

She arrived at Tommy's a little before seven, just before the early crowd so she could have her choice of seats. She chose a table at the edge of the dance floor where she hoped someone would notice she was alone and invite her to dance. She sipped on a light gin and tonic and watched as the room began to fill. Some people she knew and they smiled and spoke. Two men whom she had talked to before arrived with women on their arms and ignored her. She chuckled at their fickleness; when they were alone they were ready to take her home. Just before eight o'clock the band began warming up, random notes wafting across the room to her. Promptly at eight they launched into "Sweet Georgia Brown". She had her legs crossed, a shoe dangling from her toes as she swung her foot in time to the music. When the song ended she leaned back in her chair and glanced around the room.

A stylishly dressed man had just come in and was heading for the bar. He half sat on a stool, one foot remaining on the floor next to the stool and pushed his black felt hat up away from his face. He was a little doughy faced, she noticed, a bit pale with the vestiges of a second chin beginning to form. His finely tailored suit fit him perfectly and Twyla could see the sparkle of diamond cuff links against his pale pink shirt. He spoke to Bob then lit a cigarette and turned to look around the room while he waited for his drink. Twyla continued looking at him just long enough for him to see her then turned to look at the band. She sensed rather than saw him crossing the room with his drink in her direction.

In fact, he had two drinks. He had asked Bob what she was drinking. He set the drinks on the table then pulled the chair across from her away from the table, positioning it so he could face the room rather than her.

"I don't believe I've seen you in here before," he said.

"I was about to make the same observation. My name is Twyla."

"I'm Cliff. I'm surprised we haven't seen each other in here. It seems I'm in here all the time."

"I don't come in all that often, usually just pop in for a minute on the way home from work to relax. We have probably been just two ships in the night."

"Obviously. My loss."

Twyla smiled demurely and sipped her drink. "Thanks," she said raising the glass in his direction. "Your timing was perfect."

He smiled in return and sipped his own drink.

Twyla and Cliff talked casually about themselves. Twyla's eyes grew big when Cliff said he was a private detective. She asked if he carried a gun and whether he had ever had to use it. He gave vague answers, giving her just enough information to impress her, not enough to betray any secrets. They talked throughout the band's first set but when the musicians returned from their break, Cliff asked Twyla to dance. He was impressed with how well she followed him.

"You're like a feather in my arms," he said slyly.

"And you sir, know how to lead a lady around the floor."

They danced till the band wrapped up with "Stardust" and Cliff helped Twyla into her coat. Outside, the rain had stopped, and the streets glistened beneath the street lights like pools of crystals. Cliff offered Twyla a ride home which she gladly accepted, her aching feet eager to be released from their bonds. At the curb in front of the Searle home, Cliff leaned across to Twyla and gave her a light kiss on the cheek.

"That's all a married lady gets from me," he said quietly. "I don't like confrontations with angry husbands."

Twyla pulled up short wondering how he knew she was married since the subject hadn't come up, then she realized he had noticed her wedding band.

"He's thousands of miles away," she whispered and leaned toward him. He leaned back against the car door.

"That's not far enough." He pulled a cigarette from the pack on the dashboard. "Thanks for a nice evening. I hadn't expected it."

"I didn't either. And thanks." She opened the door and slid out, noticing he waited at the curb till she was safely inside.

Twyla was anxious to return to Tommy's to dance with the handsome, obviously well-off Cliff, but she didn't want to be too eager so she waited two weeks before returning. There he was and, before she knew it, he was leading her around the dance floor again. Once again, he drove her home, but he never asked her for a date. He must have a real paranoia about married women, she thought. But she didn't really care. Cliff was a wonderful dancer, attentive to her needs and always paid her bill, even though they were never on an official date. From time to time, he introduced her to different people then excused himself and went outside with them. She assumed it had something to do with his being a private detective and hesitated to ask any questions. Still, her interest was piqued and, after she had known him several months, broached the issue.

"You seem to do a lot of business at night," she said, three gin and tonics boosting her courage.

"What do you mean?"

"You know, meeting these people in here then going out to talk about whatever you talk about."

Cliff finished the last half of his cigarette before saying anything then he smiled slowly.

"I like you. I trust you. I think you're the type of person who likes nice things."

Twyla smiled and leaned back in her chair. He must have noticed the new dress she bought this week. It was the most expensive one she owned.

"How would you like to earn a little extra money to build that nest egg of yours a little faster?"

"Depends. What do I have to do?"

"Nothing much really. Just deliver a few packages for me. I'll pay you twenty-five dollars for every package."

"What's in the packages?"

"That doesn't need to concern you."

"I need to know what I'm getting into. Is it something dangerous or illegal?"

"No. It's just some papers, that's all."

"Twenty-five dollars is a lot of money to pay for some papers."

"Well, they're pretty important papers to the people who are sending and receiving them. They're willing to pay to make sure they are delivered safely."

"Where do I have to deliver them?"

"Different places. I'll give you directions every time I give you a package."

"I don't drive."

"You can take a bus to any place I send you."

"How often would I deliver these packages?"

"As often as you like."

The following week, Cliff gave Twyla her first package to deliver, a packet of betting slips that were to go to an unmarked building on Wyandotte. The next week he gave her two packages, one to go to the same building on Wyandotte and another that went to Griswold Street, to the home of an elderly couple. Each week, Twyla delivered the packages as ordered and each week at Tommy's, Cliff gave her twenty-five dollars cash for each package she had delivered. Initially she was afraid to deposit the money into the savings account where she was accumulating money from her paycheck and the money Ernie sent home. She didn't know how she would explain it. Instead, she carried thick rolls of bills in her purse. On a visit to Port Huron, her mother noticed the money and seemed worried.

"You shouldn't be walking around with that kind of money, Dear. That's what banks are for." She never mentioned her concern about the source of so much money.

Twyla began tucking the money in the toes of her shoes, but she became worried that the house might burn down or Lillian might discover the money when she was trying on Twyla's clothes. She decided to open a separate savings account that no one would know about. That would give her time to concoct a story before Ernie came home. When he asked about the balance in their joint account, as he sometimes did in his letters, she could truthfully tell him what was in that account while omitting the extra money.

Not all of the money she earned from Cliff's deliveries went into the bank, though. She bought a set of china at J.L. Hudson's that she had been admiring and a bedspread and matching curtains for the home she and Ernie would own when the war was over. She stored them in her sister's basement saying they were last season's clothes.

Twyla had been running errands for Cliff Malin for several months when he asked her to make a run across town on Jefferson Avenue. She had never been to that part of town before, but she knew that it was predominantly populated by Negroes. She felt a bit uncomfortable about going to that part of the city. At the end of Jefferson Avenue stood the bridge over to Belle Isle, a lush city park in the middle of the Detroit River. For some reason, Detroit Police officers had been searching cars headed over the Belle Isle Bridge. (It had been renamed the Douglas MacArthur Bridge, but no one called it that.) They may have been looking for booze, which was illegal in the city park, or they may have just been making trouble. The Negroes who went to the park had been protesting that only their cars, not those filled with white families, were being searched. On several occasions, groups of angry, combative Negroes confronted police officers at the bridge, yelling and landing a few punches to demand that the searches stop.

Two days before Twyla was to make her run to that neighborhood, she overheard a couple of women at work saying that some whites had thrown a Negro woman and her baby off the Bridge and into the Detroit River where they both drowned, but Cliff offered to double her pay if she would go, and she said she would.

She was to pick up a packet of papers at the Red Onion, a bar and restaurant on Jefferson half a mile from the Bridge. She considered taking someone with her, but the thought of having to explain why she was going to that neighborhood dissuaded her. Cliff said the papers would be ready for her to pick up by eleven o'clock. She could easily get down there and back before dark.

It was a stuffy June morning, and she rode the cross town bus next to an open window, the smells of exhaust and hot concrete enveloping her as the bus seemed to inch along its route. Twyla kept glancing at her watch. Would her contact person at the Red Onion wait if she was late? She wasn't at all interested in waiting for him to return if he had left. Get in and get out was all she could think of. Through the bus window speckled with dust she watched as the city retreated behind her, giving way to small commercial properties that housed tiny grocers, dress shops and radio repairmen. The buildings grew drabber and smaller then disappeared altogether, replaced by squalid homes with front doors hanging by one hinge and boarded-up windows. Postage stamp front yards were filled with calf-high grass and dandelions. Twyla sunk lower in her seat as she realized no white faces were to be seen.

The bus continued groaning on its route then turned onto Jefferson Avenue where Twyla was relieved to see more and better kept businesses. Small restaurants looked inviting with clean windows and bright neon signs. Customers leaving a green grocers carried fresh-looking produce and were dressed moderately but at least were clean. And, to Twyla's relief, an occasional white face appeared along the sidewalk.

"Ma'am, you was looking for the Red Onion?" the bus driver bawled back without turning around.

"Yes, thank you," she said quickly.

"You get off the next stop and walk back one block, you'll be fine."

"Thank you," she said, heading to the door.

"Thank you," she said again, as though being polite to the black bus driver would protect her in this neighborhood.

The door to the Red Onion stood open, held in place by a worn chair tucked under the door knob. Twyla stepped just inside the door and blinked, her eyes adjusting to the dim interior, her nose assaulted stale smells. Along the wall to her right stood a row of wooden booths, their seats shiny where butts had slid across but dark with grease around their exteriors. Every table held a collection of condiments and paper napkins. On her left a long, scarred bar stretched nearly the length of the room. Three men, all black, sat hunched scattered down the length of the bar sipping on beers. A tall, muscular black man leaned against the back bar wiping his hands on his apron and talking with one of the men at the bar. Twyla had been told to ask the bartender for Fred who would give her the packet of papers she was to deliver to the Great Lakes Policy House. She stepped quietly to the end of the bar closest to the door, and all eyes turned toward her. The bartender remained leaning against the bar and wiping his hands for a moment then sauntered toward her with a rolling gait.

"You lost, girl?" he asked her.

"I'm here to see Fred."

"Fred? You sure?" His deep voice rose slightly at the end of each sentence.

"I'm sure."

"Have a seat. I'll see if he's here."

Twyla remained standing as the bartender disappeared through a door at the back of the room, shifting uneasily from foot to foot, watching the door but not looking at any of the men who stared at her as though she had just flown in from another planet. The bartender emerged from the door in no particular hurry to get back to her. From the middle of the room he stopped and looked at her. Twyla felt her skin tingle and she looked away.

"Fred says get you whatever you want to drink. He'll be a few minutes."

"I'll just have a Coke," she said quietly.

"A what?"

"A Coke. I'll just have a coke," she said louder.

The bartender shook his head, and the men all snickered then looked back into their beers. Twla had nearly finished her drink when a middle-aged man virtually burst through the door at the back. He was well-dressed in a gray suit, tattersal vest, and perfectly tied tie. His hair was beginning to gray at the temples, and he removed wire-rimmed glasses as he walked briskly toward her. He carried a large leather zippered bag stuffed with papers under his arm.

"Mrs. Larson?"

"Yes. Are you Fred?"

"Yes ma'am. This is what you came for." He paused a moment and looked around the room. "You didn't come here alone, did you?"

"Yes, I did. Mr. Malin said I'd be okay."

"Normally you probably would, but things are different down here right now. I'm sure you have heard about the troubles on Belle Isle." He spoke clearly and precisely.

"Yes." The hair on Twyla's arms bristled.

"You need to leave here as quickly as you can."

Twyla suddenly became aware of a hum of voices from outside the building. An occasional shout rose above the hum, then she heard a window break.

"Come with me," Fred said, hurrying toward the back of the room.

The men at the bar turned to watch the pair as they disappeared through the door in back, Fred going through the door before the white woman.

"She gonna give him what for for that," the bartender said.

Behind the door was a narrow hallway lit only by the open door at the end. Fred stepped inside an office and grabbed the coat that matched the pants and vest he was wearing.

"Put this over your head and run," he said, pushing her out the back door. "Turn left then right at the end of the alley. Go two blocks and you'll be in a white neighborhood. You'll be okay then."

Twyla heard more glass breaking. The hum of the crowd had become a roar and seemed to be coming from the front of the building she had just left. Holding on to the packet of papers and her purse while keeping the suit coat over her head proved to require four hands, and she let the jacket fall as she ran. At the end of the alley she peered to her left and saw a sea of ebony faces, fists rising over their heads, surging in her direction. She stopped and looked behind her, then tried to open a door. It wouldn't budge. Suddenly she jerked backward as a large hand clamped around her upper arm. She dropped the packet of papers and strained against the hand as she tried to retrieve them.

"Forget about that. Come with me." It was a deep, raspy voice.

The hand released her, and she turned to see a tall, olive-skinned man, a thick wave of black hair cascading over his forehead from under his hat. His eyes swallowed her immediately.

'You can't go out there. You know what's going on? You wouldn't make it a block if they got sight of you."

He pushed her inside an open door and into a hallway that smelled of stale urine.

"Upstairs," he said gruffly.

She picked her way up the narrow staircase, arriving in a large room. The outer wall was mostly glass, from the ceiling to about two feet above the floor.

"Get down," the man behind her said, and she dropped to the floor.

The couple remained on the floor, peering over the windowsill at the mob below. A sea of nappy heads washed from the sidewalk into the street, crashing against the buildings across from where they watched. The tinkling of broken windows rose above the wave of voices that were shouting indiscernible words. Twyla watched as the black sea pushed its way across Jefferson into a grassy park where white faces stood and stared. Like waves pounding against rocks, the black sea smashed into the white pool, forcing its way into the bewildered crowd, pushing and shoving and pounding. Spurts of blood speckled blacks and whites and bodies fell to the ground. Soon the black and white faces were interspersed with blue uniforms, wooden batons rising over their heads of the policemen, battering, pounding, shattering.

Twyla and the man who had rescued her from certain doom watched, terrified they would be spotted but unable to turn away from the mayhem in the streets. By dark, paddy wagons and ambulances had separated the crowds, carrying away the injured and the arrested. Twyla's back and legs ached from being scrunched and contorted for hours. The room was dark and she realized the man next to her had fallen asleep on the floor. She was trying to decide whether to wake him or attempt to make her own way back home when he stirred. He blinked several times then stretched and said, "Who…oh yeah."

"How could you have slept through all that? Weren't you scared?" she asked him.

"Naw. I grew up around here. I know a lot of those people. Course I'm not sure that would have kept me from getting my head bashed in. You get a lot of people pissed off about something, and they don't think so clearly."

He stood and stretched, his broad shoulders and narrow hips silhouetted against the one street lamp that had not been broken in the melee. Twyla guessed from the shade of his skin and the color of his eyes that he was Italian.

"I guess I owe you my life," she said. "And I don't even know your name."

"Vince. Vince Di Grassi."

# CHAPTER 27

▼

For a December morning in Michigan, it was warm and dry. No snow had fallen in a week and the old snow was slowly disappearing. Dan Kirk was among the last of the reporters to arrive at the Courthouse for Cliff Malin's trial, something he planned. As the lead reporter on the story, he would be bombarded with questions from out-of-town reporters who hadn't bothered to do any research of their own. He didn't want to be rude to his fellow journalists, but he also wasn't about to do their work for them.

The two-page spread profiling Cliff Malin and Twyla Larson had run the previous day, Sunday, timed for the maxim readership. He also knew that these reporters would have arrived Sunday and scooped up whatever papers they could find with details about the trial and the principals involved. Marie Young from the *Detroit News* was the first person to recognize him. He knew she had done her homework and wouldn't be asking him questions. Ashe expected, though, she called out to him, denying him the opportunity to slip through the crowd unobtrusively.

"Hey, Dan, "she called out cheerily and all heads turned to see who she was addressing. Reporters and photographs rushed toward him all babbling questions at once. Dan raised his hands.

"Look, people. Pretty much everything I know was in yesterday's stories and the ones when Mrs. Larson was first discovered. I'm sure you've all read those. You'll probably get everything else you need in the courtroom. Now, if you want suggestions about where to have dinner, I can give you some help." He nodded toward the woman who had called to him. "So can Miss Young." He elbowed his way through the crowd and up the stairs.

Not far behind Dan, Judge Charles Wightman picked his way through the throng of reporters, photographers and spectators waiting in the early morning sun for the courthouse to open. Many had small bags or large purses that held their lunches and magazines tucked under their arms. If they managed to get a seat in the courtroom, they weren't going to give it up for lunch. Once behind the bench, Judge Wightman looked around at the eager spectators, mostly female, who had come to see the man accused of murder. They would go home that night to babble to their families and friends about they way the defendant or his attorney or the prosecutor had looked at them, straight at them or how you could tell Cliff Malin was guilty just by the way he put his hands in his lap.

Judge Wightman hated media cases, but it was an election year and this trial might secure another term on the bench for him. It would certainly make the voters aware of who he was.

Promptly at nine o'clock the Judge called the court to order. At the defense table attorney Leo Columbo sat before meticulously arranged files, exhibits and documents he would use in defense of his client. Judge Wightman knew Columbo to be thorough, prepared, and a tenacious advocate for his clients. He also knew Columbo was the leading attorney for Detroit's most powerful underworld families as well as for the Ford Motor Company. Since Malin was not a Ford employee, Wightman assumed he represented the other arm of Columbo's practice. At six foot two and one hundred ninety pounds, Leo Columbo created an imposing figure in the courtroom, his hand-tailored suit fitting like a second skin, his tortoise-shell glasses giving him a professorial look. He used his vice like an actor, rising while revealing important information, speaking quieter when the most critical information was elicited.

At the state's table sat Lieutenant Cunningham and, to Judge Wightman's surprise, Chief Prosecutor Lee Edgely. At only five feet four, Lee Edgely did not present the figure of a man with the formidable reputation he had earned. But standing in front of a jury box, the short man could look straight into the eyes of the jurors in the first row. It gave them a sense of intimacy with the prosecutor. That, coupled with his straightforward manner of speaking and talent for simplifying complex issues, made him a tough opponent. But there would be no jury in this hearing Judge Wightman alone would decide if there was sufficient evidence to go to trial.

Edgely rarely appeared in court himself. He was well known for his belief that the real work of a lawyer lay in research and preparation. "Do your homework and a well-trained monkey could handle a trial," he often said. Only two situations brought the acerbic prosecutor to the court room: a precedent-setting case or a weak one. Wightman was not aware that any new legal ground would be plowed in this trial which meant the state was going to have a difficult time proving its case. If this went to trail, Wightman knew it would be one of the more interesting ones of his career as both attorneys struggled to arrange what evidence there was to suit their own interpretations.

It was cold this morning after last night's heavy rain, but the Judge ordered the windows of the courtroom opened; it would soon be steamy in the room with the press of bodies. He hammered his gavel to begin the proceedings.

Lieutenant Stan Cunningham was the state's first witness, detailing where Twyla's body had been found, the bullet wounds in her head, the identification by her co-workers and her brother-in-law. In the front row, Ernest Larson sat next to his dead wife's twin sister listening to the Lieutenant's testimony. He stared at his hands while Cunningham talked, and Twyla's sister sobbed quietly into her handkerchief. Cunningham told the court of Clifford Malin's appearances at the sheriff's office and the information that led to a search for Vince Di Grassi.

"Did you consider Mr. Di Grassi a suspect in Mrs. Larson's murder?" Edgely asked.

"Yes, at first. But when we found him, he could account for his whereabouts. He was in New York City and had witnesses to that fact at the time Mrs. Larson was killed."

"What made you decide Mr. Malin was a suspect in the case?"

"Several things. He misled us on several occasions, and he outright lied other times. And he was too helpful. He seemed to want to be involved in the investigation and kept giving us information he thought would be helpful. It's my experience a person does that when they are trying to throw us off track. Then when we found Mrs. Larson's Packard in front of Mr. Malin's house, I was sure."

Cunningham answered questions about the Packard revealing that the car had been recently painted. Under the paint the police had found traces of blood that matched Twyla's and mud in the wheel wells of the same type found near the Adams Road Bridge. He testified that Cliff and Twyla had known each other from Tommy's club and that Twyla probably was involved in some illegal activities, working for Cliff. He also revealed that a Detroit citizen had come forward with the information that Malin had been married before moving to Detroit.

"Where is his wife?" Edgely asked.

"She's dead."

"How did she die?"

"Objection," Columbo said, rising to his feet. "What is the relevance of this?'

"Your Honor, this is to bear out what Lieutenant Cunningham said about Mr. Malin lying to the police."

"Go ahead, Mr. Edgely," the judge said, leaning back in his chair.

"How did Mr. Malin's wife die, Lieutenant?"

"The death certificate says asphyxiation."

"Is that what Mr. Malin told you about his wife's death, that she suffocated?"

"No. He said she died after she had been hit in the head with a basketball."

"In your experience, Lieutenant, could a hit on the head with a basketball result in asphyxiation?"

"I don't see how."

Mrs. Searle, Twyla's landlady took the stand next. She had been nervous enough when Mr. Edgely told her she would have to testify. Her poor English embarrassed her even in casual circumstances, but she was afraid that she wouldn't be able to understand anything they said to her or that she would say the wrong thing in court. Then Mrs. Otis across the street told her she should dress smartly because the newspaper reporters and photographers would likely want to talk to her and take her picture. That made her even more nervous. Mr. Edgely had met with her last night in an effort to soothe her apprehensions about the courtroom. She had decided not to waste money on a new dress for just one occasion. She had washed and pressed her brown seersucker suit and borrowed Mrs. Otis's new hat with the peach flowers on it. She was relieved when she saw that the witness stand would hide her battered shoes.

Mrs. Searle told the court that Mrs. Larson had been living at the Searle home for two years. She had been an ideal tenant, clean, polite, considerate of others. Twyla and Mrs. Searle's teenage daughter, Lillian, had become good friends, often spending time listening to the radio or going to the picture show. Twyla taught Lillian how to dance. Until early last year, Mrs. Searle said, Twyla had been a part of the family.

"What happened last year that changed that," Edgely asked.

"Mrs. Larson seemed to change. She got more quiet. She didn't talk with me or Lillian much. She don't even come home very much. I think maybe she is with her sister but sometimes her sister call and say she doesn't know where Twyla is. Then there was those men who called and all that money she carry. I don't know what was happening to her."

"Could you tell us about the money, Mrs. Searle?"

"I see in her purse one night. I didn't mean to look, but she was getting out her key and I couldn't help it. I see money in her purse, lots of money. I ask her where she get that money, and she say her rich uncle die. I tell her to put all that money in the bank. Young women shouldn't be out alone with all that money."

"What about the men who called her. Do you remember their names?'

Mrs. Searle looked at Captain Larson then down into her lap before speaking. "I remember two names. It was Vince and Cliff. That's all I remember."

"You said Mrs. Larson moved in with your family about two years ago. Did she stay with you that entire time?"

"Mostly all the time except for last summer. That's when she go to stay with her girlfriend who was sick."

"Do you know the name of the girlfriend?"

"No, she never tell me. She came back again when her girlfriend get well, I think maybe in September."

"Was Mrs. Larson any different, did she behave any different, when she moved back into your home, Mrs. Searle?"

"She was very quiet. Then one night after dinner, I take some ice cream to her. She love my homemade ice cream. I take some to her room, and she is crying. I ask her what was wrong and she say she get a letter from her husband. He wants a divorce."

"Did she say anything else?"

"No, she just sit there and cry."

Edgely handed Mrs. Searle a letter and asked her to read the marked portion. She read:

"Honey, whatever the postwar era brings to us—whether it's the army or civilian life—I want to enjoy that life with you. Even if things should come a little tough for awhile, I'm sure you'll stick by me. I'm that sure of your love for me." The letter was signed "Ernie."

"Could you read us the date on that letter, Mrs. Searle?"

The witness riffled through the papers then read, "October 15, 1945.

"Does that letter sound like it was written by a man who wanted a divorce?'

"No, sir it doesn't, but that's what Twyla told me. She said her husband want a divorce."

"Did she say anything else? Did she talk about her financial situation?"

"No, she just sit there and cry."

"Do you think Mrs. Larson might have been upset about something else and invented the story about the divorce?"

"Objection," Columbo said. "Speculation."

"Sustained," Wightman said.

Edgely finished his examination of Mrs. Searle then Columbo elicited from her that she did not know the last names of either Vince or Cliff who had called Twyla. She said the last time she saw her boarder alive was the night before Twyla's body had been found. Twyla left the house after dinner saying she had a dentist appointment.

Edgely stood up. "Redirect, Your Honor. Mrs. Searle, how was Mrs. Larson dressed when she left for this supposed dentist appointment?"

"She wore a nice suit and a flowered blouse. She look nice. She always look nice."

"Had she changed her clothes from what she wore to work?"

"Yes."

"A nice suit and a flowered blouse. Any jewelry?"

"Yes, a ring and a bracelet. And her wedding ring, of course."

"Seems more like clothes she would wear for a date than for a dentist's appointment, doesn't it?"

"Objection," Columbo boomed.

"Withdrawn."

The hearing continued for two more days during which details of Twyla's life in Detroit were exposed. Judge Wightman heard of her dwindling bank accounts. Her coworkers gold how she had become more nervous and cried easily in the weeks preceding her death. Her supervisor, Robert Gaines, one of the people who had helped identify her body, said she had talked of financial troubles. She had loaned money to someone and was having trouble getting it back, he said. Gaines said he had given her the name of a man he knew, a former policeman, who could probably help.

"What was that man's name?" Edgely asked.

"Clifford Malin." He added he didn't know the two were already acquainted.

Vince Di Grassi took the stand on Wednesday and testified for a day and a half. He told the court that he had met Twyla Larson in 1943 when he rescued her during the race riots. He said they hit it off right away, since they both liked to dance and often stayed till closing at the nightclubs they frequented. Vince said he made most of his money from shooting pool and gambling when he lived in Detroit, but sometimes he took odd jobs. After he and Twyla had been dating for several months, she mentioned the money she had in the bank.

"I started borrowing money from her, I guess about November. I always told her I'd pay it back, but I never did."

"How much did you borrow from her?" Edgely asked.

"I don't know. Twenty-five here, a hundred there. Sometimes more."

"Did you borrow money from her to buy a car?'
"Yes. A friend of mine had a 1941 Packard for sale at a really good price. I told Twyla I could use the car to collect some money that was owed to some men I knew, and then I could pay her back. I told her I would pay her for the car, too."
"Was the license plate AY1452?"
"I don't remember exactly. Could be."
"What happened to the car?"
"I had an accident with it, and she took it back. I think she sold it to Cliff Malin."
"When was that?"
"I don't know for sure. I left for New York last July, and it was sometime after that."
"That's all, Mr. Di Grassi."
Leo Columbo began his cross examination of Vince Di Grassi after lunch on Thursday. He asked where Vince was living and Vince said New York City.
"I mean right now, where are you living? Where did you sleep last night?"
Vince shifted in his chair and cleared his voice before answering.
"I slept at the Wayne County jail in Detroit."
"Why were you there?"
Vince shifted in his seat and looked down at the floor in front of the lawyer.
"When I came back from New York, they arrested me for not paying child support."
"Mr. Di Grassi, you said you and Mrs. Larson dated. Did you ever live together?"
"Yeah, for a while last summer. We got a place at the Roosevelt."
"Is that at the time Mrs. Larson told her previous landlady, Mrs. Searle, that she was going to stay with a sick girlfriend?"
"Yeah. She didn't want the old lady to know what she was up to. She had a husband, you know."
Ernie Larson's face froze as he stared at the handsome man in the witness stand. His sister-in-law reached for his hand, but he gave no indication he noticed.
Vince said they lived together for most of the summer, then one day he found a letter from her husband that said he was coming home and was looking forward to starting a life with her. When they moved in together, Twyla had said that her husband wanted a divorce, but when he confronted her with the letter, she admitted the story about the divorce was a lie. She had just said that so they could move in together. As soon as Ernie got home, though, she would talk to him and

ask for a divorce. Not wanting to be caught in some messy scandal, Vince moved out of the Roosevelt and said he would move back when her divorce was final. He moved to New York instead.

Judge Wightman kept his head down but peered out at Major Larson who sat stiffly and stared forward. The Judge wondered if this was the first time the dead woman's husband was hearing of his wife's activities. If so, he was taking it very well.

Columbo produced a document from the orderly files on his table and handed it to Di Grassi. Di Grassi identified it as a police report filed by Mrs. Larson in Detroit in June 1945 claiming that Di Grassi had swindled Twyla out of money. The report included a confession from Di Grassi with an itemization of the money he had taken from Twyla. Columbo led the witness through the list of dates and amounts: December 4, 1944, $50. December 13, 1944, $215. December 20, 1944, $100. February 10, 1945, $100.

"What were the reasons you gave Mrs. Larson for needing this money?" Columbo asked.

Vince shifted again in his seat and took a drink of water before answering.

"Well, I gave her different reasons. Once I told her I needed to pay off a bail bond. Sometimes I told her I lost money in a poker game. I don't know what all I said."

"Isn't it true that once you told her your daughter had died, and you needed money for the funeral?'

Again Vince moved in his chair and took a drink of water before answering.

"Yeah," he said quietly without looking at the lawyer.

"Were any of those stories true?"

"No. I just needed money. I wasn't working."

Leo Columbo directed the witness to read from the report he held.

"On February 17, 1945, I manufactured a scheme to swindle Mrs. Larson out of a much larger sum by telling her it was necessary to give me thirteen hundred and fifty dollars to purchase a car so I could go out collecting on some illegitimate enterprise to get the money I had already swindled from her. Mrs. Larson gave me thirteen hundred and fifty dollars with the agreement the car would be purchased and that I would immediately repay her all I had taken previously including thirteen hundred and fifty dollars. I purchased a 1941 Packard convertible couple, license AY 1452, engine number C 5903H, serial number 13895038, title number 2620839. This car was bought in my name, realizing at this time that Mrs. Larson was an easy victim for my schemes to cheat her out of different sums of money at different times."

Columbo stopped Di Grassi's reading and asked more questions about the car; the accident he had had with it, how badly it was damaged, how he knew Mrs. Larson had sold it to Clifford Malin. Di Grassi said he had been drinking and rolled the car over in a ditch. It was damaged some but was drivable. He transferred the title to Twyla so she could sell it to Cliff.

"What was Mrs. Larson's relationship with Mr. Malin?"

"I don't think there was a relationship. I mean, they never dated that I knew of."

"They never had a relationship. So there would be no reason for Mr. Malin to be upset with her?"

"Not that I can think of."

Columbo showed the witness a title to a 1941 Packard registered to Twyla Larson.

"Isn't true, Mr. Di Grassi, that Mrs. Larson never sold the car to my client? That after you had someone kill her, you had that person use the car with a key you still had to it to take her body to the Adams Road Bridge and throw her in the river then park it in front of Mr. Malin's house?"

"You're crazy. I didn't have anything to do with her getting offed."

"Can you explain why, if Mr. Malin owned the car, why his fingerprints are nowhere to be found on it?"

"How should I know? You can wipe fingerprints away, you know. Maybe that's what he did."

"Doesn't it seem odd to you that a man with the background of Mr. Malin's a private investigator and former police officer, would leave the murdered woman's car in front of his own home?"

"I don't know. He was a cocky son of a bitch."

The Judge interrupted. "Mr. Di Grassi, I'll not have that kind of language in my court."

"Sorry, Judge. Maybe he figured he couldn't get caught. Or if he did, he had the right friends to cover for him. That's what he told me when he threatened to have me arrested. He said he had friends."

"Isn't it true, Mr. Di Grassi, that Mrs. Larson found you in New York and threatened to contact the police if you didn't pay her the money you owed her, and you hired one of your friends in Detroit to kill her?"

"No, it isn't true. I never heard from her after I got to New York. Besides, if I could have afforded to hire someone to do her, I could have afforded to pay her off. Those guys don't work for the price of a steak dinner and a beer, you know."

"No, Mr. Di Grassi. I wouldn't know about that."

The lawyer returned to his table and shuffled through some papers, extracting one.

Mr. Di Grassi, do you know a man named Chester La Mare?"

"I heard of him, yeah."

"You've more than heard of him, haven't you? Isn't it true that you worked for Mr. La Mare at Crescent City Motors?"

"Yeah, when I was a kid."

"Didn't you sometimes use a car Mr. La Mare loaned you to pick up betting slips and cash for Mr. La Mare?"

"I sometimes ran errands for him, but I didn't know what was in the envelopes. I just picked 'em up and dropped 'em off wherever he told me."

"Are you aware that Mr. La Mare was gunned down in his kitchen as a result of wars between Mafia families?"

"I maybe read that in the papers, but you can't believe everything you read. I didn't know what all Mr. La Mare did, but I didn't see nothing looked like Mafia stuff."

"Mr. Di Grassi, you have admitted that you lied and cheated Mrs. Larson out of her money. With her husband coming home, she must have been desperate to restore her bank accounts to their previous levels. You were the only one she could get that money from, and you had her killed before she could make trouble for you."

"That's an absolute lie and you know it! I had nothing to do with her getting killed!"

"You have admitted to being a liar and a cheat. You are in jail for not supporting your wife and child. You have a history of illicit activities, including working for Chester La Mare, one of the most notorious gangsters in Detroit. But now, you are asking us to believe you didn't kill Mrs. Larson to protect your own hide?"

"I may have lied and cheated, but I'm no killer."

"Thank you, Mr. Di Grassi."

Friday morning, Lee Edgely's first witness was Mrs. Ethel Blumenthal. Thirty-five years of working on the farm with her husband showed in her stiff walk and hunched back. Her thinning, graying hair was pulled tight and pinned up beneath her hat, a navy blue shapeless straw with dingy white flowers, its brim showing signs of having been crushed and an attempt made to restore its shape. Her brown wool coat was worn at the cuffs and the hem hung unevenly.

Mrs. Blumenthal identified herself as the owner of a turkey farm two and a half miles from the Adams Road Bridge where Mrs. Larson's body had been found. She said she had known Clifford Malin for twenty years or more, though she didn't see much of him. He had some business with her husband, but she didn't know the nature of the business. Sometimes he would come out to the farm for a few hours and other times he stayed for days. He had once spent an entire spring at the farm, she said. They frequently had other visitors like that, she said. Her husband always instructed her not to mention these visitors to anyone. She told the court that Cliff had made a visit to their farm at the end of October or early November last year.

"What can you tell us about the visit?"

"Well, he didn't stay long. He and Edmund, my husband, talked in the kitchen for about a half hour, then he left."

'Did anything strike you as unusual about the visit?"

"Well, just that he didn't drive up to the house. Usually, if he's just going to be a little while he parks in front. If he's going to stay longer, he parks out behind the barn."

"Where did he park on this occasion?"

"Out on the road, in the dark. He didn't even pull up to the house. I thought that was kind of odd."

"Could you see if anyone was in the car out on the road?"

"No. It was too dark."

"Mrs. Blumenthal, can you pinpoint the date of this visit precisely for the court?"

"Not off the top of my head, but it's wrote in my appointment book."

"You mean you wrote down what date Mr. Malin was last at your farm?"

"Yes. I write everything down. My memory ain't so good, and my husband is always asking when something or another happened, so I write down everything I think I might need to know later and all my appointments and what days I planted and stuff like that."

"And can you produce this book you write everything in?"

"I don't have it with me, if that's what you mean, but I can get it over dinner."

Knowing that it was a long drive out to her farm and hoping to wind up early on this Friday afternoon, Edgely suggested she bring the book to court Monday morning. She agreed and stepped down from the witness stand. When court adjourned for the weekend, Leo Columbo and his client sat in whispered consultation as Edgely gathered his files and left the courtroom.

Saturday morning, Cliff sat across the table from Wingy Adamo in the visitor's room at Oakland County jail. In the twenty-five years since Cliff arrived in Detroit, he had worked for a lot of people. The Bernsteins, Chet La Mare and his various successors. When the Italians first came to town, Cliff had been accepted into the fold, but it became apparent that they valued him only for his contacts. Little by little, as they got to know the city, he was shunted into positions of lesser and lesser importance, replaced by Italians. After the Ferguson Grand Jury shut down, he had been treated as though he had a communicable disease. Now he reported to Wingy instead of to the men at the top.

Wingy Adamo was a *capo*, a lieutenant, in the family that now ran Detroit, something Cliff would never be. Wingy was included in conversations held only in Italian. In fact, Cliff remembered being told when the Italians first came to Detroit that, if they started speaking Italian, he should leave the room. Wingy got his nickname after a bomb he had built for the car of an errant magistrate had gone off prematurely, costing him his arm. He was a spare, short man with bulging brown eyes and bad teeth. He chewed on a toothpick and leaned forward as he talked to Cliff. Cliff's red-rimmed eyes and chain smoking gave away his lack of sleep.

"Listen," Wingy said quietly. "You don't gotta worry about a thing. Didn't I say I would take care of you? Haven't I kept my word? Getting Columbo for you and all? This thing will be okay. You can relax. The Boss says you can take it from me like he was saying it. Whackin' the Larson broad was the best thing you coulda done for everyone concerned. These broads. They just don't understand. That woman that offed herself and her kid a few years back and made so much trouble for everyone including you? Well, that Larson woman woulda done the same thing. It was either give her the money she wanted or get rid of her. She knew enough to hut our operations good. Once you start paying that kinda woman, there's no let up. She was a good runner for you for a while. Kept her mouth shut. Hell, she never even bellyached when she got caught in the middle of that race riot. But, hell, you can't nursemaid these people forever. She made her own bed, giving up all that money to her boyfriend. Now, she's lying in it. Course, it wasn't too bright of you to park her car in front of your house."

"It had been there less than an hour. I just got it back from getting it painted and was going to ditch it somewhere as soon as it got dark. I didn't think the cops could trace it that fast. They just got lucky. Right now, I'm worried about Mrs. Blumenthal. She's the only one who can put me in the right place at the right time."

"Don't you worry about that. Leave that to me."

"You going to dump the old lady in the Clinton River, too?"

"Just don't worry. The less you know, the better."

When court reconvened on Monday morning, Cliff looked around and heaved a barely audible sigh of relief when he saw Mrs. Blumenthal take a seat in the second row. Wingy hadn't done anything to her. She was empty handed except for a battered black handbag. Lee Edgely called her to the stand, for the first time noticing that she was not carrying the appointment book she had mentioned in Friday's testimony.

"Mrs. Blumenthal, I believe you said you were going to bring your appointment book to court today. Do you have it?"

"No, sir, I don't."

"Excuse me? You said you would bring that book to court today. Where is it?"

"I destroyed it."

Edgely stared at the work-weary woman for a moment, his mouth slightly open. "You destroyed it?" he finally stammered.

"Yes, sir, that's right." She looked straight ahead, over the tops of the heads of the people in the room, her hands firmly folded in her lap. The prosecutor wasn't close enough to notice the bruise under her chin.

"Mrs. Blumenthal, you know that it is evidence in a murder trial."

"I don't know nothing about law and evidence."

"Well, let me tell you about the law and evidence. You can go to jail for what you did."

"Then I guess you'll have to send me to jail, because the book is destroyed."

"Why did you do that, Mrs. Blumenthal?"

She took a handkerchief from her purse and dabbed her nose. "Well, Mr. Edgely, I got to looking at the book over the weekend and I realize there's a lot of personal information in that book. It's been in my family since my parents had the farm. There's lots of things in there that could embarrass my family and maybe some of the neighbors. It was kind of a diary, you know. I didn't know what you would do or what the newspaper people would do if they saw some of those things that's wrote in there. So my husband and me, we decided to destroy it."

Edgely walked back to his seat, obviously frustrated and stunned. He shuffled papers on his table for a moment in an effort to regain his composure then asked the witness if she could say with certainty what date Clifford Malin had visited her farm.

"No, sir. I reckon I can't rightly say. It was late October or early November, best I can recollect, but I can't say for certain exactly what day."

Leo Columbo rose and straightened his back, almost appearing to flex his muscles. Spectators whispered loudly and reporters leapt from their seats and rushed out of the courtroom.

"You Honor, I move that charges against my client be dismissed for lack of evidence. The state has not produced the murder weapon, cannot tie my client to the dead woman on the day of her death, and has shown no motive for his allegedly murdering her."

Judge Wightman turned to speak to his clerk for a moment then turned to the attorneys.

"You'll have my response tomorrow morning at nine. Court is adjourned."

Leo Columbo patted his client on the arm, assuring him a dismissal was imminent.

The next morning, the courtroom was again crowded. Dan Kirk stood with the other reporters at the back of the room in order to escape quickly when the Judge's ruling was in to file their stories. Judge Wightman entered the room promptly at nine o'clock, a leather folder tucked under his arm. He opened the folder as he sat and cleared his throat.

"The matter before the Court involves a motion to quash the information filed against the respondent charging him with first degree murder," the Judge began. He then recounted the facts of the case, how Twyla had been found in the Clinton River, the bullet hole in her head, the fact that she remained unidentified for several days. He talked of her association with other men while her husband was overseas and her spending habits.

Malin's history did not escape the Judge's notice as he recounted the defendant's history with the Detroit Police and the Ferguson Grand Jury followed by his employment at Carrier Tool and Die.

"There is now before the Court a motion to dismiss charges against Clifford Malin for lack of evidence. Twyla Larson was not seen by any witness produced after 7:30 p.m. October 30. The autopsy showed she had eaten about two hours before her death. No one has placed her in the car driven by the defendant, and no one has placed defendant with that car in Oakland Count on October 30 or 31.

"That is the missing link in the evidence in this case, all the argument about motive, malice aforethought, premeditation notwithstanding. The fact that this missing link in the evidence cannot be supplied is not the fault of the Prosecuting Attorney, Sheriff's Office, State Police, or City Police. Each office is to be commended for its untiring efforts to solve this crime. However, these agencies have not solved it, and the Court holds that there is not probable cause to hold defendant for trial."

Reporters rushed from the courtroom and spectators whispered among themselves. Judge Wightman gaveled them to silence.

"Despicable as is the character of the defendant and considering also that the finger of suspicion points in his direction, these elements alone are not sufficient to hold him for trial. I am of the firm opinion that any court hearing this case, either with or without a jury would be compelled to direct a verdict of not guilty at the conclusion of the proofs. By dismissing this case upon motion as presented, it will be left open for future investigation and possible solution. If presented to a jury, that door would be forever closed.

"Who murdered Twyla Larson? The record does not hold the answer. Perhaps sometime, somewhere, the defendant will answer that question. Defendant is released."

# CHAPTER 28

▼

Captain Ernest Larson laid his shaving gear on top of the few clothes in the suit-case lying open on the bed then snapped the case shut. He stood staring down at it as thoughts of the last few days flooded his brain. He had taken a thirty day leave from the Army to attend the hearing and, he hoped, the trial of the man accused of murdering his wife. The hearing was over in a week and there would be no trial, at least not for now. He would spend the rest of his leave with his parents in Port Huron.

When he had learned of Twyla's death, the blood had drained to his feet. He felt cold and light headed with the incomprehensibility of the news. Twyla dead? Murdered? How could that be? Upon arriving in Michigan from France, Ernie had gone straight to the Oakland County Sheriff's office, his brother, Barney, at his side. Lieutenant Cunningham was clearly ill at ease as he told Ernie what they had learned about the life his wife had been leading in his absence. Ernie's physi-cal reaction to the news was just the opposite of what he had felt upon hearing about her death. He grew hot and his head was full and pounding.

Lieutenant Cunningham had offered to let him read the police reports of the investigation into his wife's death. His natural curiosity was initially piqued, but he hadn't gotten too far into the reports before he dropped them back on the desk and closed the folder. The details weren't important. Twyla was dead. She had been unfaithful to him. Their money was gone. What more could matter? All those nighst he lay awake in his Army cot or on the damp ground in Europe yearning for her, she was depriving him of their future together. Every song he heard overseas reminded him of how she felt in his arms on the dance floor, but she was dancing with someone else. He often recalled how she laughed when a tune ended, and he took her back to the table or outside for some fresh air, but all the while he dreamed of her, someone else was taking her out for air. Even with the stench of battle and death all around him, he could smell her clean hair and the perfume she wore whose name he could never remember. Meantime she had been wearing that perfume for someone else. It was all over now, tragically, bitterly, sadly over. He wasn't sure he could ever trust another woman.

The hearing and the dismissal of charges against Cliff Malin left Ernie feeling empty and dull. He thought of himself as a fair-minded man, ready to give anyone the benefit of the doubt, particularly when he didn't know all the circumstances, but he didn't think the police and the prosecutor would go to the trouble of arresting a man if they didn't have a solid case against him. Ernie had come to Pontiac fully expecting the trial and conviction of Cliff Malin, but that wasn't going to happen, may never happen. The judge made it sound like the police and the prosecutor could continue trying to get Malin, but Ernie had a sense that they never would. The evidence they needed was gone.

Ernie wondered if he would ever know warmth and trust and love again. For the first few weeks after he came home, he had avoided women. Their sounds, their looks, their smells all welled up and churned inside him. He even found himself steeling his ears against his own mother's voice. That's when he realized he had to get hold of himself and put this behind him. He couldn't go through life like this, becoming a hostile, bitter old man. He had to move on. He adjusted to his mother's and sisters' voices first, then in a few weeks he found he could hear the telephone operator without a sense of revulsion. It seemed over now, that part at least, but he wondered how close he ever wanted to be to a woman again.

Ernie picked up his suitcase and left the room. In the lobby, he could see his brother's car parked at the curb. Torrents of rain poured down so hard it bounced back up off the payment. The drive back to Port Huron would be slow and hard. When he had paid his bill, he started toward the front door but was intercepted by Dan Kirk.

"Captain Larson?" the reporter said quietly. Ernie turned and recognized the reporter.

"Mr. Kirk."

"What are your plans now, Captain?"

"I'm still on leave, so I'm going back to Port Huron for a while. I am re-enlist in the service, I just don't know."

"Will you be going back to Europe?"

"No. I'm headed to Fort Bliss, Texas from here."

"I just wanted to say how sorry I am for how things turned out." He reached inside his jacket and extracted a letter. "Lieutenant Cunningham received this yesterday. It's amazing it ever found its way to him. I guess you've become pretty famous."

Ernie took the letter and glanced at it. The postmark was New Castle, Pennsylvania, and it was addressed to the Sheriff's Department in Taylor, Michigan. A nurse he had met before Twyla died was from New Castle. He remembered telling her that his mother lived on Taylor Street. Dan Kirk was right. It was a minor miracle that it had found him.

"Thanks, Mr. Kirk. I appreciate your taking the time to bring this to me."

"In my experience, men in your position get a lot of letters from women."

"Yeah, I have. They are the only thing that has made me laugh through this whole thing. My brother and I would read them over a bottle of whiskey and roar. There are some pretty desperate women out there."

"You suppose this is another one of those letters?"

"No, I think I know who this is from. A nurse I met in Paris."

"Well, good luck to you, Captain."

Dan held the door of Barney's car open as Ernie leaned inside and threw his suitcase in the back seat then slid in front. He waved to Dan as the car eased away from the curb.

The strong winds blew the rain nearly vertically and when it did touch down, it hit so hard it bounced a foot back up in the air off the pavement. Although it was noon, all the buildings and the few cars they passed were lit up against the dark sky. He squinted into the rain and shuddered, unable to make out anything that was more than a few feet away. A second shudder ran over him, and he realized it was the first time in over six months that he had really felt anything or at least been aware he felt anything. The windshield wipers beat futilely against the rain as sheets of water cascaded down the glass.

"Are you sure we should be driving in this?" Ernie asked.

"It's okay. By the time we get north of town, we'll be out of the worst of it. Grace is anxious for me to get back home," Barney said, leaning forward to wipe the fog from the inside of the window.

Across the street and a block away, Cliff Malin sat at the bar in Mitch's Tavern. He had decided to wait there until the rain abated. He stared into his drink thinking about Twyla. She had been a beautiful woman and a lot of fun. She had been a good employee, dependable and honest. But she'd been stupid. Those men she was seeing, especially Vince, were bound to lead to trouble. He had tried to tell her that once, but she said she could take care of herself. She was so typical of the young women, girls really, who had come to Detroit since the War started. They arrived with their shiny young faces and bright, querulous eyes, mesmerized by all the things that were new to them: J.L. Hudson's, gangsters, good jobs, nice clothes, nightclubs. He remembered when he was equally taken by all the new sights so many years ago.

That last night he had seen Twyla she sat huddled against the door of the car as he pressed the cold steel of the gun barrel against her head. She had cried and let out a brief scream before the bullet sunk into her flesh then her skull then her brain and out the other side. It shattered the window on her side of the car. One instant she was alive and breathing, the next she was slumped lifeless against the car seat. He hadn't wanted to shoot her, but he kept remembering what had happened when Janet McDonald wrote all those letters. So many people had gone to prison. He had barely escaped himself and then only because he was willing to provide details to Judge Ferguson. He was only just now regaining the friendships and trust he had lost. Twyla wasn't going to take it from him. Things were still okay for him with the people he was working for. The fact that Leo Columbo had defended him at trial and that the key piece of evidence, Mrs. Blumenthal's appointment book, had disappeared proved that.

He glanced at his watch and threw down the last of his whiskey and soda. The wind continued to pelt the pavement outside but, if he left right now, he could get back to Detroit in time for the afternoon poker game at the Windsor Hotel. Outside, he pulled up the collar of his raincoat and stepped off the curb just as a brown Buick rounded the corner. Neither saw the other until it was too late.

0-595-27868-X